My Enemy's Enemy

A Midge Carrington Mystery

by
Margaret Suckling

For Diana,

who has read all my books
and has been so encouraging about them.

Chapter One

"Damn you, you little runt, I want an answer."

"Then want must be your master. Why did your nurse let a baby like you out to play with the grown-ups?"

There was a sharp crack as the interrogator's gloved hand struck the suspect hard across the mouth. "Grown-ups, eh?" Peveril repeated sibilantly. "If you think questioning according to the rules is childish, let's play it by your rules. Let's be grown-up; let's play it nastily."

Denman cowered back in his chair. Peveril loomed over him, his fist still raised.

"Don't like a taste of your own medicine?" he snapped harshly. "Then the remedy is in your hands. I want the name of your Dutch contact and I haven't time to waste waiting for it."

Denman slowly wiped the trickle of blood which was dribbling from the side of his mouth. "You're not allowed to hit me," he protested.

Peveril leaned closer towards him. "Don't whine," he hissed in a low, unpleasant voice. "I don't like people who whine." He raised his head to observe the effect that this last remark had on his captive. "And don't bother to call for help. The orderly doesn't like people who whine either. It might be slightly less amusing for me if he had to hold you down to stop you crying out, but I can assure you that you wouldn't benefit at all. Not at all."

Quite unexpectedly, the door opened and the orderly entered.

"The other interrogator, sir," he announced, before retiring smartly.

Peveril looked up, only to recognise the new arrival in horror.

A hardening around the newcomer's lips suggested that he had sized up the situation accurately. "I shall take over the questioning now. Wait for me outside, please."

Two hours later, Patrick Fletcher, K.C., finished his official examination of Denman and emerged from the interrogation room. As instructed, Peveril was waiting. Fletcher turned to him.

"Well?"

Silence greeted this question. Fletcher sighed. He knew what he ought to do. He ought to storm in to the senior officer on duty and demand that Peveril be cashiered or, at the very least, reprimanded and never left to interrogate a suspect alone again. That would be the correct response – and by far the simplest and quickest course of action. On the other hand, would it make matters worse if he did a little questioning of his own? Fletcher assumed the forbidding countenance which he wore in court when dealing with witnesses of doubtful veracity.

"I assume that you are not completely ignorant of the principles of the Geneva Convention?"

Peveril shook his head wordlessly.

"Then do enlighten me as to whether you would have hit a foreign prisoner-of-war if you had been interrogating him? Or do you reserve assaults merely for the sweepings of the gaols of London?"

When there was no response, the barrister demanded, "Why did you do it?"

Unable to think of anything else to say, Peveril muttered, "Denman wouldn't tell me the name of his Dutch contact. I lost my temper."

Fletcher frowned at the younger man. "A year ago, you were less than co-operative when you were questioned, first by the police and then by me as your defence counsel. No-one treated you like that. And do you really think that evidence extracted under those sorts of conditions is likely to be reliable?"

"Wishing you hadn't defended me, sir?"

Even although Fletcher suspected that the lieutenant's cool impertinence was designed to disguise any regrets which he might have, his own patience promptly evaporated. "If I marched you in before Col. Hall-Gordon, I wouldn't be acting as counsel for the defence; I'd be the main witness for the prosecution. Be thankful that it is far more important that I spend this evening reporting the name of Denman's contact and the details of his routes than wasting my time filling in forms in triplicate concerning your conduct." He surveyed Peveril disapprovingly. "Moreover, you might reflect upon the fact that the information could be discovered without resorting to violence."

With that, Fletcher left abruptly. Peveril sank down onto a convenient chair. He knew that what he had done was inexcusable. It didn't matter that getting the information was crucial, that lives depended upon it. He should never have hit a suspect. He'd behaved exactly as his father would have behaved – even although he knew how Leo's actions had made people suffer. And, as Fletcher had said, using brute force wasn't likely to lead to reliable information anyway. Peveril squirmed. Why, why, why had it been the barrister who had seen him? And why had he made things worse by throwing Fletcher's help the previous year back in his teeth? Peveril flushed. He ought to have explained, to have told Fletcher that the officer in charge of the case had fallen sick and he'd been ordered to take over an actual interrogation, rather than simply marshalling the preliminary facts. But that would have looked like he was trying to justify the unjustifiable and Fletcher would have despised him even more. And it still didn't excuse hitting an unarmed man.

The next morning, a corporal brought Peveril a request that he report to Major Reynolds immediately. Peveril managed to treat this information with casual insouciance, but underneath he was perturbed. His concerns were not allayed by Reynolds' opening words.

"Ah, Peveril, you are to be posted away from here."

"Indeed, sir?"

Reynolds gave him an unfriendly look. When Hall-Gordon had asked him who could be most easily spared, it had been simple to suggest that the young lieutenant be transferred. It was not just that Peveril was the newest addition to the base; Reynolds instinctively mistrusted anyone who so clearly avoided joining in the social life of the mess. If anyone had to be posted to Counter-Espionage, the ideal candidate was a loner like Peveril.

"Yes. You will report to Major Collingwood in St James's at eleven hundred hours." Reynolds' face took on a vulpine glimmer of pleasure. "I gather that the colonel thinks that you will have more scope to practise your particular skills under Collingwood than here."

Peveril saluted and withdrew, before returning in shock to his quarters.

'So Fletcher did report me after all. I know I was damned rude and he probably didn't like it, but he said he wasn't going to report me. Why did he change his mind? Is it because he's a lawyer? Or did he intend to report me all along and he didn't want an argument?' Peveril scowled angrily at his reflection in the mirror. 'I can see why he felt that he had to take action; I wouldn't even have argued with him if he had hauled me before Hall-Gordon. But he shouldn't have lied to me.'

As Peveril finished packing and slammed the lid of his suitcase shut, an unpleasant thought occurred to him. Perhaps Fletcher had deliberately left him in ignorance to give him a greater shock when he found out that he had been reported. 'If that's the case I don't see why I should bother making an effort with this Collingwood chap. I'll practise some of my particular skills that Major Bloody Sarcastic Reynolds hasn't seen much of. A few weeks of airy persiflage and downright insubordination ought to be enough to get me chucked out of Intelligence altogether.'

Dragging the door open and then slamming it shut behind him after he had emerged, Peveril hastened across the parade ground, hoping that he would not meet anyone. Rejecting the offer of a cab, he stormed towards the underground station, before getting onto a tube. As the train rattled and clattered towards central London, Peveril's furious resentment died down somewhat. He still felt bitterly betrayed by Fletcher, but perhaps there were other considerations to be taken into account. Ralph remembered with some embarrassment the cutting comment which an ex-Egyptology don, now full-time Intelligence officer, had made to him during an argument at training – 'Young man, this war is not being fought to prove the manhood of individual officers'. Well, he hadn't ever exactly meant to imply that it was, but perhaps not making an effort wasn't a particularly patriotic – or sensible – approach. If he blotted his copy-book further and got chucked out of Intelligence, he might get reduced to the ranks. Wouldn't dear brother Robert crow over him if that happened. Nor did he really believe that he would be of more use to the war effort as a private.

Peveril gave a wry grin. If he didn't like being ordered around as a lieutenant, how much worse would it be as other ranks? And it wouldn't be enormously amusing explaining the reasons for his reduction in status to Hartismere. The Vice-Master of Trinity could be just as caustic as the Egyptologist when he chose and, somehow, Peveril doubted that the don would regard insubordination in a military context as praiseworthy – however much Hartismere might have practised insubordination in an academic context.

An hour later, Peveril arrived at the address in St James's, entered the tall building and gave his name to the clerk on duty. After a few minutes, the clerk informed him that Major Collingwood was free. Peveril followed the clerk upstairs, wondering what Collingwood would be like. As the clerk opened the door and indicated that he should enter, Peveril hesitated momentarily in surprise on the threshold. The officer at the desk was one who had been present during his final assessment at recruitment, and Peveril remembered with disquiet how he had fallen foul of him. Ralph made himself advance forward with every air of confidence. Perhaps the major saw so many would-be adornments of the Intelligence realm that he would not remember one who had singularly failed to shine in the firmament of eager recruits, However, the glare in the major's eyes suggested that recognition was mutual.

"I thought I remembered the name," the older man commented abruptly, after Peveril had closed the door. "You were the insubordinate young hound who thought that it was amusing to be offensive to a superior officer, weren't you?"

Peveril compromised on an inconsequential, "Sir."

Collingwood favoured him with a heavy stare. "Let me warn you that you will make yourself very unpopular if you try that sort of thing here."

"Yes, sir," agreed Peveril, wondering why on earth the major had passed him at the selection board if he objected to him so much. He was unaware that Intelligence was expanding rapidly and desperately needed new recruits. Since Peveril's brains had outweighed any tendency towards insubordination, Collingwood had authorised Peveril's recruitment, although at that stage he had had no expectation that Peveril would join him in Counter-Espionage.

Having finished glaring at Peveril for the moment, Collingwood continued.

"Cambridge man, aren't you?"

"Yes, sir."

"Trinity?"

"Yes, sir."

"Any meaningful experience since you joined?"

"No, sir."

The major grunted. "I suppose you have to start somewhere."

Ralph waited, unsure how to reply to this less-than-enthusiastic assessment of his promise.

"Well, sit down, man; I haven't time to waste."

"Sir," replied Ralph, feeling as if he were taking part in a rather bad amateur farce. However, as Major Collingwood began to outline the operation, any thoughts of amusement melted away.

"We know there's a Fifth Column in this country; we always knew that there would be. Most of the buggers who paraded around airing their views on the importance of Anglo-German friendship are safely locked up, but there are a few who had the good sense to lie low and not draw attention to themselves over the previous few years. Now that war has been declared, their main concern is either to acquire information useful to the Nazi war effort, or to wait until the Germans attempt a landing and then do their damnedest to interrupt our response."

The major scowled balefully at a pigeon which had alighted on his windowsill and was looking in, for all the world as if it

10

were an Intelligence operative eager to eavesdrop on his words. "You won't be searching for any of the big fish," he declared brusquely. "However, there's no harm keeping tabs on the lesser fry, especially when their activities serve to damage morale."

Ralph nodded in what he hoped was an intelligent manner. Major Collingwood shot him an ill-favoured glance. "You will be based at C Coy, the 2nd Battalion, East Suffolk Regiment. We've had reports of dissension in the ranks, low morale and defeatist talk. Likely as not it's some rot dreamed up by the old woman of a padre who's supposedly in charge of their souls – if they've got any souls in the East Suffolks, which I take leave to doubt. Your job will be to see whether defeatist talk does exist, whether it's any worse there than anywhere else, and, if so, if anyone appears to be driving it. You will be going under the guise of Capt. Thrigby, an expert, God help you, in the correct siting, positioning and use of semaphore stations. You can mug it up on the train down there – I don't suppose that they'd notice whether what you say is correct or not, but it won't harm you to acquire some military knowledge, even if it is about two hundred years out of date."

"Yes, sir," replied Peveril, wondering whether all senior officers in the Intelligence Corps normally sounded as world-weary, or whether Major Collingwood was merely a particularly bilious specimen.

"Thrigby joined up at seventeen and is now twenty-four. That explains how he has already attained his captaincy." Collingwood ran his eyes over Peveril's face. "You could just pass for that age, so don't act otherwise. Thrigby also belongs to the Survey Unit. That will give you far more freedom than if you were posted in the ordinary way to C Coy – you will not, for example, undertake ordinary regimental duties, although it may be tactful to help out somewhat. You will also have much greater access to petrol. It may be worth dropping some hints that your semaphores are a cover for something more important – but for God's sake don't mistake ordinary professional interest for treason."

"No, sir."

The major sighed and thrust a brown file at him. "The padre's been rushed into hospital, so you can't talk to him. But a summary of his statement is in this. Read it and the rest of the briefing, return the file to the clerk, and collect the appropriate paperwork from him – identity papers, travel permit, that sort of thing. And don't forget, you must observe the utmost security about what you're doing."

"Yes, sir."

Collingwood let Ralph walk most of the way to the door before he called out. "Oh, Lt. Peveril…"

"Yes, sir?"

A malicious smirk crossed Collingwood's face. "Very poor, Lieutenant; from now on you should only answer to Capt. Thrigby until you are given leave to do otherwise."

Peveril forced his face to remain expressionless. "Very good, sir; thank you for warning me." However, once outside the room, he cursed. 'How could I have been such a damned fool to fall into such an obvious trap?' He shrugged his shoulders. 'I suppose if I'd ignored him, he'd have blown me out of the water for lack of respect. Was it some sort of test or is he just a fire-eater? And why the devil did he have to have been at Waterbeach? Fat chance of my making a decent impression now.'

Ralph grimaced as he recollected one particular remark which Collingwood had heard. Admittedly, he'd been pretty annoyed when an anonymous naval commander who was questioning him had asked him how he would explain the presence of 'Peveril the murderer' in some cushy number which required him to be based far away from the front. Nonetheless, perhaps it had been a mistake to snap back that everyone would attribute it to his new-found wealth – or the fear of letting loose a murderer with a rifle. "Think of the damage I could cause if I decided to knock off the local brass-hats," he had drawled irritatingly. "Particularly if I were in charge of an entire platoon. No one will wonder why I'm not doin' my bit at the front; it's you who will invite suspicion, sir. The only explanation for a regular officer of your age hangin' round Whitehall is Intelligence, a breakdown, or both."

Since the unknown commander had been assigned to Intelligence duties precisely because he was still recovering his somewhat shaky equilibrium from the shock of seeing his ship blown up and most of the survivors machine-gunned, Peveril's shot in the dark had been remarkably accurate. Naturally, Peveril was unaware that he had both impressed Collingwood with his instinctive grasp of the truth, whilst at the same time repelling the major because of his apparent cold-blooded arrogance.

However, by the time that the suppositious Capt. Thrigby was sitting on a slow train out of Liverpool St. Station, Ralph had lost interest in whether Collingwood's irascibility was genuine or assumed. He was busily trying to remind himself of the details of his new persona, as set out in the file.

'I wish to goodness I'd been allowed to take notes to go over on the journey. I don't want to forget anything important.' Ralph gazed anxiously out of the window as street after street of small London houses swept by. 'I suppose it'd be a bit risky if I were found with notes of my own address and other things I ought to be expected to know automatically, but I'd rather have mugged them up than this idiotic bilge about semaphore stations. As if we'd be using them in France – or anywhere else, for that matter!'

Despite Peveril's intention to focus firmly on his new assignment, he found himself returning again and again to the humiliating fact that a man whom he admired had seen him behaving in a barbaric fashion.

'I bet Fletcher does regret saving my neck now. Why else would he have reported me? He must think that I'm a callous brute. And I certainly shan't be asked to dinner next time Midge is visiting Jenny.' Ralph swallowed hard as a thought struck him. 'Immortal gods, what if Fletcher tells Midge? He may think it's his bounden duty to warn her.' He stared unhappily at the carriage floor. He had missed Midge desperately badly when she had been in Italy. Indeed, his longing for her had made it quite clear to him that he really did love Midge and it wasn't just gratitude for her help at the trial, as he had at first wondered. But he didn't know what she felt about him. And if Fletcher informed Midge that he went around hitting unarmed prisoners, he'd never have the chance to tell her that he loved her.

Chapter Two

Whilst Ralph was worrying whether Fletcher might expose his true character to Midge, the object of his thoughts was curled up in Cambridge reading a letter from Ralph's mother.

'Ralph has been very good about writing to me regularly, but his letters seem rather tense. Has he said anything to you which might explain what is worrying him? You see, my dear, Ralph spent so much of his childhood trying to protect me that, even now, he is very unlikely to tell me anything which might upset me. He was very badly damaged by his father's actions and you are the first friend he has had whom he trusts completely. If he were to confide in anyone, it would be you. He respects your intelligence and common sense. Indeed, he told me that he hopes that his younger sister will grow up to be like you. I don't ask you to pass on to me whatever is worrying him, but I would be deeply grateful if you could let him talk to you.'

Midge sighed as she folded up this letter. All she had noticed was that Ralph seemed very worried about the progress of the war. Midge suddenly grinned. Ralph's last letter had been notable for a promise to arrange a regular supply of food to be sent from his estate for Bertie if rationing were to cause problems for cats. Midge leant over to stroke Bertie. "I don't imagine that will be necessary, but perhaps you might like the odd pheasant or partridge." Bertie yawned and settled himself more comfortably, so Midge turned to her second letter, which was from her aunt.

'You can imagine the shock when we heard – your uncle had actually interviewed him about his experiences when he reached Britain. And since he was such a fine sailor it makes it all the more tragic that he died in such a pointless manner. His poor wife is absolutely distraught – they'd fallen in love years ago, when she was a student at the Warsaw Scientific Institute. She turned up here, demanding to speak to your uncle and making all sorts of wild allegations about nameless people who wanted Serring dead. I'm afraid that I had to agree with Ellen's assessment that "she was fair mazed with grief". I can't imagine why she wanted to speak to Geoffrey, but she seemed to think that his absence was further proof of some dark plot. Once I'd convinced her that your uncle wasn't here, she refused my offer of tea and went away muttering about going up to London to "speak to people and tell them what was going on."'

Midge turned to the newspaper cuttings which her aunt had enclosed. '*Local man drowned*' was the bald heading of the first, which went on to explain that Mr Richard Serring, an ornithologist of note, had been found dead in the River Hart. '*The Hart, which has strong tidal currents at its mouth, is known for the speed with which the tide turns,*' it explained helpfully, before adding, '*It is thought that Mr Serring may have been pursuing his research into seabirds and forgot the dangers of the tide. Mr Serring, although a Suffolk man by birth, had spent many years in Poland tracing the migratory patterns of the Great Bustard, and he may not have been familiar with the treacherous nature of this particular part of East Suffolk.*' Reading this addendum, Midge could not escape the conclusion that the author was rather proud of the inimical aspects of his native shores. Presumably Serring would have been less likely to drown if he had not spent so long in strange places in Mitteleuropa.

A second cutting from the *East Anglian* reported on the inquest at which, it appeared, more details about the man's life had emerged. According to Serring's widow ('*dressed in deep black and speaking in a faltering voice wracked with emotion*'), the dead man had been accustomed to spend a considerable amount of time on the seashore. Furthermore, since his main interest was observing the activities of birds at daybreak, he generally secreted himself in a convenient position to watch their early-morning flight. When asked by the coroner whether Serring kept to one particular location, Mrs Serring had stated that he moved about to ensure that he collected the greatest data. If he expected to be in one place for several weeks he would build a rudimentary hide, but most of the time he contented himself with scraping a hollow in the sand where he could lie unobserved.

'*Readers of the East Anglian will remember the daring escape of Mr and Mrs Serring from Poland last autumn,*' concluded the report. '*Faced with the invading hordes of Herr Hitler's warriors, Mr Serring concocted a plot which would put the late Erskine Childers to shame. Loosing his small vessel from its mooring close to Danzig, he sailed through the Baltic Sea, accompanied only by his Polish wife and their terrier, evading all German vessels. This epic voyage was a feat of navigational exactitude and only when Mr Serring reached the North Sea did he feel safe to sail by day, sure in the knowledge that the Royal Navy was patrolling the waters which surround this sea-girt isle.'*

Despite the somewhat exaggerated conclusion to the tale, Midge could not help agreeing with her aunt. Imagine managing to complete such a journey, practically under the eyes of the German Navy, only to meet your end by drowning in a creek. And how dreadful for Mrs Serring to have thought that they had escaped to safety only to lose her husband scarcely six months later. Midge shivered, unwilling to envisage what it must be like to be caught in an undercurrent, tossed and battered against the beach, unable to escape the predatory clasp of the sea. Thank goodness that wasn't something which she was likely to face, but how many men in the Navy were going to meet that end? Why couldn't Hitler have been satisfied with ruling Germany? Why had he insisted on dragging Europe into another conflagration?

Chapter Three

When Ralph eventually arrived at the small seaside town of Newton, which was the temporary home of C Company, it slowly became apparent that others apart from him had their doubts about the value of his supposed professional expertise. However, the pointlessness of his cover-role appeared not to rouse any suspicion as to Ralph's real identity – it was clear that months in the army had inured the officers to tasks which had no possible utility.

"Ah, Thrigby, good to see you," greeted the major who was in charge of the company. "HQ said that you'd be down today or tomorrow."

"Sir," replied Peveril, as he flung up a stiff salute.

"You don't need to stand on ceremony with me," responded the major. "We're a pretty relaxed bunch on the whole. There's not a lot happening, but that's no bad thing whilst we find our feet. Come and meet the rest of the chaps."

Major Goodwin's assessment of the company as being a relaxed bunch seemed to be borne out by his introduction of Corporal Trent, the mess-waiter, to Peveril. "Trent's the most important man in C Coy," he joked. "He's the man in charge of drinks. And talking of which, will you join me in a spot, Thrigby? We tend to gather for a snifter at this time if there's not much on."

"Rather," agreed Peveril, instinctively feeling that a hearty response would go down well. "Dashed dull journey out here."

"Not even a pretty girl to cheer it up?" enquired Goodwin. "Devilish, these trains are."

Ralph was left distinctly unsure whether the slowness of the trains or the lack of pretty girls who chose to travel on them was the main area of weakness in LNER's lines to Ipswich, Norwich and stations in-between. He sank his nose into his gin to avoid the need to make any coherent response.

"I'm Hetherley," declared a portly 2nd lieutenant, who had been chatting with Trent. "And this is Snellgrove. What's your role to be in our glad throng?"

"Semaphores."

"Semaphores?" repeated Hetherley, in surprised tones. "Do you mean those windmill things the navy use?"

"Not just the navy," retorted Peveril, hoping that Hetherley did not number Garst-Perkins' *The History and Use of the Semaphore in Modern Military Training* (published 1871) amongst his favourite bedtime literature. Plagiarising shamelessly, he added, "The semaphore has been a key component in both sea-to-shore signalling practice and also in land-to-land communications. The first use of the semaphore can be traced back with certainty to Roman times, although they did not have quite the subtleties available to the modern signaller."

"Such as Morse Code?" suggested Snellgrove. Behind him, Ralph heard Major Goodwin mutter something uncomplimentary about the War Office having sent down a right dull beggar when they really needed someone who could play a decent hand of bridge. Feeling that he had established his apparent professional expertise as much as was needed on the first evening, Ralph turned to his questioner.

"What about you, Hetherley? What's your task?"

Hetherley grinned. "Trying to stop Pte. Wetherill from thumping Pte. Catchpole was this morning's pleasant duty."

"What were they quarrelling about now?" sighed Goodwin. "I really don't want to have to deal with them again. They create so many unnecessary problems."

"Catchpole said that Wetherill's grandmother was a witch who put the evil eye on Catchpole's sister-in-law's youngest but one."

"You're making that up," accused Goodwin. "We're not living in the sixteenth century."

"But we do currently live in darkest Suffolk," joked Hetherley. "Mind you, my spies tell me that it's even worse in Norfolk. They still eat babies there."

"Lots of sixteenth-century crime is coming back into fashion," remarked Snellgrove acidly. "The way people react to a perfectly sensible remark about the Maginot Line makes you feel as if you'll be lucky to escape being boiled alive in oil for High Treason."

Goodwin glared angrily for a moment at Snellgrove. Trust

him to make that sort of bitter remark in front of a newcomer. If that got back to HQ, he'd have Durrant complaining about his company not functioning as a team. What did Durrant expect with a pessimist like Snellgrove always seeing the worst?

After the quick snifter had turned into three fairly large glasses, Goodwin suggested that Hetherley might as well take Thrigby for a tour round the camp.

"It's getting a bit late to pick out good sites for windmills," he added, "but at least you'll get a feel for the layout of the tents. I'd come with you, but I've got some rosters to fill up."

As they picked their way round the camp, Peveril asked whether the officers were housed in tents, too.

"Gad, no!" expostulated Hetherley. "We've got quarters above the mess. I rather draw the line at boy-scoutery."

"Beastly in winter," agreed Peveril, absent-mindedly. "It looks quite pleasant now."

"Just wait until the first lot of bad weather," warned Hetherley. "It's foul with a gale blowing in off the coast, summer or winter."

"What's the battalion doing at present?" enquired Peveril with interest.

"D Coy's in France along with nearly half of our men. It's left us beastly under strength, but I imagine they're more needed over the Channel than spread along the coast." Hetherley shrugged. "We're supposed to be improving or guarding coastal defences, but I can't see much point in it. We've still got a Navy, thank God!"

"They need to earn their rum ration somehow."

This comment was well-received and by the time the two returned to the old farm-house which housed the officers' mess, Hetherley had clearly decided that Thrigby might not be such a blot as he had initially feared. For his part, once Peveril had managed to detach himself from the jovial atmosphere of the mess, he found it much harder to sum up his impressions. If he were making a report to Collingwood, how would he describe the men he had met? Goodwin – medium height, mousy hair, unsuccessful moustache, breath smelling of coffee. Those were the externals, what about the rest of him? Well, he seemed quite jovial, but did that mean anything? After all, perhaps someone who knew Collingwood well might not think that he was a martinet. Peveril shrugged and returned to his mental report. Snellgrove – thin, with a hard-bitten face reminiscent of turn-of-the-century cartoons of cavalry officers. What else? Did an acid tongue and a resentful manner match the cavalry officer type? Probably not. As for Hetherley, he was overweight, but so far otherwise indeterminate. Trent, on the other hand, was markedly nosey and clearly a privileged specimen. Was that because he controlled the gin supply, or did he possess any other more important traits?

'It all seems so damned normal,' Peveril growled under his breath as he threw another grey army blanket over his iron bedstead. 'I suppose that Snellgrove's talk of heresy sounds a bit suspicious, but if he really were a traitor would he discuss that sort of thing so casually in front of a stranger? And if I'm meant to seize upon Hetherley's remarks about having spies in Norfolk and deduce that his subconscious mind has betrayed him, then all I can say is that I'm not cut out for this game.' He yawned. Either the sea-air or the large amount of alcohol which had circulated during dinner had made him sleepy. 'I'll worry about things tomorrow,' he resolved as he turned out the light. 'Something may occur to me then.'

Ralph's impression of the innocuousness of the company was reinforced over the following days. Cautious investigation revealed that Hetherley was quite correct to say that C Company was horribly under strength. However, Goodwin merely laughed when Ralph asked if the men were downhearted at having to carry out a full company's work when at half-strength.

"No, no, there's no problem at all. We present an air of hard work and that's all HQ cares about." The major suddenly frowned. "Of course, I've ended up with a lot more on my plate, but that is one of the responsibilities of command."

Peveril made the appropriate noises of sympathy, while admitting to himself that morale did seem strong. True, C Coy did not seem to achieve a great deal of work and, even to Peveril's Cambridge-educated eyes, the officers appeared to drink more than he would have expected. Nonetheless, there was nothing especially sinister in men with nothing much to do resorting to the bottle to liven up yet another dull evening. He thought that he would have taken to drink himself if he had been on a genuine posting, stuck talking to the same few men night after night. Even when he had volunteered to act as Duty Officer, there had been no excitement – let alone anything of interest in the company rosters, which he had assiduously investigated in the hope that they would reveal something crucial to his real role.

Peveril soon got into the habit of devoting part of each day to long walks along the coast. He had begun doing so partly to improve his knowledge of the local terrain and partly to reinforce his cover, since he could claim that these excursions were vital for investigating possible positions for a new, advanced system of semaphore stations. Before long, no-one showed any interest in his activities, and he only maintained his exercise as a cast-iron excuse to get away from the torpid boredom of the camp and to have the chance to think.

On the ninth day after his arrival, Ralph was reluctantly returning to what he strongly suspected would be yet another evening devoted to bridge, the sole possible excitement being if Snellgrove were to enliven matters by protesting to Goodwin about the need to set a proper camp guard. As he turned in at the guard-post, manned somewhat slackly by a corporal and a private, Peveril spotted an unfamiliar back entering the officers' mess.

'Surely the colonel hasn't paid an unexpected visit?' speculated Peveril edgily, wondering whether he could really convince the battalion commander that he was an expert on semaphores. Then he reassured himself. 'Of course he hasn't. If Durrant were here, Cpl. Jackson would be showing rather more enthusiasm about guarding the gate. It must Poole back from leave.'

Acknowledging Jackson's sketchy salute, Ralph hurried over to the officers' mess. He had little doubt that 2nd Lt. Poole would prove to be as unpromising a suspect as the other three officers, in which case he would have to either report failure or try to dig up something against the padre who had first raised the alert. He suspected that neither response would gain him much praise from Major Collingwood in London, but he was running out of ideas and a brief visit to B Coy had not suggested anything useful.

Poole proved to be about the same age as Ralph and seemed to be popular in the mess, although less lively than Hetherley had led Peveril to believe.

"About time you returned," remarked Hetherley. "Thrigby's not much of a hand at bridge."

"Poker's more my style," agreed Ralph helpfully. "Bit livelier, what? I can't stand the sort of piddling affairs that are on hand here. Plunge properly into a game is my rule."

"Oh, ah, quite," agreed Poole, running his hand through his fair hair in a distracted manner.

"How are things at HQ?" demanded Snellgrove. "Weren't you meant to spend a few days there before you rejoined us following your leave?"

"Nothing new," Poole grunted, as he nodded his thanks to Trent for bringing a pint of beer. "Same old invasion scare. Durrant's surrounding himself with plans and more plans, but doesn't want to share anything with us."

Hetherley grinned. "You can't really expect a colonel to share his thoughts with junior officers. We subalterns are there to do as ordered, not to provide criticism."

"Especially not when whatever plan Durrant's using will have been thought up by some brass hat in the War Office who probably hasn't been near a battle for twenty years," growled Snellgrove, his thin face twisted in disapproval. "We ought to have men with experience at the top. Our brigadier hardly compares to Guderian."

"Ibbotson's not a tank man," agreed Poole, "but this isn't Poland and Jerry won't be bringing over tanks on the first wave."

Snellgrove snorted. "There was nothing wrong with the Poles' spirit. They made damned brave soldiers – I shouldn't care to tackle a tank on horseback as they did. But the point is that our top men aren't up to the Wehrmacht's. Guderian and von Runstedt will make mincemeat out of Gort and Alexander."

Major Goodwin looked mildly perturbed by this comment. "Come off it, Snellgrove. Things in Poland may not have been too bright, but there's always the Channel – we saw off Napoleon that way, why shouldn't we see off Hitler too? Leave that sort of worry to the brass hats – that's what they're paid for; I want to know what Poole got up to in London."

Chapter Four

On the following day, Peveril had gained leave to go to Cambridge, rather than pursue his normal duties searching for semaphore sites. He would have preferred to have slipped off without saying where he was going, but that seemed too risky. If someone chanced to see him at the railway station it might give rise to awkward questions, whereas a plea of needing to attend to urgent personal affairs had received casual acceptance from Goodwin. Moreover, Ralph's excuse was entirely true. He had come of age three days after being posted to the East Suffolks and he was eager to sign his will.

"It's not that I have any expectation of dying," he muttered to himself as he stared out of the window at the flat landscape, broken by magnificent oaks and elms, "but I want to make sure that Mother and Honor are protected if something were to happen. I don't want to rely upon that informal will; it wouldn't cover the entailed estate." He shivered suddenly. "Goose walking over my grave," he mocked. "At least I can relax for a day – I think I'll scream if I hear the word semaphore again."

After the unnerving business of signing his will had been complete and he emerged from his solicitor's office, Ralph glanced at his watch. Could he go and see Midge? He had enough time. Then his face contracted. Midge certainly wouldn't welcome him if Fletcher had seen fit to enlighten her as to his methods of dealing with unarmed prisoners. Ralph shrugged. There hadn't been any change in tone in Midge's last letter and the K.C. would probably prefer to pass on any such information face to face. Anyway, if Fletcher had told her, better that he find out now.

Minutes later, Ralph was striding through Newnham, hoping that Midge would not be out. Having keyed himself up to test Midge's reaction to him, it would be unutterably disheartening to come away without seeing her. To his relief, Midge answered her door and – still more to his relief – appeared to be pleased to see him.

"Ralph? Is it really you?"

"It is indeed," agreed Ralph, before glancing down at Midge's feet, where a huge, great black cat was twining round her legs. "Two cats?" he questioned, momentarily distracted from his own concerns. "I thought you only had one."

Midge grinned. "Last year's problems have had unforeseen benefits. I'm terrible popular with the Newnham authorities now, so when my old housemistress needed someone to look after darling Boris, I had no difficulty in getting permission."

Ralph looked rather dubious. "Doesn't Bertie mind?"

"No. They're old friends." Midge laughed. "I don't suppose that you came to Cambridge to talk about cats, enjoyable though the subject is. And aren't I supposed to be felicitating you on becoming twenty-one?"

"Oh, that," replied Peveril dismissively.

Midge looked slightly surprised at this response, but was too busy passing on her congratulations at Ralph's new rank to pursue the matter further. For his part, Ralph glanced down as his pips in horror, appalled that he was masquerading as a captain in front of Midge.

"You must have done frightfully well," praised Midge.

"Yes… well… no, not really."

Midge appeared not to be put off by this incoherent response. "Come in and I'll make some tea. You won't want to discuss your promotion in the corridor."

Ralph entered suspiciously. "Why?"

"Well, you're in Intelligence, aren't you?"

"Midge!" expostulated Ralph in shock. "Who told you that? Surely Fletcher didn't? Was it Hartismere?"

Despite herself, Midge giggled. "Honestly, Ralph, it's just as well I don't know your C.O.; I can't think what he'd make of you exposing yourself and two other contacts like that. Come to think of it, I didn't know that Mr Fletcher had any involvement with Intelligence. Jenny's never said anything."

Peveril scowled at the fire.

"Don't look so annoyed," coaxed Midge. "I've suspected since last year that Dr Hartismere had links with Intelligence. And how else could you have gained such rapid promotion?" She looked thoughtful. "Of course, the other solution is that you're pretending to be a captain because you're undercover, in which case I think it's a bit risky to visit me."

"Risky?"

Midge sighed. "Some of the Newnham porters know who you are. It would be simple for anyone who was following you to find out what your real name is."

"I always said I wasn't cut out for Intelligence work," snapped Ralph savagely. "No wonder I've not discovered anything so far. You'd be much better than I would."

Now it was the turn of Midge's face to tighten. "At least you're doing something. What can I do?"

"Your place is here. You've got another year left in your degree."

"That didn't stop you," pointed out Midge unanswerably. "How does my degree help the war effort?"

"It gives you a trained mind," replied Ralph firmly.

"You sound like Dr Hartismere," grumbled Midge. "He said something similar."

"Which proves that it's good advice," answered Peveril, carefully avoiding admitting that he was merely parroting his tutor's arguments.

"You didn't listen to it."

"But you're a girl."

"What's that got to do with it?" Midge snarled. "Plenty of girls worked in munitions and on the land last war. I can't do either."

"You'd loathe being a Land Girl," retorted Ralph, in an attempt not to lose the argument. Somewhat belatedly he realised that this was hardly the best response to someone whose physical disability meant that she had no chance of becoming a Land Girl, whether she would enjoy it or not. However, rather than leaving his remark hanging awkwardly in the air, he ploughed on. "It sounds unutterably hearty. M'sister wants to join them."

"Honor?" queried Midge, in a voice of shocked incredulity.

Ralph sighed with relief at Midge's response; at least she had not raged at him for his tactlessness. "Hardly! No, it's Geraldine. I know that the Land Girls are doing a vital job, so it's dashed important that people do volunteer – especially since Land Girls don't have the glamour that the WAAF has. All the same, everyone else'll hate her. We had one of those keen types in the Territorials and I couldn't bear him always telling us that we should be leaping out of bed, eager to greet the new day."

"Don't you like the idea of getting up at four o'clock?" enquired Midge mischievously.

"Is that a joke?"

"Yes," replied Midge, somewhat surprised. Ralph didn't normally mind being teased.

Peveril grinned. "That's all right. For a moment, I thought that you were serious. What would it suggest about my investigatory credentials if I had misinterpreted your character so badly?" Encouraged by Midge's laugh, he added, "I blew some of my inheritance on an Alfa and I collected the keys today. Do come out for a spin, Midge, and I could show you her paces. I can wangle petrol as part of my cover, so we don't need to worry how far we go."

Midge reluctantly shook her head. "I'd better not. Considering that I raised the danger of someone finding out who you really are, we can't add to the risk by driving round the countryside."

Wishing that he could swear in front of a girl, Ralph contented himself by jabbing at the fire with the poker. "I suppose not," he replied, trying to disguise his hurt. "Best to be sensible."

"It's nearly the end of term," Midge pointed out. "If no-one were following you, maybe you could visit me at Brandon."

"I'd soon show a clean pair of heels to anyone who tried to tail me," boasted Peveril, relieved that Midge's invitation appeared to be genuine. "The Alfa'll lose anyone on the road."

"Good," remarked Midge somewhat absent-mindedly. She had suddenly been reminded of her cousin John's proud enthusiasm for his Lagonda. Normally, this would not have been a concern, but, given John's letter of the previous week – a letter clearly designed to warn her that he might not return from active service – she wasn't sure that she wanted to think about John in front of anyone else. Then, realising that it was rather poor form to go off into a day-dream when Ralph had made the effort to visit her, she pulled herself together. At least Ralph's assignment would provide a distraction from her current fears.

"You'd better tell me what your supposed name is," she remarked. "I don't want to deny all knowledge of you."

"Capt. Ernest Thrigby, currently on secondment to C Coy, 2nd Battalion, the East Suffolks," replied Peveril smartly. "My cover is researching sites for semaphore stations, but actually I'm checking up on morale in the battalion."

"Semaphore stations?" repeated Midge. "Aren't they rather Napoleonic?"

"They may indeed be, but they make a splendid cover story. When I tell people what I'm doing, half the chaps are too busy covering up their incredulity to pursue it further and the other half are bored rigid before I've got through the first paragraph of my set text."

"What else have you had to learn about the captain?" enquired Midge with interest. "What are you like?"

Peveril's face closed over.

Aware that she had somehow disturbed Ralph, Midge attempted to laugh the matter off. "Not Ralph Peveril, you clot; I mean this Capt. Thrigby. What's he like? Clever? Friendly?"

"He's a rotter," growled Ralph. "If he's not being arrogant and sneering, he's hearty and unreflecting. I can't bear him."

"Then why did you make him like that when you've got to live with him?"

Ralph gave a reluctant grin. "Mainly because I'm lazy and his behaviour is very easy to mimic. I also thought that people might be more inclined to let things slip in front of that sort of person compared with any other type. But I wish I hadn't made him quite so frightful."

Midge kept to herself her inevitable reflection that Ralph had modelled himself on certain members of his family. "Just don't get caught reading a Penguin Poetry special."

"Poets? Long-haired layabouts with no guts."

"Can you snort contemptuously as well?" enquired Midge admiringly.

"I shall practise assiduously," promised Ralph, before

remarking. "More to the point, Midge, I've spent ten days trying to track down some blighter who's supposedly spreading alarm and despondency, but so far I've done nothing more exciting than lose money playing cards on wet afternoons."

"Playing cards?" repeated Midge in surprised tones. "Aren't you doing something to keep the men occupied? No wonder they're disheartened."

"If you think that I want to crawl around digging gun emplacements in the rain…," began Ralph, before Midge interrupted him.

"No, I should very much doubt that you or any other sane person would want to. But surely you can see that if you don't keep the men occupied they'll just fall into bad habits. The officers, too, by the sound of it."

Ralph suddenly realised the source of Midge's outrage. Her father was a regular officer. Naturally his daughter would disapprove of such a slipshod approach to duties. "But I'm not there to encourage the growth of a tip-top detachment," he teased. "I'm there to investigate nay-sayers, gloom-merchants and, with a bit of luck, outright traitors. What better chance than if I do nothing to improve morale?"

"Do you really think that there is anything behind this story of someone deliberately lowering morale?"

Ralph shrugged his shoulders. "Increasingly I doubt it. To be quite honest, I've started to wonder whether I'm being tested for suitability – can I maintain my cover for a fortnight in the field? – that sort of thing."

"I suppose that would be quite a good exercise," nodded Midge thoughtfully. "Gosh, Ralph your superiors must think quite highly of you."

"Eh? Surely it must mean that they're not at all certain whether I'm good enough."

It struck Midge that, whatever was going on in his battalion, Ralph had sounded quite despondent himself several times during their conversation. She decided that now was the time to cheer him up, even if what she said was totally unsubstantiated.

"Why should they waste a fortnight if they doubt your suitability? After all, it'd be a waste of their time as well as yours.

Perhaps there really is someone whom you need to discover. Perhaps someone's been asked to pretend to be a dubious specimen to see if you could track him down. Think how highly you'd be rated if you discovered who he is."

"That's all very well, Midge," Ralph pointed out, "but I simply don't know what to do next." He repeated to Midge the various conversations which he had held with the other officers in the mess. "As I say, Snellgrove is the only one who makes comments which might argue a tendency towards defeatism, but I can't really see that there is any proof that he is an actual danger."

"Your Capt. Thrigby hasn't made any political remarks so far, has he?"

Ralph shook his head. "Any blighting remarks he makes are entirely aimed at boosting his prestige – he certainly doesn't talk politics."

"Possibly it's just as well that you took that attitude," murmured Midge. "That way you won't contradict yourself now."

"Won't contradict myself now?" repeated Peveril suspiciously. "What do you mean?"

Midge grinned. "It'd have been rather disastrous if you'd already nailed your colours to the mast as a good democrat. I had in mind that you might make a few remarks which suggest that you have more than a little sympathy with our Fascist friends."

"What?" demanded Ralph in horror. "I'm damned if I'm going to pretend to be some filthy Mosleyite!"

"Lt. Peveril isn't one, but Capt. Thrigby might well be one for a few weeks. Don't you see, if you trail your coat a little, then any genuine Fascist sympathiser may start paying attention to you?"

"And then I investigate him?"

"Exactly. If it doesn't work in C Coy, you could try the other companies in the battalion. Have you looked into them?"

"D Coy's in France, but I went to B Coy last week."

"And?"

Ralph winced. "They seemed to think it was awfully funny to mock Hore-Belisha."

"Because he's been pushed out of the War Office?"

"Nothing that sensible. There's a rather ghastly marching-song which the men were singing and none of the officers who were around did anything to stop them."

"What is it?" demanded Midge, wondering why Ralph was so reluctant to quote it.

"*Onwards Christian Soldiers, Ye shall have no fear, Israel Hore-Belisha leads you from the rear.*"

Midge grunted her disapproval. "His name's Leslie, quite apart from any other considerations."

"Now do you see why I don't want to play at being a Mosleyite? Confound it, Midge, I know I've made some pretty beastly remarks in my time, but I've never mocked a chap's race and I don't want to start now, even when in disguise."

"You don't have to."

"I'd look like a damned – sorry, Midge – deuced odd Fascist if I didn't."

Midge chewed on her thumb thoughtfully. She could see Ralph's point. Furthermore, she could see that an unconvincing denunciation of the perfidy of world Jewry might raise suspicions that Capt. Thrigby was not all he seemed. "Couldn't you pretend that you haven't read Il Duce's most recent communications to the faithful? After all, he used to claim that he wasn't anti-Semitic – he said so in his autobiography. You could be an old-fashioned admirer of Musso who approves of the fact that he made the trains run on time."

Ralph hunched his shoulders. "I think it's vile going around checking up on people's political beliefs. We might as well be in Germany – or Russia."

"It is vile," agreed Midge, "but if there's something fishy going on in your regiment it's your duty to hunt it out. That's why you've been sent there."

"Or it may just be some idiotic training exercise," growled Ralph angrily. "In which case I'm simply wasting time which should be devoted to the war effort. And I don't like all this pretence."

Midge bit her lip, wondering whether she dared tell Ralph that it must have been because of his capacity for pretence and subterfuge that he had been recruited into Intelligence in the first place.

Chapter Five

Although Ralph had been deeply relieved that Midge had been genuinely pleased to see him, by the time he had returned to the coast he was exceedingly perturbed about what he had revealed. Just because he'd had a shock when Midge had guessed that he was in Intelligence, that was no excuse for him to have confirmed her suspicions. And it certainly didn't justify him telling Midge the specific details of his mission. Ralph bit his lip edgily. When he had left, Midge had reassured him that she wouldn't say anything – she'd even pointed out that he oughtn't to have said anything to her. So she must be safe. She had to be. But what if she let something slip? It was all very well telling himself that she hadn't said anything about his mother last year; that hadn't involved national security.

As he tried to think what he could do to improve the situation, Ralph dismissed a nagging thought that he ought to have gone to Trinity to ask Hartismere's advice. He didn't want another vilely embarrassing interview with the Vice-Master, but, much more importantly, Hartismere would never be satisfied with a casual statement that Peveril had accidentally given away that he was in Intelligence. The don would drag out that he'd revealed every aspect of his mission, and that would leave Midge in a terrible position. In those circumstances, could Hartismere really restrict himself to simply warning Midge not to talk? It seemed unlikely. In fact, the only certain way in which Midge could be prevented from revealing anything would be to lock her up.

Ralph cursed. He was damned if he was going to repay Midge for saving him from the gallows by having that happen. Why had he been such an idiot? He'd been warned at training not to talk about his work and now he'd given himself away at the first opportunity.

Fortunately, when Ralph reached camp, any potential surprise as to his despondent demeanour was swallowed up in admiration of his new motorcar.

"I can quite see why you said that you had urgent personal

affairs," commented Major Goodwin, unable to keep a note of envy from his voice. "How fast does she go?"

"Very!"

"Lucky devil," breathed Hetherley, running his hand over the bonnet in an acquisitive fashion. "She'll be wasted on you – you don't know the roads round here, so you won't be able to let her out properly."

"Avoid Newton," warned Poole. "The constable there doesn't approve of 'them fast machines'."

"And you don't want to take her over the Newton causeway," agreed Goodwin. "It's too salty – you might damage her paintwork."

While momentarily amused by this interest in the Alfa, Ralph thought nothing more of it until later that evening when he became aware that Poole was paying him more attention than before. To start with, Ralph assumed that Poole must be angling for an invitation to drive the Alfa. However, whilst that shiny marvel of automobile workmanship certainly began the conversation, Poole soon brought up the subject of poker.

"Why don't you join me in a hand or two?" he suggested. "Bridge is a bit flat and, since we always play the same people, it becomes dreadfully predictable what will happen."

"Frightfully bad form to keep winning money off one's company commander," gibed Peveril. "Not that I do, actually, but bridge isn't really my game. Goes on too long for a start."

"Hetherley sometimes joins me," Poole remarked, "but he's tied up tonight. A rumour went round that the colonel's visiting tomorrow and Snellgrove's determined to make sure that everything is all spick and span. Goodwin, of course, is claiming to be too busy with paperwork to help him, so Snellgrove dragooned Hetherley in."

"How beastly dull," replied Peveril with a cavernous yawn. "I'm dashed glad I've been seconded to semaphores; it gets me out of all sorts of tedious rot, even if I have ended up in a ghastly hole like this place."

Poole signalled to Trent, the mess waiter, to bring them drinks, before finding a pack of cards and dealing them. Peveril had learnt to play the game competently years earlier, but was happy to appear as a bold and over-confident player. It struck him that Poole might be less inclined to take him seriously if he thought that he was reckless and slapdash. Nevertheless, despite his air of languid insouciance as his losses piled up, Ralph was surprised at how high the stakes were. Could Poole and Hetherley – as mere lieutenants – really afford this sort of play or did they break even against each other?

Although Peveril felt that his game of poker with Poole had given him an interesting sidelight into the habits of the mess, his investigations on the following day were rather less successful. Snellgrove had spent most of the morning and afternoon on tenterhooks in case Col. Durrant turned up. Unsurprisingly, he had reacted badly to Hetherley's remarks about not believing rumours until they were proved to be true.

"Don't be such a purblind idiot," he snapped. "How the devil do you think that I could have ensured that the men were properly organised if I'd waited until Durrant's staff-car actually showed up at the gate?"

Hetherley shrugged. "You're not the company commander; Goodwin'd get the blame, not you."

"I am very well aware of the fact that Major Goodwin is in charge of the company," retorted Snellgrove stiffly. "However, you seem to be unaware of two facts. First, that we all have our duty to do, no matter what attitude those at the top take, and, secondly, that blame is always passed down from the top. I may consider this company to be stagnant and damnably badly run, but I'll bet you five pounds that Durrant would have been told that it was the fault of junior officers that the men aren't smartly turned out and a credit to the regiment."

"Must you take things so seriously?" complained Hetherley. "We're not Prussians, so you can hardly expect their standard of drill."

"In case you hadn't noticed, there's a war on!"

Strolling off, Hetherley encountered Peveril and warned him to keep clear of Snellgrove. "He's like a bear with a sore head, but it's his own stupid fault. Anyone would know better than to believe Cpl. Trent's rumours. He may make a good mess waiter, but he's a frightful gossip. Personally, I think he invents things to make the time pass more quickly."

Peveril was delighted by this information. If Snellgrove were half as disgruntled as Hetherley appeared to believe, then this was a most opportune moment for testing some defeatist talk on him. Surely the lieutenant might let something slip out of frustration and irritation?

Eventually, Peveril found Snellgrove in the mess, downing a stiff whisky.

"Damned bad show you having to hang around all this time," opened Peveril.

Snellgrove grunted wordlessly into his whisky.

"Good for the men, though," persevered Peveril. "Keeps them on their toes, what?"

"Hmm."

"Slackness is the danger. You need real leadership to inspire men."

The lieutenant shot the supposed Captain Thrigby a suspicious look. "What do you mean?"

Sticking firmly to character, Peveril gave a hearty laugh. "Just think about chaps at school. Do they admire weedy intellectual types who never do anything more energetic than climbing the library steps to find some musty tome? Or do they look up to the rugger captain who doesn't shirk a hard struggle?"

"I was a cricketer myself."

"But not a weedy bookworm," chortled Peveril. "Dash it all, Snellgrove, you must know what I mean. Sport trains a man to command and that's what we need in this country – a few more men to take command."

Snellgrove deliberately drank a mouthful of whisky before responding. "I don't know what you're up to, and I don't want to know. But might I suggest that you try your wiles on someone else and leave me alone?"

On the pretext that he wanted to check that the Alfa was properly housed, Peveril retreated, wondering whether he had been too obvious. 'Did he think that I was trying to trap him into praising Mosley or was he just chary about slanging off Goodwin?' Ralph stared absent-mindedly at a greasy handprint which suggested that the Alfa had admirers other than Pte. Catchpole, who had eagerly volunteered to fill her up with petrol and polish her over. 'It's probably just as well that I'm going to visit A Coy tomorrow. Perhaps Snellgrove will have forgotten what I said when I get back.' He gave a rueful laugh. 'And how prescient of me to volunteer to accompany Hetherley on the rounds of the camp tonight. That'll enable me to avoid Snellgrove after dinner.' He sighed. 'I hope to goodness I manage to sleep tonight. Thank the Lord there isn't anyone sharing the room with me at the moment.'

Whilst Ralph was retreating ingloriously before the guns of Lt. Snellgrove, Midge had returned to Brandon, where she lived with her uncle and aunt. Geoffrey Carrington, a noted diplomatic correspondent, was absent in London, but when Midge tentatively tried to commiserate with her aunt about John being posted on active service, it was abundantly clear that the older woman preferred not to talk about it.

"There's no point discussing things, Midge. John is serving his country, just as his father and your father did in the last war. I learned to wait then and I can wait now."

Since Midge felt incapable of taking such a stoical line as Alice, she had resorted to distracting her mind by considering whether there really was a Fifth Columnist in the East Suffolks. She sighed, wishing that she knew the personalities involved. 'I'm sure it would be easier if I'd met the rest of his mess, but I can't imagine how Ralph would engineer that – I can't pretend to be his sister or cousin because his cover hasn't got any immediate family, and it would look deeply suspicious if he suddenly discovered a long-lost cousin.' She nibbled the corner of her thumb thoughtfully. 'Actually, I wonder whether it would be that much simpler if I did know the people. How easy, for instance, would I find it to spot a Fifth Columnist in Brandon?'

Mildly distracted by this conceit, Midge ran her mind over the people she knew locally. The trouble was that it was difficult to imagine any of them having much truck with Hitler's crew. Col. Gregory, although quite an authoritarian figure, had been mouthing curses for years at the German Reichschancellor.

Indeed, on the outbreak of war, the colonel had, with considerable smugness, pointed out that he had been absolutely correct to warn that the Hun would rear his ugly head again. The vicar, to whom this shaft had been addressed, made an equally unlikely Fascist sympathiser. In fact, he and Col. Gregory had fallen out over what the Rev. Halliday had termed Col. Gregory's excessive glorification of war. The idea of the scholarly, gentle vicar encouraging the hounds of Hell (as he had denounced the Nazi troops following the Blitzkrieg on Poland) to run loose over the Suffolk countryside which he loved was so ludicrous as to be laughable. As for the doctor, he had lost his only son in the Great War and in no circumstance could Midge imagine him having any sympathy with a regime which seemed determined to unleash a storm of horror even worse than that seen in the trenches of 1914-18.

Midge stirred uncomfortably, not wishing to contemplate how her uncle and aunt would react if they, too, lost their only son at the end of a German rifle. Then she frowned. There was somebody she knew who might have flirted with Fascism; certainly he had been inclined to make very approving remarks regarding Mussolini's ability to lick a notoriously divided and ill-disciplined nation into shape. Might he fit the description of a likely Fifth Columnist? And, even if he were not an actual traitor, his controversial views might well have brought him into contact with out-and-out sympathisers.

'Gosh,' she murmured unhappily, 'this is a bit foul. Surely I must have got carried away to even think this sort of thing.' She sat up, apologising to Bertie as he plaintively protested at her movements. 'Nevertheless, I suppose I really ought to consider this seriously. It's all very well assuming that General Whitlock is just a Poona veteran who regrets the days when he could command regiments and bark at a bevy of servants to carry out his every wish. But what if he isn't just a fiery old man? What if he thinks that 'the lower orders' need to be ordered around and bossed into shape by those who are born to lead and command? He'd be exactly the sort of person who would be extremely useful to the Germans. He's a trained soldier: he must know all the strategic points round here and he could lead an invasion force straight towards London. And he could be in contact with a whole series of like-minded officers who are actually serving, not retired as he is.'

Midge shivered, telling herself that she had let her imagination conjure up a nightmare vision of treason spreading secretly through the country, hedgerow by hedgerow, field by field. Surely the whole point of living in Britain was that you could make remarks which did not fit in with the viewpoint of the majority? And undoubtedly General Whitlock was a patriot; he still grew red, his moustache quivering with rage, when he discussed the fate of Abyssinia and the spinelessness of the British government in their failure to challenge Mussolini over it. But, another voice commented coldly in Midge's head, a man who despised the government's record on foreign affairs might be precisely the sort of man who welcomed the prospect of establishing firm rule based on the sound traditions of the army.

'The authorities must know that the general holds pretty strong views,' Midge countered her inner voice. 'They'd lock him up if they thought that he were a real danger. It's nothing to do with me. I was only posing a hypothetical question so that I could see whether Ralph's missed anything. It's absolutely none of my business and it would be hideously embarrassing even to suggest the possibility.'

Chapter Six

The following day, Peveril snaked the Alfa through winding, narrow country lanes to A Coy. Although it was situated only about eight miles up the coast from C Coy, the precautionary removal of all signposts made it difficult to find and Peveril lost his way twice. By the time he finally found the correct turn-off for the camp, he was distinctly fed-up.

'Why didn't I listen to Snellgrove's directions, rather than Goodwin's? That man has about as much idea as to how to command a company as a glandered baboon. I bet A Coy will be just as bad.'

However, it shortly became apparent that Lt.-Col. Durrant took a rather different approach to his work than did Major Goodwin. Not only was the guard at the gate extremely alert, but Peveril had had to pass through a road-block a mile away from camp. Even the Alfa's gleaming presence had not distracted the sentries until they had assured themselves of Capt. Thrigby's bona fides. 'Durrant clearly runs a tight ship in camp,' reflected Peveril, mixing his metaphors badly in his anxiety. 'I hope to goodness he doesn't realise that I'm a fraud who knows next to nothing about these wretched semaphores.'

After Ralph passed through the sentry-post, a private conducted him to Col. Durrant's quarters. Peveril, who was becoming nervous, followed the soldier, noting as he walked through the camp the many signs of efficiency which were not present in his own company. All too aware that he was not in the casual atmosphere of C Coy, Peveril snapped off his sharpest salute as he was ushered into Durrant's presence. The battalion commander acknowledged Peveril with a grunt. He did not approve of these peculiar specialists who got wished on a decent battalion. Mind you, he'd heard a dashed odd rumour last leave that several Survey Units were doing something a lot more interesting than positioning guns. It wasn't very likely that this Thrigby chap would let anything slip, but it might be worth following up. If it came to that, why was the man attached to Goodwin's mob – however loosely – rather than HQ? Again, something to keep an eye on.

Durrant growled under his breath. If he'd had his way, Goodwin would have been transferred, but Ibbotson had said that, whatever his faults, at least Goodwin was a trained man on the spot. Moreover, Ibbotson had pointed out that if you removed Goodwin, you would have to promote Snellgrove, which was impossible while Snellgrove's brother was behind bars as a danger to the state. Durrant growled again. It was a great pity that HQ was taking that line; Snellgrove could have been of considerably more use to him than Goodwin. But it was quite clear from Ibbotson's words that Snellgrove would not be promoted, so there wasn't much point in suggesting it again.

All these thoughts raced through Durrant's head as he cast a searching glance over the newest officer attached to the battalion.

"Thrigby, isn't it?"

"Yes, sir."

"Semaphores?"

"Yes, sir."

"And what use will they be here?"

"Well, sir," began Peveril, wishing that he did not feel as if the grizzled man in front of him could see straight through his pretence.

"Don't 'well, sir' me," spat Durrant. "Come out with what you have to say or say nothing at all."

A tiny imp of humour made Peveril wonder what would happen if he stayed mute when asked of the possibly utility of his supposed speciality. However, as Durrant's eyebrows snapped together menacingly, he made haste to outline his excuse.

"There is a strong chance that the enemy will be able to interfere with wireless transmissions. If that occurs, it will be essential to have a secondary means of communication to fall back upon. I have been sent to survey this coast not only to ensure that there can be rapid communication along possible areas of invasion, but also to ensure that ship-to-shore communication will be feasible."

"What's wrong with Morse?" demanded Durrant. "Surely you're not telling me that the Navy has forgotten how to signal?"

"No, sir. However, semaphore stations can send signals over a greater distance than Morse lamps can reach."

"Except at night," snorted Durrant.

"Yes, sir," agreed Ralph respectfully.

"I suppose Brigade know what they're doing," sniffed the colonel, giving every impression that he did not believe that they did. Peveril deemed it appropriate to maintain a tactful silence and, after a further glare, Durrant dismissed him.

As Ralph left Durrant's office, he encountered a fellow-captain whom he had met as Hetherley's guest at C Coy. Chatham was a regular soldier who had spent a fair amount of time studying German infantry tactics. As he had freely admitted, a lot of his knowledge had been proved out-of-date by the Blitzkrieg on Poland, but he still maintained that learning about your opponent was vital. Moreover, he had argued that visiting Germany had given him an insight into the German character which others lacked. Peveril had noted with some surprise that Hetherley had cross-examined Chatham in some depth on this point – it had seemed rather unlike Hetherley to take anything seriously.

"What brings you this way?" demanded Chatham, as he steered Peveril in the direction of A Coy's mess.

"I've surveyed everything south of C Coy's position and now I need to move north," explained Peveril, sticking to his cover-story. He glanced round conspiratorially. "Your C.O.'s a bit of a tartar."

Chatham grinned. "Durrant likes to keep everyone on his toes, isn't that so, Jervis?"

A tall lieutenant sauntered over to join them and Chatham introduced the supposed Capt. Thrigby.

"What you have to remember, Thrigby," explained Jervis languidly, "is that Durrant's a regular officer. He's got rather different standards from some of the jumped-up office clerks who think that because they're in khaki they know how to win a war."

Grateful that whatever else Thrigby's failings were, he had never been a clerk, Peveril gave an appreciative laugh. However, Jervis was not finished.

"Has Poole recovered from being rapped over the knuckles by Durrant last week?" he demanded.

Peveril pricked up his ears. "What do you mean?"

"He got bawled out by the C.O. when he was here a few days ago. We were laying bets on whether he cried on his way back to your lot."

"I didn't see any signs of it," responded Peveril cautiously.

Jervis sniggered. "I don't suppose you did – after all, you're in C Coy too."

Peveril thought swiftly. How would hearty Capt. Thrigby react? Angry loyalty. That was the line to follow.

"I fail to grasp your meaning," he replied stiffly.

"Come off it, Thrigby," chimed in Chatham. "I know you're attached to them, but even if you've only been there a fortnight, you must surely have spotted that they're a damned slack bunch. God knows how they get away with it – they wouldn't in the Wehrmacht."

Jervis grinned, his mobile face lit up with sardonic amusement. "Last time we were on manoeuvres, Goodwin completely failed to set a guard on a bridge two miles south of his position, so we simply marched round and took him in the rear. Hopeless, quite hopeless!"

"How did Durrant react?" enquired Peveril with interest, finding it difficult to imagine how any half-decent regular officer, let alone a stickler like the battalion commander, would respond to such an obvious mistake.

"Blew Goodwin up, and then blew Poole up for having the temerity to suggest that the bridge had been booby-trapped and mined."

"Quick thinking on Poole's part," commented Chatham, "but no-one believed him, especially as – according to the rules of the exercise – he ought to have left some sign to prove that he had mined it."

"And," agreed Jervis, "he ought to have left a platoon to mop up any survivors. So you can see why your lot aren't exactly popular round here."

"Doubtless," Chatham added smoothly, "your expertise will help to improve matters and bring 'em much more up-to-date."

"Oh, ah," replied Capt. Thrigby meaninglessly, whilst 2nd Lt. Peveril's hackles rose at the scarcely-concealed suggestion that he was just as useless as the rest of C Coy.

As the conversation grew more general, Peveril seized the opportunity to throw in a few pessimistic comments regarding the conduct of the war. These were rigorously debated, but when Peveril added a remark about the need for more forceful leadership, Jervis eyebrows rose. He waited until Chatham had excused himself for a moment and then turned to the visitor.

"I shouldn't talk quite so loudly about strong leaders if I were you," he advised. "That sort of line doesn't go down terribly well."

"What do you mean?" blustered Peveril.

"Well, old boy, it's entirely up to you, but our mess doesn't respond frightfully well to remarks which imply that what Britain needs is our own pocket Hitler. We rather leave that sort of comment up to Mosley and his crew."

"Dash it all, I'm not a Blackshirt," protested Peveril, wondering how sincere he ought to sound. "But I do think that we shouldn't be in the muddle we are in if we'd had someone with a bit more grit than Chamberlain. He didn't precisely achieve a lasting peace, did he? What's the point of going to war over some faraway country that is nothing to do with us?"

"Peace isn't always worth having if it means signing away all honour," grunted Jervis, before changing the subject to the less controversial one of the illness of the regimental padre.

Chapter Seven

Two days later, Ralph decided that he might just visit the small village of Brandon on his way from C Coy to report to Major Collingwood in London. The fact that this could in no way be described as the most direct route he dismissed as unimportant. Had Midge not suggested that he might visit her? And was it not the case that she might have some ideas which he could present to Collingwood? After all, he had failed to discover anything at A Coy apart from the fact that it was very well run and that the padre who had first raised the alert was expected to die in hospital. Surely it was only sensible to turn to the only person with whom he could discuss the problem? He'd already given his mission away, so he wasn't going to make things worse. If nothing else, it might prevent him from being forced to admit complete failure to the irascible major.

As Ralph pressed down the accelerator on the Alfa, he was aware that his heart was thumping uncomfortably. In Cambridge, he had bidden goodbye to Midge with a chaste kiss on her cheek, but had stored up the memory of her body tantalisingly close to his. He could still smell the delicate scent which she had been wearing, with its fragrance of oranges and summer. Would Midge realise that he was interested in more than just discussing what little he had discovered? Might she suspect...?

As Ralph drove past Brandon church, he pulled himself together. He recollected that Midge had once said that her uncle's house was slightly outside the village itself and was approached through a bluebell wood from one side and a gravel drive from another side. Suddenly noticing two worn sandstone pillars topped with sandstone pineapples, he braked the car and managed to make out the name of the house carved into the smooth stone. Gratified that he had discovered the Grange by sheer luck, Ralph drove sedately up the drive. Perhaps his luck would continue to hold. If nothing else, it would be interesting to see what sort of place Carrington came from. His erstwhile supervisor had never been noted for giving away personal information, and one wit had suggested that Carrington's unreasonable demands of at least a modicum of work from his students indicated that Carrington must have hauled his way out of poverty by his bootstraps. However, the grey house with the elegant, wide windows which had now come into view showed every indication of gentility.

Peveril pulled a face. What was the point of thinking about asinine jokes concerning a chap's background in the middle of a war? A bullet certainly didn't pause to take account of where you had the good fortune to be brought up. After parking his car to one side of the heavy oak door, Ralph rang the doorbell. Now that he was here, he rather wished that he had not come. What if Midge were to be busy or resting? What if Fletcher had written to her?

Just as Ralph was wondering whether he could leap back into the Alfa and drive away, an elderly countrywoman opened the door and ushered him indoors. After ascertaining his name, she disappeared along a passageway, leaving Ralph a prey to nervousness. Then a middle-aged woman appeared, with a welcoming smile on her face. Forcing himself to appear nonchalant, Ralph sprang forward to shake hands and introduce himself properly to Midge's aunt. As he did so, he decided that Carrington must take after his father; Mrs Carrington's countenance lacked the expression of sardonic humour which frequently crossed her son's face. For her part Alice Carrington saw a tall young man with a thin face – too thin, she thought – and dark, intelligent eyes. So this was the young man whom Midge had saved from the hangman's noose. Busily wondering what significance his visit boded, Alice chatted for several minutes until Midge appeared, accompanied by Bertie and Boris.

"I hope you like cats," remarked Alice, wishing that her niece did not look so pale. It was most unfortunate that Midge should have been worrying about John just when she had a visitor and ought to be looking her best.

"Yes, I do like them," agreed Peveril firmly, well aware that Midge would react badly to any contrary statement. "Anyway, Midge looks like some sort of Classical goddess flanked by her guardian spirits."

Alice's ears twitched at this remark. In her view, any reference to a goddess meant that a young man was interested in a woman. She murmured something about needing to talk to Ellen about afternoon tea and departed to leave her niece alone with young Captain Peveril. Midge, meanwhile, was merely amused by Ralph's comment.

"Dionysus was often depicted with panthers. Are you suggesting that I am some sort of Maenad or Bacchant?"

Embarrassed at the thought of discussing drink-fuelled orgies with a girl, Peveril changed the subject to what Midge had been doing since she had returned from Cambridge.

"Reading a rather decent book about bats," remarked Midge, somewhat surprisingly.

"Excellent preparation for May exams," teased Ralph. "Think of the abstruse information which you could introduce into a verse composition."

Midge laughed. "That's rather a good idea. After all, Virgil wrote about bees."

"You could get lots of metaphysical concepts in – consider how bats communicate, but humans can only hear their squeaks when young. Is that not a metaphor for the human condition?"

"And there's hibernation," agreed Midge enthusiastically.

"Hanging upside down."

"Hands at the end of their wings."

"Warm-blooded."

"Active only at dusk."

"Perhaps even predicting the future from their flight."

Midge grinned. "It's good to be able to talk nonsense again."

"Nonsense?" declared Ralph in a shocked voice. "I am quite serious in my attempt to aid your academic career."

"And what about your career?" demanded Midge. "Have you made any progress?"

Ralph sighed. "I feel as if I'm going round and round in circles." He related what had been happening, including his various attempts to indicate that he might have some sympathy with the Fascist movement. "And if I get quodded," he concluded, "I'm deuced well relying upon you to swear that I'm only trailing my coat in the hope of catching some real Blackshirts."

Midge ignored this remark. "Do you think that Snellgrove or Jervis' reactions are significant?"

Peveril shrugged his shoulders. "Goodness knows. Jervis might be a thoroughly decent chap who disapproved of what I was saying, or he might have wanted to shut me up because he doesn't want some blundering oaf to attract the attention of the police whilst he's carrying out some deep-laid plan. Equally, Snellgrove may be completely innocent or he may suspect that I've been sent to sniff out Fascist sympathisers."

"Maybe you need to keep making dubious comments," suggested Midge. "That way Jervis and Snellgrove will be sure that you're a genuine sympathiser and one of them might approach you – or one of the men might. You don't seem to have had much of a chance to mix with them."

"I haven't," Ralph agreed. "It's the main problem with my cover – I have no obvious reason for talking to any of them other than the chap who's looking after the Alfa and the mess waiter, who hangs around the bar." He frowned in thought. "Actually, I think that an officer is the most likely source of trouble – we have far more freedom than the men. Presumably, this traitor has occasional meetings with other people to collect supplies or take instructions. It would be tricky to do that even as a corporal like Trent – you're far more likely to be assigned some duty which you can't get out of."

"Then I suppose you ought to concentrate on the officers first. Apart from Jervis and Snellgrove, have any of them done anything odd?"

Ralph nodded. "Chatham made a sarcastic remark that C Coy's inefficiency wouldn't be allowed in the Wehrmacht. He ought to know – he seems to have spent a lot of time in Germany."

Midge's eyebrows rose. "And he's friendly with Jervis, who told you not to talk about Mosley." Then she sighed. "The trouble is, it's not surprising that a professional soldier would be interested in his likely enemy. Once you start looking for reasons to suspect someone, it's very easy to find them."

"I know – and it would be very easy to overlook someone who hasn't drawn attention to himself by an offhand remark."

Ralph sighed. "As for making more political comments, I do see the point for doing so, however unpleasant it is, but I don't want people wondering why I've not been locked up under 18B. If I go too far they'll be bound to suspect that I'm not whom I appear to be."

"What about the colonel?"

"Are you mad?" demanded Peveril unromantically. "Durrant'd eat me alive."

"You don't know that for sure," disagreed Midge. Then she sighed. "Actually, I suppose you've got a point. Jervis is only a junior officer, so he can slip you a friendly warning, but a battalion commander would be forced to take action if he really thought that one of his officers was a Blackshirt."

This admission from Midge forced one from Peveril. "Quite frankly, Midge, I don't think that I've got the nerve to try it. In any case, I cannot imagine any circumstance in which I could casually introduce my supposed admiration for Mussolini into a discussion with my battalion commander. So far, I've not said much more than 'Yes, sir' or 'No, sir' to him. He doesn't give the impression of wanting to chat to junior officers."

Midge giggled. "How unenterprising you are, Ralph. Surely you could respond to a question about where you're planning to site a semaphore station with the helpful information that you've chosen to go north because there's a very decent bunch of Mosleyites nearby with whom you often dine."

A grin crossed Peveril's face. "For a moment I thought you meant it. Anyway, I'm going up to London tonight – supposedly for overnight leave, but actually to report to Collingwood, as per instructions. I think he wants to check whether I've been wasting my time or not. If he doesn't decide that I'm completely hopeless, I'll soon be back with C Coy, wandering along the shore again."

Midge suddenly frowned. "You are being careful, aren't you, Ralph? If someone suspected what you were up to, it would be terribly easy for them to follow you and push you over a cliff or throw a rock at you."

The thought that Midge was worrying about his safety delighted Peveril. Reluctantly, he decided that he ought to try to reassure her. "Don't worry, Midge, no-one's in the slightest bit interested in me. I'm so alone that I can sing Elgar to the sea, with only the seagulls to complain about my wrong notes."

"Elgar?" repeated Midge.

Ralph failed to pick up the odd intonation in Midge's voice. Instead, carried away by the memory of the pounding, battering waves hurling themselves to destruction on the shore, Ralph responded eagerly. Midge was one of the very few people with whom he could talk about music and not be laughed at. "Yes, Honor sent me a copy of *Sea Pictures*. I know it's for mezzo, but even in a tenor voice you achieve something. It's splendid, Midge; full of the grandeur and majesty of the crashing, surging surf."

Midge sighed. She normally greatly enjoyed discussing music with Ralph, particularly since he had a much wider knowledge of vocal music than she had. However, there were complications in this instance. "That doesn't sound much like Capt. Thrigby, and how do you intend to explain away the score if someone finds it?"

"I'll say m'sister sent it," explained Peveril, before stopping. "Oh. I'm supposed to have only an aged great-aunt. Damn. Music as another casualty of war." He scowled. "Do you know, Midge, I think that m'father would have made a dashed good Nazi."

Midge grimaced. Perhaps that sentiment explained why Ralph had sounded tense in his letters to his mother. Nor could it be pleasant to have tasted freedom and then have to return to living a lie, constantly considering every word and action, in case it betrayed your true feelings. With this in mind, Midge tried to encourage Ralph. "I don't imagine you much like pretending to be Thrigby – he sounds ghastly – but you need to live and breathe every moment as him; you can't behave like Lt. Peveril or you'll give yourself away."

"I suppose you're right. It wasn't something that was dealt with much during training." Ralph gave a sarcastic laugh. "Perhaps they thought I already knew it all – apparently, Hartismere told them that I'm good at mental disguises; he wrote something about 'adopting a mask', whatever he meant by that."

"How did you find that out?"

"I read it upside down on my interviewer's desk."

"That was a bit careless of him."

"Indeed. I didn't know whether to point it out, thus confirming that I was a good recruit, or to stay silent." Ralph suddenly grinned. "At least I didn't ask him to turn the page over so that I could read the rest."

Midge laughed. "That would have given him something of a shock." She glanced at Ralph. "You won't sing anything which could give you away, will you?"

"No, even although I still think that C Coy are a bunch of barbarians who would simply think that I was singing a music hall ditty." Ralph bent down to stroke Bertie, who had wandered over to see him. "I just wish I felt that I was achieving something."

"That's because it's difficult to discover anything," responded Midge consolingly. "In any case, you ought to have been given more information about the chaps involved. Why weren't you able to read their service records before you came down here? They might have supplied a number of clues."

"Possibly, but I didn't think of it, and Collingwood's manner doesn't exactly encourage the asking of questions which could be construed as passing oblique criticism of his orders."

"Poor Ralph," sympathised Midge. "Just imagine how much worse it'd have been in the Roman army."

At this comment, Ralph managed a faint smile. "When I fail, at least Collingwood won't be able to order me to stand outside his tent all day with an entrenching tool as a mark of humiliation." He sighed. "Frankly, Midge, I always thought, that after leaving school, I shouldn't have to concern myself overly much about observing status. But last night I watched Goodwin toadying up to Durrant, because Durrant outranks him. At the same time, Goodwin snubbed Jervis and Cohen because they're lieutenants. And, back in C Coy, Trent toadies up to Goodwin and Snellgrove. The concern with status is just the same."

"That's because you're dealing with institutions. It's no different in a college. Senior dons want to be the next Master, while junior dons strive to come to the admiring notice of the college authorities."

Peveril grinned in sudden amusement. "Is that the sort of thing which Carrington tells you? I never realised that he spilled the secrets of the SCR to members of other colleges quite like that – and, as a undergraduate, you don't even rank as a 2nd lieutenant like Cohen. At best you'd be a corporal."

"I am talking in general terms," stated Midge repressively, "and what I have to say bears no relation to John's position within college."

"I don't believe you," Ralph teased, finding it distinctly amusing that his supervisor gossiped about Trinity politics with his undergraduate cousin.

"Who is this Lt. Cohen?" demanded Midge, rapidly changing the subject. "You haven't said anything about him before."

"There didn't seem much point. I mean, dash it all, the man's a Jew – he can't possibly be a Fascist sympathiser. He'd have everything to fear if an invasion succeeded, or even if we only got a home-grown dictator."

"You need to suspect everybody," urged Midge firmly.

"As it happens, I was deuced fortunate not to rouse his suspicions."

Midge looked worried. "Why?"

"He was the lucky specimen ordered to show me round the environs of battalion HQ. He seemed fearfully eager to learn about semaphores and kept asking me about their modern use. Appeared to expect that I'd know all about their historical use as well, which led to my first mistake: knowing the Greek roots of the word."

"Sema – signal; phoros – bearing," agreed Midge intelligently.

"Quite. At least I could claim that knowledge on the grounds of professional curiosity. Then he let slip that he'd studied history at Cambridge and I nearly went and asked him which college." He waved away Midge's protest. "Yes, I know, Midge, if I'd been more in my role as Thrigby I would have despised Cohen as a wet layabout, but I promise I shall remember from now on that I am a hearty barbarian through and through. More to the point, I didn't actually ask him – I turned my question into a meaningless grunt, before beginning a monologue about the difficulties of acquiring sufficient quantities of suitable material for making semaphore flags."

"Are there such difficulties?"

Ralph shrugged. "I haven't the faintest idea, but everyone's always complaining about shortages so it sounded convincing – and a dashed sight more convincing than a discussion about the historical uses of the semaphore. I know enough to bore most people rigid, but I'm not an expert on the Napoleonic Wars and Cohen seemed to be. Anyway, I've wasted enough time talking about my rather dull little problem. I'd much rather hear about what you're doing."

Midge sighed internally. Clearly Ralph had become uncommunicative again and she suspected that there was little point in attempting to force him to speak. She allowed him to turn the conversation onto her own affairs, unaware that she was just as uncommunicative regarding certain aspects of her life as Ralph was about his.

Chapter Eight

It was dark by the time that Ralph approached the outskirts of London. He glanced at his watch in concern, realising that he ought to have left Midge earlier. Unless he had dashed good luck, he was going to be late, which wouldn't make him excessively popular.

When Ralph reached St James's, he was relieved to have arrived with two minutes to spare, and he hared up the short flight of outside stairs. As he entered the gloomy hallway, the duty-clerk looked up and asked his name.

"Thrigby, reporting to Major Collingwood," replied Peveril, hoping that he had given the correct name. Still, Collingwood had told him to use Thrigby until given permission to do otherwise.

The clerk signalled another soldier to escort the visitor to Major Collingwood's room on the first floor. The office had a pleasant view over the trees at the front of the building, but at that precise moment Collingwood was uninterested in both the vista and – it appeared – Capt. Thrigby.

"Oh, it's you, is it?" he remarked in unwelcoming tones. "I can't see you now. I've got something very urgent to deal with. I'll see you tomorrow."

Peveril's hackles rose. If he'd known that he wouldn't have been needed, he could have motored to Huntingdonshire and looked up his mother, rather than forcing the pace through a series of devilish bad country roads in a pointless attempt to arrive on time.

"Sir," he responded, some of his irritation showing in his voice.

Collingwood looked Peveril over slowly. "May I remind you, Lieutenant, that the war does not revolve around your personal convenience? I shall expect to see you at 0800 hours sharp tomorrow morning and, in the meantime, don't go anywhere where you're known."

Resisting the temptation to retort that the war ought not to revolve round inefficiency either, Ralph saluted, before stalking out the door.

Peveril's mood was not improved by the difficulty of finding a hotel room in London. By the time he had done so and safely garaged the Alfa, he was in a state of considerable irritation. 'I could have gone home and seen m'mother. I could have remained later at Brandon – Midge might even have invited me to stay for dinner.' He threw his overnight bag down on the bed. 'Were I as incompetent and immature as Collingwood clearly thinks, I'd go out and get drunk.' Then, remembering the last time he had pursued this course of action, he cursed viciously. 'I suppose that's out of the question. Damn and blast Hartismere for getting me involved in this ridiculous escapade – what am I contributing to the war effort? I might as well be propping up the bar of the Ritz drinking poisonous cocktails.'

Suddenly, a smile crept over Peveril's face. Collingwood had ordered him not to go anywhere where he was known. The major probably meant not to go anywhere at all. But he wasn't 'known' at Covent Garden and he couldn't imagine that he'd run into too many of the East Suffolks listening to *The Marriage of Figaro*.

Since Ralph was both musical and a former chorister, his choice of evening entertainment proved to be an ideal distraction from his cares. He had heard the odd aria sung live and had recently begun to listen to opera on the wireless, but the Royal Opera House came as a revelation to him. The setting itself, with the gilded plasterwork and the glittering chandeliers, was magnificent, but the quality of the music was exceptional. Three hours later, Ralph was heading towards Leicester Square tube, scarcely aware of the throng of people crowding around him. Count Almaviva's final aria was reverberating in his head and he felt as if it were the urgent semiquavers of the violins, rather than his feet, which carried him forward. For the first time in months he was utterly relaxed. 'I've heard Cherubino's love aria before,' he reflected, 'but it made so much more sense in its proper setting. And, thank goodness I don't have the *Requiem* going round and round in my head any longer.'

Wishing that he could go back and watch the production again, Peveril strolled on, ignoring the chilly night air which encouraged others to seek the underground more quickly.

Suddenly, his thoughts were assailed by a drunken voice recalling him to his daytime concerns. "Gad, look who it is; it's m'brother the murdering coward!"

Peveril swung round, his musical dream shattered. Even despite Robert's slurred speech, he could recognise his brother's voice – and the jibe about cowardice made the recognition all the more certain. Without stopping to think, Peveril hit out with all the force at his command. Robert had not been expecting such an immediate response and put up his guard too late. A straight right from Ralph knocked him down to the ground. A crowd instantly gathered to watch the fun, evenly split between those who believed that Ralph ought to have given warning before striking out and those who suggested that Robert must have done something to provoke such an attack.

As a friend leant forward to help Robert up, the younger Peveril was spitting with drunken rage, "Damn you, you filthy bastard. Take off your greatcoat and have it out man to man, once and for all."

Ralph was only too delighted to accept this invitation to fight his brother, despite the inconvenience of doing so in a crowded street. He'd endured months of Robert calling him a murderer and now, finally, he'd been granted the chance to deal with him without upsetting their mother. Rejecting the offer of a greengrocer to act as his second, he began to undo the buttons on his greatcoat before stopping dead. "Damnation take it," he cursed beneath his breath, before doing up the buttons again. "I'm not soiling my hands with you, you contemptible little louse," he snapped. Then he strode into the underground station, ignoring the mocking jeers which came from behind him.

Thirty minutes later, without being entirely sure how he had reached it, Peveril found himself on the Embankment. The black, oily waters of the Thames reflected his mood. 'That little brute will never let me hear the end of this,' he growled. 'But what else was I supposed to do?' He scowled angrily across the lapping waves. 'I'm damned glad I knocked him down and I wish I'd done it before. In fact,' he snarled as his rage mastered him again, 'I wish I could seek him out tomorrow and thrash him properly. What the devil was he doing in town anyway? It's not half-term. And,' Ralph added angrily, 'I wish I'd never chucked up Cambridge. If I get accused of cowardice when I am in uniform, I might as well have stayed at Trinity and done what I wanted to do.' He swore out loud in his frustration. "Oh, *damn* everything. Why has life got to be so complicated?"

Chapter Nine

Whilst Ralph was angrily cursing his younger brother, Midge was facing problems of her own in Suffolk. Although she felt that her reasons for postulating that General Whitlock might have links with Fifth Columnists were defensible, she baulked at the idea of putting them to the test. Nevertheless, remembering a dinner invitation which she had previously turned down, she approached her aunt with a request that she might, after all, accompany Mrs Carrington to the general's house that evening.

"Really, Midge," replied Alice crossly, "you simply can't reject an invitation and then turn up. It's frightfully bad manners, not least because it suggests to your host that you had intended to do something more interesting and then fell back on his invitation at the last moment."

Midge muttered something apologetic.

Alice sighed. "I suppose I can think of some sort of excuse and telephone them to explain that you are also coming. Mind you, considering that you always complain of being bored when you do go to the Manor, I can't imagine why you want to go tonight."

"I'm feeling at a bit of a loose end," murmured Midge, in embarrassed tones.

Alice heaved another sigh, thinking that Midge must be worrying about her cousin. Catching her aunt's sigh, Midge's colour deepened as she guessed what was in Mrs Carrington's mind. The fact that Aunt Alice was taking pity on her did not make it any easier to infiltrate herself into the Whitlocks' house under false pretences. Indeed, as the time of departure approached, Midge would have been deeply relieved if some excuse for her not to attend had suddenly presented itself. The more she contemplated what she was about to do, the more it loomed in her mind as an unforgivable breach of hospitality.

Neither General nor Mrs Whitlock seemed to be in the slightest put out by the fact that they had had to rearrange their seating plan to accommodate an extra female at a time when women were in excess supply and men all too scarce.

"Delighted to see you, m'dear," exclaimed the general.

"Yes," chirruped his wife. "I'm glad you've recovered enough to come. It must be such a trial to you to be so delicate."

Midge's colour rose, on the one hand irritated by the reference to her constant battle with illness and on the other embarrassed by the general's hearty welcome when she had only come to test his loyalty.

"It's very kind of you to ask me," she replied. "Is Naomi here or is she visiting school friends?"

This query about her granddaughter distracted Mrs Whitlock from the question of Midge's health. "Naomi still has a few more weeks' holiday. I'm sure she'll have lots to tell you about school. She seems to be doing very well, though I can never see the point of expecting sixth formers to work as hard as they do at Rushford nowadays." She tittered. "I contented myself with playing lots of hockey and getting ready for my coming-out ball. Ah, those were the days, my dear! I remember being presented to the Queen and being terrified that my curtsey would not be good enough, even although I had practised for weeks. You modern gels don't have anything like as much fun. There's Naomi pottering around with test-tubes in some funny old laboratory and you spend hours in a library." She shook her head. "I suppose you can't look forward to balls in the way in which I could – all those handsome Guards officers twirling their moustaches and beggin' the inestimable pleasure of the dance – but why Naomi wants to waste the best years of her life worrying about atoms and other silly things is quite beyond me."

Naomi herself suddenly appeared on the scene and practically dragged Midge off to one side.

"Hope you're all right," she declared abruptly. "It's good to see you again."

Since Midge had been to the same school as Naomi and had, indeed, overlapped with her for two years, the time before dinner was dominated by catching up on news, not least the fact that Naomi had blossomed into a prefect.

"It came as a bit of a shock to me," admitted Naomi with some amusement. "I'd always assumed that my Past would rule me out."

Midge grinned. "Most of us grow up eventually – even I did."

"And," whispered Naomi, after a swift glance to see who was in earshot, "they want me to sit a Science scholarship for Cambridge."

"Congrats.," murmured Midge, realising that she was not meant to draw attention to Naomi's news. "What do your grandparents think?"

"I'm maintaining a diplomatic silence at the moment. Grandmother will hate the idea, but I might be able to persuade Grandfather – he was fearfully bucked when I got made a prefect."

"Tell your grandmother about May Week balls," suggested Midge, unaware that there was a slight edge to her voice. "You can meet lots of young men there – some of them have private incomes as well as hopes of getting a degree."

Naomi shot Midge a swift, uncomfortable glance. She had not caught everything that her grandmother had been saying, but experience had taught her both that Mrs Whitlock made the most tactless comments and that Midge detested remarks about her disability. If, as she strongly suspected, something of that nature had been mentioned, it was clearly time to move off the subject of balls and on to whether Girton or Newnham was better for science.

Whilst Midge was quite happy to drop all discussion of dances which she had no hope of attending, when the guests filed into the dining-room it was clear that Mrs Whitlock had not exhausted her fund of reminiscences. Currently, she was discussing the ball given in honour of a Russian duchess at the turn of the century.

"Her diamonds, my dear! If it had been another woman I might have said that the display was vulgar, but I suppose these Russian aristocrats were used to sprinkling diamonds over their dresses as we might use sequins. Not that they'll have any diamonds now, poor things. Do you know, I met the most extraordinary man the other day in a Kensington tea-shop." She gave a tinkling laugh. "Not that I should like you to think that I belong to *that* set, but I was meeting a friend who has lost a lot of money in investments in Germany and who insisted that I must not pay for her afternoon tea, which ruled out more sensible places.

"So, there we were, drinking our tea when the owner appeared. Such an exquisitely dressed man, Alice, you'd have thought that he would have been more at home in the Ritz. But he pattered over to check that we had had everything that we wanted. And then – well, my dear, the excitement! – I recognised an order which he was wearing on his coat; just a miniature, but enough to tell me that I was dealing with a Russian. And when I asked him whether he was wearing the Order of St Peter and St Paul, he admitted it. He said that the Czar had pinned it on to him with his own hands, so he wore it every day to be reminded of the Martyrs of Ekaterinburg. And he told me that he had been an admiral, but no longer used the title because his estate was now reduced to a tea-shop. Then he added that he regarded us as his honoured guests, just the same as he would had we been escorted to his palace accompanied by ratings from his squadron."

Since Midge chose this moment to go into a rather bad-tempered reverie about how any foreign-sounding man with a shapely black beard could pass himself off as a Russian admiral, she missed the remainder of this fascinating anecdote. However, Mrs Whitlock appeared to be indefatigable that evening, because she was soon back discussing the ball for the Grand Duchess Olga.

"I was worried that my dress would not meet with approval. I was wearing white, of course, but it was just a little bit more daring than some of the other girls' dresses. And the officers were queuing up to dance with me – my dance card was full almost before the orchestra first struck up." She sighed, remembering past glories when every man in the room had been smitten by her now-faded beauty and when she had not had to worry about such mundane things as attracting decent servants who were prepared to work in the country without demanding ridiculously high wages. She turned to her granddaughter rather pettishly. "I simply can't imagine why you don't want to come out, Naomi. All this dull fuss about science won't last. You'll wake up one morning and discover that all the other girls are married and you're not."

Since Naomi was, at that precise moment, enjoying flirting with a very good-looking young army officer, she did not take kindly to her grandmother's remarks. "Lots of girls do things nowadays," she replied with a sniff. Searching round for an argument, she picked on Midge to illustrate her point. "Midge is up at Cambridge and lots of her friends went to university as well."

Mrs Whitlock cast a pitying look at Midge, which made all too apparent her view that Midge was a special case who could not possibly hope to attract a man. "Yes, dear, I'm sure it's lovely for Midge to be at Cambridge, but it's not what I want for you."

In the pause which followed this rather pointed remark, Midge leapt in with one of her own. "You must have met so many interesting people, Mrs Whitlock. Didn't you once say that you'd met Mr Mosley and his wife?"

Mrs Whitlock seemed not to notice anything odd about this question or to feel any embarrassment in admitting that she had known and admired Britain's most famous Fascist. "Yes, such a handsome man. And his wife is so poised and elegant. Of course, she's a Mitford and all the Mitford gels were quite, quite beautiful. They took the shine out of anyone whom they were with." She gave a braying laugh. "Naturally, they were a little bit too intellectual for my taste, and I was always relieved, Naomi, when your dear mother didn't take up with them, although she and Diana had quite a number of mutual friends."

To judge from Naomi's silence, she appeared to be blessing the fact that her mother had died years ago. However, as Mrs Whitlock's fund of reminiscences were now leading her on to reveal what Goring's wife had confided to her when she was in Baden Baden taking a cure, Naomi was spared any further revelations about her mother. The general adroitly moved the discussion on to one of whether the Germans really would bomb British cities and the conversation became less fraught.

Soon afterwards, the ladies left the men to their port, but when the men rejoined them, General Whitlock manoeuvred Midge into an isolated spot behind a large potted fern and began to reprove her.

"I'm not quite sure what you were after over dinner, m'dear, but since you are a guest in my house, you might allow me to point out that it is bad form to attempt to pump your hostess for information." Looking Midge up and down, he added, "I can't say I understand why you wanted to get m'wife to talk about Mosley, but the next time you try something like that you might do it rather more discreetly than you have done."

Midge made what she hoped was a suitable apology, adding somewhat unconvincingly that she had not been attempting to get information from Mrs Whitlock.

The general retained his frosty air. "In my young day, gels knew how to behave. Your uncle ought to know better than to tell you to ask questions like that, and you ought to have better manners than to ask them."

Midge winced, wondering whether it was fair to leave her uncle to take the blame, or whether any further explanation would merely make things worse. Meanwhile, the general had more to say.

"I can't say that it's particularly flattering that Carrington has been casting doubt upon my integrity. Just because I believe in firm government and he believes in a lot of liberal, mealy-mouthed pap does not – yet – make me a traitor. Do you really think that I'd want to see a Hun in charge of one platoon in the British army, let alone the entire army itself?" He snorted, sounding remarkably like the charger which he had once ridden. "The sort of fellers who believe in that sort of rot aren't found in the army, by God! They're found skulking around avoiding their call-up papers and pretending to be doing war work when they're doing nothing of the sort. If Carrington wants to hunt Fifth Columnists, he ought to be asking why nothing's been done about Cosford. Why has he been left in a coastal town like Newton?" He snorted again, even more forcefully. "But the real scandal is why so many of those filthy Bolsheviks are still at large in vital industries rather than being locked up – they're all pals with Germany now and ought to be exposed for what they are."

The general's cold anger and the awareness that she had, indeed, broken several codes of civilized conduct left Midge shaken. Moreover, she had not expected anyone, least of all the general, to have seen through her as easily as he had done.

Perhaps it was easier to fool strangers than people who actually knew you. Perhaps her success in the Fletcher case had made her inclined to over-estimate her own ability. If nothing else, she was sure that Ralph would have carried off this appallingly embarrassing incident much more insouciantly. For her own part, she simply could not think of any words which would soothe the justifiable anger of her outraged host.

Whitlock, noticing that Midge was looking distinctly upset, softened somewhat. He had known Midge on and off for several years and tended to think that she had guts, even if he could hardly approve of the evening's activities. "We'll say no more about it; just tell your uncle to do his own work in future, eh?"

Midge nodded, hoping desperately that her aunt had not noticed the altercation. 'In future,' she thought grimly, 'I'll make sure I have a water-tight plan before I attempt anything of this sort again. Or, even better, I'll leave it all up to Ralph – he's the one in Intelligence, not I.'

Chapter Ten

The swift changes which could take place in Intelligence were well illustrated by two snapshots of Collingwood's activities taken less than a day apart. At twelve o'clock on the evening of April 8th, Collingwood had allowed himself to be distracted for a few minutes away from his immediate task and onto the question of how Peveril was shaping up. Notwithstanding the young officer's disrespectful annoyance at being pushed to one side, Collingwood was prepared to acknowledge that Peveril seemed to be doing quite well in Suffolk. Certainly he had managed to retain his role as a semaphore specialist without anyone spotting that he was a fraud. And – despite a small nagging suspicion raised at Peveril's first assessment – surely it was safe to assign him to a purely information-gathering role? Hartismere had sworn that he was good material. Collingwood smiled reluctantly – if he were to start doubting Hartismere's choice of recruit, he'd have to investigate himself as well as Peveril.

Six hours later, Collingwood was approaching the question of Ralph Peveril's suitability for his current task with much greater caution. A telephone call from Newton had suddenly made it critical to discover whether Peveril was likely to lose his nerve. Hence when Peveril reported, as commanded, at 0800 hours on the 9th of April, he was unpleasantly surprised to be greeted with every sign of dislike by a stony-faced major.

"Sit," ordered Collingwood curtly, waving in the direction of an upright chair placed exactly where the table-lamp shone brightest.

Peveril, who had not had anything like enough sleep to cope with the unexpected, sat down, wondering what on earth was up. The first issue was a searching cross-examination as to what he had – or had not – discovered at the East Suffolks.

At the end of Peveril's report, Collingwood responded much less antagonistically than Peveril had expected from his original greeting.

"Not much to go on," the major noted, "but that's perhaps not surprising."

He then made some general points about how investigations into morale had been run in the past, without any obvious negative comparison with Peveril's efforts. Just as Peveril was cautiously starting to relax, Collingwood snapped without any warning. "Does your mother think that you are a coward?"

Peveril rocketed up from his chair. "Damn you, take that back."

Collingwood appeared to be unmoved at the sight of Peveril leaning menacingly over his desk. Mentally, however, he noted the young man's fury with approval; clearly there was some red blood in him. Nevertheless, he continued to attack Peveril. "Is the reason why you've failed to discover anything that you're too afraid to investigate properly? Are you too cowardly to put yourself in danger? And are you too craven to admit that you're no good?"

Peveril suddenly remembered a warning which Fletcher had made before he had given evidence at his trial. A successful cross-examiner might attempt to anger a witness so much that he forgot to watch his tongue – precisely the method which Collingwood appeared to be adopting now. Peveril forced himself to resume his seat, even although there was nothing more he wanted to do than get his hands round Collingwood's throat and choke him into admitting that his words were lies. "The reason I've not discovered anything," he remarked as airily as possible, "is because of poor staff work higher up."

This time it was Collingwood's turn to lean forward menacingly. "I didn't take to languid superiority when I was at Trinity, and I'm certainly not going to listen to it now, when it counts as insolence towards a commanding officer."

Peveril froze in shock. If Collingwood had been at Trinity then he must know Hartismere. Had Hartismere recruited Collingwood too? And, if so, what had Hartismere told Collingwood about his newest recruit? How much did Collingwood know?

"I thought that you might find that information of interest," remarked Collingwood grimly. "And now I'd like some information from you. What the devil were you doing in Soho?"

"Soho?" repeated Peveril, fighting for time.

"Yes, Lieutenant, it's a place in London and you were in it last night. Why, when I explicitly ordered you not to go anywhere where you might be recognised?"

"No-one does know me there."

"Indeed?" queried the major. "Then perhaps you can explain the interesting experience which you had in Leicester Square. It was an odd sort of contretemps to have with a complete stranger."

Despite himself, Peveril could not stop an angry flush from mounting his cheek. If Collingwood suspected him of having spent the night on the town with Robert he was very far out. "I had no expectation of meeting anyone I knew," he snapped. "Nor did I want to."

"Does your brother know what you're doing at the moment?" Collingwood demanded suspiciously.

"No. I should have thought it was perfectly obvious that I don't waste my time talking to him."

The major glared at Peveril balefully. "Address me with proper respect and don't make sarcastic remarks," he hissed. "As for last night, you are entirely to blame. First, you wilfully disobeyed orders. And secondly, far from sinking yourself into your role as Capt. Thrigby, you completely ignored his habits and chose to indulge your own. You told me that you had portrayed him as an unlettered barbarian. If you had made any attempt to live up to your part, you wouldn't have been in that area and your cover wouldn't have been jeopardised."

This repetition of Midge's concern about burying yourself in your character and living his life surprised Peveril so much that he nearly blurted out that Midge had made a similar point and that he hadn't entirely believed her. He hastily attempted to pull himself together, unaware that Collingwood had noticed his shock. Fortunately, the major attributed Peveril's change of expression to the effect of his reprimand. Moreover, he had other things on his mind.

"Cigarette?" he offered.

"No, thanks," Peveril replied, wondering what trap Collingwood was trying to lay now. "I don't smoke."

"And it's a bit too early in the morning to offer you a drink," grunted Collingwood. "Now, look here, Peveril, if you don't think that you're up to things, I'd prefer you to say so outright." He held up his hand. "Hear me out, before you speak. First, I need to know that you can preserve your identity as Thrigby and not do damn silly things like being seen where your cover would never be. Secondly, I need to be certain…"

He paused to light his cigarette, whilst Peveril wondered how he should respond to a question about his bravery when the simple truth was that he had no desire whatsoever to die. Several months spent under the conviction that his life would be snuffed out early one morning on a scaffold had strengthened that view a thousand-fold.

His cigarette now lit, Collingwood continued. "I need to be certain that you have yourself sufficiently in hand that you won't blow your cover by losing your temper at idiotic accusations." He shot a surprisingly approving glance at Peveril. "For what it's worth, my informant tells me that, although you forgot yourself enough to brawl in the street like a costermonger to begin with, you did preserve sufficient sense to walk away from a direct challenge."

"Your informant?" repeated Peveril slowly, ignoring the implied criticism of his actions. "It was you, wasn't it, sir?"

Noticing with grim amusement that the younger man appeared to have suddenly remembered to show the respect due to his superior, Collingwood waved his question away. "Never mind that. The point is that, despite every provocation, something stopped you from slaughtering that tedious young drunk. What was it?"

Peveril shrugged. "I might not have slaughtered him; he's more heavily built than I am. But I couldn't fight with my greatcoat on and if I'd taken it off, he would have seen that I wasn't wearing the correct rank badges. And I thought that it would have made an interesting scene in the charge-room if we'd been picked up by the police – m'brother busy calling me Ralph Peveril and my papers saying that I was Ernest Thrigby."

"If you can conquer your bellicose streak, you might possibly achieve something in Intelligence," came the rejoinder. "You did well to remember that complication. But, for God's sake, do as you're ordered in future. Why on earth did you go to the opera of all things?"

Sensing that Collingwood was no longer as irate as before, Peveril thought that he could risk the partial truth. "I was annoyed about having come up to London last night when I could have done something else and turned up this morning."

The major sighed. "Last night Norway was invaded by Germany."

Ralph stared at his C.O. in disbelief.

Collingwood continued. "I was rather too busy to be worrying about what is going on in the East Suffolks." Collingwood toyed momentarily with the idea of warning Peveril to steer clear of the opera house, since it was being used as a letter drop by enemy sympathisers. That, after all, was why he had been in the vicinity and had been able to observe the meeting of the Peveril brothers. Then he rejected the idea as being unconnected with Peveril's investigation. "Actually, it was just as well that I couldn't see you. Col. Durrant was shot last night."

For a second time in as many minutes, Peveril gaped at Collingwood. The major laughed sardonically. "Just make sure you show that level of surprise when you get back and are greeted with the news."

"But who?" stammered Peveril. "Why?"

"That may be something which you will have to investigate," retorted Collingwood. "Durrant was shot at some point between whenever he left battalion HQ and four o'clock this morning, when his body was discovered."

Peveril frowned. "How did you learn of it so quickly, sir?"

"I was informed early this morning."

Peveril hesitated, unsure whether he could pursue the matter further. Presumably, if Collingwood had wanted to tell him how he had found out he would have done so. Nevertheless, there were other things which he needed to ask.

"You said I might have to investigate, sir. Does that mean that you think that there may be a connection between possible Fascist infiltration of the East Suffolks and Durrant's murder?"

Collingwood suddenly looked extremely tired. "Yes, I think

they may very well be linked. Naturally, the police are handling things at the moment, but it won't do any harm to have a man on the spot. In particular, given your concerns over Snellgrove, it would make a lot of sense for you to spend as much time in C Coy as possible."

"Do we have anything to go on?"

"Not yet; even the times are uncertain. God knows what Durrant was up to leaving HQ in the middle of the night, but he seems to have taken every precaution against being spotted leaving camp – no-one saw him go out, not even the sentries."

Peveril frowned again. "Presumably, sir, the first thing to establish is the time of death."

"The medicos will be of some help there," agreed Collingwood, "but it was damned cold last night and his body was outdoors. Both points will make it harder to be certain when he died. I would suggest that you start by trying to find out who was the last person to see him in camp, and then attempt to discover if that person is trustworthy or whether he is making things up in hope of providing an alibi for himself."

The major pulled across a piece of paper and started scribbling on it. "I am well aware of your brush with the law and there is always a chance that you may be recognised, particularly if the local constabulary requests help from the Yard. This is my telephone number. I want you to memorise it. If you do have trouble with the police, get hold of me on it. However, you must not tell any of the local police what you're up to and certainly not anyone under the rank of inspector."

"Sir."

"And, Peveril…"

"Sir?"

"When you made that remark about bad staff work, did you have something in mind or were you merely being offensive for the sake of it?"

Peveril hoped that he was not flushing. The accusation was one which he had heard before and, given the news about Durrant, it was not one which reflected particularly well upon him. He hastily plucked at Midge's remark to provide an excuse for what he had said. "I thought that it would have been useful if

I'd seen the service records of the officers involved."

Collingwood's eyebrows rose. "Why?"

"I thought they might suggest some lines of enquiry, sir."

"Quite," snorted Collingwood. "They might also incline you to think in certain directions only. We are not completely without experience of conducting these operations, Lt. Peveril, and we have not overlooked such an obvious source of information."

'Thought he wouldn't stay as gentle as a sucking dove for long,' opined Peveril disrespectfully to himself. However, no trace of his inner amusement showed in his voice as he replied smartly, "Yes, sir." Then he saluted and departed.

After Peveril had left, Collingwood gazed reflectively at the door; there was something about the stillness with which Peveril had received his orders regarding the police which was worrying. The major sighed. He could quite see that, if you had been through the strain of standing trial for murder, you wouldn't welcome any contact with the police. Nor did it appear as if Peveril had a particularly supportive family, if his brother was anything to go by. Collingwood shrugged. It was damned bad luck on Peveril, but there was a war on and he could not afford to extract an operative from a mission just because he felt sorry for him. That wasn't the way to discover what was going on in the East Suffolks, let alone defeat a ruthless enemy. In any event, all the evidence suggested that Peveril was a pretty callous specimen – there wasn't much point wasting sympathy on him.

II

Chapter Eleven

Had Midge risen as early as Peveril she would have learned of Durrant's death at about the same time as he did. However, it was not until half-past ten that Midge eventually made her appearance at the breakfast table. Alice Carrington was normally very sympathetic towards the fact that polio had left her niece a prey to exhaustion, but that morning she was practically champing at the bit and rushed into conversation immediately Midge appeared, yawning.

"Ralph Peveril's in the East Suffolks, isn't he?"

"Mmm," muttered Midge, who was still half-asleep.

"Their colonel was found dead on the Harting mud-flats early this morning."

Midge dropped her teaspoon in shock. "Are you sure?"

"Yes. Ellen heard it from the milkman, who heard it from Mrs Halliday's Nora, who heard it from Col. Gregory's batman. Baldock's got a nephew serving in the police, who was told to guard the body until the divisional surgeon could look at it."

Accustomed to the ways of villages, Midge had no doubt that the news was true. "You didn't say anything about my knowing one of the officers, did you?" she quizzed edgily.

"I haven't been married to a newspaperman for over thirty years without learning when not to talk," responded Alice with dignity.

"Sorry. It's just that I don't think that it would help Ralph if people gossiped about him."

Since Mrs Carrington had every intention of fostering what she trusted might be a fruitful relationship between Midge and young Capt. Peveril, she did not take offence at this remark.

"What happened?" enquired Midge, hoping that Ralph was not in any way involved.

"Apparently," hissed Alice with relish, "the colonel was shot in the middle of the night!"

"Good grief!"

"Quite!" Alice could not prevent herself from laughing. "Mrs Halliday's Nora has attributed it to 'heathen Nazis' whilst the milkman thinks that it was a spy disguised as a nun."

"What would a nun be doing on the mud-flats in the middle of the night?"

"I gather," replied Alice cautiously, "that the fact that a nun ought not to be there proved that she was there."

Midge clutched her head. "There are times when I wonder whether a jury-system is a good idea, when you see how credulous people are."

"Better than state-sponsored trials with pre-arranged verdicts," remarked Alice dryly. "Anyway, you can't really blame the villagers; they're putting in a lot of time as coast-watchers. Half of this gossip stems from the desire to feel that their job is vital. Obviously it is, but a little local excitement must help the hours to pass when you're stuck in a freezing cold outpost."

"I'm not sure I'd want to think about murder and sudden death on guard-duty," admitted Midge. "I'd start imagining assassins and ghosts."

"It must have been something more substantial than a ghost which Col. Durrant encountered last night."

"Quite. What else did you hear?"

"The Newton constable is Baldock's nephew; he was alerted around four o'clock to the presence of a body on the Harting mud-flats."

"By whom?"

"A coast-watcher coming off duty early. Apparently he'd got a cow in calf and he'd arranged for his young son to relieve him when it looked as if the birth was due. He took a short cut along the riverbank and practically stumbled over Durrant's body."

"Bit of a shock, surely?"

"Ghastly, I should think. Anyhow, he went haring off to Newton for the local bobby and alerted half the street banging on the station-house door and shouting. Once he'd conveyed his message, he returned to his cow and young Baldock told his wife to ring up the police surgeon whilst he raced off to mount guard."

"In the hope that he'd come across a parachuting nun," murmured Midge.

"Since rum-runners have had their activities curtailed, a spy or a drowned man like poor Mr Serring were the most likely options," agreed Alice. "I should imagine that young Baldock must have been distinctly taken-aback to discover an army colonel in full uniform. I'm sure the body ought not to have been touched but there's not been a murder round here for the best part of twenty years, and young Baldock can't be more than twenty-five. I suppose that, once he'd established that the poor man was dead, he couldn't resist taking a closer look to see whether he could discover what had happened. Hence how he discovered that the colonel had been shot through the chest."

Midge frowned. "Baldock really oughtn't to have told everyone about it. How does he think that the murderer is going to be tracked down if half the county knows what's going on?"

"He didn't tell half the county," remarked Alice mildly. "He only told his wife and his uncle."

"Hmph!" sniffed Midge. "I bet whoever's in charge of the investigation won't be anything like as understanding as you are."

"The chances are that Scotland Yard will be sent for. No-one will let on to some foreigner from London that young Baldock talked. They'll all close ranks and pretend that nobody has said anything."

"What if the Chief Constable sends for someone from Ipswich?" enquired Midge, interested in these revelations, which made her feel as if she were living amongst an exotic tribe on the far side of the globe.

"In that case," Alice pointed out, "he'll be related to half the farmers and fisher-folk in the county, so he might find some sources which are prepared to hint at the truth."

"Golly," ejaculated Midge faintly. "I never realised that police-work had quite so many ramifications. Does the same thing apply to journalists?"

"Naturally. Your uncle may be a diplomatic correspondent who has spent most of his working life abroad or in London, but young Baldock wouldn't think that he was speaking to the press if he talked to him. He'd just think he was speaking to Mr Geoffrey, who employed him as a gardener's boy when he left school."

"Isn't that a bit feudal?" asked Midge, who was not entirely sure that she approved of the picture her aunt was painting.

Alice shrugged. "Call it what you like. Round here it counts as local loyalty and knowing whom to trust. Why would young Baldock trust some anonymous journalist from London who will swan in here, scoop up the news and disappear off, never to be seen again? He knows that Geoffrey wouldn't treat him like that, therefore he would be prepared to talk to him." She sighed. "Not that there's much chance of Geoffrey coming to report on a local matter."

Chapter Twelve

Even allowing for poor driving conditions, Ralph ought to have been back with his battalion by luncheon. Since the roads had, in fact, been exceptionally clear, and since the Alfa had eaten up the miles, it was all the more surprising that by one o'clock Ralph was not carefully ensconced in the mess, attempting to pick up as much information as possible. Instead, he was sitting in his car in a lay-by, repeating the arguments which he had been making throughout the drive from London.

'What have I got to be afraid of? No-one has recognised me so far in the mess and my photograph was in all the papers. Either no-one cares any more about the trial or altering my hairstyle has prevented anyone from realising who I really am. And even if some clod-hopping constable does recognise me, what can he do? If he thinks that I'm Peveril, my papers show that I'm Thrigby. And he can't arrest me for murdering Durrant, because I have an unbreakable alibi. So there's no reason for me to funk things.'

Despite himself, Ralph shivered. 'I suppose Collingwood *will* come to my rescue if I get arrested for using false papers. If he didn't, no-one would know what had happened to me.' A thought suddenly struck Peveril. 'I could tell Midge what's going on. She'd do something if I disappeared.' He bit his lip nervously. 'Collingwood would be simply livid if he found out.' He shook himself. 'Pah! Am I afraid of him? Even if he clearly disapproves of me he can't actually *do* anything to me.'

Notwithstanding these reassuring remarks, a small voice in Ralph's head pointed out that Collingwood could probably do rather a lot to someone who casually flouted the Official Secrets Act. Moreover, even if Ralph were not afraid of his C.O. – which the same small voice took polite leave to doubt – he damn well ought to be.

'I wish I could think straight,' Peveril cursed. 'No wonder Robert thinks that I'm a coward.' The memory of his brother's drunken sneers stirred Ralph to anger. 'Damn it all, I will go and see Midge. After all, two heads are better than one. And surely it won't tire her too much to talk things over.'

Hence, to her considerable surprise, Midge saw the unmistakable shape of Ralph's motor draw up outside the house shortly after she and her aunt had finished lunch. Wondering what had brought him back so soon after his last visit, Midge made her way slowly to the hall, reaching it just as Peveril rang the doorbell. As she ushered him in, it struck Midge that Ralph was looking distinctly tired; his skin seemed bleached and stretched tight over his cheekbones.

"I didn't expect to see you again so quickly. Have you heard the news about Durrant?"

"Durrant?"

"He was discovered dead last night."

"How on earth did you find that out?" demanded Ralph.

"Have you just come from battalion HQ?" Midge replied, realising that she was not breaking fresh news.

"No, London. But how did you learn?"

"It's all over the place," answered Midge with pardonable exaggeration. "Everyone's talking about it."

"So much for the official policy of blanket silence on Durrant's death."

Midge shrugged. "Considering that his body was discovered by a civilian in the middle of the night, it'd be quite surprising if the news hadn't started to spread by now."

Peveril gave a reluctant laugh. "You'll have to forgive me, Midge, but I'm still recovering from the shock of being told to investigate his death. It is, shall we say, something of a reversal from my previous role."

"I suppose it makes sense since you're on the spot. But, if you ask me, it was ridiculous sending merely one officer to investigate possible Fascists in the first place. There ought to have been several of you and, as I said yesterday, you ought to have seen everyone's records before you went to the battalion."

"I asked to see them," admitted Peveril, "but Collingwood wouldn't show me them."

"Why?"

"I don't know. Maybe Collingwood doesn't trust me."

"That's ludicrous. Why would he send you on a mission if he doesn't?" Midge's colour rose at having to speak of Ralph's past.

"If Collingwood were worried about the trial, he'd have never chosen you for this mission in the first place. And what other reason could he possibly have for not trusting you?"

Peveril's mouth twisted as he wondered how Midge would respond if he replied that the most likely reason was Fletcher's report on his interrogation technique. Then he shrugged his shoulders. "Let's forget about Collingwood. Tell me what you've heard about Durrant's death."

Midge limped over to a tall bookcase on the far wall and drew out a large map. Ralph immediately took it from her, before unfolding it on the table. Midge flashed him a look of gratitude for seeing what needed to be done without commenting upon it – sticks got horribly in the way of maps. She lent over the table and eventually found the spot she was looking for.

"The village gossip is that Durrant was found on a mud bank about half a mile from Harting Magna." She pointed to a coastal inlet. "I remember John telling me that smugglers used to make their way inland along the River Hart on misty nights. The river was too shallow for Revenue cutters to navigate, but duck punts had no difficulty in keeping afloat, even if laden with brandy kegs." She gave a slight laugh. "I can't imagine that the Germans would choose to send an invasion force up the Hart – not least because the tide turns without any warning whatsoever – but it was a coast-watcher who discovered Durrant's body at four o'clock this morning."

Ralph craned his head over the map. "Good grief. Look here, Midge, our base must be only about three miles away."

"Which base? C Coy or battalion HQ?"

Seizing a convenient pencil, Ralph pointed out the relevant positions. "Roughly speaking, the two are equidistant from the body. A Coy is just under five miles to the north, and C Coy is three miles south-east."

"Glory," breathed Midge, who had not entirely grasped the geographical distribution of the various companies before. "Where's B Coy?"

"About another five miles north of HQ. I think the idea is to have HQ centrally positioned between the two subsidiary companies." A thought struck Peveril. "Midge, do you know exactly where the body was found? Was it on the north or the south bank?"

"Ellen said the south bank." Midge glanced at Ralph. "That doesn't necessarily mean that her information is true or that C Coy is involved. Remember what I said about the tides. The murderer might have left Durrant's body there hoping that it would be swept out to sea on the morning tide. He couldn't possibly have anticipated that some coast-watcher would race home to check on whether his cow had calved and instead trip up over a dead colonel."

A brief smile illuminated Peveril's face. "Dashed bad luck on him." Then he frowned. "Do you think that suggests local knowledge? I hadn't heard anything about dangerous tides in the creek."

Midge shrugged. "There was quite a lot in the local press nearly a month ago about an ornithologist who was drowned on the sea-shore nearby. Perhaps that gave the murderer the idea. In any case, anyone might guess that a river which debouches into the sea a few miles away is bound to be tidal at that point. Or it may have been pure chance that Durrant was killed there."

Peveril traced his index-finger along the coastline. "Newton's only a few miles further along from C Coy. The murderer may not be in the army at all."

"But he may be," retorted Midge firmly, "so you'll have to be very careful that you don't give yourself away."

Ralph gave her an unexpected grin. "Now, if Collingwood had said that to me, I'd have resented it hotly, but I might just possibly listen to the woman who saved my life. No singing Elgar?"

"No Elgar," agreed Midge, wondering how Ralph had managed to conceal his personality for years and now made such simple mistakes. Prompted by a mixture of curiosity and concern, she pursued the question, although she chose to approach it rather obliquely. "You avoided running risks at Eton, didn't you?"

"I wasn't precisely ordered to report to m'housemaster before breakfast every other morning," Peveril drawled, "but I wasn't a penitent Eric either."

Midge had no difficulty supplying from her own youthful literary explorations the reference to Dean Farrer's ill-fated schoolboy. She attempted to suppress her momentary amusement. "I should hardly have thought that you were," she admitted, before growing more solemn. "On the other hand, Ralph, you simply can't afford to throw things away now, when the consequences are potentially so much more serious. You're dealing with treason and murder."

"I know. I wouldn't be keeping you off your work otherwise." More out of a desire not to have Midge worry than because he believed his words, Ralph added, "Anyway, Durrant may have met his end for some purely personal reason – there are, presumably, pretty girls in Newton who may have attracted his attention." He glanced at his watch. "I'd better go, Midge. There's a limit to quite how late I can return to camp." He looked at her awkwardly. "Err... thanks for letting me talk to you."

Chapter Thirteen

On his way back to camp, Peveril wrestled with his conscience. Midge normally rested in the afternoon, but now she'd spend her time thinking about the murder rather than resting or working. And Newnham wouldn't take kindly to Midge devoting her time to Durrant's murder – however important solving it might turn out to be. Ralph grimaced. It was all very well saying that he didn't want Midge to suffer, but he'd done the wrong thing. He shouldn't have gone to see Midge, and he should have left immediately he had noticed that she looked tired. Blast.

Peveril's concerns regarding Midge distracted him from his earlier fears that he might be recognised by a policeman investigating Durrant's death. Hence he received a distinct shock when he discovered a constable talking to the sentry at the camp gate; a constable, moreover, who looked him over carefully as he drove in. Hastily remembering that he was meant to have no knowledge of the events of the previous night, Peveril demanded to know why the constable was there.

"Unforeseen events, sir," replied the constable, who appeared torn between a desire to preserve the portentous gravity suitable to his new-found importance and an all-too-human desire to gossip. In the end, he contented himself with a gnomic remark that 'things had happened'.

"Very well," snapped Peveril, certain that Capt. Thrigby's pride would have been offended by a mere constable refusing to explain matters to him. "If you won't tell me what's up, I'll speak to Major Goodwin." With that, he parked the Alfa and strode across to the officers' mess.

When he entered the sequestered farm building, Peveril made his way immediately to Major Goodwin's office. The company commander looked extremely harassed and shaken out of his usual attitude of lazy good humour.

"Where the hell have you been?" demanded Goodwin. "It's nearly seventeen hundred hours and your leave expired at thirteen hundred hours."

Despite Goodwin's remarks several weeks earlier that the chaps in C Coy did not stand on ceremony, Peveril felt that this was a moment when a Guards' standard of salute was appropriate.

"Sir."

The major scowled at him with displeasure. It was all right for Thrigby, he was one of those cursed specialists who didn't appear to have to answer to anyone, whereas he, Goodwin, had been up half the night dealing with an unhelpfully-minded police sergeant. Goodwin's scowl intensified. If it came to that, Thrigby must have been on a devil of a bender – he looked like he'd had no sleep either. Typical rich young idiot; more money than sense and probably some well-connected relations to keep him out of the front line. Well, young Master Thrigby'd have to do some work for a change, instead of floating around in that bloody motor, showing off his wealth to all who cared to speculate how much it had set him back.

"Where the devil were you?" he snapped for a second time, although fortunately in too much of a hurry to wait for an answer. "Don't you know what's happened?"

"There was a policeman at the gate," admitted Peveril cautiously, "but he just muttered something about events having occurred."

"Events?" repeated Goodwin with a snarl. "Events? Damn it, man, Poole's just been arrested for the murder of Durrant!"

Peveril had been gearing himself up to show sufficient surprise at the news of the colonel's death, but he had no difficulty in appearing shocked by Goodwin's announcement.

"Poole?" he stammered. "Poole's been arrested for killing Col. Durrant?"

"You heard me correctly. They've just carted him off in a Black Maria to Newton."

"But why?"

"If you'd been here a few hours ago, you'd know all that," snapped Goodwin irritably. "Durrant's body was found lying on the banks of the Hart at some god-forsaken hour of the morning. We're the closest camp, so the police came here first." Goodwin scowled at his desk, before adding pettishly, "I told them that the only colonel round here was based at HQ – I don't see why they couldn't have gone there first. They might have arrested someone else if they had."

Peveril was momentarily amused by this indication of his company commander's devotion to justice. However, he seized the opportunity to press for more details.

"Why did they arrest Poole? Surely they must have had a reason?"

"Presumably."

Peveril wisely chose not to pursue this remark. Goodwin didn't sound any too happy about what the police had done.

"Now that you *are* here," remarked Goodwin, working off some of his sense of inadequacy by pouncing on Thrigby, "you can do something useful."

"Sir?"

Goodwin forced a smile, suddenly realising that it might not be a good idea to have Thrigby complaining about how ratty his company commander had been. Durrant, curse him, had made some pretty unpleasant remarks on the subject of inadequacy and ill-preparedness last time he'd visited C Coy. The last thing he needed was a suggestion that he was out of his depth when faced with the unexpected problem of Poole; pretending to take a fatherly interest in Poole might prevent any hurtful and deeply damaging gossip taking hold.

"You seem to have become quite friendly with Poole."

Peveril was uncertain whether deliberately losing a decent-ish amount of money at poker counted as becoming friendly, but waited obediently for more information.

"Get Poole's batman to pack him some small kit and then run over to Newton with it. Talk to Poole and see if you could encourage him to speak to the police inspector. He wouldn't say a word when he was arrested. If he talks, we might get this all cleared up one way or the other."

"Sir," agreed Peveril, trying to sound enthusiastic. It was all very well Goodwin casually suggesting that he talk to Poole, but Goodwin didn't know what had happened last time he had been faced with a prisoner.

When Peveril appeared at the Newton police station, he was greeted by the inspector in charge of the case.

"I'm Woolf," he remarked in a country burr. "What can I do for you, Captain?"

Ralph noticed with surprise that the man was running to fat – the once strong jaw-line was blurred with flesh and Woolf's body bulged under the uniform. He'd always thought that the police were meant to keep in good shape. The Cambridge ones had been. Peveril gave a mental shrug. Maybe it didn't matter in rural districts. But what did matter was whether the inspector recognised him; it was vital that he didn't make a false move.

"Goodwin sent me," explained Peveril. "I've brought some things for Lt. Poole."

"Well, since you're here, p'raps you might persuade your pal to talk about what he's been up to."

"Has he said anything?" demanded Peveril, conscious that Inspector Woolf was asking him, in effect, to be a Judas.

"He swore he was innocent and then shut his trap tight," admitted Woolf. "That's typical, though. They all say that they didn't do it, but that doesn't make them any more innocent than a fox swearing he didn't go into the hen-coop. Poole will swing for murder on the evidence we've got."

"Evidence?"

"Of course, sir; we can't arrest people because we don't like the look of them. This isn't Germany."

"Can you tell me what the evidence is?" enquired Peveril, adding cunningly, "I might have more chance of persuading Poole to talk if I could demonstrate to him that things were serious."

Woolf regarded his visitor thoughtfully. It was no part of his job to be encouraging speculative gossip about Poole's guilt but, on the other hand, there was a very slim possibility that Poole might claim that he had killed Durrant in self-defence. Certainly, Poole had an impressive bruise on the side of his head and Durrant's gun had been fired. It would be useful to know what Poole's explanation of that was. And this chap wouldn't be bound by Judges' Rules and all that ridiculous nonsense about not trying to trick a suspect into a confession. The magistrates had been unpleasantly sceptical about the last confession which had been presented to them.

Woolf suppressed a snort. You'd think that magistrates would realise that the police didn't bring a man before the Bench without good reason. Moreover, if he sent this chap in, it would end those unhelpful complaints from battalion HQ about civilians investigating a military crime – they must be mad if they thought that he'd hang around waiting for the Military Police to be brought from Ipswich or London. That would just give Poole the opportunity to pull himself together and escape justice.

"You point out to Poole that denying what's in his personal accounts isn't very sensible when we have them and when we're about to interview his bank-manager." Woolf coughed. "A lot of people think that police work is about clever theories, but it isn't. It's about careful, routine checking of all the ends and when we tie up those ends, we tie up the criminal. If Poole's got an explanation, he'd be better coming out with it now than leaving it 'til the trial when no-one will believe it."

"Doubtless his lawyer will say the same," agreed Peveril smoothly, wondering what all this talk of accounts meant. Had Poole been bluing his money? Why should that lead to Poole killing Durrant? He could hardly imagine Durrant gambling with Poole or lending him money at extortionate rates of interest.

"His lawyer," grunted Woolf with hostility, "will do well to get him to co-operate with the police."

Peveril's instinctive response was that Poole would be a fool to admit anything. However, he was loath to make any statement which suggested that he had inside knowledge of criminal procedure, so he restricted himself to requesting to be shown into Poole's cell.

"If I might trouble you to leave your parcel with me, sir," replied Woolf. "Regulations are that my sergeant checks everything sent into the prisoner. And I'm afraid that I'll have to search you, sir."

"Of course," Peveril agreed stiffly, trying not to resent this perfectly sensible precaution. If nothing else, at least the inspector's words had alerted him to the fact that there would be no point in trying to win Poole's confidence by smuggling in a knife.

There was nothing to criticise regarding the punctiliousness with which Woolf treated his prisoner when he ushered Peveril into the cell. However, Ralph had no time to worry about how the inspector addressed Poole; he was too busy trying to fight off a feeling of doom.

'Nothing is going to happen to me just because I'm involved in this mess,' he thought savagely. 'I'm a friend of the prisoner, not the prisoner himself. Blast Poole for getting me dragged into this damned affair – why couldn't he have shot Durrant three weeks ago?' Aware that this was not, to put it mildly, the most generous of reactions, Peveril scowled angrily at the cause of his troubles. Somewhat to his disgust, he could not help noticing that Poole was shivering, despite the warmth of the cell. Sticking to the helpful excuse provided by Goodwin, Peveril explained why he had come.

"Very good of you, Thrigby," responded Poole in lacklustre tones, accompanying his greeting with a flabby handshake.

"Must have come as a ghastly shock to be run in," Peveril trumpeted in Thrigby-like tones. "Damned bad luck, old chap. What happened?"

"I... I... I...," stammered Poole.

"Good Lord," remarked Peveril after a few moments. "That bad, eh? No wonder Goodwin seemed so upset. He wants to know whether he can do anything."

Poole cast him a furtive look and shook his head.

"Well, now that I am here, why don't we talk about things?"

Poole shook his head again.

"Don't be an ass," declared Peveril heartily, deciding to stay in character as Thrigby for the moment. "How am I supposed to play poker with you in quod? And you'd had quite a winning streak lately, too."

"It doesn't matter any more now," muttered Poole gloomily. "It's too late."

Peveril frowned, unsure what Poole meant. "Is that intended to be a confession, old boy?" he asked with a breezy laugh. "The bluebottle out there was buzzing about accounts and your bank. Did Durrant catch you embezzling the mess funds?"

"Damn you, shut up!" snarled Poole. "It's not some inane joke. And what's it got to do with you anyway? You may have your captaincy, but you're not in command of me. Why are you here? You're just a specialist in a load of footling rot, not a real soldier who'll serve on the front line."

A spurt of rage flashed through Peveril. So this filthy little cad was going to sneer at him, was he? Suggest that he had no authority? Suggest that he was a coward? 'By God,' thought Peveril furiously, 'I may have been frightened when I was arrested, but I'm damned if I ever showed tears to the men sent to interrogate me.' Thrusting aside the unhelpful recollection that he had once more-or-less cried in front of Midge, he glared at the hapless Poole, determined to teach him who was the coward. He leant forward.

"Blubbing already?" he asked cruelly. "Well, you'll soon blub a bit more. How are you going to cope with police questioning when you can't even cope with a few friendly enquiries from me? They'll probably send someone down from the Yard. Do you really think that you'll be able to hold out against them?"

There was no reply.

"But," hissed Peveril, unaware that he had cast off his adopted persona, "of course, you despise specialists, don't you? You think that they ought to be serving on the front line. Would you say that swinging from a rope's end counts as the front line? It's not the same as risking bullets, but it's certainly more final."

Peveril watched with warped satisfaction as Poole covered his face with his hands. Clearly his words were striking home. He continued remorselessly.

"I shouldn't be so keen to thrust away the few friends you've got," he murmured ominously. "Don't you realise that no-one will want to talk to you when it comes out what you've done? Your friends will shun you; your family will curse you for bringing disgrace upon them; and the regiment will cast you off, utterly and completely. Do you really think that Goodwin will bother with you any more if I report back that you're as guilty as hell? This is your only chance to speak out about what happened and convince me that you didn't kill Durrant. If you don't, you'll be left here to rot until you are sent to trial or are shot at dawn."

Poole's body suddenly heaved convulsively. "Be quiet," he pleaded, his voice muffled and thick.

Peveril stared at him with dislike. Didn't Poole have any backbone at all? Didn't he realise that he was asking to be pushed harder and harder, until he finally broke? A small, twisted smile crossed Peveril's face.

"Oh no," he whispered, "I shan't be quiet. I shan't be quiet until you tell me what I want to know."

Poole could not stop himself from glancing at his visitor. "Who are you? You're not a semaphore specialist, are you?"

"Don't you worry about who I am." Peveril allowed his eyes to run over Poole lingeringly, as if he were already measuring him for the drop from the scaffold, before adding with silken menace, "More to the point, you need to worry about what's happening to you. Do you know what they do to murderers after they've hanged them? They put them in the cold, cold ground and cast quicklime over their bodies until even their bones are no more. Do you want that to happen to you?"

"Don't; please don't."

"Only cowards beg," taunted Peveril unpleasantly. "Only cowards or those with guilty consciences. Which are you? A coward or a murderer?"

Poole held up his hands as if he were almost physically trying to push Peveril away from him. "Leave me alone."

Peveril laughed. "I shall leave when I choose and I haven't heard anything to make me leave yet."

"You inhumane devil," Poole cursed miserably. "Go away."

"Very well spotted," purred Peveril. "I am an inhumane devil. But haven't you realised that you can't drive the devil away, especially not if you've killed? Perhaps that pricking you can feel isn't your conscience. Perhaps what you feel is my talons taking their grip on your soul already."

Poole shuddered, but Peveril's voice went on and on, questioning him, hectoring him, cajoling him to speak. It seemed to Poole that his interrogator would never leave but, eventually, Peveril decided that he would get nothing more out of the prisoner. He rapped on the door of the cell and, as he heard footsteps approaching, he turned to Poole, who was sitting with his head sunk on his arms.

"I'll be back; the devil always comes back. Think about Faust,

Poole; think about Faust." With that uncomfortable thrust, Peveril left.

Chapter Fourteen

When Peveril made his way to the front desk of the police-station, he found Woolf still present.

"Any luck, sir?"

"Not yet, Inspector," admitted Peveril, unwillingly to reveal a piece of information which might potentially prove to be of interest. "He seems a bit shocked. Would it be possible for me to come back another time?"

"I think so," agreed Woolf slowly. "I'd have to be present to give permission, sir, but I can't see any harm in it at present. After all, there's something of an overlap between Army and police jurisdiction in this matter, so some co-operation might be useful."

"Thank you, Inspector; I'll tell Major Goodwin."

With mutual handshakes, the two men parted, Peveril to drive off in his Alfa and Woolf to return thoughtfully to his office.

As he headed back towards C Coy, Peveril was decidedly pre-occupied. In his mind he could hear Fletcher's voice saying 'no-one treated you like that'. He scowled at the steering-wheel. His case was completely different. That had been a private murder; this was potentially linked to treason. So it didn't matter if his questioning had been rather harsh. It didn't matter at all. It wasn't as if he'd actually hit Poole; all he'd done was point out the facts. Poole was in a mess, and he would hang if he were convicted. So there was nothing wrong with having said so. And no-one had observed him interrogating Poole, so it didn't count.

Ralph thrust away a half-formed wish that Fletcher had indeed walked into the cell. The consequences would have been horribly unpleasant, but at least the K.C. might have acquired the necessary information – and told him how to conduct an interrogation. Ralph scowled. That sort of thought was stupid – you didn't run begging for help when you were twenty-one, and all that would have happened if Fletcher had observed today's exhibition was that he would have informed Midge what the man she'd saved from the gallows was really like.

Ralph shook himself. Since he was meant to be undercover, the sooner he reverted to thinking like Thrigby, the better.

Thrigby suffered from no qualms or self-doubt. He certainly didn't worry about what nameless barristers might say about his conduct. And since Thrigby wasn't keen on anyone, he didn't have to wonder about how the girl he loved would respond, either. And why the hell was he driving so slowly when he had nothing whatsoever on his conscience?

When Peveril returned to camp, he dutifully reported that he had seen Poole, before retiring to the mess bar, which was a whirl of speculation and gossip. Hetherley, who was decidedly interested in what Poole might have said, was the first to seize upon him.

"Is it true that you've been to see him?"

"Whom?"

"Poole."

"Yes. Goodwin asked me to take some things down to him."

"Is Poole in gaol?"

"Where else would he be?" demanded Peveril irritably, before suddenly remembering that Thrigby probably would not have reacted in quite this manner. On the other hand, Thrigby wouldn't have spent over an hour intensively interrogating Poole either. "Sorry, old chap," he replied, swiftly returning to his assumed manner, "didn't mean to snap at you. Just a bit of a shock seeing Poole in clink." He turned to Trent, who was busy polishing the bar. "Beer, please, Trent."

Snellgrove joined them. "It strikes me that you were lucky to have been away last night."

Peveril buried his nose in his glass, wondering if Snellgrove was hinting anything.

"The police have been crawling round the camp all day," added Snellgrove angrily, his thin lips pursed in disapproval. "It's a disgrace. I know that Durrant's body wasn't found on Army land, but, in matters relating to two officers, the Army ought to be investigating, not the local police."

Peveril looked rather blank, wondering if his apparent years of experience meant that he ought to understand such issues of jurisdiction. "I suppose Newton's a lot closer."

Snellgrove snorted. "There's been plenty of time to call in the

Military Police. And even if they are grossly understaffed, this is a very serious affair."

Hetherley shrugged his shoulders dismissively. "That's all very well, Snellgrove, but Goodwin has no intention of wasting time arguing with bobbies as to what they can or can't do. And don't forget that the MPs know a thing or two about military matters. At least Woolf pushes off back to Newton; think what a couple of regular officers staying here might make of our set-up. They might even report adversely upon our general lack of organisation and readiness."

Snellgrove glared at him. It was quite true that there were a number of things which it would be much better if the MPs did not discover, but need Hetherley declare it quite so openly? He reverted to the question of Poole. "I hear that the police were up questioning A Coy as well." He snorted. "The inspector asked them some damn fool questions."

"Such as?"

"Whether 'there had been any record of disagreement' with Durrant. That's what I mean about damn fool questions – who's going to admit to quarrelling with Durrant when they've just heard that he's been shot?"

"Goes to show which way the police are working," murmured Peveril.

"If you ask me," replied Hetherley, "they were probably expecting to hear about rows with local tradesmen, not about any squabbles within the regiment."

"One of the chaps up there said something about Durrant having bawled out Poole," commented Peveril slowly. "Did anyone mention it to the police?"

"Be your age, Thrigby," recommended Snellgrove unkindly. "Of course they didn't. Jervis told me that there was a sudden frozen silence, followed by polite, professional courtesy and interest. I can't imagine that the police got anything of the slightest use from A Coy, and I shouldn't go around mentioning Poole's misfortune if I were you."

"I should think that Durrant had bawled out half the regiment at one point or another," agreed Hetherley, adding with no apparent concern, "he certainly didn't mince his words with me.

In fact, he taught me some new ones."

"Then why was Poole fixed upon as the guilty party?" queried Peveril, wondering whether what Woolf had told him was public knowledge.

"No alibi for the time of the crime."

"Surely Poole can't have been the only one without an alibi, Snellgrove," Peveril protested. "Why pick on Poole?"

"Because A Platoon was up at B Coy, being taught how to guard a camp properly. That left one other under-strength platoon – and Poole."

"And the officers," pointed out Peveril.

"Quite," agreed Hetherley. "All the officers were here apart from you. But it was Poole who had the time 0.45 scrawled in his diary for last night; it was Poole who denied having left camp at all; and it was Poole's boots which were still damp with sea-water when the coppers arrived."

"How did you learn all this?"

"*We* didn't," replied Hetherley regretfully. "Catchpole, Ulph and several others managed to place themselves in strategic positions when the posse of police turned up. There's been a roaring trade in information all afternoon, but we're the last to hear of it."

Back in Brandon, Midge had evinced a most unusual interest in joining her aunt at a Women's Institute meeting at the vicarage that evening.

"I suppose you want to hear all the gossip about that poor man's death," observed Alice dryly. "I trust that Mrs Halliday will have realised that she is likely to have a very full attendance tonight and that hardly anyone will attend because they want to sew comforts for refugees."

"Out of evil good may come," Midge murmured.

"That's all very well," countered Alice, "but I don't want you dropping any more bricks like that dreadful comment about Mosley. You have to remember that you're not in Cambridge, Midge. In the country, young women simply don't make remarks like that – not unless they want to gain a shocking reputation."

Midge attempted to adopt a meek expression. It did not seem

a fruitful time for launching into a plaint that women were expected to lock their mouths when men were not.

Alice laughed reluctantly. "Butter wouldn't melt! I suppose I can't really blame you for being interested; half the village will be panting to hear whether Maria Gregory has acquired any further information from Baldock's nephew."

Since Midge could not walk down to the vicarage, Alice requested that Evans motor them to the village. This had the considerable additional benefit that they were able to call in at the colonel's house on the way.

"Come to offer my good lady a lift?" enquired the colonel, with an amused lift of his eyebrows. "Now, that's what I call a sound piece of tactical manoeuvring. Intercept the source of information before the enemy has the chance to seize it." He winked at Midge. "Not that I'd call the Hallidays the enemy, but the principle stands: secure your intelligence and it puts you ahead of the other feller."

"My aunt knew that Mrs Gregory was intending to bring some old sheets along to cut up," replied Midge. "We thought that we could save her the effort of carrying them along the lane."

Col. Gregory guffawed. "And the second principle is never to admit that you're on the hunt for information or the price'll go up no end. I managed to maintain the polite fiction with my Azeris that I took only a nominal interest in odd goings-on in the up-country passes. Naturally, they didn't believe me, but we all observed the rules of the game." He sighed, thinking of the most recent letter from the War Office declining his services in the current conflict. "The question is, m'dear, what do you propose to trade for the latest news from Newton?"

Wondering what the colonel would reply if she answered that she could tell him the name of an undercover operative at work in the East Suffolks, Midge looked inscrutable. "If I traded news, surely that would suggest that I really was interested in collecting information?"

"Aha!" declared Col. Gregory in glee. "A splendid reply! You shouldn't be wasting your time at Cambridge, Midge; you should be out in India, tracking down information in the bazaar!"

Midge forced a smile, not wishing to hurt the colonel's feelings. He could hardly be expected to realise she indeed sometimes felt as if she were wasting her time at Cambridge when other girls were doing their bit towards the war effort.

"In any case," concluded the elderly man, "we can't let your splendid tactics go awry. If you turn up too late, all the tables will have been bagged and you'll get separated from m'wife. Can't have that happening when you're the only person in the village who's ever solved a murder!"

Fortunately for Midge's blushes, Maria Gregory bustled into the room at that precise moment, apologising for the delay.

"The thing is, I laid down the parcel of linen but I simply cannot remember where I had put it."

"It's on the hall table," interjected her husband.

"Silly me! I'm afraid that my mind was on Higher Things."

Knowing that this admission was unlikely to be related to matters of ecclesiastical doctrine, the colonel urged her towards the waiting motor-car. Midge only devoted a fraction of her attention to Mrs Gregory's latest fad – deep-breathing exercises which toned the mind as well as the muscles.

Once they arrived at the vicarage, Midge picked her way carefully up the path in the wake of her aunt and Mrs Gregory, who was still discoursing on the benefits of Swedish breathing. The vicar's wife must have observed their progress, because the door opened as they approached.

"Mrs Gregory, Mrs Carrington, how good to see you. And you, too, Midge. Splendid! The more the merrier." She ushered them into the long low room which was set aside for such pastoral excitements as tonight's affair and suggested that they sit where the light was best. "Since you've arrived first, you may as well benefit from having the pick of the seats."

By half-past, the room was sufficiently full for Mrs Halliday to suggest that some people could move to another room, if they wished.

"Do let's stay together," disagreed the elderly Miss Clayton, her nose twitching in disapproval. "It would be simply wasteful to use more coal when we can manage as we are."

"Quite," sniffed Miss Thurleston. "We must remember the

War Effort, even if we have to sacrifice some of our own personal comfort to do so."

Midge bit back a grin. If she were as farouche as her aunt had suggested, she would be tempted to point out that the two elderly ladies were significantly more interested in not being left out of any discussion of Col. Durrant's death than in any concerns about coal shortages. However, this was unlikely to advance her own particular wishes so she merely bent her head over a peculiarly uninspiring piece of grey linen and hoped that someone else would raise the topic. Eventually, young Mrs Otley, whose husband was said to be in the RAF – although more unkind tongues had pointed out that had he not yet visited his wife – obliged.

"What's the latest news from Baldock's nephew?" she enquired breathlessly. "I've been dying to hear."

Seven faces turned disapproving looks upon her. True, she was only asking what they all wanted to know, but there were ways of approaching a subject and this was not one of them. However, what could you expect of a young woman who painted her nails scarlet and positively showered her drawing room with large numbers of photographs of different young men in uniform?

'Most unsuitable,' reflected Miss Thurleston damningly, while even Mrs Halliday felt that Mrs Otley really needed to learn to conduct herself more appropriately. Maria Gregory, who had looked as disapproving as Miss Thurleston, secretly rejoiced. Her dramatic instincts were well to the fore, but she assumed an air of diffident reluctance.

"I'm sure no-one will want to talk about these dreadful events."

"Of course not," trumpeted Miss Clayton, peering over her narrow glasses, eyes flashing at the idea of being deprived of her evening's entertainment. "Naturally, it is a great trial to be forced to speak of them, but we all know our duty. What if one of us happened to know something which would be of use to the police? I, for one, shrink from discussing so distasteful a matter, but we must put our Duty To The Authorities ahead of our own personal desires."

This convenient explanation of sheer curiosity was greeted with widespread agreement.

"If you feel that it is my *duty*, then naturally I must speak," proclaimed Mrs Gregory. "I've been married to an army man for long enough to know that some things must be tackled, however difficult they may be." Having made that disclaimer, she promptly threw a verbal hand grenade into the conversation. "There's been an arrest!"

"Who?"

"When?"

"Is it a local?"

This excited reaction to her statement reassured Mrs Gregory that she was, indeed, first with the news. Encouraged, she proceeded to pass on further information which she had garnered shortly before she had left the house.

"It's rather a worry for the Baldocks – they want young Joe to do well, but they don't like him being mixed up in murder. So, naturally, when I was arranging menus for the coming week with Mrs Baldock, she wanted to talk to me about what's been happening."

Her auditors' heads nodded intelligently, appreciating that Maria Gregory had established a valid reason for why she had been encouraging tittle-tattle.

"Apparently there's a young man from the regiment who has been behaving oddly for some time – rather a nervous specimen, I gather. He seems to have had an argument with the colonel and the police arrested him this afternoon."

This remark brought more excited discussion, but Midge was willing Mrs Gregory to hurry up and finish her story. She was conscious of a dreadful fear that perhaps the police had made a horrible mistake and had arrested Ralph.

"Yes," twittered Mrs Gregory happily, unaware that she was putting one member of her audience under considerable strain. "I don't really understand which company is based where, but apparently this young man is based very close to where the colonel's body was found."

'C Coy,' thought Midge with foreboding. 'Please don't let it be Ralph.'

Mrs Gregory leaned forward. "Apparently..." She paused, seemingly reluctant to continue.

"Go on," urged Mrs Clayton.

"Apparently, he was seen returning to camp at around two o'clock in the morning, but, when he was questioned about it, he denied everything."

Midge felt a flurry of relief. Ralph was in London at two a.m. and he could prove it. 'Gosh,' she reflected, 'I'll have to resort to Swedish breathing to calm my nerves soon.'

Mrs Gregory was nearly finished, but she had kept the best to last. "He's denied everything to the police *and* to a young officer the Army sent down to question him. He won't say anything at all." She looked round, ensuring that everyone was listening attentively. "But how can you explain away a gun which has been fired?!"

The sensation which greeted this remark satisfied even Mrs Gregory. Speculation broke out as to the importance of the gun. Mrs Clayton, who was a keen reader of all the crime news in the press, pointed out that if the police found the bullet which had killed Col. Durrant, they would be able to test to see whether it came from the gun of the arrested man.

"What do you think, Miss Carrington?" enquired Miss Thurleston, adding pointedly, "You've got more experience than any of us of this sort of shocking affair."

Hoping that she did not appear embarrassed, Midge waved her hands airily. "Proving that the bullet came from a gun is not the same as proving that the owner fired the gun."

"I shouldn't think that the police will have much difficulty," snorted Mrs Gregory. "The gun was found in the man's quarters, wrapped up in his socks. Coupled with the fact that he was seen returning in the middle of the night, I'd think that would be enough for any jury."

Chapter Fifteen

When Midge returned back to the Grange, she wanted nothing more than to have some peace to consider Mrs Gregory's revelations. However, when she entered the house, she was greeted by Ellen.

"Is the mistress with you?"

Midge shook her head. "She stayed to talk to Mrs Halliday. I came back in the car. Is everything all right?"

Ellen pulled a face. "Not exactly, Miss Midge. That Mrs Serring has turned up again, wanting to speak to the master."

"How silly! My aunt told her that he was in London."

"Yes, but she's here all the same. And she's brought her dog and Bertie's scared of it."

"I'll see if I can persuade her to go away before my aunt returns. Is she in the drawing-room?"

Ellen nodded and Midge made her way to the drawing-room. When she entered, Midge saw a middle-aged woman, shrouded in black clothes. Nonetheless, despite the drab nature of her garments, there would be no chance of overlooking this woman in a crowd – her fiery eyes shone with determined intelligence, while her nose, curved like the beak of a hawk, gave her a predatory air. The alert terrier at her side added to the impression that Mrs Serring could have stepped out of a hunting-scene in a mediaeval painting.

"Who are you?" the woman demanded. "Why are you here?"

"I'm Midge Carrington. I'm Mr and Mrs Carrington's niece, and I live here when I'm not at Cambridge."

"Cambridge," repeated Mrs Serring softly. "Dickie was a student there. He loved it. He promised to take me." Her tone changed. "You could be anyone."

"Let me fetch my identity card."

"No, no. I will not let you run away."

"I can't exactly run anywhere," pointed out Midge, with an edge to her voice.

Mrs Serring ran her eyes over Midge's sticks. "It is a good disguise."

"Don't be so perfectly ridiculous," snapped Midge,

overwhelmed by a sudden rage that anyone had suggested that she was inventing her dragging gait and the constant, unending pain which was the legacy of polio. "I had infantile paralysis. Look at my leg – it's clearly weaker than the other. And," she added as she dragged up the sleeve of her blouse, "do you think that I did this to myself?"

Looking at Midge's right arm, which was thin and fragile compared to her left, the woman seemed momentarily convinced. Then she laughed unpleasantly. "Not one of the Herrenvolk, then. But why should I trust you?"

Midge limped over to the piano and picked up a cabinet photograph. "Look at this," she ordered. "That's my uncle – he interviewed you when you escaped from Poland – and you can quite clearly see that he's standing next to me and my aunt, whom you have also met. Either we can wait for her to return from the village or you can trust the evidence of this photograph."

Mrs Serring appeared to fall into a reverie. "Why do they not send someone? Why does no-one come? If only I knew to whom Dickie spoke. Why does no-one come? Did they not care about my message? I might as well have died too."

Although Midge was intrigued by the widow's reference to a message, she suspected that Mrs Serring would close up if she asked about it. Instead, Midge attempted to answer the widow's final point. "You have your dog. What would she do without you?"

Unexpectedly, the woman's eyes filled with tears and she whispered something in a foreign tongue. Then she turned on Midge. "And what do I do without him? He whom murderers killed – my Dickie."

Midge remembered that her aunt had said that Mrs Serring had some conspiracy on her brain that her husband had been deliberately killed, rather than dying in a tragic accident. Mrs Serring seemed to sense her disbelief.

"Ah, you think I am mad. Well, what if I were to tell you of what Dickie spoke before he died? What if he spoke of people and lights where there should be none? What if he had seen vessels on the water where there should be none? And what if he came back from London saying that his friend was worried?"

"Who was his friend?" asked Midge gently.

The animation on Mrs Serring's face died. "I don't know," she admitted hopelessly. "Dickie suddenly became very secretive. He said he was trying to protect me. He wouldn't tell me where he saw the lights. He wouldn't even tell me to whom he spoke."

"Was it a policeman or a soldier?"

"I have said enough to make you kill me if you are an enemy."

"But I am not an enemy. And you approached my uncle for help." Midge thought rapidly. "He is not here and will not be for some time, but I might be able to visit him in London and pass on what you wish to say."

Mrs Serring shrugged fatalistically. "If you are false I shall die sooner, but I do not care. I gamble so I can get revenge upon the killers of my Dickie." She made a gesture of despair. "I think he spoke to someone in your Intelligence department – when we were in Poland he said that he knew someone there. But I don't know how to contact him."

"You said you wrote to London?" urged Midge.

"I tried writing to the War Office, but the reply said that my letter would be considered in due course. Why can you people not see that British traitors exist too? My Dickie knew there was something wrong, but I cannot make anyone care. They say that I am mad and foreign. That inspector at the police station refuses to see me any more and the sergeant laughs behind my back."

Midge was both appalled and excited by these revelations. If Mrs Serring were even partly correct, her information might provide a very important clue towards Ralph's mission. On the other hand, how dreadful if her husband really had been murdered. Midge regarded the older woman uncertainly for a moment, well aware that her next question might encourage a lot of jaundiced spite. "Is there anyone whom you do not trust?"

"I trust no-one now that my Dickie is dead."

"Err, yes. But is there anyone locally who disliked your husband or has behaved oddly to you?"

A spasm of hate crossed the widow's face. "There is my

neighbour." spat the widow. "He looks me up and down and sneers at me. He calls me a Russian Jewess and laughs. He pretends to be sorry for me when my Dickie is killed, but it is a lie. Does he think that I forget what he says before?"

"Who is your neighbour?"

"Basil Cosford."

"Cosford? The bookseller in Newton?"

Mrs Serring mistook Midge's surprise for incredulity. "Yes. Do you think that booksellers have no politics? There are plenty who think as he does." She scowled angrily. "No-one would listen if I reported that he is a danger. They would say it was another Jewish plot."

Trembling in case she betrayed her interest, Midge asked, "What makes you say he is a danger?"

"He has visitors who stay late – but late! They often leave after midnight and they do not lower their voices. They drink. There are army officers, too. I have seen them. And they gamble. Some complain of losing money; a few boast of winning. They should be preparing for invasion, not gambling. He distracts them from their duty."

"Did your husband say anything about Cosford?"

Reluctantly, Mrs Serring shook her head.

"And he didn't give any details at all about whom he saw?"

"No."

"Not even whether they were men or women?"

"No. Nor where he saw them. Do you not believe that I have thought and thought about what he said? Or do you think that he did not say anything and I invented the lights and the people and the boats?"

Ruefully recollecting Ellen's description of Mrs Serring as 'fair mazed with grief', Midge shook her head. "I do believe you. If I didn't, I shouldn't have listened to you."

"So you will help?"

"I'll try. Do you have a list of dates when your husband had noted something suspicious?"

"Naturally. I sent a copy to your War Office. But you may have them. Just promise me that you will use them. Don't laugh at me. Investigate."

Hearing the exhaustion in the older woman's voice, Midge realised that it was probably only her fiery determination to see her husband's killers pay which was keeping her going. Quite how she would react if it were proved that the ornithologist genuinely had died in an accident, Midge hated to contemplate.

Chapter Sixteen

Several hours later, Peveril was staring sightlessly out of the window of his quarters. If he turned his head, he could just catch the sound of the surf combing the beach over a mile away, but he could see nothing since the camp was concealed by the thick velvet of night. He sighed, feeling that the problem of Durrant's death was equally shrouded in darkness. The atmosphere over dinner had been a bit sticky, but that wasn't particularly surprising. And nobody seemed to be behaving oddly. If anything, their individual characteristics were accentuated – Snellgrove had a dashed cutting tongue, Hetherley was desperate not to miss any excitement, and Goodwin was rushing around to cover up for the fact that he didn't know what he was doing. As for Trent, he had clearly been listening to the conversation, so it was just as well that nothing new had been discussed.

Peveril turned to considering what little he had gained from Poole that afternoon. After he had mentioned treason, why had Poole kept refusing so emphatically to respond? It had almost sounded as if he were trying to reassure Peveril that he would not talk. Why should he think that that would please his interrogator? Or was it all of a one with his desire to annoy Peveril by his comments about Peveril having no authority over him? Peveril flushed at that last recollection. Maybe he hadn't responded frightfully sensibly to Poole's insults, but they had sounded dreadfully like Robert's constant sneers. Peveril bit his lip, aware that that was not much of an excuse. Anyway, was it so surprising that Poole was scared and lashing out? Oh hell, why hadn't he shown a bit more understanding towards the man? Quite apart from any issues of humanity, Poole would be more likely to reveal whatever he knew if his interrogator treated him decently.

Eventually Peveril dropped off into an exhausted sleep. The work of the camp went on quietly, but with unaccustomed efficiency. The sentries were thoroughly alert and hoping for excitement; Snellgrove, as the duty officer, was determined that nothing would go wrong, whatever might have happened the previous evening; even Goodwin put in an atypical presence.

Indeed, the only creature to articulate its resentment at the unusual activity was the resident screech owl, which protested long and loud at the company commander prowling along the perimeter.

"I wish that damn bird would shut up," grunted Goodwin. "It gets on my nerves."

That someone else was suffering from nerves was demonstrated by another shriek, albeit soundless and issued by a human throat. Unnoticed by anyone, up in his quarters Peveril threshed around in the bedclothes, before clawing his way upright.

"Christ," he panted, "no, no, no." Then, as the music which was resounding in his head began to lessen in volume, he attempted to pull himself together. 'Hell and damnation take it; it's ludicrous to have nightmares like some scared kid.'

Ralph grimaced in distaste as he discovered that his pyjama jacket was soaked with sweat. He pulled it off and threw it into the corner, before shivering as the moisture on his torso evaporated in the cold night air. Realising that he had better find something else to wear, but reluctant to turn on the main light in case it attracted attention, Ralph lit a candle which stood on top of the chest of drawers. Then he halted in shock at he caught sight of his reflection, illuminated from beneath by the fluttering flame of the candle.

'Don't be an ass,' Ralph rebuked himself. 'It's only the way the shadows are falling. You're not an El Greco saint undergoing one of the more esoteric forms of torture. And,' he added grimly, 'if you are looking a bit tormented, whose fault is that? Your own. Sneering at Poole for being a coward doesn't prove that you are brave. In fact, it rather proves the opposite. You should never have spoken to him like that, even if he is a murderer. It was despicable.'

The next morning, following a nearly sleepless night, Peveril arrived at the Newton police station shortly before eight o'clock.

The burly inspector soon appeared, all good humour.

"Good morning, sir. Back for another chat with our little friend?"

"Yes."

Woolf eyed him thoughtfully. "I take it that you disapprove of an officer being killed, just as much as I do?"

"Naturally."

"Well, perhaps you might help me out, sir." Woolf coughed. "You'll maybe have heard a bit of discussion about jurisdiction up at the camp. Currently, it's the police, not the Army, which is running this investigation. You're an officer, not a policeman. That means that anything you say to Poole can't affect the police case. So you could do your country a bit of good by putting some pressure on Poole."

"What do you mean?"

"I need to know how he's going to explain away what he was doing. He won't talk to me, but it would help a lot if you softened him up a bit mentally."

"Presumably," remarked Peveril bitterly, "you'd like me to soften him up a bit physically, too."

Woolf appeared genuinely appalled at this suggestion. "Good God, certainly not – he'd just lie to keep you off him."

This response made Peveril feel sick. It sounded as if some country bobby would have restrained himself rather more effectively when dealing with Denman than he had. All the same, what Woolf was asking him to do was pretty unsound. It was all very well arguing that an irregular interrogation by an army officer didn't count, but what if the Military Police did then take over? Wouldn't that undermine the chances of using in court anything which Poole did reveal?

Woolf seemed inclined to take his agreement for granted. "So you'll help me out, won't you, sir?"

Telling himself that he'd be a fool to lose the chance to acquire further information, Peveril nodded. "If that's what you want."

The inspector escorted Peveril along to Poole's cell. Just as he was about to unlock it, the sergeant appeared.

"Very sorry, sir, but the Chief Constable's on the phone."

"Damn." Woolf glanced apologetically at Peveril. "Do you mind waiting a minute, sir? I'll be as quick as I can."

"That's all right," agreed Peveril, thinking that at least that put off the moment when he had to meet Poole again. Once the inspector had left, the sergeant glanced at Peveril.

"The prisoner seemed quite upset last time I saw him – maybe you'll be able to get him to speak."

"What do you mean?"

"When I walked in, he was weeping. He said that nobody could ever believe him and that he'd be killed."

Ralph grimaced. That sort of fear did seem horribly credible. "Did he say anything else?"

"No." The sergeant glanced discreetly at his watch. "I don't imagine Inspector Woolf will be much longer."

Sure enough, Woolf soon reappeared. Ralph adopted a bored tone.

"Got the Chief Constable under control?"

"I've reassured him that we have the culprit safely under lock and key. I didn't mention you, sir; I thought he might not approve of you speaking to Poole."

Peveril gave a sarcastic laugh. "If I do persuade Poole to talk, you're welcome to all of the credit. It won't make me excessively popular with the regiment if it gets round that I'm acting as a policeman's nark."

Woolf's offended dignity made it clear to Peveril that he had made an error, but Peveril found it hard to care. Obviously, any half-competent police officer would be keen to tie up a case, but it hadn't previously occurred to him that Woolf's eagerness to do so was dictated by local politics. Presumably, the Chief Constable's approval could lead to promotion. God, what a reason to hang a man!

He turned to the police officer. "I'll speak to him, but I doubt if I'll get much from him."

"We don't need much," remarked Woolf. "All we need is the motive for killing Durrant. I know that Durrant ticked him off severely, but that seems a pretty feeble motive for killing someone." He shrugged. "Mind you, Poole seems a pretty feeble character, so perhaps he thought that it was a good enough reason."

Peveril preserved a discreet silence on this point, merely urging Woolf to let him get on with the interrogation. The inspector agreed, apparently regarding this remark as a sign of Peveril's enthusiasm for his job.

When Peveril entered Poole's cell, the young officer appeared to have pulled himself together somewhat, much to Peveril's relief. Nonetheless, Poole was no more communicative than he had been the previous day. Eventually Peveril, remembering what the sergeant had told him, lost sympathy with Poole's silence.

"For God's sake, man, buck up," he snapped. "If you have got an explanation for what happened, come out with it. You won't do yourself any good by refusing to speak. And the longer you wait to explain, the less likely you are to be believed."

"I have nothing to say," declared Poole. "Absolutely nothing at all, do you hear?"

Peveril caught a slight note of hysteria in Poole's voice. Disgusted with the whole business, he stood up abruptly. "If you want to speak to me, ask one of the policemen to contact me." With that, he hastily strode out of the cell. He bid a swift goodbye to Woolf and hurried out on to the main street. Gunning the Alfa's motor unnecessarily, he shot off, ignoring the superior claims of several pedestrians to their right to cross the road.

'Collingwood told me not to trust the local police with my real identity and purpose,' he reflected bitterly. 'I don't suppose he realised that the local inspector is so keen to earn the Chief Constable's praise that he uses Army officers to try to trick a suspect in police custody.' He snorted. 'Gad, how naïve I must be! I thought that it mattered. I spent half of last night castigating myself for crossing a moral Rubicon, and then I discover that the local police inspector is happy to break the rules himself.'

After driving purposelessly for a couple of miles, Ralph's expression changed. 'I'll go and see Midge.' He glanced down at his wrist-watch. 'I suppose I'd better give her a few more hours; her aunt won't take kindly to my crashing in just after nine.' He grimaced at the walnut dashboard. It might not be very pleasant observing Midge's disgust if he were to admit everything which had happened, but at least she would be disgusted. That, in itself, made her a haven of sanity in a world where boundaries appeared to have become very blurred.

Chapter Seventeen

More to kill time than out of any real belief that it would be useful, Peveril took the turn-off for Harting Magna. After drawing up his car in the lee of a fisherman's cottage, he set off along the track which he hoped would lead down to the mud-flats and the River Hart; certainly, the narrow path which branched off it looked too overgrown to be used regularly by the villagers. Pulling his British warm more closely around him, he shivered. There was a deuced icy wind and the whole setting gave him the creeps. The sedge stood up stiffly against the grey sky, but there seemed to be no colour – only tracts of rushes, interspersed with isolated pools of standing water. The eerie, desolate nature of the scene was emphasised by the unexpected silence; the only sound which Peveril could hear was his own breathing. Suddenly, the muddy track veered to the left and Peveril was presented with a view of dark sand on which lay a small boat, its paintwork scuffed and bleached, the tiller rusty and uncared-for. He slowly made his way towards the dinghy, listening to the voracious sucking as he stepped across the glutinous mud.

'I hope to goodness I've not strayed onto quicksand,' reflected Peveril nervously. 'Beastly place; I'm surprised that coast-watcher chose it for a nocturnal short-cut, but perhaps he's used to it.' When Peveril reached the boat, he found it harder than he had expected to raise it off the ground. Squatting down to get a good purchase, he noted with some surprise that the oars had been carefully tucked underneath the shell of the dingy. "That's odd; I thought all boats were meant to be immobilised," he murmured in surprise. Then he shrugged. 'I suppose this is so out of the way that the chances of a German spy arriving from a U-boat are very limited.' He gazed around, trying to get his bearings. 'If this is where the Harting boats are normally berthed, then I think I have to go upriver for around five hundred yards.'

Scrambling up to the top of the riverbank in the hope of getting a better view, Peveril was disappointed to see that the rushes continued to dominate the landscape. Eventually, he spotted an even narrower track.

'That must have been the path I saw earlier,' he decided. 'Now, do I go back and join it where it branches off from the main track, or shall I cut across to it?' Looking with some distaste at the muddy reed-beds which lay between him and the path, he decided that he would get soaked if he attempted to reach it at this point. Equally, he was reluctant to try to retrace his steps, since that would involve a tedious journey almost to the village itself. Dropping back to the bank, he began to follow the river upstream, only to reach a dead-end after a few hundred yards. The river curved steeply at this point, and either its own force or the tidal stream had scoured away the shelving earth, so that the bank rose steeply above the water with no way round.

'Blast,' cursed Peveril. 'Either I'll have to go back or cut across country.' Feeling fed-up with the whole expedition, he decided to stop wasting time and head straight for the place where Durrant's body was found.

'All I have to do is keep going until I strike the path,' he concluded. 'It won't take more than ten minutes, even if the going is a bit damp.'

That this estimate had been over-optimistic came home to Peveril after twenty minutes. He had already slipped into a pool of water and been forced to wring out the sleeve of his greatcoat; now he was facing another interminable clump of reeds. 'Where the hell is the path?' he swore. 'I can't have missed it. I wish it weren't so damned flat; I simply can't get a decent long-distance view.' Glancing round, it suddenly occurred to Peveril that the lack of hillocks was not the only reason why he could not see where he was going. "Zeus on Olympus," he breathed as he stared in horror at the thin miasma curling lovingly towards him. "Mist!"

Ralph gulped as the seriousness of his situation struck him. He was lost in the middle of a featureless marsh with mist coming in. There were no points to aim for, and he was pretty certain that he had changed directions slightly when he had been forced to take a detour to avoid a particularly noisome pool of stagnant water. He fumbled in his pockets urgently, before pulling his hands out empty. 'No wonder they didn't let me join a regiment on active service; I don't even have a compass. I could go round and round in circles without even knowing.' He suddenly remembered Midge's warning about the swiftness of the tidal surges which affected the Hart and how the luckless ornithologist Serring had died within a mile of the spot.

'It will help the investigation enormously if I get swept away into the North Sea,' he cursed, before shaking himself. 'I don't suppose that the water reaches where I am, except in the midst of winter floods. Well, it's not winter, so I'm not going to drown, even if I am the sort of stupid, brainless nincompoop who manages to get himself lost within yards of a village.'

As the mist crept closer, Ralph wondered what he ought to do. He knew perfectly well that the advice to those caught on mountainsides was to stay where they were, but it seemed so beastly feeble to remain stuck like a scarecrow in a field, particularly as the atmosphere was growing decidedly chilly. 'God only knows how long these wretched things last,' he snarled. 'I've no desire to go down with exposure. Apart from anything else, I should look the most utter ass attempting to explain what happened.'

Reassuring himself that he could still see a few feet ahead of him, so was unlikely to plunge headlong over a bank into the river, Peveril set off cautiously, hoping against hope that he would strike upon a path. 'Even a boulder would help,' he reflected. 'Then I could sit down and wait things out.'

An hour later, Ralph was still wandering round in circles and growing distinctly panicky. 'It's all very well thinking that all I have to do is wait,' he thought, 'but this could last for days. Damn this silence; it's driving me mad.'

Suddenly realising that, however lost he might be, he did not have to tolerate the oppressive silence which locked him into a small, frozen world of wisps of white mist and traces of grey-brown sludge, Ralph laughed humourlessly. 'Midge warned me against music. There's nobody to hear me, so I can, for once, do what I like.' Shuddering at the idea of summoning up the sea by resorting to Elgar, Peveril reluctantly rejected his favourite Schubert lieder. 'Imagine trying to explain away being picked up singing in German *and* having false identity papers. Not quite what is expected of our promisin' young recruit. Curse it, if

Poole gives me nightmares, then I'll give my own private nightmare a life of its own here. Come, Signor Verdi, do your worst. Fight me face to face, stop lurking in the dark to snatch me whilst I sleep.'

Shivering, Peveril glared into the mist. When on trial he had repeatedly dreamed that he was abandoned and alone, wandering lost through the Underworld, with no friendly Sibyl to guide him as Aeneas had been granted. Since he had been quite clearly dead in the dream, it had never occasioned much surprise that the music which accompanied it was always a requiem mass – sometimes Byrd, sometimes Mozart, sometimes Verdi. After his acquittal, Peveril had hoped that the nightmares would go away, but they had not. At times, they had seemed to increase in intensity and vividness until he felt that the world of the dead was closer to him than the daytime world in which he floated as a visitor. Thinking it cowardly even to speak of what he dreamt, much less use it as an excuse for irritability or the inability to concentrate properly on his work, Peveril had attempted to defeat his private nocturnal world. Instead of realising that he was on the edge of a breakdown, he had forced himself to read and re-read Virgil's account of Aeneas' visit to the Underworld, surprising his supervisor with a series of markedly brilliant essays on it. Now, with wraiths of moisture swirling round his head and all colour bleached from the world, Peveril felt that day and night had finally come together.

"I saw your rust-coloured boat, Charon," he declared to the empty whiteness, "but where were you? Not ferrying souls to the Underworld; you'd need your boat for that. Are you lying in wait for me, just as I said I was waiting for Poole? Then show yourself or leave me forever. And whilst I'm waiting for you, hear the music with which you haunt me."

He proceeded to whistle with great precision the *Recordare* of the Verdi *Requiem*. The lilting melody appeared to lick round the still figure standing in the midst of the mist; caressing him, shielding him, protecting him from the threatening menace which hovered on all sides. Moving on to the *Domine*, Peveril could almost imagine that the trailing wisps of mist were indeed the flickering, bloodless wraiths which inhabited the

Underworld. "Avaunt, ye shades," he whispered. "I have dug no trench to fill with blood, the thick venous blood which gives life back to you for an hour of a day. I have no white ewe and black ram to sacrifice in the place where three rivers meet. This is not Acheron or Styx; I am not ready yet to inhabit Erebus."

Suddenly aware that the droplet of moisture on his hand was not vapour from the fog, Peveril shook himself. 'I must be mad. Absolutely stark, staring mad. Imagine going around challenging Verdi and Charon to a duel!' He shuddered as he looked round at what he could see of the barren landscape. 'Mind you, I could hardly think of a better setting.' He licked his lips, aware that his nightmare of the previous night remained unconquered. 'All right, damn it; it may be completely insane, but I'll do it. If I can cope with the *Dies Irae* now, in a world enclosed by mist and peopled by nothingness, then I can cope with it in the darkest recesses of night.'

Hearing again in his head the menacing, threatening chords which spoke of Furies and black pestilence, Ralph could feel his nightmare closing in upon him. 'Blast it,' he cursed desperately. 'I called down this music. It is not summoning my soul to judgement. It is not the ululating wails of the damned. The brass section is not falling into the fires of Hell. It is simply a particularly effective piece of writing and if I can't fight if off now, I shall always fall before any test I set myself. I am a rational human being. I am not going to hang. I may be shot in this hellish war, but I am not going to hang.'

Seconds later, Ralph found himself kneeling on the ground whilst he vomited up his breakfast. When he had recovered, he retreated somewhat.

'How perfectly revolting,' he spat in disgust. 'I've got to stop over-reacting to things.' He kicked a piece of sludge moodily. 'Mind you, it might be a bit easier if I got more sleep. Still, I don't suppose the Norwegians are getting much at the moment.' Looking up from a reverie about how beastly it would be to have to fight in the snow and ice, it struck him that the mist seemed less thick. As he watched eagerly, he dimly perceived a streak of light in the distance. "Thank you, Helios," he murmured. "If this wretched stuff lifts I can clear off out of here." He blushed hotly. 'And I can stop acting like some idiotic Romantic poet. I can't think what made me behave like that.' He sniffed contemptuously. 'Imagine what Hartismere would make of his 'natural' recruit to Intelligence running round lost in a marsh, whimpering like a brat of seven.'

Chapter Eighteen

As the mist began to slowly lift, Ralph caught sight of a track only fifty yards away.

'What an idiot I am,' he thought crossly. 'How could I have missed that?' He cast a hasty glance at his wristwatch. 'I'm sure that a conscientious officer would go and inspect the scene of the crime, but I'm sick of this beastly place and I don't suppose that there's anything to see. I can always come back another day if I really need to.'

By hurrying, Ralph was soon back at the hamlet where he had left his motor-car. Conscious that he might be a little mud-encrusted, he bent down to check his appearance in the Alfa's wing-mirror. His eyebrows rose in some surprise and embarrassment.

'A touch, how shall I say?, chiaroscuro,' he murmured, as he attempted to remove a mud-streak from his cheek. 'Not quite the urbane, man-of-the-world appearance that an Old Etonian normally cares to present – particularly not if he is about to seek out a gel of whom he is enamoured.' He winced as he rubbed his cheek too hard. 'I really ought to go back and change, but most of the mud is on my greatcoat. Anyway, if I do return, Goodwin's bound to want to know what's happening with Poole. Poole's my alibi for sneaking off to see Midge.'

Having avoided running down two curious fisher-brats on the road out of Harting Magna, Peveril made good speed to Brandon. This time, Alice Carrington observed his arrival with less pleasure than she had on earlier occasions. It was all very well hoping that Midge was acquiring a boyfriend, but Alice had a nasty suspicion that young Capt. Peveril's most recent appearances were linked with events at the East Suffolks. Certainly, Midge did not appear to be full of the bloom of a girl embarked upon her first serious love affair and, if Capt. Peveril really were pursuing her, why was he looking so dishevelled? Geoffrey had never appeared before her in anything less than the most immaculate of outfits. Even when he had gone down on one knee to beg for her hand, he had contrived to look positively dashing, despite the heavy dew. Alice pushed aside the memory of her lost youth and stepped forward to welcome Capt. Peveril, unaware that – as far as Ralph was concerned – he would far rather turn up looking extremely unkempt than not see Midge.

For her part, Midge appeared not to notice that Ralph was not looking quite as slick as usual. Indeed, her aunt observed with some worry that Midge's opening remarks were entirely connected with Col. Durrant's murder. Alice quite understood that Midge might be interested in the event – after all, the entire village was waiting with baited breath for the latest instalment – but Midge was not strong and John had emphasised to his mother how important it was that Midge kept her energies for her degree. At the time Alice had suspected that John meant that Midge was not to worry about him, but it could hardly be said that getting involved in another murder enquiry was likely to improve Midge's health. Hence Alice fussed around Midge, before reluctantly taking herself off.

"Have I done something to annoy your aunt?" enquired Ralph in some concern.

"No," replied Midge, who had also noticed her aunt's unusual manner but did not want Ralph to feel unwelcome. "Boris caught a mouse in the kitchen this morning," she commented, before going on to add slanderously, "Aunt Alice is probably worried that there's nothing fit to eat."

At the mention of food, Peveril's stomach contracted unpleasantly. "I'm not hungry, thanks. What I really want to do is pick your brains."

Midge grinned. "And I want to pick yours. What's all this about Poole's revolver having been fired?"

Peveril gaped at her. "I didn't know that. How did you find out?"

"Through great personal sacrifice on my part," commented Midge smugly, before taking pity on Ralph. "The village grapevine was working apace last night and I attended a sewing party purely to hear the latest news from the Harting constable."

"A sewing party?" repeated Ralph in surprise. "Do you…" He broke off hastily, but Midge was not offended.

"Do I know how to sew? Sad though it is to admit, yes, I do, and the vicar's wife happily pressed me into service last night.

However, since the sewing party was regaled with the news that Poole's revolver was found hidden amongst his socks, I feel that the sacrifice was worth it." She grinned at him. "What can you offer in exchange?"

Ralph grimaced. "I was sent to question Poole," he admitted.

"Gosh, how did you wangle that?" queried Midge admiringly.

Faced with Midge's approbation, Ralph's courage failed. He couldn't, he simply couldn't watch her admiration turn to contempt before his very eyes. Promising himself that he could always explain later, the subaltern briefly outlined how Goodwin had ordered him to visit Poole. Then, hastily moving away from the subject of interrogation, he related to Midge what the other officers had told him.

"Apparently there was a note in Poole's diary which showed an appointment for 00.45 – the police think that this means that he intended to meet or intercept Durrant at that time."

Midge looked sceptical. "I can see that it reads like an appointment, but I don't see that it proves that he was due to meet Durrant. And I certainly don't see how it proves that Poole was intending to murder Durrant."

Peveril shrugged his shoulders. "I suppose that their line of argument is that anyone who was meeting Durrant at such an odd time was up to something fishy."

"But that's not logical," protested Midge. "It's taking at least three different postulations and sweeping them into one."

Peveril groaned. "Please don't quote Plato at me," he begged. "I always hated having to read any philosophy, and I had more than enough of it from the Dean last autumn."

Midge attempted to look superior. "At Newnham, we tackle all branches of Classics with equal rigour." Then she admitted, "Actually, you have my full sympathy. I had to translate Aristotle's *Rhetoric* and it was the most ghastly bilge – I never knew whether I'd translated it correctly, because it didn't make sense even in English."

"What do you mean about the police argument being illogical?" asked Ralph, returning to the question.

"Point one, the time in the diary may not be an appointment. Point two, even if it were, it may not have been with Durrant.

Point three, the police don't know when Durrant was shot, so the time in Poole's diary may be completely irrelevant. Point four, even if Poole did have an appointment with Durrant, it does not follow that he was the one to shoot him."

"Why?" interrupted Peveril.

"The police can't have it both ways," argued Midge firmly. "If they say that the time was a reminder to Poole to go and intercept someone else having a conversation with Durrant and that Poole then shot Durrant, why can't it equally well work the other way? Perhaps Poole did have an appointment for 00.45. But perhaps it was Poole who was intercepted and the unknown – not Poole – who killed Durrant."

"Logically that makes sense," Ralph admitted. "But to be frank, Midge, I can't see that washing with a jury. Look at the facts. Poole lied about not having left camp, but someone saw him returning. Poole's boots were damp with water, so he could well have been at the river mouth. Poole's revolver had been fired. All of that adds up to pretty impressive circumstantial evidence against him. He even had a nasty bruise on his face, although I suppose he could have got that when he was arrested."

"Circumstantial evidence isn't proof," argued Midge. "Why's he supposed to have killed Durrant, anyway? Was he the Fifth Columnist? Have they found a whole lot of leaflets preaching alarm and despondency hidden amongst his shirts to match the revolver in his socks?"

"Not that I've heard, but the inspector hinted that Poole had serious money problems. I can't say that I understand how that's supposed to link up to Durrant, but I do know that Poole had a row with Durrant. When I was up at HQ, half of A Coy were sniggering over the fact that Durrant had given Poole the very devil of a dressing-down after he returned from leave. If the officers know what happened, you can be sure that the men do, and that means that, sooner or later, the police will find out."

"Don't they know already?"

"No. The A Coy officers refused to let on anything about it, but I'm sure it'll leak out."

"Didn't Poole give any explanation of what had happened?"

demanded Midge curiously.

Peveril suddenly looked harassed. "No."

"What did he say?"

"Nothing really."

Midge sighed in exasperation, wondering why Ralph had suddenly become uncommunicative. "Did you think that he seemed guilty?"

Peveril shrugged his shoulders. "He kept blubbing. He's the most frightful coward." Then, impelled by a sense of fairness, he added, "He doesn't think that he could be believed."

Midge frowned. "He said he couldn't be believed? Or that he wouldn't be?"

"I didn't actually hear him – it was the sergeant, but he definitely said couldn't."

"It's an odd way to phrase it."

"Yes," agreed Peveril. "I got the impression that the sergeant walked in on Poole when he was talking to himself, so I don't suppose that Poole intended him to hear. Apparently, Poole also talked about being killed." Ralph fiddled with a pencil. "I rather wondered about that."

"Why?"

"I don't understand why he used the phrase 'be killed'."

"Murder carries the death penalty," Midge pointed out, somewhat unnecessarily.

"Yes, but when I was locked up in gaol, I always phrased it as being hanged, not being killed." Peveril scowled at the ground. "I thought it sounded odd, but I suppose I'm being fanciful."

Midge looked thoughtful. "Do you mean Poole's afraid of someone else killing him?"

Relieved that Midge had not laughed at him, Ralph nodded. "That's precisely what I thought. And that may mean that Poole isn't guilty of killing Durrant." He sighed. "But he won't talk to me."

"Can't you try to gain his trust?"

Ralph paced over to the window. "It's too late for that. I pushed him too far yesterday." He ran his hands through his hair in a distracted manner. "I don't think I'm much good at interrogating people; I don't have enough patience." He swallowed again. "I was vile to Poole; he'd be a fool to trust me."

"Might he talk to me?" suggested Midge hesitantly. "I'd be a new face. He might think that a woman was less threatening."

"How could I explain your presence to Woolf?"

Midge wrinkled her brow in thought. "Could you say that I was a relative?"

"And what would you do when Poole said that you weren't?"

Dimly remembering a friend's jest that she might end up becoming a woman police officer, Midge tentatively put forward the idea that Ralph might introduce her as being sent from London to question Poole.

Ralph shook his head. "Woolf would immediately check with Scotland Yard. And if you claimed that you came from some unnamed branch of the War Office, the police would promptly suspect that Intelligence was involved and then everyone would hear about it. I can't take that risk."

"Could you take the risk of telling Poole who you really are? If he realised how well you understood his position, he might decide to trust you."

"Absolutely not," Ralph snapped.

Midge picked up an odd tone in Peveril's voice and reluctantly forbore from pushing him further. It might be possible to change his mind later, but today was clearly inauspicious.

"All right," she agreed peaceably. "Poole is your lead, but I may just have discovered a lead of my own." She proceeded to outline what Mrs Serring had told her.

Ralph greeted this information with enthusiasm, particularly after he had performed a number of calculations.

"If the woman isn't bats, that might explain why I was sent down here. She wrote three days before I got my orders. If you allow a couple of days for her letter to filter through to Collingwood, that would fit very nicely."

"It might also explain why Collingwood may have another operative in place," agreed Midge. "Perhaps he was sent down when Mr Serring first alerted his 'friend' in Intelligence."

"How old was Serring?"

"Forty-five or forty-six, I think. Why?"

"I wondered whether he knew Collingwood from Cambridge, but the ages don't quite match."

Midge shrugged. "I don't suppose it matters, though I'd like to be able to pass on something directly to Serring's friend for Mrs Serring's sake. Goodness knows what she's been through."

"She must have been extraordinarily determined to contact the War Office and the police." Ralph grimaced. "I don't suppose that Polish Jews feel much trust in the authorities – she must be terrified of being interned as a suspicious foreigner."

"Quite."

Ralph suddenly looked embarrassed. "It rams home the point of the war, doesn't it? No woman should suffer as she's done. It could be my mother or your aunt next." Then, as if ashamed of this outburst of emotion, he turned resolutely back to the facts. "Mrs Serring mentioned mysterious vessels. Serring must have been a competent sailor if he managed to cross the Baltic and North Sea without being picked up. I can't imagine that he would start a scare over a couple of fishing-vessels out to sea. He must have thought that there was something dashed underhand going on."

"Which may explain what he was doing on the Hart," agreed Midge. "It doesn't just owe its nasty reputation to the tide – there was a really ruthless gang of smugglers based there at the turn of the century and memories die hard in country districts."

Ralph frowned. "I hope the poor devil didn't get killed because he intercepted a bunch of rum-runners, but I can't see Collingwood wasting his time doing the Revenue's work for it."

"Yes," nodded Midge, "and you might be able to work out who Collingwood's other operative is if you can discover when they were posted to the East Suffolks."

Grabbing the neat list of dates which Mrs Serring had provided, Ralph saw what Midge meant. "Of course! You are clever, Midge. Anyone who came before mid-January can't be an operative unless Collingwood has second sight." He shivered momentarily. "Mind you, he may have. I thought he was just another fire-eater to begin with, but I'm rapidly changing my mind."

Midge ignored this uncharacteristic remark. "I think that it might be worth looking into a possible Fascist who lives in Newton. Mrs Serring made an accusation against him, and General Whitlock said that he was a dubious customer, too."

"What have you in mind?"

"Since Cosford's a bookseller, I thought that I could visit his shop on the perfectly good excuse of wanting to buy some books."

"Do you think that anything will come of it?"

Midge shrugged. "Not really, but at least it is something specific." Glancing at Ralph she added, "Could you exploit the fact that there's been a quarrel about administration? You're Army, and Goodwin asked you to talk to Poole. Could you persuade Woolf to share his information with you?" She shot an urchin-grin at Peveril. "*Much* better for you to see the actual notes he's made than for me to try to persuade Aunt Alice to arrange a meeting between me and Constable Baldock."

Peveril ran his hands through his hair again in frustration. "I'm no good at this sort of thing. It hadn't even occurred to me to ask to see Woolf's notes." He sighed. "Have you any other ideas?"

"Well," Midge replied slowly, "it did strike me that Collingwood must have some sort of contact down here. How else did he learn of Durrant's death so quickly?"

"He merely stated that he'd been 'informed' of it," answered Ralph. "Mind you, I thought it was pretty quick work, too. I saw Collingwood at 08.00 hours and Durrant was discovered at 04.00. I had presumed that, if Collingwood has another operative in place, it would be as an officer, but could his informant be someone in the police?"

Midge frowned. "Why would Woolf contact someone in Intelligence to report the death of an army colonel? Surely, if he reported it to anyone it would either be the Brigadier or the War Office? Also, he appears to have been pretty short-handed in dealing with the body – he only had a constable and a sergeant, and I simply cannot see Baldock in the role of secret Intelligence agent."

Ralph grinned. The constable seemed a pleasant enough chap, but Midge was right about the unlikelihood of the idea. Nor did the sergeant seem much more likely, even if he had actually been the one to arrest Poole. Most policemen regarded Intelligence with considerable disfavour and, last time Ralph had spoken to him, the sergeant had proudly referred to his many years service in the Force – would he choose to become involved with an unacknowledged, semi-underground operation? Then Peveril's expression darkened again. "The trouble is, was Collingwood informed because Durrant was in Intelligence, or because there's something deuced wrong in the East Suffolks? For all we know, Durrant may have been killed by a fellow-conspirator."

"Perhaps it was the murderer himself who alerted Collingwood," suggested Midge frivolously. She glanced at Ralph before asking cautiously. "Do you think that Collingwood would tell you who his contact is if you asked him? Apart from anything else, if we knew for certain that there was already an Intelligence agent in position, it might suggest that we don't need to worry too much about investigating civilian reasons for his murder. A military cause is much more likely if there is something going on which requires an Intelligence operative on the spot."

"I can't possibly waste time going up to London," Peveril argued, unwilling to tell Midge that he felt distinctly queasy at the thought of how Collingwood might react to this implicit questioning of his orders.

"But you must have a code to communicate with him."

"Well, yes, but I don't want to use it again at the moment." Changing the subject, Ralph asked, "How do you propose getting to Newton?"

"You promised me a spin in your Alfa," Midge pointed out mischievously. "Don't you think that you might point her towards the coast?"

"So long as you also allow me to run you back, and so long as we've worked out a decent cover story for who you are and how I know you."

After a certain amount of wrangling, it was agreed that Midge was the god-daughter of Capt. Thrigby's putative great-aunt. Not only was this eminently more believable than Midge's facetious suggestion that she might be a dryad of some woodland grove, it also avoided the possible complication of someone remembering that Capt. Thrigby had no relatives. Moreover, it explained why Thrigby had suddenly made the acquaintance of a girl when he was meant to be busily concentrating on semaphore sites.

"The thing is," Ralph drawled, "I don't want Great Aunt Wilhelmina to leave all her money to you because she's offended that I didn't show you sufficient attention."

Midge laughed. "How mercenary of you, Ernest. Or do I call you Cousin Ernest?"

"You watch that I don't feed you cyanide in the hope of inheriting the entire estate," threatened Ralph. "I don't trust your influence over Great-Aunt Wilhelmina and, even if she doesn't rewrite her will to increase your share, I'm not sure that I'm terribly happy with how much she's left you as it is." He pulled a mock-solemn face. "Death duties eat up so much of an estate these days that it's wise to take sensible precautions."

Chapter Nineteen

Whatever Midge's supposed influence over Ralph's imaginary great-aunt, Mrs Carrington appeared to be uneasy about Midge's sudden desire to visit Newton. Moreover she, quite correctly, attributed this wish to Capt. Peveril's presence. Cornering Midge on her own, Alice raised her anxiety that Ralph was dragging Midge into something which did not concern her.

"I'm sure that Ralph Peveril is a nice boy," she conceded, "but there is no need for you to get involved in whatever he's mixed up with."

"Ralph wants to take me for a spin, and I want to chase something up in a bookshop," answered Midge, lying manfully. "If I can find it in Newton, it'll save me having to send to Cambridge for it."

Alice cast Midge a suspicious look. "I do wish you'd leave things alone," she murmured fretfully. "It's all very well for Captain Peveril; he's a man and he's in uniform, but he has no business dragging you into things."

"He isn't," replied Midge abruptly. She was unwilling to see Ralph blamed for her own suggestion, but she was even more unwilling to explain that she felt tormented by her inability to help the war effort. Many of her friends had helped to get the harvest in and were planning to devote their vacations to other useful causes, but she could do nothing like that.

"You're as stubborn as your uncle," was Alice's uncomplimentary retort, before abandoning Midge to the doubtful pleasures of being driven too quickly along country lanes by a driver who wanted to impress.

Since Midge was used to her cousin's speed of travel, she gained credit in Ralph's eyes by not wincing too obviously or covering her eyes when he took a corner too quickly. Once he felt that he had demonstrated sufficient mastery of the road, he slowed down enough to allow normal conversation to take place.

"Do you want me to drive right up to the door of Cosford's shop?" he enquired.

Midge frowned thoughtfully. "Perhaps not. If Newton's anything like Brandon, half the inhabitants will have learned by now that an army captain has been interrogating Poole. It might put Cosford on the alert if he saw me with you."

The conversation stalled whilst Ralph sought out a parking-place in a side-street near to the bookshop. Once the Alfa was safely parked, he looked at Midge anxiously. "You will be careful, won't you, Midge? Are you sure I can't go instead of you?"

Midge shook her head. "You're an army officer; it would make Cosford suspicious. And even if Cosford were Himmler in disguise, I don't see how he could abduct me from the shop."

"Do be careful," urged Peveril again. He had not believed that Cosford would prove to be anything more than a disgruntled enemy of General Whitlock, but now that Midge was about to enter the shop, Ralph had a sudden fear that he was exposing her to danger. "I'll hang around here," he promised. "Then we can have lunch so that you can reassure your aunt that we were merely on an expedition of pleasure."

"Yes," replied Midge, suddenly conscious that her mouth was dry. It was all very well airily considering who might, or might not, be a traitor, but it was rather different to step deliberately across the enemy threshold. What if Cosford guessed what she was doing? What if it were General Whitlock who was a traitor and he had, in fact, laid a trap for her? On the other hand, what would she do if the bookseller were not actually present? It would be something of a let-down to say the least, but it might also be a relief.

Telling herself not to be a coward, she entered the shop, admiring the unusually musical chimes of the door as she did so. A thin man stepped forward, with a worn face and hair trimmed so close to his head that in the dim light he appeared practically bald.

"What can I do for you?" he asked civilly.

"I need two notebooks and a sheaf of lined paper," replied Midge, before adding. "I'd like to browse through your books as well."

"Certainly, miss. I'll show you what we have in stock."

Since Cosford's stock of notebooks was rather limited, Midge was soon able to use one of her prepared lines. "These shortages are so difficult," she sighed. "I really need a hard-bound notebook, but none of these is suitable."

"It requires less paper to make the soft-covered ones," replied Cosford neutrally.

Midge sighed fretfully. "I can see that, but it's very frustrating having so little choice. How can some clerk in the Ministry of Supply know what sort of notebooks I need?"

Cosford contented himself with a murmur which could have meant anything. Midge carried on complaining. "There are shortages everywhere. And someone quite high-up whom I know says that things will only get worse. It must be very difficult for you trying to sell books when there is such a shortage of paper to print them."

"It is," agreed the bookseller with feeling. "And people don't understand why you can't stock what they want. Or they complain about the quality of the paper."

Midge waved idly at a stack of brightly-coloured volumes entitled *Why We Are Fighting*. "They seem to be able to find paper for propaganda, but I don't want to keep reading that sort of thing. I want something light and entertaining."

"That's a change from what you've had before."

Midge's eyes widened in surprise. Ralph had been correct about the danger of being recognised, even although it was nearly a year since she had last been in Cosford's shop. She had better get to the point, before he remembered anything else about her.

She limped over to where there were more books on politics and rapidly ran her eyes over them.

"Do you have a simple introduction to Communism?" she enquired hopefully. "I've got a friend who keeps sending me things from the Left Book Club, but I don't understand them. I think I need to read some basic information first."

Cosford's colour had been rising during this speech. "I don't hold truck with Reds," he snapped angrily. "I don't stock their filthy lies and I'd prefer not to serve them."

Midge tittered in embarrassment. "Oh, please don't misunderstand me. I don't believe that Russia is a land of paradise, whatever my friend tells me. But I need something which explains to me why it isn't – preferably a short book."

Cosford regarded her consideringly. "I've got a few old pamphlets tucked away. Let me fetch you one."

As Cosford opened a door which led to the back quarters of the shop, Midge repositioned herself swiftly. There was a mirror attached to one wall of the shop – presumably to try to lighten the somewhat gloomy atmosphere created by the small shop windows. But at that moment Midge's interest was focussed less on questions of interior design and more on the heavy bevelling round the mirror's edge. The main body of the mirror showed an uninteresting image of the shop's bookcases. However, the right-hand edge was cut at a sufficiently deep angle that, instead of reflecting what was directly in front of the mirror, it revealed a partial view of the back quarters. Watching carefully, Midge could see Cosford fumble with a panel, pull it to one side and then rifle through a stack of pamphlets, before securing the one which he wanted. As he stood up, Midge moved away from the mirror – it was unlikely that the bookseller would guess that she had, by chance, realised the mirror's serendipitous properties, but there was no sense running risks. When Cosford returned to offer Midge *The Red Menace and How to Defeat It*, by A Former Naval Officer, she was innocently occupied in choosing a detective story from the shelf of green Penguins which was sited conveniently near the mirror.

"This will probably suit your needs best," he commented. "If not, I have a copy of *Twenty Soviet Lies*."

"Twenty?" remarked Midge in horror. "That sounds frightfully detailed. I'll stick to this, thank you."

Once Midge had returned to where the Alfa was parked, she was grateful for Ralph's suggestion that he drive to the hotel where they would have lunch. She was conscious that her legs were suddenly very shaky, and that this response had nothing to do with infantile paralysis. 'I'm losing my nerve,' she told herself. 'There was nothing threatening in that encounter.'

Over lunch, Midge explained what had happened. "Cosford's certainly not a Red," she concluded. "He could be putting on an act, but I'm sure he had lots of leaflets and books like this – the cupboard went a long way back. And why should he respond so aggressively to any mention of Russia if he weren't fairly right-wing?"

Ralph, who had been flicking through the pamphlet, whistled softly. "I must say, this is pretty hot stuff. Listen to this. '*The Soviet menace threatens the whole of Western civilisation and the only method of countering it is if Western nations wake up to the threat of hidden Jewish influences in their midst.*'" He skimmed forward. "'*While some European nations are taking active measures to suppress Bolshevism, others – such as France and England – are so fearful of Bolshevist reaction that they believe Communist complaints that their revolutionaries are being badly treated.*' I'd say that was a coded argument that Germany and Italy are correct to shoot people after only the most derisory trial."

"Why on earth did he sell me it?" demanded Midge incredulously. "I know that I was pretending to be a pretty vapid specimen, but presumably I have relatives who might come across this and want to know where I got it."

Ralph shrugged. "It doesn't actually say outright, 'Let's become allies of Herr Hitler'. Nevertheless, I begin to see why your general doesn't approve of friend Cosford."

"I suppose he must have been so annoyed that I sounded pro-Bolshevik that he seized the opportunity to counter my beliefs," reflected Midge, before looking at Ralph speculatively. "Do you have to go back to camp soon?"

For a blissful moment, Ralph thought that Midge was suggesting that she wanted to spend the whole afternoon with him. Then she explained her plan.

"I thought I could be a Mass Observer and survey the street where Cosford lives."

"Why?"

"People talk," declared Midge, somewhat obviously. "And the war means that people have got used to strangers asking intrusive questions. I'd pretend to be conducting a survey of the effects of the blackout on early morning and evening activities. Cosford looked prosperous enough to have a maid or a cook. I could quiz her about whether he goes out at odd times."

Disappointment made Ralph blunt. "And how do you think

130

he's going to react if he discovers that, immediately after you purchased some dubious pamphlet from him, you questioned his servants? He'd recognise you instantly from their description of their interlocutor."

Midge's colour rose. "They probably won't tell him. After all, that would mean admitting that they had been gossiping instead of working."

"And if he's married and you meet his wife? What happens then?"

"By that point, it would be too late for him to do anything."

"No. It's too much of a risk for you, and it would undermine everything if you were recognised."

Midge sighed. Ralph was probably correct, in which case her only alternative lay with Poole. It might not be a new idea, but perhaps Ralph would agree to it this time.

"Poole thinks that the police won't believe him even if he speaks out. Well, surely it would be obvious that I wasn't connected with the army or the police?"

Peveril thrust away his disappointment and tried to consider this suggestion more carefully than he had earlier. "Honestly, Midge, I don't see how that would help. If Poole's mixed up with something, he'd just think that you were one of the people he's afraid of. You could be involved to make money, rather than because of political convictions. Also, if you question him at the police-station, he'd be sure that you are connected with the police."

Midge gave a frustrated growl of annoyance. "In that case, it will be impossible for me to speak to him. I do wish you could arrange something which would give me access."

Suddenly fearing that Midge was sneering at his caution, Peveril responded without thinking. "I might be able to."

"Really?" Midge sounded relieved. "That would be very clever of you, Ralph."

Peveril improvised hastily. He couldn't possibly admit that he had had no plan in mind and had only said he did because he didn't want to sink in Midge's estimation. "I'll give Poole a chance to escape and then follow him to see where he goes. Given Mrs Serring's eagerness to help, I'm sure I could use her house to spy on Cosford and spot if Poole turned up there."

Midge stared at Ralph. "Are you going to ask Woolf if he'd mind awfully leaving the key in the lock one night?"

"Not exactly," drawled Ralph, inventing details as he spoke. "I thought that I could blow up the end wall under the window and get Poole out that way."

"But you'd need to use explosives – they're dangerous if you don't know what you're doing. How would you feel if you harmed Poole? Anyway, he might not take the chance to escape. And, even if he did, you're not an expert follower. Either you'd have to rush ahead to be in position at Cosford's in the hope that he chose to appear there out of the whole of Newton, or you'd have to lurk a long way behind him lest he heard you."

Ralph promptly selected the one comment in this comprehensive list which he could easily attack. "How like a girl to be afraid of explosives." Then he saw Midge's face. "Sorry, I had no business saying that. I didn't mean it. Honestly, I didn't. I'd be dead if it weren't for you. And I know you've never said so."

"More to the point," stated Midge coolly, "at Cambridge we'd compete on equal terms in an examination. My essays might be just as good, or better, than yours, even if I am a girl."

"I know." Ralph looked at Midge apologetically. "And I have just enough sense to see that if your grasp of logic enables you to write better essays, you might think more intelligently about how to deal with Poole." Ralph swallowed. "I am sorry, Midge. I... sometimes I sound like my father, even when I don't want to be like him in any way whatsoever."

Midge's mind flickered back to the letter she had received from Ralph's mother. She had little difficulty in believing that Leo Peveril had damaged Ralph badly. And Ralph was, presumably, under strain from operating incognito. So now was not the time to have an argument about the place of women – particularly not when Ralph's operation was so important.

"I don't suppose Leo would have bothered to apologise."

"No," muttered Ralph unhappily.

"If you really do think that it would be worth letting Poole escape, why don't you give him a file to cut his way out of his cell."

"I thought about that, but parcels are searched. And I've been searched when I visited. If a file were found on me, I shouldn't be allowed in again."

"Then slip up to the window one night and pass him a file." A thought struck Midge. "If you tell him in advance what you intend to do, he might even trust you enough to speak to you."

Ralph pulled a rueful face. "A very practical suggestion which demonstrates that you are better at my job than I am." He frowned momentarily. "The only problem is how long it may take to file through the bars – and the noise. But if I take some oil and help him from outside, it might be quicker and quieter." He hesitated, wondering whether it was contemptible to try and place himself in a better light with Midge. "Look here, Midge, I know I sounded like a supercilious swine, but I don't despise women – or their brains. If I did, I wouldn't have sent my younger sister to your old school. She was frustrated and bored at her previous place; all it did was teach accomplishments rather than develop a trained mind. I... I think that she ought to have a proper opportunity to use her brain."

Unsure how much she was meant to know about the rest of his family, Midge restricted herself to saying, "That was good of you, Ralph."

Peveril suddenly admitted one of his fears. "It's not much good if I send her there and then don't write to her because I've gone undercover. I can't write to her from Suffolk when I'm meant to be in London. I can't even receive her letters." He gave a sour laugh. "I know I should never have told you anything about my job, but I do observe security precautions normally, which is why I'm letting m'sister down. Clara hasn't the confidence to keep pursuing her intellectual interests if someone doesn't encourage her."

"The teachers at Rushford will."

"But it makes all the difference if a family member does it. I don't want Clara to think that I don't care about her, or her intellectual growth. I know what it's like when nobody is interested in that sort of thing."

"Won't Honor write to her? And your mother?"

"Yes, but it's important that I do." Ralph tried to explain. "I don't mean that Clara likes me more than my mother. Obviously, she doesn't. But I'm a man and..."

Midge continued. "And all the males in your family sneer at any academic pretensions?"

"Yes. Thank God you understand." Ralph glanced shyly at Midge. "Please forgive me for what I said, Midge. I do respect your ability. Honestly, I do. And I'm terribly grateful that you didn't fire up at me for what I said. I'd have deserved it if you had."

"That wouldn't have helped to discover Durrant's killer."

At this reply, Ralph's heart sank. Midge was only thinking in terms of the murder, not whether she liked him or not. Well, he could hardly blame her. He tried to pull himself together. After all, he was meant to be on duty, not enjoying himself. "In that case, perhaps we ought to discuss the practicalities of how to deal with Poole. After that, I'll drive you home."

Chapter Twenty

After Ralph had driven Midge back to Brandon, he returned to the police-station and requested to speak to Poole. The constable on duty subjected him to a long scrutiny, but when the inspector appeared, Woolf agreed to let Poole be questioned again.

"Since it's still unclear whether this is a military or civil crime, I'm grateful for your co-operation. However, we have to observe strict precautions when any other officer visits, so I'll need to search you, sir." Woolf sighed. "I apologise; it's nothing personal."

"Regulations, eh?" returned Peveril. "Must be a frightful bore for you."

"Indeed, sir. But crime's crime, whether in an army camp or outside it."

"Quite so."

Once inside Poole's cell, Peveril was unsure where to start. Eventually, he said, "Look here, Poole, I know I've behaved despicably to you and I'm damnably sorry about it."

Poole gave a derisive laugh. "Really?"

"Yes. I don't know how to interrogate people and I lost my temper. I... I got carried away. I shouldn't have. I'm devilish sorry." When this attracted no response, Peveril carried on. "I've been thinking matters over and I'm not at all sure what's going on. That's why I propose to do something unorthodox."

Poole stared at him suspiciously. "What do you mean?"

"I want to get you out of here." Peveril gave an embarrassed cough. "I'm afraid I don't have any authority to get you out officially, so I'll act unofficially."

"Go on."

"If I passed you a file one night, do you think that you'd be able to saw through the bars? They aren't that thick, and I might be able to help from the outside." As Poole was still regarding him with deep suspicion, Peveril added, "I know it'd take a bit of time, but it's a lot safer than trying to blow up the end wall, which is what I thought about to begin with."

"Why are you proposing this?"

Since it was clearly impossible to reply that he hoped to trap a traitor, Peveril lied, "To prove that I am on your side. Then perhaps you'll trust me enough to talk."

"I don't believe you."

"All right, but when you get the file, you'll see that I'm correct."

"And when do you intend to do me that honour?" asked Poole sarcastically.

Peveril calculated hastily. "It can't be tonight. Say Tuesday."

"You want me dead," stated Poole flatly. "But a death in gaol will look suspicious. It'll be much easier to deal with me in the open. That's why you're going to treat me like a pheasant and flush me out."

"No. Honestly, I'm not. I'm trying to help you."

"Honestly, you're not," mimicked Poole. "Do you think I'm going to believe you just because you're not sneering at me any more? I'm not a fool. You can go to hell."

Since Poole refused to say anything more after this, Peveril reluctantly gave up and called for Baldock to let him out. He could hardly blame Poole for disbelieving him, but what the blazes was he going to do if Poole refused to co-operate when he appeared with a file and a means of escape? If Midge's information from Mrs Serring was correct, the situation was even more serious than Durrant's murder suggested, so it was vital to get Poole to talk. After all, vessels which appeared where they ought not to be implied the possibility of espionage. On the other hand, Midge might have dug up a mare's nest. The Serring woman had said herself that the police thought that she was mad.

Ralph thrust away these fears and attempted to concentrate. Even if Poole wouldn't co-operate, perhaps Woolf's notes might show something useful. However, this hope was soon blighted. Woolf was clearly amused by the idea that Peveril could extract the solution to who killed Durrant from reading through his notes.

"You're very welcome to them, sir. If you can pick out what trained policemen can't spot, then we'll all be grateful to you." Woolf gave a slight grin in the direction of Baldock. "I know that some of you military men don't approve of an officer being held in a police gaol, rather than army custody, but, if you ask me, Major Goodwin knew exactly what he was doing when he called us in. He can no more solve this crime than I can run an army camp. Best for each to stick to his own lathe, sir."

Peveril thought that this was a fair enough comment, but he repeated the complaint which Snellgrove had made. "Goodwin could have called in the Military Police."

Woolf's grin widened. "Well, sir, I've heard that they're rather overstretched at the moment, what with the army having expanded considerably. And I don't suppose that their experience runs much to murder – more to brawls and lads going absent without leave."

Annoyed at the man's amusement, Peveril turned to the notes which he had been offered. As he read through them, Ralph's heart sunk. Woolf was quite correct. There was nothing here which pointed to the murderer. The only interesting fact was that it had been Trent who had observed Poole returning to camp on the night of Durrant's death. Since Trent was the biggest gossip in the battalion, it seemed to Peveril just as likely that Trent was only repeating what he had heard from someone else who really had been there.

More for the sake of it than because he thought that anything would come of it, Peveril spent another hour jotting down notes. Then he left. As he drove back to camp, he wondered what, if anything had been achieved that day. The only real information had come from Mrs Serring, but was it going to lead anywhere? The dates which she had supplied might help him to identify Collingwood's other operative – if such a being did actually exist. But even if the idea weren't another mare's nest, he might not gain much useful information from it – after all, the other chap hadn't spotted Durrant's killer either. Investigating a murder suddenly seemed a lot harder than when Collingwood had ordered him to do so. No wonder Woolf had been so amused at the idea of army personel – whether officers or members of the Military Police – being able to solve the crime. But it was critical that someone did so.

When Ralph entered the mess, he received a distinct shock.

"Well, well, Thrigby, who's the fair lady?"

"Christ, shut up, Hetherley," hissed Peveril, casting round hurriedly to see whether Goodwin had overheard.

"Absent without leave, were you?" sniggered the portly Second lieutenant, who appeared to have been watering himself fairly liberally. "Risking a bit of a reprimand, aren't you, old boy? Whatever new form of semaphore you're involved with, they don't require a girl to operate them."

"Do keep your voice down."

"But my dear chap, why did you take the risk? She's hardly a looker, now, is she?"

Ralph forced himself to stick to his prepared story-line. It seemed unlikely that Capt. Thrigby would respond with an impassioned plea that Midge should be judged upon her cleverness and loyalty, rather than the fact that she could not walk properly. Instead of protesting, Ralph managed a vulgar wink. "Don't want m'great-aunt leaving all her money to the gel if she hears that I'm ignoring her altogether. Very touchy, m'great-aunt."

"Relatives are," agreed Hetherley, whose father had just sent him a most unreasonable letter on the subject of gambling debts.

"Gad, the woman's not a relative," snorted Peveril, as if horrified at the idea of being related to a disabled female. "She's m'great-aunt's god-daughter. Ghastly creature. Cries a lot, that sort of thing."

"Very tedious," nodded Hetherley, before expounding the charms of a rather hot filly whom he had met in Ipswich last leave.

By the end of dinner, Ralph was conscious of an overmastering desire to sleep. Instead of retreating into the arms of Hypnos, he was forced to listen to a long diatribe from Goodwin on the subject of duty, with particular reference to the duty owed to one's battalion. Since Goodwin made a number of barbed remarks about the battalion including even those officers who happened to be very loosely attached to it, it was abundantly clear to all who cared to listen that Capt. Thrigby had somehow attracted the company commander's ire. For his part,

Peveril refused to rise to any of the jibes which Goodwin made. As far as he was concerned, he had more important considerations to deal with. One of those was Trent.

After Goodwin finally stopped lecturing him, Peveril retreated to the bar and ordered a brandy. Trent gave it to him, scarcely hiding a grin as he did so. Ralph felt his hackles rising. The corporal might be a privileged specimen, but in a half-decent regiment a mess-waiter would disguise his amusement at an officer being in trouble rather more effectively. However, since reprimanding the man was unlikely to lead to any useful information, Peveril settled for following up something from Woolf's notes.

"It must have been a bit of a surprise to see Poole returning to camp on the night of the murder."

"What do you mean, sir?"

"You were the one to see him, weren't you?"

"Yes. How did you learn that, sir?"

Peveril smiled. "The police inspector is quite friendly – he told me."

"Ah."

"And what did you see?"

Trent shrugged his shoulders. "Just Mr Poole returning in rather a hurry. I didn't think anything of it at the time."

"Really? I'd have been a bit surprised."

Trent allowed himself a faint grin. "You're not from round here, sir, are you?"

"No." Peveril pushed some change across the bar-top. "Pour me another brandy and get yourself something at the same time."

"Thank you very much, sir."

"Why would someone from round here not be surprised to see Mr Poole returning to camp in the middle of the night when he wasn't on duty?"

"Mr Poole liked a bit of excitement of nights – and he liked the odd pheasant or trout, too."

"Oh. Poaching."

Trent laughed. "You see, sir, round here even the gentlemen see it as a bit of a sport. But it'll maybe be different where you're from?"

Peveril realised two things. First, that Trent was fishing for information and, secondly, that, even if he had no desire to shoot pheasants himself, he'd be damned annoyed if he caught anyone in his plantations. "So Mr Poole went out regularly, then?"

"I'm surprised he hadn't told you, sir. He seemed to spend a bit of time with you."

"He was good at cards," declared Ralph, before adding, "and, of course, he was interested in what I'm doing."

"Indeed, sir?"

"Yes." Peveril knocked back the rest of his brandy. "Semaphores seem damned boring until you understand all the details. Then you realise how important they are going to be."

A third voice came from behind them. "Really? I thought that they were as dull as ditchwater."

Cursing Hetherley's interruption, Peveril attempted to sound slightly drunk. "Well, old boy, that's because you don't have the technical knowledge to appreciate what they can achieve."

"They get you out of all sorts of duties," pointed out Hetherley. "So the least you can do is tell me a bit more about them in return."

Wondering quite how far he should go, Peveril adopted a secretive air. "Ah, my orders don't allow me to do that."

"I don't suppose I'd understand the technicalities, but surely you can explain what you hope to achieve with them."

"More than just a bit of signalling," declared Peveril in slurred tones, before standing up. "I'm going to push off now. Goodwin's coming this way and I don't want to listen to any more from him this evening."

Meanwhile, back at Brandon, it was abundantly apparent to Alice Carrington that her niece was not in the best of moods. Midge had attempted to pull herself together when asked whether she had found what she wanted in Newton, but Alice had seemed unconvinced by Midge's avowal that she had.

"Capt. Peveril must have fairly light duties at the moment."

"If you mean that he's keeping me off my work, don't worry," remarked Midge, with a valiant attempt to sound unconcerned. "I know I need to get on with it."

"Have you had a disagreement?"

"No, not really." As her aunt raised her eyebrows in polite disbelief, Midge's worries spilled over. "I know it's not Ralph's fault that he spent his childhood listening to his ghastly father making blighting remarks about women, but do you think that constantly hearing that sort of thing rubs off on people?"

Alice sighed at this confirmation of her fears. "Men like to feel that they are guiding and helping. They don't like women showing signs of independence – it undermines them. That's why they seek rest and support at home, not ideas which challenge them when they want to relax."

Suddenly feeling very disloyal to Ralph, Midge added, "Ralph wasn't objecting to being challenged; it's just that he made a stupid remark. And I'm sure he does respect women. But if he can say dim things, what does that suggest about men in general?"

"Men are the breadwinners, Midge. They make the rules at work and think that gives them the right to make the rules at home as well."

"In that case," snorted Midge, "they're going to get a bit of a shock when this war is finished and a whole lot of women return from the Services or working on the land or in offices. What's the point of training WAAF officers if they have to become shrinking violets when they return to civilian life?"

Alice shrugged. "Perhaps that will indeed be the case. But have you also considered that there will be far more single women than available men? Women who make bold demands to be treated equally will find that men can easily look elsewhere."

Midge scowled. If marrying and breeding were the only rationales for a woman's existence, it seemed rather pointless to waste time and money educating them in schools or colleges. However, she suspected that Aunt Alice might feel hurt if she articulated this belief. Still more tactless would be to point out that, if John were lucky enough to survive, he had better not be too old-fashioned in his approach to life with Jenny, since that putative barrister would not take kindly to anyone suggesting that she should not practise law. Hastily changing the subject, Midge explained how Mrs Serring had come to the Grange earlier.

"Oh dear. Was she still very odd?"

"She was certainly upset." Midge glanced at her aunt, thinking that now was a propitious moment for testing another idea which had occurred to her. If Ralph was determined upon engineering Poole's escape, she could act as a witness by lurking in the bushes which separated Mrs Serring's garden from Cosford's house. If Mrs Serring was correct that Cosford's visitors often spoke openly when they left, perhaps she might overhear something interesting. "She has prevailed upon me to come to dinner next week. She's even offered to put me up for the night so that I don't have to worry about travelling in the blackout."

Mrs Carrington looked distinctly unhappy at this revelation. She had every sympathy for Mrs Serring's grief, but she also had a strong suspicion that the widow had caught Midge's attention by claiming that Dickie Serring had been murdered. Alice groaned inwardly. First young Peveril and now this. However, since she could not say outright that Midge should not be wasting her energy on the ravings of a very distressed woman, she contented herself with making a protest that Midge had to consider her work for Cambridge.

"I know," agreed Midge, before adding in an uncharacteristically mulish manner, "but I still intend to go, not least because it might prevent Mrs Serring from going up to London to seek out Uncle Geoffrey." She grinned at her aunt in a way which took the sting out of her next words. "'Men need rest and support at home, not ideas which challenge them when they want to relax.' Don't you think that I'm being frightfully noble and feminine in helping Uncle Geoffrey to do so?"

"I must say, if you can keep Mrs Serring away from here I shall be grateful, whatever she does in London. However, please don't get involved in any of her crazed claims about poor Mr Serring's death not being an accident."

"I shall endeavour to be the epitome of reason and commonsense."

"Hmm," muttered Alice disbelievingly, before moving the conversation on to the – for once – more soothing topic of the latest developments in Norway.

III

Chapter Twenty-One

Although Peveril had dropped into a heavy sleep, his sleep was not destined to remain dreamless. Shortly after three o'clock, he juddered upright, clawing the blankets off him. "No," he begged in a thin, breathless voice. "No, no, no." Coming to, he tried to drive away the vision of the jury returning to their box and refusing to meet his eyes whilst the foreman stood to deliver their Guilty verdict. So vivid was the dream that he looked round the darkened room, unable to understand why he could see nothing. Was he dead already? Surely there was a delay before the sentence was executed? It was only moments ago that the judge had slowly placed the black cap upon his snowy wig and pronounced sentence of death upon him. Ralph felt his neck carefully to reassure himself that it was not broken, before shivering.

'Another nightmare. I ought to have known it. The judge looked exactly like Fletcher. Whatever he may have thought of me for hitting a suspect, he'd hardly put me to death for it.'

Despite this manful attempt to make light of his nightmare, Ralph stared into the darkness of the room miserably. As a Classicist, he had spent years supplying sense to texts which, on first reading, lacked any. Hence it required little difficulty to supply a fitting interpretation to his dream. Fletcher had defended him, but he had shown no interest in defending Poole. Instead, he had automatically assumed Poole's guilt.

'I know the evidence is pretty convincing, but where would I be if Midge – or Carrington – had assumed that I was guilty? Rotting bones in the cold, cold ground, that's where.'

Peveril got up and crossed to the window, wishing that it was dawn. 'Midge was correct then. So maybe she's correct now about Cosford being a fishy customer.'

The upshot of Peveril's lucubrations was that Midge received a telegram which consisted of one word – 'Tuesday'. Midge was apprehensive, realising that Ralph had decided to put his plan into action after all. What she did not know was how hair-raising Ralph had found it to send the telegram. A curt request from Goodwin that he might be more noticeably evident round C Coy had made it very clear to Peveril that, if he were to swan off to Brandon again, he was liable to find himself in receipt of a formal reprimand. Even although Ralph was fairly sure that Collingwood was bound to have put some sort of mechanism in place to deal with any such queries about Capt. Thrigby's status, it seemed too dangerous to risk something going wrong.

'If I keep my head down for the next few days,' Peveril calculated, 'nothing will happen to give me away before I spring Poole from his cell. Goodwin's a lazy blighter; he won't do anything unless I obviously break his orders. Thank God I'm supposedly a captain; I'd never get away with being so casual if I were a mere subaltern.'

Nevertheless, despite Ralph's decision to understudy the ideal young officer who was not distracted by extraneous females unconnected with his duties, he still faced the difficulty of alerting Midge. Since the sole telephone in camp was to be found in Goodwin's office, Ralph's first instinct had been to sneak in when the major was absorbed with an inspection of the men – something which had become suddenly dear to Goodwin's heart since a rumour had spread that Durrant's replacement would be appointed very soon. Peveril could not decide whether Goodwin had ambitions in that direction, or whether the major had realised that whoever was appointed was bound to begin by inspecting B and C Coy.

Having carefully allowed Goodwin ten minutes in which to return for anything which he might have forgotten (such as the orders for the day), Ralph slipped into the company commander's office and lifted the receiver. He had just been connected to the operator and was on the point of asking for Brandon 25 when he glimpsed a shadow pausing by the frosted glass of the door. Thinking feverishly, he realised that it would look highly suspicious if he suddenly stopped speaking. Instead, he raised his voice. "Ah, operator, can you tell me the number of the biggest bookmakers in Ipswich?" When the operator had supplied the information, he hastily scribbled it down, before refusing her query as to whether he wanted to be put through. 'Not likely,' he thought. 'It'd give the show away completely if I had to have some complicated discussion about the 4.15 at Epsom when I haven't the faintest idea what's running.'

Peveril waited for a few moments, wondering whether Goodwin was about to burst into the office full of ire and condemnation. When nothing happened, Peveril cautiously relaxed. Perhaps the shadow had not been interested in him – or perhaps it was someone on a similar errand. Wondering whether he dare risk a second attempt to telephone Midge, Peveril suddenly caught sight of a familiar figure crossing the parade-ground. Perhaps the heavy drizzle had something to do with Goodwin's lack of enthusiasm for inspecting the men, but it was clear that the company commander's office was no place for someone who wanted to make a surreptitious telephone call. Hurriedly slipping out of the room, Peveril hastened down the corridor, where he encountered Cpl. Trent busily counting bottles in a store-room at the back of the officers' mess.

"Morning, sir."

"Morning, Trent. Have you seen Major Goodwin?"

"He's outside, sir. Mr Snellgrove was looking for him, too."

Peveril kept his face emotionless as he thanked the corporal. However, his mind was racing. 'So it was Snellgrove. I wonder what he wanted and why he didn't enter? I suppose he might have just been going past, but I could have sworn that he stopped. If he wasn't trying to listen, then he was peering in, presumably in the hope of trying to spot if the office was occupied.'

Snellgrove made no reference to having seen Peveril in Goodwin's office. However, he did allow himself a barbed remark when he observed Peveril spreading out a series of Ordnance Survey maps on the mess-room table.

"You seem to have waited rather a long time before attempting to tabulate your results, Thrigby. Surely that is something of a bad habit to acquire – what would happen if you were in a fighting zone and you were shot? Or, indeed, what if you were caught in a raid in London? All your information would die with you."

"Plannin' on shootin' me just to prove the point, old boy?" Peveril drawled, wondering if Snellgrove was indeed threatening him.

"I am merely pointing out that lax record-keeping is no assistance to the battalion."

"But this isn't for the battalion," argued Peveril unhelpfully. "It's for the Survey Unit."

Snellgrove lent over the map and indicated one of the few supposed semaphore sites already marked in. "That's an odd place to position a semaphore, when it's out of sight of anything else."

Peveril stared at his map. Damn. Snellgrove was correct. "I must have misread my co-ordinates."

"Indeed? Or has the Survey Unit created a new type of signalling system? Signalling – or perhaps receiving?"

Ralph tried not to show any interest, but he was speculating wildly. Why was Snellgrove so interested? Was he an enemy agent trying to acquire key information? Had those hints to Hetherley and Trent that the Survey Unit might be doing something rather important attracted Snellgrove's attention?

"Naturally, we undertake a certain amount of research to improve the use of our semaphores."

"I can't see much sign of you doing so," commented Snellgrove disapprovingly.

Peveril laughed. "My dear chap, why should I work harder than is absolutely necessary? After all, once I'm finished here, I'll have to go back to London and all sorts of dashed dull duties which I'm currently escaping."

Snellgrove shot Peveril a look which strongly suggested that he would have liked to have the younger man under his direct command for a few days, preferably as a private.

"Such an attitude in wartime is disgraceful."

'That,' reflected Peveril as he watched Snellgrove stalk off, 'is either a very conscientious man who is being slowly driven to distraction by incompetent leadership or someone who is playing a very careful double game.' He grimaced. 'Not that I can see how I'm supposed to tell the difference.' A sudden shaft of amusement lit up his face and disguised the pallor and the dark rings under his eyes which told of repeated bad nights. 'Imagine if he were Collingwood's other operative and he reported back that I spend all my time placing bets and playing poker. I rather think that my Intelligence career, such as it is, would disappear in an explosion of vitriolic abuse.' He stared down at the maps in front of him, conscious that he had failed map-reading on his first attempt. 'What was it that grizzled old sergeant said to me? 'Now, Mr Peveril, if you be wishful of leading all your troops into the drink, holding the map the wrong way up is a good start.' Thank goodness we're on the coast. If I keep the North Sea to my right and avoid sand-dunes, I can pretty much place my blasted semaphores anywhere I like.'

By lunchtime, Ralph had amassed a reasonably impressive series of notes. His spirits had risen when Goodwin had announced that he would have to pay a brief call to HQ. Surely this was his chance to slip into Newton and make a quick telephone call to Midge? However, the major seemed determined not to leave Capt. Thrigby to his own devices.

"Since, Thrigby, you possess the fastest motor in the company – and doubtless the battalion – I am sure that you will have no objection to driving me to HQ this afternoon."

"Sir."

"I don't suppose that your semaphores will suffer too much from lack of attention. I imagine that they are quite used to it."

"Sir," repeated Peveril, conscious that the other officers – and Trent – were drinking in this public rebuke.

"You may draw some petrol from the company store," Goodwin added patronisingly. "I would not like you to feel that you were out of pocket for using your machine on Army business."

"Thank you, sir," returned Peveril politely, whilst savagely thinking that if Goodwin were to be found with a bullet in him it would serve him right. This resentment grew even stronger after lunch. Ralph was quite prepared to admit that it must have been extremely irritating for Goodwin – the commander of a company which already had a reputation for slackness and inefficiency – to have appeared thirty minutes late for a meeting which was intended to enable the new battalion commander to introduce himself and discuss the priorities facing the different companies. Nonetheless, Ralph could not see how he was personally responsible for the fact that he had sprung a puncture half-way between the two bases. Indeed, if Goodwin had either assisted him to change the tyre or had walked to HQ, he would have arrived practically on time. As it was, faced with changing a tyre for the first time in his life, Ralph had taken twice as long as necessary, mainly because he was distracted by snide and increasingly angry remarks from his company commander. When he had finally achieved the desired result, the rest of the journey had been undertaken in frosty silence.

Once they had arrived at A Coy, Peveril had hoped that he might be able to find a telephone and have three minutes' conversation with Midge. However, his appearance was greeted with muted pleasure by Jervis and Chatham, who were eager to hear from the horse's mouth what, precisely, was happening at C Coy.

"Is Poole really going to stand trial?" demanded Jervis.

Peveril shrugged somewhat uncommunicatively. "Looks like it."

"But do the coppers genuinely have anything on Poole, or have they arrested the first person whom they saw?" Chatham queried.

"They seem to think that they do – and when they learn about his row with Durrant, the case will only be strengthened."

"I say," Jervis protested, "you're surely not going to tell them?"

"Don't be an ass," retorted Peveril wearily. "I wasn't a witness to it, so I can hardly tell anyone anything. All the same, hasn't it occurred to you that people are bound to have talked about it? I bet the police will learn about it before the end of the week."

Jervis grimaced. "I can't honestly believe that Poole would kill Durrant just because Durrant tore him off a strip. I mean, would you?"

Repressing the insane desire to say that he'd been accused of worse, Peveril contented himself with shaking his head. Then it occurred to him that he might attempt to fish for information regarding when various officers had been posted to the battalion. Casting a disparaging glance out of the window, he groaned. "It's going to rain again. What on earth did you chaps find to do to pass away the time in winter?"

Chatham laughed. "Thankfully I was only posted here in February – that was bad enough, but I think I'd have gone mad spending Christmas here."

"We had some dashed good duck-hunting," argued Jervis vigorously. "I know it can seem a bit dreary when the mist is creeping in over the saltings, but there are recompenses. I went shooting every week in December and January. You have to be careful not to fall into the water, but the shooting is splendid up the creeks."

Peveril fought down a shudder at the idea of voluntarily setting out into the haunted other world of mists and miasmas which he had experienced the previous day. Instead, he focussed on the fact that Jervis could not have been sent in response to any suspicions reported by the Serrings. It seemed unlikely that Jervis was lying outrageously, particularly given that Chatham had not looked surprised at his statement. However, Peveril groaned inwardly as he realised that, even if Jervis were ruled out of being a putative operative of Collingwood's, that did not rule him out of being a possible murderer.

"Shame Poole's been run in," Jervis added thoughtfully. "He grew up fairly near here and knows the inland waterways very thoroughly." He grinned. "We went out on Harting Broad in the company of a frightful old pirate. I should imagine he'd poached every river and wood in a fifteen-mile radius – God knows how Poole first met him."

"Poole doesn't seem an outdoor type," replied Peveril. "Frankly, his sole interests appeared to be fast cars and cards."

Chatham laughed. "We can't shake off all traces of our past."

Peveril shivered unconsciously.

"I should imagine Poole spent most of his childhood tracking long-tailed tits and all that sort of ornithological rot," added Chatham. "When he grew older he shot the birds and, now that he's joined the army, he's decided to shoot men."

"I must say," Jervis grumbled, "I wish C Coy had shot their

own company commander, not Durrant. I don't like the look of the new man at all. He's got a gleam in his eye which speaks of new brooms sweeping clean."

"Deeply tedious," agreed Peveril absent-mindedly, before suddenly frowning. "Durrant didn't exactly strike me as being lax. Will this new chap be any worse?"

"They claim," commented Chatham, in a voice of heavy scepticism, "they claim that he's meant to be Ibbotson's man, but if you ask me he'll have been sent in by Intelligence to see what the devil's going on."

Peveril blessed the fact that his past meant that he could maintain an inscrutable countenance in the face of shocks. "But the police have arrested Poole," he protested. "Why should Intelligence get involved?"

"Gad, you're naïve," scoffed Jervis. "If this part of the coast is sufficiently important that no-one other than residents are admitted, do you think that an unsolved murder isn't going to attract attention?"

"But it isn't unsolved; Poole's been arrested."

"You C Coy types are so dim," Chatham sighed. "Have the police discovered why Poole shot Durrant?"

"No," admitted Peveril.

"Exactly. There's no way that Leake is from Scotland Yard – he's got regular army stamped all over him – so what's left?"

"An ordinary replacement?" suggested Peveril, hoping to move the subject on from the rather sensitive one of Intelligence.

"Don't be an ass. Even Cohen was forced to agree with us," declared Jervis, "and – although I hate having to admit that a second lieutenant has any brains at all – Cohen is no fool."

"Your resident Jew-boy?" enquired Peveril nastily, sticking firmly to his Thrigby persona. "Are Old Testament prophets really reliable when it comes to modern affairs?"

An expression of distaste crossed Jervis' face. "Was that why you were posted to C Coy when most specialists end up at Brigade HQ?"

"What do you mean?"

Jervis gave a false laugh. "I should imagine that you and

Snellgrove must hit it off extremely well."

Peveril was genuinely puzzled. "Snellgrove?"

"Yes, Snellgrove's brother's in quod for being a Blackshirt." Jervis exchanged a glance with Chatham, before adding, "I'd watch your step unless you plan to join him."

As the two officers rose and walked off, Peveril was left wondering whether he had made a mistake by sneering at Cohen's racial origin. On the one hand, he had gained a potentially useful piece of information about Snellgrove; on the other, he had clearly annoyed Jervis, who might no longer speak as freely with him. Peveril winced. It was all very well staying fully in character and making remarks which could have come straight out of his father's mouth, but it was damned unpleasant doing so. And while Midge was correct that appearing to have Fascist leanings might encourage other similarly dubious characters to approach him, it hadn't worked so far.

Peveril tried to shake off his despondency. Since he didn't believe the remarks he was making, he was unlikely to turn into a Fascist. In any case, other people were suffering much worse things than having to make vile comments. The Serring woman must be in despair. She'd lost everything. And although she might have been able to cope with losing her country and her home while her husband was alive, now she had lost him as well. Ralph shivered. If the Nazis crossed the Channel, what chances would his mother and sisters have? Honor would never accept dictatorship – he was sure of it. So she would end up being shot, which would break his mother's heart. And even if he didn't like Geraldine, he didn't care to contemplate how invading troops might treat an attractive woman. As for Clara, ought he to have sent her to America? At least she'd have been safe there, whatever happened. Currently, it felt as if nobody were safe – and that included Midge.

Chapter Twenty-Two

When the conference between Leake and the other senior officers broke up, Goodwin, who was clearly still in a bad mood, ordered Peveril to drive back to camp as quickly as possible.

"I don't want a repetition of the drive here."

"No, sir."

"So you can damned well take more care."

"Yes, sir."

"Why the devil you didn't check your tyres before we set out is beyond me."

"There was a flint on the road, sir."

"A flint wouldn't have made any difference if you had checked things properly."

"Yes, sir."

"That's what happens when men are taken out of proper battalions and seconded to all this specialist rot. Semaphores, indeed."

"Sir."

"Well, get on with it. I don't intend to waste the afternoon waiting for you."

"Yes, sir."

As Goodwin settled himself into his seat, he allowed himself a moment's pleasure at having put Thrigby in his place. The younger man was just the sort of arrogant puppy who gained promotion owing to family connections, rather than any real ability. As if there was any chance that Thrigby deserved to be a captain at his age, war or no war. Goodwin snorted. It had taken him a lot longer to gain his promotion, which just proved how unjustified Thrigby's was. No wonder the army was so badly run when competent chaps were passed over and conceited youngsters swanned into posts they were incapable of holding. It was all very well Leake being so demanding – and Durrant before him – but neither of them had the sort of useless material which he had to work with. At least Poole was now in gaol, rather than sneaking around the marshes in the middle of the night. But it made it damned difficult to run things as they ought to be run. Blast Poole. And blast Thrigby.

Once they had reached camp, Peveril remained conspicuously present for some time, before slipping out to let Midge know what was planned. The telephone in Goodwin's office was far too open – better to risk someone wondering where he was than for him to be caught sending a wire to Midge from the camp.

By ten o'clock on Tuesday evening, Midge was safely – if uncomfortably – ensconced in the depths of an overgrown lilac bush in the Serrings' garden. She knew perfectly well that Ralph was unlikely to make a move before eleven o'clock, but she did not want to risk cutting things too fine. 'If Poole does aim for here,' she reminded herself, 'he won't be disposed to chatter on the door-step. Thank goodness the night is so still; I may hear him approaching.' She tried to calculate how long a frightened man might take to cover the distance, but gave up when she considered the imponderables in the equation: whether there would be passers-by from whom he would have to hide; how cautious he was; and, indeed, whether he headed somewhere completely different. 'I hope to goodness that Ralph can follow him if that happens. Otherwise Ralph may well lose his only lead. I can't help thinking that something will go wrong.'

To pass the time, Midge fell to reflecting on some further details which Mrs Serring had given her. 'I wonder if she will lend me her husband's jottings. They looked pretty comprehensive to me – each of them has a date and a note of where he was.' She shook her head crossly. 'The trouble is, just because Serring saw something strange in place A doesn't mean to say that the same odd occurrence is going to happen there again. Apart from anything else, tides could greatly affect matters.'

The minutes went by. Midge was grateful for the town clock chiming the half-hour as well as the hour. By the time that eleven o'clock sounded, she was keyed up with excitement. The half-hour tolled out. Minutes continued to tick past. Then, just as Midge was beginning to assume that Ralph had changed his mind or been unable to carry out his plan, she caught the sound of a sharp crack from the direction of the gaol. Her eyes widened in shock. That sounded like an explosion. Surely Ralph hadn't decided to blow up the gaol after all? Surely she had convinced him not to?

For his part, Peveril was even more keyed up than Midge, although he had been surprised at how easily he had been able to slip out of camp. 'Snellgrove has a point about things being a bit slack,' he mused as he strode towards Newton. 'If I could cut a hole in the wire and get out, then anyone could get in. Why isn't there a proper section patrolling along the perimeter? Is it because it's raining, or is it because Goodwin's lost interest now that Leake has been appointed as the battalion commander?' Smothering an exclamation as he nearly tripped over a tussock of grass, an alternative point presented itself unexpectedly. 'Much of the supposition that Poole is guilty has rested on the fact that this is a secure camp. Only he was seen returning, thus only he could have been involved. But what's to stop someone else from cutting through the wire as I've just done?' He frowned thoughtfully. 'I suppose any such cut would have been discovered by now. Even if Goodwin doesn't care about patrolling, Snellgrove's conscientious enough.'

Ralph suddenly sucked in his breath. Could it be that Snellgrove did discover such a gap and had deliberately kept quiet about it? Or was Snellgrove the one who made it? Snellgrove normally drew up the patrolling rosters. He could easily arrange to leave a section unguarded so that he could disappear out of camp unnoticed. And he was lurking outside Goodwin's office that morning. Was he the murderer? Or was he Collingwood's operative?

Pausing to check his compass to ensure that he was heading in the correct direction, Peveril's enthusiasm for his theory died. 'It's all very well speculating, but what actual evidence do I have? Snellgrove suspects that my semaphores may be a cover for something more important – but Hetherley and Trent were equally interested in them. And while Snellgrove's brother is apparently locked up, that doesn't prove that Snellgrove also has dubious views. Nor does it prove that he wouldn't have been recruited into Intelligence.' Peveril grunted sarcastically. 'They let me in, so they clearly can't care too much about what Leo said when he was in his cups with Admiral Domvile.' He shrugged. He might not fancy passing on information about chaps' relatives, but for the moment he'd better concentrate. The gaol might be better guarded than C Coy's camp. In any case, the chances were that Collingwood knew all about Snellgrove's brother – it was probably all in the notes which Collingwood had refused to show him.

Reaching the street which led to the gaol, Peveril stopped at the corner, craning his ears to hear if there was anyone else present. He was conscious of how quiet everything was – not even the hoot of an owl. Only the steady lapping of the waves broke the silence. After several minutes, Peveril decided that the street was empty and he crept forward cautiously. Eventually the gaol loomed as an indistinct black bulk on his left. Peveril inched forward, seeking the gateway which led round the back to where Poole's cell was. Having found it, he paused again before softly pushing the gate back, praying that it would not squeak. It seemed to be darker as he entered the courtyard and he forced himself to wait until his eyes had adjusted to the more intense gloom. If he rushed things now, he'd wreck the whole idea and he'd never get another chance because Poole would be moved to a bigger gaol elsewhere.

Peveril slowly began to edge across the yard. A sudden vision of what would happen if there were a guard on duty did not encourage him to leave the apparent safety of the wall, even although he knew that an alert guard was just as likely to shoot him there as in the middle of the yard. Peveril could only marvel at how strong was the instinctive desire not to be caught out in the open. 'Probably dates back to when we were trying to avoid sabre-toothed tigers or something. I must put that question to Midge's cats.'

Finally, Peveril reached the wall of the gaol and crept along it to Poole's cell. It was too risky to speak, but he pushed the file in through the window and heard it fall upon the floor. There was a sound of movement inside. Good, that meant that Poole knew that he was there. Now to start filing through the bars from the outside. If Poole helped, they'd get it done relatively quickly.

At this point, Peveril suddenly heard the noise of footsteps.

Conscious that he would have some difficult explanations to make if he were found lurking near Poole's cell window, Peveril retreated round the corner furthest from where he had entered. Once he was most of the way along the side of the gaol, he halted. There was a convenient bush behind which he could hide. It might be that the footsteps belonged to whoever was on duty in the police-station. If so, at least he'd know that there was a regular patrol round the building.

While he was waiting, Peveril thought he heard the footsteps retracing their steps. Just as he was deciding that it was a bit odd for a patrol not to circle the whole building, a loud bang came from the back. Peveril automatically crouched down, wondering what on earth had happened. Then he realised that there had been an explosion. For a moment he stayed where he was, fixed immobile by the shock; then he moved. He had to find out what had happened to Poole. Had someone thrown a grenade into the cell to kill him? Or had a bomb fallen from an aircraft? But that was impossible – nothing had flown over.

As Peveril edged cautiously round the corner, he caught sight of a shadow flitting across the yard. Then he heard a door banging at the front of the police-station and cursed. Of course, whoever was on duty would be bound to investigate. Damn. Aware that if he retreated, he was likely to run into a policeman, Peveril took a chance and followed the shadow. Scrambling over the wall, he thought that he heard a shout, but he ignored it and dropped to the ground on the other side. He paused momentarily, cursing the fact that he had no idea where the shadowy figure had gone, nor whether it was Poole or whoever had planted the explosion. But if he had stopped to check the state of the cell, he'd have been arrested by the police – which wouldn't have done much to preserve his undercover identity.

Finding himself in a dark alleyway, Peveril proceeded carefully. If he were to crash into an iron dustbin, the noise would alert anyone who was listening. When he reached the end and was faced with a choice of two directions, he paused to think. Was it likely that a fugitive from justice – or a potential murderer – would keep to the main street, or would he stick to the side streets? Deciding that Poole would probably avoid the main road, Ralph tried to follow his possible route through a tangle of small streets which seemed to weave around with no discernible logic. Wishing that when the Romans had been busy slaughtering the Iceni they had at least imposed a grid street-plan on the town, Peveril suddenly recognised where he was. That was Cosford's shop, so he must be in Whelk Street. As he followed the street out onto where it joined the front, Peveril decided that he would stick to the coast road to gain time. A quick walk and he would soon be at Cosford's house, perhaps before Poole turned up – if he did.

Such was Peveril's relief at gaining his bearings that he momentarily forgot that he might not be alone. He was sharply reminded of it a few seconds later when he heard the tramp of marching boots. Thinking hurriedly, he hauled himself over the low wall which divided the street from the beach below and ducked onto the ground. To his horror, he found himself on shingle, rather than smooth sand. His plan for moving soundlessly away from the patrol disintegrated and, instead, he lay flat on the damp shingle, as close to the sea wall as he could get, hoping desperately that the patrol wouldn't take it into their heads to turn their torches onto the beach. He'd had it if they did.

As Peveril lay there, wondering whether he was imagining the fact that the patrol had halted practically above him, he suddenly heard the sound of running feet. The jingling of metal suggested that the patrol had also heard the noise and was deploying for action. As the command to halt was barked out, the running feet slithered to a stop.

"Just wait there, if you please, sir," came an educated voice. "We're a detachment of the Local Defence Volunteers and I should like to check your papers."

"M… m… my papers?" stammered the newcomer.

"Yes, sir. Shine a light on him, Dennis."

Clearly, the unknown Dennis obliged, because Peveril could quite distinctly hear the sharp intake of breath which followed.

"Good God, that's Poole, the murderer."

"How did he get out?"

A cry of "Hey, you, stop!" suggested that Poole was not

waiting to answer this question. Amidst the hubbub, there came the sharp crack of a revolver and an exultant exclamation of "Winged him, by God!"

"You've done more than wing him," responded Dennis' voice. "I'd say you've killed him."

Chapter Twenty-Three

As Dennis requested the other member of the LDV to cut along and call for an ambulance, Peveril lay in hiding, clutching the shingle beneath him in an agony of horror.

'What have I done? I've killed Poole. I really am a murderer now. I shouldn't have hesitated. I should have intercepted him much more quickly. Then I could have got him to safety.' Peveril stared sightlessly at the beach, wondering if he had gone mad. 'How could someone have adopted my idea? And how could it have led to this?'

Fighting down a spasm of retching, Peveril momentarily buried his face in the shingle, before thinking hastily. 'I mustn't stay here. I have to get away before the ambulance comes. 'Dennis' will be so busy with Poole's body that he won't be looking this way. I'll have a chance to escape. The operation will be exposed if I'm caught here.'

Thankful that the scene of the incident did not lie between him and his route back to the camp, Peveril cautiously crawled over the sea wall and surreptitiously set off up the street, expecting at any time to hear a shout behind him. When he was sufficiently far enough away not to be heard, he broke into a steady lope, wondering if he was doing the right thing. He couldn't risk being caught, but he might have made things better for Poole if he'd explained that it wasn't Poole's fault that he had escaped. And he'd never find out now what Poole knew.

As Peveril approached the camp, he was forced to avoid a detachment marching down the road at double speed. It was obvious that they must have been called out in response to the explosion, and Ralph felt a momentary tremor of fear that someone might have spotted that he was missing. However, when he sneaked back into camp, no-one accosted him to demand where the devil he had been. By the time that morning came, only his bleached, taut expression marked Peveril out from the other officers at the breakfast table. As they were all busily exclaiming over the latest news which Trent had imparted, no-one remarked upon Peveril's look of strain.

"So they think that he will die?" questioned Snellgrove.

"Bound to," nodded Goodwin. "He was shot at close quarters. I'm surprised he didn't die at once. In fact, it might have been better if he had, poor devil."

Peveril's stomach turned. Then he remembered that this news was meant to be a surprise to him. "What's happened, sir?"

"Poole broke out from gaol last night, and was caught and shot by the LDV. He's in Ipswich Hospital now – the ambulance men took him to the nearest place with decent facilities."

"I still don't understand how he got out," commented Hetherley. "A chap can't just blow up walls when he feels like it. Trent said that there was talk of a German plane dropping bombs, but there was only one explosion last night. "

"Perhaps Poole had an accomplice," suggested Snellgrove. "What do you think, Thrigby? You've seen more of him lately than we have."

Hoping that he did not look as guilty as he felt, Peveril asked for more details.

"Woolf's hopping mad," remarked Hetherley, with a good deal of relish. "He turned up here practically at dawn."

"A slight exaggeration, although perhaps pardonable in the circumstances," noted Goodwin patronisingly. "He merely wanted to check that none of Poole's friends had concocted a hare-brained scheme to release him." He smiled unpleasantly in Peveril's direction. "You can eat your breakfast without fear, Captain. I don't suppose that Woolf is likely to arrest you, either, after he's spoken to you."

Glancing down at his plate, Peveril wondered how Goodwin would respond if he knew the truth. He forced himself to eat some of the fried egg which lay congealing on his plate. However, as the discussion passed on to the details of Poole's injuries, he found his gorge rising. Hetherley noticed that his neighbour was starting to look distinctly green.

"Squeamish, old boy?"

"That's probably why you stick to semaphores and leave real soldiering to the rest of us," purred Goodwin, happy to pay Thrigby back for the embarrassment of the previous day.

"Excuse me, sir," grunted Peveril, "I think that Trent must have added arsenic to my egg this morning." With that he removed himself hastily.

Five minutes later, as he wiped the sweat from his brow and swilled out his mouth with water, he attempted to reassure himself that no-one would suspect the truth. 'All they'll think is that I'm a physical coward. They won't think that I'm as good as a murderer.' His stomach heaved at the thought and he fought down another spasm of retching. 'I must pull myself together before I see Woolf – unless that was an invention of Goodwin's.'

It soon became apparent that the company commander had been speaking the truth when he said that Woolf wanted to speak to Peveril. However, the inspector seemed inclined to treat Peveril as an ally rather than a potential suspect. Having led Peveril outside until they had reached a spot where they could not be overheard, he turned to the officer.

"You will have heard what has happened to Poole, sir?"

"Yes, it was the main topic of conversation at breakfast."

"Good, then I don't need to fill you in. What I want to know is how everybody reacted."

Peveril frowned. "What do you mean?"

Woolf sighed. "I don't have much time to waste, Capt. Thrigby. Cell walls don't blow themselves up. Someone let Poole out – presumably someone who wanted to help him. Who is more likely than one of his mess-mates? You've only recently joined."

"Oh," muttered Peveril, who had wondered if Woolf was suspicious of him. "I hadn't thought of that," he added, in an attempt to fill an awkward pause.

This remark restored Woolf's good humour – clearly the young man was learning quite why the police were investigating the murder, rather than military officers as he had suggested a few days earlier. "Well, sir, how did they react?"

"They didn't seem pleased, precisely," Peveril admitted, "but they were pretty heartless. After all, they've known Poole for months."

"Since November," agreed Woolf. "And none of them seemed especially upset, either?"

"No," Peveril agreed, thinking that what he had said was technically true. Woolf had not asked him for his own views on the matter.

"I'd be grateful if you'd keep your eyes and ears open for any odd behaviour," requested the inspector. "You never know what might help – even something very small."

"Is Poole fit to have a visitor?" demanded Peveril, making a hasty decision.

Woolf laughed. "Thinking of trying your hand at questioning him again, sir? I'm afraid that rather greater security precautions will be observed from now on. Anyway, the doctors won't let anyone speak to him at the moment."

"I see." Peveril decided to pretend that he was not especially interested. "If he's dying, that will solve your case for you."

"Quite so, sir, although we prefer a proper trial, rather than this sort of ending."

With that he was off. Peveril stared after him, before eventually rousing himself. 'I suppose I'd better go and pretend to play with windmills, otherwise someone might wonder why I was reacting oddly to Poole's fate.' A slight frown crossed his face. 'Mind you, what *was* a bit strange this morning was Hetherley's expression when I made that quip about Trent putting arsenic in my food. Was it because he despised me for not being able to keep my breakfast down, or was something else behind it?'

Chapter Twenty-Four

In the end, Peveril decided to not to return to his semaphore maps, and instead drove into Newton to make two urgent telephone calls. The code-words which had been arranged between Collingwood and him did not cover everything which he wanted to say, but he did manage to alert the duty-officer to the fact that a very urgent request would be arriving by telegram. He followed this up with a coded wire asking for Collingwood to arrange the authority for him and another to question Poole at Ipswich Hospital. Finally, Ralph telephoned Mrs Serring to ask Midge whether it was safe for him to drive up to the house. It took some time for Ralph to convince the widow that he was who he said he was, while all the time he was worrying about the possibility of someone at the exchange listening in to his cryptic comments.

As he left the sleepy post office and turned the Alfa towards the area where Mrs Serring lived, Peveril was conscious that he had burnt his boats. Once Woolf found out that he had authority from London to speak to Poole then there was very little chance of hiding up his true role. Peveril shrugged. In many respects it was ludicrous not to have revealed who he was to the police – it would have made a lot of sense to co-operate and save time. But he wasn't exactly keen on the idea of giving away his real identity, and Collingwood had been clear not to reveal his role unless it was absolutely imperative to do so.

At the thought of his C.O., Peveril grimaced. Collingwood would be incandescent with rage if he discovered that some unauthorised woman had become involved in an Intelligence operation, but what else could he do? Somehow, he must discover what it was that Poole knew – and which his own plan had put so dreadfully at risk. Midge was far more likely to persuade Poole to talk, particularly if the man was gravely injured. Whatever happened later would just have to be endured, however bad it was.

Observing security precautions, Ralph met Midge at a rendezvous several streets away from Mrs Serring's house. The delay left Ralph imagining Poole dying whilst he waited to collect

Midge. However, when Midge finally got into the Alfa, it became apparent that she had been a prey to nerves as well.

"Are you all right, Ralph? What happened last night?"

Peveril swiftly explained, adding his apologies for not appearing at Mrs Serring's. "The thing is, after Poole was shot, there was the devil of an uproar and I was worried that the LDV might ring through to camp. I'd have blown my cover if I'd been caught out of camp. I'm sorry – I should have thought earlier of the complication that someone might alert the camp."

"Don't worry," replied Midge, lying valiantly. "I realised that you might not be able to reach me last night." She suddenly frowned. "Are you sure that you can spare the time to run me home today?"

Peveril gave a short laugh. "I'm not here to run you home. I'm here to do what I ought to have done before – to take you to Poole and leave you to question him. I know it's awful cheek of me to ask you after I rejected your offer before, but please say you will, Midge."

Wondering whether Peveril's intensity of manner was caused by his fears for Poole's life, Midge agreed. "I don't suppose I shall discover anything, but I'll do my best."

Even although the speed of Ralph's driving suggested the urgency of the affair, it was after one o'clock when they reached Ipswich. Once at the hospital, Peveril was faced with persuading the staff to let him speak to Poole.

"No-one is allowed in," stated the matron of the ward implacably.

"But I've come specially to see him. It is imperative that I question him."

"It is imperative that the patient is able to rest."

"But…"

"I don't want a dead man on my hands."

Midge decided to take a part in the proceedings. "No, indeed not, and nor would we be disrupting hospital routine unless it were very important. We know that you and your nurses must be extremely busy."

Matron Roberts' frown diminished slightly.

Encouraged, Midge continued. "You must think that we are

making most unreasonable requests, but it really is vitally important that we can speak to Lt. Poole."

"Why?"

Faced with this bald question, Midge murmured something about it being a police matter.

"I know that," retorted the nurse. "The police told us to keep him quiet and not to allow him any visitors."

Peveril reached inside his tunic and pulled out his identification. "You will have had authorisation from London that I am to speak to Poole." Following Midge's lead, he added emolliently, "It is only because the matter is so serious that I am asking you to let us allow access to your patient. Otherwise, I should not have dreamed of taking up your time in this way."

Very, very reluctantly, Matron Roberts gave in and led them to the private room which held Poole.

"Anyone else who's turned up has been sent away," grunted the sick man resentfully, as Ralph and Midge appeared. "I heard one of the nurses tell some policeman that I was far too ill to be bothered by questions. You must have enormous pull."

"It's not I, it's the people above me," contradicted Peveril, who was looking rather white. "What you need to know is that I'm not Ernest Thrigby at all. I'm not a specialist in semaphores, either."

Poole scowled at him. "I suppose you're in the police."

"Quite the opposite. I'm Peveril the murderer. And this is Miss Carrington who saved my life. She may be able to save yours."

"Really?" muttered Poole suspiciously. "Are you sure that this isn't another of your games? How can I trust this woman? She could be anyone."

Midge blessed the fact that she had brought some newspaper cuttings with her in case she needed to re-convince Mrs Serring that she was who she had said she was. "I admit that press photographs generally look dreadful, but I'd say that we were both fairly recognisable in these, if you ignore Ralph's different hairstyle."

Poole looked at them carefully. "Ye-es," he agreed slowly, "but press clippings can be forged. And how do I know that

Thrigby or whatever he calls himself isn't a Fascist? He seems to behave in a remarkably authoritarian manner."

Midge giggled unexpectedly. "Honestly, there's no way that Ralph's a Fascist. A year ago he couldn't have named more than three of Hitler's ministers. Do you think that any normal person would choose the outbreak of war to shift allegiance to Germany?"

Poole seemed disinclined to engage in exercises of political logic. Instead, he stuck strictly to the personal. "Why should I trust you? You know Thrigby."

Midge limped forward so that she was more clearly in view. "Do I look like a Fascist?"

As the sick man was considering this point, Peveril spoke. "I kn... kn... know you must think that I've behaved like a brute," he stammered, "and that will make you suspect my motives, but I couldn't have managed to get authorisation from London to speak to you unless I am who I say I am."

Poole appeared to be making a complicated mental calculation. "All right," he eventually murmured in a weary voice. "But I'm not talking to you. I'll talk to her."

Once Peveril had left to pace the corridor outside Poole's room, Midge turned back to the sick man. "Lie back down," she suggested. "I don't want to tire you."

Poole gave a sour smile. "Being tired is the least of my worries."

"You mean, you're taking a risk talking to me?"

The sick man nodded. "If either of you is not what you say you are, then I'm as good as in my coffin." He shrugged fatalistically. "Mind you, I nearly was. The surgeon said that if the bullet had come an inch closer the state would have been saved the cost of a trial. It still could be."

Midge winced, wondering whether Poole thought that he was dying. "Whatever you know makes you a danger to the real killer," she urged. "Your sole route to safety is to speak out. Once you've told what you know, then there will be no reason for anyone to want to kill you."

"Except to get revenge," muttered Poole gloomily.

"It'll be difficult for the guilty party to take revenge on you if he is locked up in gaol," pointed out Midge. "Honestly, Lt. Poole, your best course is to explain what really happened on the night of Durrant's murder."

"Are you connected with the police?"

Midge shook her head cautiously, hoping that this would not damage her standing with the accused man.

Poole breathed a shaky sigh of relief. "If I do talk, I don't want the local police brought in at this stage. They didn't believe my denials. They think I'm a liar. And I don't trust my regiment – I think that one of them is involved. Someone must have overheard me at HQ."

"I shan't talk to them," promised Midge.

Poole fidgeted for a moment with his bedclothes, before giving a hollow laugh. "I gamble too much, but I'll take a gamble on you. You don't look like you're about to threaten my life and I can't stand the uncertainty any more. You don't know what it's like having a secret gnawing away at you. And it was much worse after I was arrested – it was impossible to ignore what was happening, even for a minute." He looked round, wishing that he could have a drink of something stronger than water. "Frankly, it's a relief to tell someone. I warn you, though, it's not a particularly edifying tale." He grimaced. "Anyway, here goes. Durrant was there to meet me, because I'd discovered something fishy. I don't know if Thrigby has told you anything about the set-up in C Coy."

Midge nodded.

"Well then, you'll know that it's a damned dull posting – and it's still worse in winter. There's nothing to do and Goodwin's a slack commander, so we don't even have much work to keep us busy. Naturally, some of us sought entertainment outside the joys of the mess." He shrugged his shoulders and then turned even paler as the action tugged at his wound. "It wasn't long before I discovered that there was a group of chaps which met regularly in Newton itself. It wasn't just army types who went there, there was also a sprinkling of local businessmen."

"Where did you meet?"

"At Cosford's house. He's the local bookseller – it was much easier than meeting in the mess." He laughed humourlessly. "No

Snellgrove looking on disapprovingly, and Cosford could be surprisingly welcoming once you got to know him."

"What went wrong?" asked Midge, suspecting that she knew the answer already.

"What you'd expect. I hit a losing streak and kept on playing, hoping that my luck would change. It didn't, and the long and short of it was that I was left owing a sum which I was utterly unable to pay."

"Was there anyone from whom you could borrow?"

Poole snorted. "Not likely. My bank had thrice written unpleasant letters drawing attention to the fact that I was significantly overdrawn. I couldn't possibly get any more funds from it and I'd already mortgaged my next month's pay to a couple of chaps in B Coy. It seemed as if I had only two options – embezzle the mess funds or blow my brains out. Then, just whilst I was drowning in a sea of my own making, Cosford threw me a lifeline." He snorted again. "Some lifeline – it'll prove to be a noose round my neck."

"Cosford offered to pay your debts?" prompted Midge.

"Not exactly, but he suggested a way whereby I could earn enough money to pay them off." Poole glanced hesitantly at Midge. "You'll probably be terribly shocked, but I grew up round here and learned all the local traditions, so it didn't seem terribly wrong to me."

Midge hazarded a guess. "Smuggling?"

"Exactly. To be honest, I was a bit unsure at first, because I did wonder whether men ought to be spending their energies on smuggling during a war, but smuggling was rife during the Napoleonic Wars and we still won those."

Midge refrained from making a tart comment about how smuggling had undermined a system of tariffs specifically designed to block essential war goods from reaching the Corsican Bandit. Reluctantly, she decided that any such argument would have to be left until she had discovered what, precisely, Poole had been roped into. "Presumably you felt that you had no choice if you were to avoid being prosecuted for non-payment of debts and lose your commission into the bargain."

"Yes," agreed Poole, thankful that Midge appeared to understand his dilemma. "Apart from anything else, my gov'nor would have cut me off with a shilling if he'd learned that I had contracted debts of honour and proposed to welsh on them."

"What did you have to do?"

Poole looked edgy. "How far is this going to go?"

"Ultimately, to someone in London," replied Midge, skating over the issue of Ralph for the moment.

"Are you absolutely sure that it won't leak out round here?"

"Quite," reassured Midge. "I have no connection with the local police. I've never even met any of the Newton constabulary."

There was a pause, whilst Poole fiddled with the top of his sheet and stared at Midge with a worried air.

"You can trust me," urged Midge. When this reassurance had no effect, she added dryly, "Frankly, Lt. Poole, if you're having second thoughts, it's a bit late. If I were in league with your enemies I'd tell them that you had to be silenced immediately."

Taken aback by such ruthlessness from a frail-looking girl, Poole blenched and appeared to be calculating whether she was about to put her threat into practice. Midge attempted to encourage him. "What did Cosford ask you to do? Betray military secrets? Show him the regimental orders for if an invasion happens?"

"Certainly not," replied Poole, shocked out of his fear. "I'd have wrung his neck if he'd asked for anything like that."

"So what did he want?" asked Midge patiently.

Poole's anger disappeared and he merely appeared embarrassed. "There were some nights when I was overseeing the guard duty and... well... I rather hinted to the men that they didn't need to do much more than guard the gate and the northern perimeter where it can be seen from the mess." He ran his hand through his fair hair. "The thing is, Miss Carrington, everyone knows that our C.O. wants an easy life and it would seem only natural to the men that I was following his example – particularly on nights when the weather was foul."

"When you say that your detachment only had to guard the gate, what else ought they to have been guarding?"

"They ought to have patrolled the entire perimeter of the camp, and a couple of them ought to have been told off to take in the eastern section which overlooks where the Hart joins the sea."

Midge frowned in thought. "So, if your men were sticking to the main part of the camp, there was no-one to spot anything coming in from the sea?"

"Precisely. I was told that brandy was going to be run in upriver." Poole suddenly sounded very unhappy. "Dash it all, Miss Carrington, it never occurred to me that there was anything else happening – the Hart's beastly shallow in places, so it was hardly as if an invasion force could have landed there."

"Something clearly made you suspicious, though."

"Yes, but that was later."

"What was it?"

Poole sighed. "There's a man I've known practically all my life – he's an old fisherman and he taught me how to sail." He glanced at Midge rather guiltily. "I don't want to give you his real name, so I'll call him Abel. Anyway, Abel didn't just make his living from the sea; he had other interests too."

"Such as rum, brandy, and other spirituous liquors?"

Poole raised his head in alarm. "I say, you're not from the Revenue, are you?"

Midge grinned. "Of course not. I just read books."

Poole sank back into his pillows. "Your choice of words sounded a bit too legalistic for my liking."

"Abel the smuggler," Midge prompted.

"I ran into Abel one night and stood him a couple of drinks. In the course of them, I made some dashed silly joke about there being plenty of business at the moment. He gave me a very old-fashioned look and asked me what on earth I meant. So I said that I gathered that trade was busier than before. He poked away at his pipe for a bit before saying that if I meant fishing, then it was harder than ever, what with mines and safe zones and restrictions in harbour, and if I had any other trade in mind, then I was still more wrong because how could it take place with most of the youngsters off serving the King in the Navy?

"Well, naturally, I felt a bit of an ass after that, but I managed to get him outside and ask again if there was anything going on. He looked at me as if I were mad and repeated his arguments about mines and half the lads being away. So I made some sort of damn-fool remark about being bored and wanting to go on a spree. I don't know whether he believed me, but he snorted something about there soon going to be the biggest spree the country had seen since old Duke William had come over from Normandy. Then he stumped back into the tavern and I cleared off."

"Do you think he was telling the truth?"

"About there being not much smuggling? I don't see why not. Anyway, the point was it made me think rather a lot about what I was doing." Poole stared down at the hospital blankets. "If I wasn't helping out in rum-running, then there seemed to be only one other answer."

"Espionage."

Poole nodded. "I didn't do anything for a bit because I didn't know what to do. Abel might have been wrong. There might have been a new group of smugglers active – perhaps they had moved in from a different part of the country, although that didn't seem very likely as only locals would know the tides and the Hart. But if ordinary smuggling were going on, then I didn't want to get anyone into trouble by reporting them. Eventually, I dismissed Abel's comments as caution or jealousy on his part, and I convinced myself that there wasn't anything terribly wrong in what I was doing." He paused. "I suppose I didn't want to believe it was anything else – after all, I hadn't quite paid off all I owed." He swallowed. "I'd have been cashiered if the gambling had come out – Arrowsmith got dashed unpleasant at one point when I was putting off paying him."

"What made you change your mind about the smuggling?" enquired Midge patiently.

"The fourth time I was asked to avoid patrolling the eastern edge of the camp, I made a joke about whether I could come and help land things or – still better – do some sailing. Cosford froze. Then he made a nasty remark about my still owing a good deal of money and that, if I intended to pay it off, I'd have to do what he asked of me."

"Was he threatening you?"

"It certainly felt like it." Poole sighed heavily. "The thing is, Miss Carrington, I grew up near here. People know that I can handle a boat. Why should Cosford be so shocked at the thought of my going on his boat unless there was something odd about what was going on?"

"I suppose," pondered Midge, striving to be absolutely fair, "he could have been smuggling drugs or something else of which you might not have approved. Or," she added with more conviction, "perhaps there wasn't a boat at all."

"Eh?" demanded Poole, forgetting in his perplexity the manners due in the presence of a woman. "Sorry, Miss Carrington," he added swiftly.

Midge grinned. "Do call me Midge, I feel frightfully old and staid when you call me Miss Carrington."

"Then," Poole replied, in a breathy whisper which belied his efforts to act normally, "you must call me Edwin. But I still don't understand what you mean about there not being a boat. Why would Cosford want me not to patrol near the Hart if a boat weren't coming up it?"

"Perhaps someone was signalling out to sea."

"Gosh, you could be correct," muttered Poole. "There isn't a coast-watcher at that precise point on the bluff where the river joins the sea because C Coy is meant to deal with the headland. There is a watcher based further down the coast, but he's too far away to be able to watch the river."

Midge was busily cursing Ralph for not having informed her of this important fact when she remembered that the inland watcher had at least served his purpose by discovering a corpse. "How did Durrant get involved?" she demanded.

"I know I ought to have gone to the police," muttered Poole, "but I've got a reputation for being wild – I don't know whether they would have believed me. They'd have probably treated it as a hoax and, if they'd talked, then the cat would have been out of the bag with a vengeance."

"Hissing and snarling," agreed Midge. "And from what I've heard of Goodwin, he probably wouldn't have taken much action."

"Quite. I didn't want to be told to leave the matter in his hands only to find that nothing happened. That's why I went to Durrant. By that point I was practically seeing spies under every bush." He groaned. "I thought that I was very clever. The offices at HQ are in a converted barn. The walls there are very thin and they don't reach up to the roof of the barn. I didn't fancy explaining my suspicions to Durrant in his office where it would be easy to eavesdrop. And I didn't much like the idea of his adjutant casually letting slip that I'd requested a meeting elsewhere than in Durrant's office."

"What did you do?"

Poole forced a grin through his pain. "Obeyed the best manuals of military tactics and made full use of the existing lie of the land. It was an open secret that Durrant couldn't bear Goodwin and thought that the rest of us in C Coy were tarred with the same brush of slackness. So when I appeared in front of him with my uniform askew and bearing a supposedly urgent report from Goodwin which was, by that point, two hours overdue, what do you think Durrant did?"

"Bawled you out, I should imagine."

"Yes. Fortunately, he didn't believe in dressing down officers in front of the men, so we went inside his office for our chat. That gave me the opportunity to slip him a note asking to talk to him where we couldn't be seen or overheard." Poole rubbed his forehead wearily. "I have to say, for a martinet he was dashed quick on the uptake. Instead of asking me what the blazes I thought I was doing passing notes, he asked me when in Hades I had left Newton since it was now nearly one o'clock. I thought that he put a slight emphasis on the 'when' and I was sure that he emphasised the 'where' when he asked where the devil I'd been. Then he fished out a map and, in exceedingly sarcastic tones, requested me to oblige him by tracing my exact route so that he could calculate an approximate top speed for my motorcycle, since he hated to waste army petrol on something so useless that it took so long to cover the distance. He added that clearly I needed a replacement means of transport – such as a donkey."

"Ouch," remarked Midge with a wince. "Pretty hideous for

you, but I suppose he wanted to let you pick a rendezvous."

"That was what I was devoutly hoping when I did so. And I assumed that the reference to one o'clock was code for 01 00, since Durrant would normally have said thirteen hundred hours."

"Couldn't he just have scribbled something down for you?"

Poole shook his head. "The adjutant was sitting there drinking it all in. I'm sure he was merely enjoying seeing C Coy get it in the neck again, but I was only too thankful that Durrant didn't take any risks. He carried on chewing me up for a bit longer, then finished with some sarcastic comment about 'presumably we should be thankful that you have arrived at all, rather than coming tonight'."

"Thus providing you with the date of your meeting?"

"Exactly. He – and somebody else – kept that appointment."

Midge nibbled her lip thoughtfully. "Could anyone other than the adjutant have overheard what you said to each other?"

Poole shrugged. "Probably. Don't forget, Durrant was supposedly reprimanding me – it would have been exceedingly unlike him to have hissed at me. So anyone in the offices on either side of his and anybody in the central corridor could have easily heard everything he said."

"But from what you say, there was very little to rouse anyone's suspicions – just a slight emphasis on two words and a reference to one o'clock rather than thirteen hundred hours."

"Unless whoever was listening thought that it was suspicious that I was speaking to Durrant at all."

"But why shouldn't you take a despatch from Goodwin? Capt. Thrigby – Ralph – has taken quite a few already."

Despite the seriousness of the situation, Poole laughed. "So your colleague has been promoted to whipping-boy in my place, has he? Goodwin pretends that some of his despatches are too important to be trusted to mere other ranks, but it's his method of reminding recalcitrant subalterns of their place in the army hierarchy. He's probably jealous of Thrigby's Alfa. In fact, I know he is – I found him looking round it one morning. I sheered off hastily before he knew that I had discovered his guilty lust."

"Do people outside C Coy know that Goodwin likes to make his junior officers run pointless errands?"

"I'm not sure," grunted Poole. "Jervis – that's one of the chaps in A Coy – once made a comment about Goodwin having a vindictive streak when feeling challenged. Perhaps that's what he was referring to. All the same, I suspect that most of them believe that we make Goodwin's despatches an excuse to escape from C Coy and that Goodwin's too lazy to do anything about it."

"That doesn't narrow things down much," protested Midge. "Practically anyone from A Coy – officers or men – could have observed or heard you talking to Durrant. If they didn't believe that Goodwin had sent you, then they might have surmised that you were there on important business of your own."

"Don't forget anybody who was visiting from B Coy could also have seen me," pointed out Poole. "And anyone from C Coy could have learned that I was up at HQ that morning."

"You'd think that in an army it would be easier to trace people's movements," Midge complained, before sighing heavily. "In any case, the person who observed you talking to Durrant need not have been the person who killed Durrant. He could have tipped off someone outside the camp altogether."

"And whoever it was came dashed close to killing me, too," declared Poole with a shiver.

Midge, who had been trying to tactfully lead up to this point, waited hopefully. Poole glanced round the room nervously, his fears seeming to flood back as he reached the key point in his narrative.

"Are you sure that we can't be overheard?"

Midge limped over to the door and opened it. Peveril was leaning against the opposite wall, with a faraway expression in his eyes.

"Has anyone approached?"

"No. Are you finished yet?"

Midge shook her head. "Shriek if anyone does come."

Ralph nodded. Kicking his heels in a corridor might be frustrating, but at least it seemed as if Midge were getting somewhere.

Chapter Twenty-Five

When Midge returned, Poole appeared to be making a manful effort to conquer his fears. "As you say, I've done for myself already if you're a Fifth Columnist, so I've nothing to lose."

"And everything to gain," declared Midge firmly. "After all, if the real killer of Col. Durrant is caught, then you'll be freed."

"Only to stand my trial for treason," grunted Poole, almost inaudibly.

"That's another reason to talk," urged Midge. "Don't you see, err..., Edwin? If you refuse to co-operate, the authorities may think that you are a died-in-the-wool Fascist and they will prosecute you for treason. However, they're bound to be grateful if your evidence helps to track down a nest of spies."

"Then let's hope they tell that to the magistrate who tries me for smuggling," Poole murmured. "Still, I can survive a fine and a harsh lecture from the Bench."

Midge, who doubted whether Poole would get off so lightly if he were to be prosecuted for smuggling, preserved a tactful silence on this point. "Who got there first – you or Durrant?"

"I think that it must have been me. I was beastly nervous and sneaked out of camp before midnight."

"Did you think that someone might follow you?"

Poole shook his head. "No, I was scared stiff that Durrant wouldn't believe that there was something fishy going on. And, I suppose, I was a bit scared that he might think that I was a traitor who was having second thoughts. I didn't much fancy being clapped in irons." He glanced down at the pyjama jacket which hid the bandages round his chest. "Remarkably far-sighted of me." Suddenly conscious that he was growing very tired, he pushed on. "Have you been to see the scene of the crime?" he asked abruptly, before looking at her leg. "No, of course you wouldn't have. Sorry, Miss Carrington, I wasn't thinking."

"Do call me Midge," urged Midge, only her heightened colour indicating that she was in any way put out by this reference to her disability. "I've studied the map and think I've got a fair idea of the topography. Col. Durrant's body was found at the point where the Hart narrows considerably."

"Yes. If the tide's low enough and you don't mind getting your legs wet, you could probably cross it on foot. Anyway, I was waiting, telling myself that there was nothing to worry about and that it wasn't half as risky as trying to break out of my house at school. Finally, I heard a noise from the river. I assumed that it was Durrant and waited for some signal from him, but nothing happened. Then it occurred to me that there was still a quarter of an hour before the rendezvous and that he might not realise that I was there."

"I suppose you didn't have a signal arranged?"

"No, that was the only weak point about the plan, but I imagine Durrant couldn't think of a way to tell me in front of his adjutant. Anyway, I waited for a few minutes and then thought that I could risk giving an owl-hoot."

"Are there any owls round that part of the shore?" asked Midge dubiously. "I thought that it was all sedge and mud."

"I wasn't expecting to chat about natural history with Durrant, so I didn't care what he thought of it," pointed out Poole, with some asperity. "The point was, it was a dashed sight better than calling out his name."

"Was he... was he still alive at that point?"

Poole nodded. "I suddenly felt the most perfectly foul sensation that there was someone creeping up on me. Unless Durrant had managed to circle round me in complete silence that meant either that I was letting my nerves get the better of me or there was a third person there."

"What did you do?" asked Midge, with a sympathetic shudder.

"Took off like a champion sprinter, keeping as low as I could to the ground. Then all hell broke loose. There was a shot from behind me and I heard Durrant's voice."

"From the same direction of the shot?"

"No. Definitely not. Durrant's voice came from the side, but that first shot was from behind." He grimaced. "If I hadn't been weaving like a snipe I'd have been winged. In fact, I thought that I had been hit, because I promptly tripped and took a header onto the ground. I knew that I was for it if the other fellow got close, so I snapped off a shot from my revolver to keep him away, whoever he was." Poole bit his lip. "I've always had pretty quick reactions, but I swear I didn't shoot at Durrant, Midge. He wasn't behind me. I shot at the man who shot at me."

"Was there any other gunfire?" questioned Midge, knowing that Durrant's gun had been fired. If Poole denied hearing any other shots, that would suggest that he and Durrant had shot at each other. It was, Midge reflected, a great pity that the bullet which had killed the colonel had passed straight through his body and been lost. Even knowing what calibre it had been might have helped untangle the mystery.

"I didn't fire again," whispered Poole, who was beginning to look grey and exhausted. "I heard another two shots, but I didn't want to call attention to my position. I had only one idea and that was to get back to camp as quickly as possible before anyone could discover that it was I who had been out on the marsh talking to Durrant."

"Why were you so nervous of Cosford knowing you'd spoken to Durrant?"

"It's not Cosford I'm afraid of," muttered Poole grimly, "it's whoever is behind him." Seeing Midge's expression of surprise, he allowed himself the luxury of explanation. "Come off it, Miss Carrington, do you think that a slimy little man like Cosford is really capable of organising espionage? He couldn't even run a smuggling enterprise – if he'd tried, then the French side would have taken his money and failed to supply the goods. You need to convince people that you mean business in the trade, and that little runt wouldn't."

Disliking the ruthlessness in Poole's voice, and perturbed that the apparently 'innocent man' had just let slip that he had a closer acquaintanceship with the smuggling fraternity than he had previously suggested, Midge struggled to maintain an even tone. "Was that why you didn't want to talk before now?"

"Exactly," grunted Poole. "I went along with Cosford's little pretence that he was in charge of the operation, but I never believed it after the first hour. I was sure that someone else must be involved, if only to provide the financial backing."

Midge wrinkled her brow. "What do you mean, financial backing."

Poole sighed fretfully. "If it was worth paying me thirty pounds a time to look the other way, then there must have been a pretty large profit involved. If there's a large profit, then there must be a high-cost cargo, not to mention the wages of the crew. I know Cosford's got a reasonable house and a servant and all that, but I can't believe he's got enough ready money to organise major runs of cargo."

"He may have money stashed away in several bank accounts," objected Midge.

"No," disagreed Poole. "Take my word for it, there are others involved in this."

"Very well," responded Midge peaceably. "How did you get back to camp?"

"My retreat was cut off, so I was forced in a westerly direction. I thought about making a circle round to the south, but I'd lost my bearings a bit in the excitement and I wanted to get back as soon as possible. So I weighed the odds and decided to risk following the river-bank. Of course, if anyone had been waiting for me, I'd have been in a tricky situation, but at least I knew where I was."

Reflecting that Edwin Poole appeared to be constitutionally inclined to take risks, Midge asked how far downstream he had gone.

"Below Harting Magna. I scrambled up the bluff there and sneaked back into camp. I didn't even know that Durrant was dead until those wretched coppers turned up and ransacked my room."

Listening to the fretful tone in Poole's voice, Midge realised that the young subaltern was growing very tired. "Only one or two more questions," she encouraged him. "First, do you have any suspicions of your fellow officers in the regiment?"

Poole gave a harsh, rasping laugh. "I suspect the whole boiling now that I've learned that Thrigby is some sort of police spy. I thought he was a rich ass with no brains to speak of." He laughed again. "There was I thinking that I could win enough money off him at poker to settle some of my debts and all the time he was eying me up for the hangman."

"And the men in C Coy? Have you noticed anything

suspicious about them?"

"No."

"When you escaped from gaol, where did you intend to go?"

"Frankly, my first thought was that someone had tried to kill me and I half wondered whether I'd be safer staying in gaol. You see, ever since your colleague informed me about his plan to blow up the outer wall, I'd taken to staying at the opposite end of the cell." Poole gasped in pain as moved incautiously. "I congratulated myself on my foresight when it did go up. Then I thought it might have been a Jerry bomb and I might as well take advantage of it. The plan was to find C…, that is, Abel and seek his help. I thought that he might be able to get me to Norfolk, where I could join the Navy."

"Was that why you went towards the beach?" enquired Midge, wondering whether the mysterious Abel lived in one of the shore cottages.

"No, I hoped to be able to find a boat and row offshore where the police wouldn't search for me." He shrugged. "Not that I had much expectation of success, since all oars are meant to be stored apart from dinghies and locked up away from the hands of would-be saboteurs."

"So you didn't intend to seek help from Cosford or any of your gambling cronies?"

Poole stared at Midge as if she were mad. "Certainly not! I didn't want to get knocked on the head and chucked down some old well." He grimaced. "In fact, that was the only point at which I wished I had taken the risk of telling the inspector what I knew. I'm sure the constables at the station must have guessed that I hadn't talked. If they knew that I was keeping silent, then Newton in general will have known. But if it had been widely known that I'd talked, there would have been much less reason to risk the gallows by killing me."

"If you would feel more secure," stated Midge seriously, "I could arrange for the rumour that you have talked to be spread pretty quickly."

"Couldn't you," whispered Poole, with a mordant attempt at humour, "spread the rumour that I've died? That would save everyone any amount of trouble, and Sprowston could be commended on having shot a real murderer – it must be most frustrating for a patriotic type like him to know that he only badly wounded me."

Midge forced a grin. "Keep your spirits up – and for goodness send a message to Ralph if you remember anything else. You never know when something apparently small may turn out to be vital."

Chapter Twenty-Six

Feeling guilty that questioning him so closely had left Poole looking rather like the very death which he had joked about, Midge restricted herself to a few more short questions before asking Ralph to summon a nurse. The nurse fussed round Poole and glared at Midge in a way which made apparent her views about women who badgered the sick with unnecessary questions. Then Ralph ushered Midge back to his car.

"Find out anything useful?"

"I think so. But, equally, Poole's evidence raised almost as many questions as it answered."

"You'd better tell me whilst I run you back to Brandon," suggested Ralph practically. "I don't want to be too late getting back to camp."

"I could catch a train."

"Don't be ridiculous, Midge. I'm not leaving you to shiver on some station platform whilst I swan back to Newton in comfort."

Secretly relieved that she would not have to deal with the vagaries of wartime cross-country trains, Midge subsided gratefully into the passenger seat of the Alfa and even allowed Ralph to tuck a travelling-rug round her. Once Peveril had negotiated a path through the centre of Ipswich, he was able to listen attentively to Midge's narrative. At the end of it, he asked her what she made of Poole.

"Do you mean Edwin the man, or Edwin the potential murderer?"

"Edwin?" repeated Peveril. "Why do you call him Edwin?"

"He asked me to. And in any case I was trying to look at him with fresh eyes. We've spent so long talking about 'Poole' that I thought that it might be easier to see the question anew if I thought of him as a fresh character called Edwin."

"Have you tried thinking of your dons by their first names?" asked Peveril with interest. Then he grinned. "I find it rather hard to imagine that approach working the other way round – 'Now, Ralph, you broke Gate Hours last night – that'll be three and six'."

Midge laughed. "Do you mean to tell me that you only respected the Dean when he was being highly formal and calling you Mr Peveril?"

Ralph shook his head. "If the Dean attached 'Mr' to my name then I knew I was safe. When he wished to draw attention to my many collegiate misdemeanours, he dropped my title altogether. Occasionally, I thought that he wanted to address me as 'boy'. Those were the moments when I sprinkled as many 'sirs' as I could into the conversation." Ralph grinned again. "Quite what would have happened had I addressed him by his first name, I dread to think. When I get sent down, I should prefer it to be for something more interesting than gross disrespect to a Senior Member."

Midge looked at him uncertainly. "You'll avoid disrespect to a senior officer, too, won't you?"

Ralph grimaced. "Yes, of course I shall. Anyway, I'm a captain, which helps no end. All I've got to do is not annoy Goodwin, even when he's making pointless demands. More to the point, what do you make of Poole? Do you believe his story?"

"I think I do," replied Midge slowly. "I'm not quite sure what to make of him, though. He clearly knows far more about smuggling than he intended to let on. If I were inclined to gamble as much as he seems to, I'd wager that, before the war, he'd helped bring in at least one illicit cargo from France, either as part of a reception committee or on the boat itself."

"You grew up round here – is his excuse about smuggling being regarded as normal actually credible?"

"'*Brandy for the Parson, 'Baccy for the Clerk, so watch the wall, my darling, while the Gentlemen go by*'," quoted Midge. "I'd be dashed surprised if it were. He may have known the odd dubious fisherman, but I can't imagine that rum-running was looked on favourably by Poole's home circle." She grinned suddenly, "I can't begin to picture how my uncle would have reacted if John had taken up smuggling as a vacation activity."

"It might explain the superior quality of Trinity brandy," suggested Ralph, attempting to keep a straight face.

"Quite," declared Midge, in what she hoped were repressive

tones. She gnawed her lip thoughtfully as she returned to Ralph's main point. "Poole's clearly got considerable presence of mind – look at how he managed to get back to camp without being hunted down by the murderer. And he's probably brave physically. All the same, I'm not sure that he displayed much grit when confronted with a moral challenge."

"What do you mean?"

"He simply must have known that something fishy was going on. In fact, he said himself that he suspected that he might have got caught up in espionage, but he vacillated and pretended that there was nothing wrong." Midge blushed. "I don't want to sound all Edwardian, or to trumpet about duty, but I do think that Poole acted pretty reprehensibly."

"A bit of a shock to discover that the man you're meant to be helping isn't the decent, honourable type you expected?"

Midge stared at Ralph in some confusion. His words sounded sympathetic enough, but his tone was hard and contemptuous. She opened her lips to speak, but Ralph continued to grind out words in the same bitter manner.

"You disapprove of Poole because he shunned his duty, don't you? You think that he ought to have run the risk of being cashiered by reporting a possible security threat which might not even have existed. You think he was a coward." Ralph suddenly slammed on the brakes and the car screeched to a stop. "It's a nice safe feeling, thinking that others are cowards. It makes you feel much less of one yourself."

Midge saw with concern the grey, pinched look round Peveril's mouth. Any angry suspicion that Ralph was insulting her died away instantaneously. "What do you mean?"

"I despised Poole for blubbing and whimpering in front of me. I called him a coward. But so am I. You said that Poole was probably quite brave physically. Well, I'm not. I'm a physical coward. And – what's worse – I'm a moral coward as well."

"Ralph, that can't possibly be true."

"Oh, it is. I'm afraid of being shot at. I'm afraid of being killed. I pretend that I'd rather fight in the front line than be in Intelligence, but that's all a lie."

"It's perfectly normal to be frightened of dying," argued

Midge cautiously. "Most young men assume that they won't be killed. You're different; you've already been in a position where it seemed as if you would hang. That's bound to affect your outlook."

Ralph stared ahead meaninglessly. "I never wanted to leave Cambridge. I only joined up because I didn't want everyone to guess the truth. I'm like young Manlius in Roman legend – I'm goaded into combat because of taunts about being a coward."

Wondering what the new science of psychology would make of Ralph's identification of himself with a Roman who was put to death by his father for disobeying military orders, Midge stuck to her point that it was perfectly sensible to be scared of being shot at.

Ralph refused to be comforted. "But I'm afraid of everything else as well." He rubbed his forehead with a shaking hand. "Midge, I'm even afraid of myself. I'm growing more and more like Leo. In a few years' time, I'll have turned into a brute who bullies his wife, and hits his children, and goes off into vicious rages when he's drunk."

Hoping that Ralph would not realise quite how much he had given away about his youthful life, Midge attempted to speak, but Peveril was not finished. "I was glad when Leo was dead. If I become him, then one day other people will want me to be dead, too." He shuddered. "I'll want myself to be dead."

Midge felt very uncertain as to how to answer this cry from the depths, but tried her best. "Ralph, you're currently working under cover and you've deliberately adopted a different persona from your own one. Don't you see? You're behaving like Leo because – consciously or unconsciously – you chose to mimic him in your character of Ernest Thrigby. Just because you act like him whilst you're pretending to be Thrigby doesn't mean that you have to turn into him in reality."

Ralph bit his lip edgily. "But it has an effect, doesn't it? Why else did I make that stupid remark about girls being scared of explosives? That's what I meant about the people you help not necessarily being white-hearted angelic innocents."

Midge struggled to respond. Ralph glanced at her. "Sorry, Midge. I should have admitted the truth to you before today."

He laughed bitterly, "Chalk it up to a lack of guts on my part. I couldn't bear telling you and watching you despise me, too."

"I do not despise you, nor do I believe that other people do," declared Midge firmly.

"No? Then why do complete strangers write to tell me that I am a filthy coward?" Peveril thrust his hand inside his tunic and drew out a packet of letters, wishing that his hands would stop shaking. "Look at these. This one's a pretty explicit indictment of my poltroonery and I'm too much of a beastly funk to reread the rest of 'em."

Midge cautiously unfolded the open letter before sucking in her breath in shock. No wonder Ralph looked so haggard and drawn if he was subjected to vitriolic hatred which claimed that he would be more use to his country dead rather than alive and skulking in an office, enjoying the ill-gotten gains of his successful murders.

"Ralph, have you had many of these?"

He nodded. "I've had them at home and care of my solicitor. They've even been sent to m'sister."

Midge glanced at him cautiously. "People write this sort of thing either because they hate someone, or because they feel inadequate themselves and want to bring someone down with them." She grimaced. "We had an outbreak of this sort of thing when I was at school. It was pretty beastly. Everyone's weak points were targeted."

Ralph looked up. "Did you…?"

"Did I receive them? Oh yes. They told me how useless I was at the cello. I cracked up in a concert, in front of the whole school." Despite herself, Midge shivered at the memory. "It was foul; all that malevolent hatred directed against you, and the knowledge that someone was watching you in secret and laughing at you."

"What happened?"

"In the end she was caught. I'd said something which had offended her, so she tried to break me for revenge." Midge flicked through the envelopes again. "Ralph, is there someone who hates you?"

Peveril frowned. "What do you mean? Most of them are

made of cut-up newspapers inside, but there is different handwriting on each of the envelopes – they can't all be disguised. So that means that the letters can't all be written by one person."

"True, but they could be co-ordinated by one person." Midge hesitated momentarily. "Ralph, has it occurred to you that it might be your brother Robert?"

"Robert?" repeated Peveril in incredulity.

"Yes, he's at Rugby and look at the postmarks on these. They're all either from Huntingdonshire or Warwickshire. Why should those two areas be the only parts of the country from which people write anonymous letters to you?"

"But I've had a few from London."

Midge shrugged dismissively. "Everybody goes through London. Presumably some of his friends go home for exeats."

Ralph sounded close to tears. "But why would complete strangers – boys who have never met me – write this sort of ghastly stuff?"

"Robert might ask people to address the letters, pretending to have hurt his wrist. Or he'll have told them some garbled version of the truth. He's probably told them that you did him out of his inheritance."

"But what could he possibly gain by doing this? He's not even near me to see my reaction – what sort of revenge is that?"

"Revenge might not be his only motive," pointed out Midge. "Think how convenient it would be if you were forced into the front line and then got helpfully shot by some German. Robert'd inherit without having any burden on his conscience." She shrugged. "And, if his conscience is a bit more elastic than yours, perhaps he hopes that you'll break under the strain of being constantly hounded by poison-pen letters. After all, he'd still get the money if you decided to take your own life.

Ralph was absolutely appalled. "Good God, what a perfectly foul thought."

Midge grimaced. "I don't suppose that he's thought it all out quite as logically as that. But it would give him a good reason for attacking you."

"If… *if* he sent them," retorted Ralph in unconvinced tones.

"Why should he?"

"It must be someone close to you or how would they know that you're serving in London, rather than abroad? Moreover, you and Robert clearly don't get on."

Ralph stiffened at this intrusion into his private life. "I am unaware of having said anything which would give you that impression."

Midge sighed heavily. "Ralph, you never mention him. You obviously like Honor, you don't like Geraldine, and you're trying to look after Clara. But you never speak about Robert at all. It's hardly an enthusiastic endorsement of his relationship with you."

"Oh," said Ralph, reflecting not for the first time that Midge was better cut out for a career in Intelligence than he was. He glared down at the steering-wheel. "It's dashed decent of you to try to suggest solutions, Midge, but there's nothing I can do to prove that it is Robert sending me the letters – or to choke him off if it were."

"Don't forget the postmarks," advised Midge, who had the germ of an idea as to how to deal with Robert if he were, indeed, responsible. "One person sneering at you is a lot easier to deal with than imagining that the whole world is." She hesitated, before adding. "Robert liked Leo, didn't he?"

"Yes."

"Perhaps that's why he's been persecuting you – he must realise that you aren't sorry that Leo was murdered."

"How could I pretend otherwise?" demanded Ralph in a choked voice. "Don't you think that m'mother's suffered enough without having that brute elevated to the status of a martyr just because he's dead? I wouldn't insult her like that – whatever Robert chooses to make of it."

Midge tactfully moved away from the subject. "Anyway, the point is that lots of people who aren't on active service – or even in the Army – are very brave. Look at firemen dealing with bombs."

Ralph shrugged. "I know. They're braver than many soldiers. But Robert thinks just like Leo did."

A flicker of memory stirred in Midge's brain. "Leo sneered at Capt. Askill for not returning to his regiment after he was badly wounded, didn't he?"

"I can't remember," declared Peveril, in tones which indicated that he had no intention of talking about the matter.

Midge sighed. Clearly Mrs Peveril's cousin was not to be discussed. All the same, she was sure that she had remembered correctly – and that Capt. Askill had ultimately died of his wounds. But if Leo had chosen to torment his wife by sneering at her cousin, no wonder Ralph was sensitive about where he served. She tried to encourage Ralph. "I know of an example which may help: James Parry's been called up."

"Yes?" enquired Ralph, wondering why it ought to make him feel better that even a foppish young barrister could manage to swap his extremely well-cut suits for battledress, whilst he was stuck confessing his cowardice to a girl.

"Are you imagining James in France?" enquired Midge impishly. "He's been sent to the Judge Advocate's department. According to Jenny, he's absolutely furious because he thinks that everyone will assume that he wangled a nice safe billet for himself."

"You don't need to explain the analogy," remarked Peveril dryly, before forcing a laugh. "Tell him to speak to me if he gets any anonymous letters on the subject." He suddenly became aware of the fact that it had begun to rain. "I'm sorry, Midge, you'd have been home by now if I hadn't decided to talk a lot of rot."

"It's only rot in the sense that you aren't a coward," retorted Midge. "Nor do I think that you are turning into Leo just because you've been mimicking him. Do you think that Leo would have worried about the sort of things you've just told me? Don't forget, I met him and he didn't seem the type who was given to introspection or reflection."

"If I spend the next thirty years drinking myself stupid most nights then I probably shan't be given to introspection or reflection either," grunted Peveril gloomily, before looking at Midge and wishing that he could kiss her. However, since he could imagine no worse point at which to indicate your interest in a girl than just after you had admitted that you were a coward, he restricted himself to a shy thank you.

Chapter Twenty-Seven

The next day, Peveril left camp to alert Collingwood by telephone to the fact that he had significant and detailed news to report. Unsurprisingly, the major was not been prepared to take the risk of discussing information over an open wire. Instead, he ordered Peveril to drive to London and report in person. As Ralph spurred the Alfa towards London, he found himself mentally thanking Collingwood for having arranged the cover that Thrigby belonged to a Survey Unit. If he'd been properly attached to the battalion, rather than just using it as a base, he'd have had to provide all sorts of excuses as to where he was going and why. As it was, some gnomic mutterings about new survey sites ought to keep him out of trouble, even if Goodwin were to suspect that he'd taken the day off.

As Ralph approached the outskirts of the capital, it dawned upon him that he ought to be less concerned about Goodwin's possible annoyance than Collingwood's likely response if he learned of Midge's involvement. If the major did not trust him with the name of a colleague in Intelligence, how would he react to his newest recruit gladly bandying Intelligence secrets around with a girl? Ralph winced. Doubtless he would soon find out.

To begin with, Collingwood appeared pleased with the information which Peveril had unexpectedly acquired from Poole. "How did you manage to get him to change his mind?" he enquired. "I thought that you said that he didn't want to talk before."

"It must have been the shock of being shot following his escape."

"Hmm," grunted the major. "There's something deuced odd about the way he got out. It sounds to me as if someone was trying to kill him, not release him. Nobody who wanted to free him would be such a damned fool as to run the risk of blowing him up along with the cell."

Peveril swallowed hard, then swallowed again. He could see horrible vistas opening up in front of him, but if he didn't say anything, his C.O. might neglect a potentially vital area of investigation. Perhaps a murder attempt was more likely than a traitor helping Poole to escape, but what if that weren't what had happened?

"Sir, I had planned to do just that."

"You *what?*" demanded Collingwood incredulously. "You planned to blow up a police station and set a suspected murderer loose? What are you, a closet Feinian?"

Peveril shook his head, unwilling to trust his voice.

"Why the devil did you think of doing something so stupid?"

"P... Poole was frightened of talking," stammered Peveril. "I didn't think he'd ever give anything away to me or the police. I thought that I could follow him to see where he went and that might lead me to his allies."

"Instead of which he got shot and nearly killed in an effort to keep him from escaping," Collingwood pointed out curtly. "I suppose you wouldn't have cared if he'd died. After all, what's one prisoner more or less?" He glared at Peveril. "Are you quite sure you didn't let him out?"

"Yes, sir. I changed my mind. I thought I'd give him a file to cut through the bars. I had given him it and then I heard someone approach. I retreated and that was when the explosion happened." Seeing that Collingwood looked unconvinced, Peveril added desperately, "I didn't do it, sir, but it did lead to Poole talking. He gave a lot of information in hospital."

"Then I want to hear it again – all of it."

When Peveril had finished repeating his story, Collingwood shot him a considering look, before asking several apparently trivial questions. Then he pounced. "You told me Poole's wound was on the right hand side of his chest, now you say that it was on the left. Which was it?"

"I... I can't remember."

"You seem to have a bad memory, Lieutenant. That's not the only contradiction which you made. Did Poole actually tell you any of this interesting information?"

"I didn't take notes, sir," stammered Peveril, realising that Collingwood did not believe him, "but Poole did say all of those details."

"Ah," Collingwood purred, "but did he say them to you?"

Instinctively not wishing to expose Midge to Collingwood's

wrath, Peveril attempted to bluster his way out. "Do you doubt my narrative of events?"

"Put bluntly, yes. What's all this regarding some girl you know?"

"A girl, sir?" repeated Peveril, startled and unaware that he sounded as if he were trying to avoid answering.

Collingwood glared at him. "You can wriggle and equivocate as much as you like, Peveril, but it is imperative that I establish certain facts and I don't want to waste any more time than I absolutely have to. In particular, I do not intend to trail off to some god-forsaken fen because you've decided that now is the moment to be unhelpful."

Deciding that a remark about the telephone having reached Suffolk was unlikely to be received with much approbation, Ralph reluctantly admitted the truth. Collingwood looked as if he could not believe what he was hearing.

"Are you mad? Have you no concept of security? Good God, man, I'm not trying to cut you off from all female society, but you don't go blurting out every detail of your job here to some girl. Damn it all, you don't even blurt out the fact that you work here – not if you want to go on working here, that is. You invent a perfectly good excuse – if you need one – that you have a job in the War Office, or that you are seconded to X, Y or Z department. You certainly don't tell a woman the precise details of your cover and your mission, and then discuss in what ways you can best undermine the peace of His Majesty's realm." Collingwood breathed heavily in exasperation. "If you must talk to a female, tell her you work on Army Staff and don't encourage her imagination to run riot."

Resenting the fact that Midge was being described as a 'female' and that he could not defend her properly, Peveril assumed an air of languid interest. "Is that what you do on such occasions, sir?" he enquired recklessly.

The expression on Collingwood's face made Peveril step back involuntarily, suddenly regretting that he had chosen to bait Collingwood. Apart from anything else, he knew that, were he on Collingwood's side of the desk, he would react damned badly to any underling speaking to him in a similar manner.

The major leant forward menacingly. "When I require your contribution, Lt. Peveril, I shall ask for it."

Since it was clear that Collingwood was awaiting a response, Peveril forced out a strangled, "Sir".

Collingwood looked him up and down, before stating coldly, "I am unsure why, precisely, you feel the need to make that sort of asinine and impertinent remark. However, let me inform you that I am not impressed by office-boy bravado. It convinces me of your immaturity, not your courage."

Observing with grim satisfaction that Peveril was looking rather sick, Collingwood twisted the knife further. "Leaving aside for the moment your indefensible breach of security, I may state that I do not tolerate insubordination. If you practise it again, you will leave my command. As for where you will go, I am informed that there are numerous vacancies for office-boys at the Ministry of Supply. Doubtless your particular brand of studied insolence would fit in perfectly among the other clerks."

"But I'm an officer."

Collingwood allowed his eyes to travel over Peveril contemptuously. "You wear the uniform, yes."

Peveril's face flamed. No-one had ever previously pinpointed the reasoning behind his actions, only to dismiss it so brutally and contemptuously. But while Collingwood had every justification in biting his head off, need he have made his contempt so apparent? And if Collingwood – who hardly knew him – had seen through him so easily, what must others think? Had his father realised that he had adopted a mocking, don't-care air precisely to ward off the many accusations of being feeble, weak and cowardly? He had always assumed that Leo was too stupid to see through the pretence, but what about Hartismere? Hartismere was certainly clever. Did Hartismere realise that he laughed in the face of danger in the hope that danger would leave him for an easier victim? Did Hartismere despise him? And – hideous thought – was that why Midge had been so unconvinced by the bomb plot? Did she think that he was all hot air and braggadocio? Peveril shuddered. He thought that he would die of humiliation if she did. And he would have to face her again with that particular maggot gnawing away at his trust in her.

Peveril opened his mouth to speak, then thought better of it as he encountered a ferocious glare from Collingwood, who was not finished dealing with the younger officer.

"Were it not for the fact that it would arouse deep suspicion if you did not return to your battalion, you would be placed under close arrest for talking about your work. As it is, the investigation into your reliability will have to wait until you are finished in Suffolk. However, you can tell me one thing – did you inform this girl that you had planned to blow up the gaol?"

Peveril turned white. Collingwood must think that Midge was involved. "Sir, she couldn't have done it."

"Did she know?"

Peveril stared at Collingwood helplessly. A lie would probably make things even worse, particularly if the major chose to check. But if he didn't lie, Collingwood would suspect that Midge had been talking. What the hell should he say?

"Well, Lieutenant, did your girlfriend know what you had planned? Your silence hardly suggests otherwise."

"She did know, sir, but she thought it was a dangerous idea. That was why I changed my mind and decided to use a file. And she couldn't have blown up the wall because... because she can't walk properly. She wouldn't have been able to get away in time."

"Perhaps not, but she could have talked about it. How else did someone come up with the identical plan which you had proposed?"

"She wouldn't talk, sir."

"Then if she didn't, you did."

"I didn't, sir."

"I see. You didn't tell anyone – except your girlfriend. And you're sure that she didn't tell anyone, despite having no evidence to prove your claim."

"But she wouldn't, sir. She doesn't talk about things. And she wouldn't have talked about something she thought was a stupid idea."

"Perhaps she told her parents."

"She lives with her aunt. And I don't think she would tell even her."

"Not quite so certain now, are you?

Ralph bit his lip. "I'm sure she wouldn't, sir. And her aunt wouldn't have said anything, either."

"Then you might explain how the idea leaked out. Where did you talk about it?"

"In... in... in a hotel, sir."

"In a hotel? Are you quite mad?"

"There was no-one anywhere near us, sir."

"Are you absolutely sure?"

"Yes, sir."

"No waiters?"

"No, sir."

"No other diners?"

"No, sir. It was very quiet."

The major regarded Peveril thoughtfully. "Don't you see that if you had been overheard, that would give a lead as to a possible traitor?"

"Yes, sir, but we couldn't have been overheard. We didn't say anything when the waiter served us."

"Then how was it that your exact plan was copied?"

Peveril thought feverishly for something which might satisfy Collingwood. "Maybe... maybe it was coincidence. There aren't many ways in which to kill someone who's locked up if you don't have access to them."

"And you can't think of any other possibility?"

"No, sir."

Collingwood subjected him to a long scrutiny. "I don't entirely believe you. Even if what you claim is true, I can't say that your behaviour reflects well on the man who recruited you."

At this statement, Peveril turned very white. However much he might resent the fact that Hartismere had practically dragooned him into Intelligence, he had no desire to see his erstwhile tutor suffer for his own insufficiency and incompetence. He tried to pull himself together. "What's happened isn't Hartismere's fault, sir."

"Isn't it? He knows you like this woman?"

"Yes, sir."

"And that you talk to her?"

"Yes, sir."

"So he ought to have anticipated that you would be reckless enough to discuss Intelligence secrets with a woman who has promptly gossiped about them."

"She hasn't, sir. I swear to you she hasn't. And Hartismere knows that she doesn't gossip." Peveril hesitated for a moment, before asking, "Sir, couldn't you draft Miss Carrington into this? I... I know I shouldn't have told her anything, but she is totally trustworthy."

"Certainly not. Didn't you listen to any of the lectures on security you were given during training?"

"Yes, sir. All of them, sir. And it's because I know that Miss Carrington wouldn't breathe a word to anyone that I thought that she could be of use over this." Ignoring the look of fury on his C.O.'s face, Peveril made a final appeal. "Sir, Miss Carrington wouldn't talk. I'd have been hanged if she couldn't keep her mouth shut."

"Then it is a great pity that you seem incapable of following her earlier example." The major glared at him. "If you speak to her again about this operation, I'll have you court-martialled and her arrested. Do you understand?"

"Yes, sir."

"Then get back to Suffolk and obey your orders for a change."

Chapter Twenty-Eight

As Peveril drove back towards Newton, he was both confused and angry. Collingwood quite clearly suspected that he was involved in blowing up the gaol, but why couldn't the major see that he wouldn't have said anything about the plot if he'd actually carried it out? It wasn't in his interests to admit anything, and the only reason he'd revealed his original plan was because he'd thought that his C.O. needed all possible information.

Peveril cursed. He'd have been much better off keeping quiet. The trouble was, while he might have been a fool to tell Collingwood about the aborted plan, he most certainly had been every kind of fool to make that idiotic remark about how Collingwood dealt with women. Oh God, how could he have been so stupid? Any C.O. would have been furious, let alone a fire-eater like Collingwood. All he'd achieved was to endanger Midge – what if Collingwood did arrest her? Could he ask Hartismere to do something, or would that simply inflame the situation and confirm Collingwood's view that Hartismere had made a mistake in recruiting him? Ralph bit his lip unhappily. It wasn't going to be an enormous disaster if he spent the rest of the war as an unimportant, disgraced 2nd lieutenant, but imagine being deemed unreliable at Hartismere's age. It certainly wasn't much repayment for the don's faith in him the previous year – and he had quite enough on his conscience regarding Hartismere as it was.

If Peveril had been able to overhear a conversation which took place between Hartismere and Collingwood after he had left London, it is unlikely that he would have been any more reassured as to the depth of Collingwood's trust in him. After listening to the major's summary of the conversation, Hartismere appeared somewhat puzzled.

"I can see that Peveril was distinctly irritating, but why did you need to see me so urgently?"

"I haven't dragged you down here to teach some impertinent puppy his manners," growled Collingwood. "I'm perfectly capable of licking him into shape myself. What I am concerned about is whether he's reliable. When I said his behaviour reflected badly upon you, I thought that the boy was going to faint. And he was a shade too keen to defend your judgement – it was as if he were scared that someone else less partial might check up on him. What's going on, sir? Is there something you know to his discredit which you haven't told me?"

"Enormous quantities, I should imagine. Do you really want a recital of all of his undergraduate sins?"

"I'm deadly serious," warned Collingwood. "I doubt if he's got the discretion for this sort of job. And I certainly wonder whether he possesses the common-sense. He's lucky not to have ended up in gaol himself over that damn silly idea of blowing up Poole's cell. Why couldn't he see how stupid it was?"

"I don't think that you're being entirely fair to him," demurred Hartismere mildly. "He should still be at Cambridge. Most undergraduates end up getting into a fix at some point or other. Nor is the species noted for its commonsense – not amongst the ones I meet, anyway."

The major made a disbelieving noise. "I don't remember being a bag of nerves when I was up."

"Never?" enquired the Vice-Master maliciously. "I can remember the small matter of the tobacconist's daughter, even if you've forgotten."

Collingwood turned brick-red. "The less said about that the better."

"Nobody likes being reminded of their undergraduate follies," agreed Hartismere urbanely, "but Peveril's folly was to get mixed up in a murder trial and he's not had the chance to get over it properly. Ideally, he'd have had time to finish off his degree, followed by a couple of years with just enough to do sorting out his inheritance to prevent him from turning into a drone. When he'd grown bored with the life of a country squire ruralising on his estates, then you could have had him with my enthusiastic blessing. After all, you prefer them wealthy, don't you? Makes 'em less liable to be bribed – or resort to blackmail."

Collingwood's colour rose again. "Damn it, Hartismere, you know that I'd have paid up – and generously, too – if she'd really been about to have my child."

"Yes, you are, at least, a gentleman. And so, for all his faults, is Peveril. Moreover, Peveril showed absolutely no interest in politics at Cambridge until it became obvious that war was imminent."

"Perhaps," shrugged Collingwood, "but I cannot ignore direct evidence of unreliability – he could be talking to more than just the Carrington woman. I wouldn't take it as seriously if it weren't for the fact that there was already a slight query over him."

Hartismere looked up alertly. "Go on."

"He was too good on preliminary selection – too good for a raw recruit, that is." Collingwood paced around like some wild beast. "Part of the exercises included a mock interrogation, so we could see what they were like under pressure. Peveril remained very cool, even when I sneered at his sister's Socialist tendencies." The major allowed himself a slight grin. "I have to say, that was something of a relief to me – the previous candidate threatened to knock my block off and did his very best to put his threat into practice. Mind you, I'd just made a slighting remark about his girlfriend, so I sympathised somewhat, even if it suggested that he did not have the correct temperament for Intelligence work."

"But Peveril?"

"Alpha grades all the way through and then one of my subordinates raised a doubt. Was he too good to be true? Had we some sort of would-be double-agent on our hands? It was the trick at the end of the interrogation which bothered him." Collingwood watched his cigarette smoke floating lazily in the air. "Normally, when you tell them that the exercise is over, and they can sit down and relax and have a drink or a cigarette, they take you at your word, particularly when you go on to discuss what they did well and badly. But Peveril treated him with exactly the same caution as he did when under interrogation and refused point-blank to provide any explanation of where he had learned to keep his mouth shut so successfully."

"So he avoided the trap?" mused Hartismere. "Good boy!"

"Very good indeed. Which is why I'm now worried that I've taken on someone who's already been through some sort of training – and who else would train him other than the Nazis or the Soviets?"

"He's been through training all right;" agreed Hartismere grimly, "a brute of a father and a bully of a cousin who was set on him to spy upon his every move. Naturally he learned to keep his emotions under control when the alternatives were so, ah… unattractive. Add to that the normal hell endured by a sensitive boy at boarding school and you arrive at Peveril. I find it very difficult to conceive of him having any sympathy with any totalitarian regime; he knows what it's like to suffer at the hands of unelected dictatorships."

"It doesn't always work out that way," warned Collingwood. "Sometimes people who have had a rough time when young want to get their own back – I bet that weedy runt Goebbels was bullied at school. In fact, I hope he was: hard." Aware that he was drifting from the point, he hastened to return to the reason for Hartismere's presence. "Now do you see why I'm worried? If your Peveril proves to be unreliable then I will have thrown away a vitally important mission purely on the chance that some unblooded neophyte will come up with the goods. Anyone looking in from outside would say that I was a fool to leave Peveril in position when he could be spilling the beans directly to the enemy – or to whichever girl takes his fancy."

"Don't forget that Miss Carrington saved Peveril's life," answered Hartismere, hoping that his argument did not sound too much like special pleading for his erstwhile student. "I shouldn't imagine that he even thinks of her in relation to the war." He allowed himself a dry laugh. "He is, after all, a man, and Miss Carrington is not an unattractive girl. And," he commented, "whilst we're on the subject of ability, it might do no harm if you were to give Peveril some sort of encouragement."

Collingwood sniffed derisively.

"Oh, I know," agreed Hartismere. "I can quite see that, from your point of view, at best he's acting like an irresponsible idiot. Furthermore, I agree that he's not knee-deep in mud and blood in the trenches. All the same, if he thinks that he's about to be cast off into the outer darkness, he may do something even more stupid than merely not letting you know what he is up to in

Suffolk."

"I didn't know that you were such a whale on psychology and, in any case, you told me months ago that Peveril didn't give a damn what people thought of him."

Hartismere shrugged, "I should imagine that that is Peveril's basic standpoint, but he was pretty badly knocked about by the trial and I think he fears that he'll never live down the fact that he was tried for his life. He's certainly a lot more sensitive than he wants anyone to ever realise. That's why he adopts that pose of arrogant insouciance."

Collingwood frowned. To a certain extent, what Hartismere said made sense, even although he did not particularly see why the older man thought it essential to tell him. He proceeded to say so. "Frankly, I can't see what relevance that has to me."

Hartismere waved his hand airily. "In a field like Intelligence, there has to be a reasonable degree of trust between the operative on the ground and the man directing the operation. Currently, Peveril's working pretty closely with you. He's going to notice your attitude towards him. If he thinks you don't trust him, he won't trust you." He pulled a rueful face. "As I know to my cost, he's like a dog that's been ill-treated; he snarls first before anyone can snarl at him."

"An ill-treated dog," remarked Collingwood, who had grown up in the countryside, "rarely recaptures its trust in humanity. And, even if it does, its trust exists only to a limited extent."

Hartismere sighed. He felt that this assessment was only too likely to apply to Peveril, which seemed to him to be unfortunate. "Allow Peveril the odd snarl," he requested.

"And what did he snarl at you?"

"The sort of idiotic thing which undergraduates say when they are annoyed. As it transpired, I received a heartfelt letter of apology the next week. Plenty of my colleagues are offensive and never trouble to apologise."

"Anyone can make an apology, especially a written one," retorted Collingwood.

"True, but if I'd told Peveril to go down on his knees and beg my pardon, he would have done it." Hartismere gave a dry cough. "I saw no need to humiliate the boy by making such a demand; he's been humiliated enough already, and it hasn't done him much good on a personal level, however much use it has been to train him as an operative. And while his experiences may have left him as an adequate operative, they also leave him with other, less happy, traits. Studying him a little may enable him to move from being a tolerable operative to a rather good one."

"I'm studying him all right," retorted the major. "According to the man I set to follow your half-tame whelp, once I'd finished with him he went to the nearest pub and downed three brandies in quick succession. Then he retreated to St James's Park and muttered to himself, before setting off back to Suffolk."

"He spoke out loud when there was someone who could overhear him?" questioned Hartismere disapprovingly.

"If he'd been talking about his mission, he would already be in custody. Apparently, all he did was swear and curse himself."

"A tribute to how much more frightening you have become since you first decorated the courts of Trinity. Perhaps you did learn something in those supervisions on mediaeval kings."

Collingwood grunted his acknowledgement of Hartismere's pleasantry. "Nevertheless, one more mistake and he's out. If it weren't for the fact that I trust your judgement – and that I can't afford to alert anybody in Suffolk as to his true role – I'd have thrown him out on his ear already."

Hartismere sighed, aware that he could do no more.

Chapter Twenty-Nine

When Peveril reached C Coy, the first person he met was Hetherley.

"Aha! The wanderer returns! Shall we slaughter the sacrificial lamb in your honour? More importantly, do you plan to reveal where you've been?"

"What the blazes do you mean?"

"Goodwin seemed rather perturbed by your absence. So perturbed, in fact, that he left instructions that you were to report to him immediately you returned."

Peveril groaned. The last thing he wanted was to have to invent a lot of lies for the benefit of the company commander. "Can't you pretend you haven't seen me?"

Hetherley sniggered. "I don't think you could make it worth my while. He's just spotted you himself."

Peveril turned round and noticed Goodwin staring through the window of his office. "It might be a trifle tactless to go and have a stiff gin first, but Lord knows I could do with it." With that, he set off, ignoring some ribald remarks from Hetherley as to his likely fate.

When he entered Goodwin's office, it was clear that the major was highly annoyed. "I don't know whether you think that you are superior to the rest of us because you are using this unit solely as a base, but, in case you weren't aware, it is normal to alert the Senior Officer to any absences which you may have planned."

"Quite so, sir. That was why I left a message for you, sir."

"And what, may I ask, demanded your attention so urgently?"

Since Peveril had struggled to think of a convincing cover-story which could not be immediately checked, he had resolved to produce only the barest explanation. "I'm afraid, sir, that it was imperative that I investigated a potential base to the south of here. There have been developments within the Survey Unit in relation to communications-siting, and I was needed at short notice."

The major fumed visibly. Technically, Thrigby did not fall under his command. And Leake had mentioned some inter-

Service liaison which was taking place. If Thrigby had spent the day discussing signalling with a boatload of sailors, he'd only make himself unpopular with the Survey Unit if he insisted on demanding details. If it came to that, Thrigby looked pretty tired; maybe he hadn't been swanning around on an errand of pleasure in that damned Alfa of his. Goodwin scowled. Thrigby might have checked him, but he could spoil Thrigby's evening.

"Now that you have returned, you can take this despatch to HQ. It's urgent and you will have to wait for an answer."

Peveril maintained an emotionless façade. He was well aware that Goodwin was exacting a petty revenge, and the last thing he wanted was another drive in the dusk. However, he had no intention of gratifying the major by protesting about a direct order.

Hetherley was lurking to intercept Peveril when he emerged. "Had your knuckles rapped, old boy?"

Ralph yawned contemptuously. "Apparently there is a despatch which is so urgent that it had to wait until I returned. I wonder what Goodwin will do when the invasion comes? Will he hang around out of sight on the excuse that he's waiting for someone to give him a rifle?"

Hetherley laughed. "I shouldn't talk too much about rifles, if I were you. Leake turned up today and insisted on a snap inspection of stores. There were ten rifles missing, three revolvers, and a load of ammunition, among other things."

"And how did our dear company commander account for that minor oversight?"

"Blamed Snellgrove, of course, even although Snellgrove's said for months that the ammunition book isn't being kept properly." Hetherley glanced round conspiratorially. "What Goodwin doesn't know is that Leake got hold of Snellgrove later on his own."

Despite his more pressing concerns, Peveril whistled. "That could set the cat among the pigeons."

"Exactly. What price Goodwin getting the push?"

Peveril shrugged. "Don't forget that Snellgrove may think that he ought to back Goodwin up loyally."

"That merely makes the chances all the more interesting,"

declared Hetherley. "I'm thinking of starting a book on it – what odds will you take?"

"What about ten to one in rifles?"

Hetherley was still sniggering over this jest when Peveril set off towards HQ. He felt curiously detached, almost as if he were watching someone else drive. Even when he reached HQ, he found it hard to shake off the feeling that he was an observer gazing down on insubstantial souls flitting around in the half-dark. '*As many as the birds which gather when the icy season puts them to flight across the sea*,' he quoted, as he watched the activity swirling around the parade-ground. 'Leake must have some sort of exercise on. I'm sure he'll be delighted to deal with my 'urgent' communication.'

Since the adjutant looked doubtful when asked how soon the colonel would be able to read the despatch from C Coy, Peveril sought refuge in the mess. With a bit of luck, he'd be able to observe how HQ had responded to the shooting of Poole – surely that would count as 'obeying orders for a change'? When Peveril reached the mess bar, it was practically deserted. Cohen was deep in conversation at one end with Arrowsmith of B Coy, whilst Jervis and Chatham greeted him with a guarded welcome. Peveril sighed. Clearly his dubious remarks the previous time he had visited had not been forgotten.

"You look a bit low," commented Jervis. "Is C Coy getting sick of murders?"

Peveril decided that Thrigby would respond to this by grunting and ordering a large gin.

Chatham laughed, "Must be damaging your chances of a quiet life – first the police dropping in at odd moments to turn up their noses at how you guard the camp, and then old Leake deciding to launch all these exercises. Goodwin must be tearing his hair out."

Peveril gave a perfunctory smile at this pleasantry.

"Are C Coy having to work a bit harder than usual?" enquired Jervis. "Serves you right – your murderer started all this fuss."

"Thrigby isn't working harder," commented Arrowsmith maliciously. "He's got his eye on a girl."

"Indeed?" remarked Jervis, regarding Peveril with interest.

"You've only been in the district for a month."

"Quick work," agreed Arrowsmith, before shrugging. "Mind you, you can tell that Thrigby's only in C Coy."

"What the devil do you mean?" demanded Peveril dangerously.

Arrowsmith laughed. "C Coy are so useless that they put a murderer in charge of their weapons and a Fascist in charge of guard duty. They're all lame ducks. No wonder Thrigby's squiring a lame girl. He's just… "

Whatever other remarks Arrowsmith intended to make were cut off as Peveril hurled himself at him and bore him down to the ground. As Arrowsmith struggled to pull himself up from the floor, Peveril got his hands round Arrowsmith's neck and began to choke him. Hardly able to breathe, Arrowsmith clawed at Peveril's face in a desperate attempt to free himself. Suddenly, Peveril felt his own throat being grabbed from behind and he momentarily slackened his grip, giving Cohen the opportunity he was seeking. Wrenching one of Peveril's arms free, he hissed in Peveril's ear, "Drop him, or I'll have your arm out of its socket." Still in a blind rage, Peveril hardly took in what Cohen had said and struggled to throw himself back onto Arrowsmith. A swift, sickening pain brought him up short.

"Let him go or you'll regret it," warned Cohen. "I'm trained in unarmed combat and I know exactly what I'm doing." With that, he dragged Peveril off Arrowsmith and out of the bar. Since Peveril appeared to have forgotten the army maxim about it being acceptable to surrender to overwhelming force and was still writhing in a vain attempt to free himself, Cohen proceeded to bang Peveril's head on the wall several times to bring him to his senses.

"For God's sake stop struggling. I don't want to break your arm, you silly ass."

Peveril suddenly went limp. Cohen regarded him suspiciously. "You aren't going to try to get back in there if I let you go, are you? Arrowsmith will have left now."

Conscious of an excruciating pain in his shoulder, Peveril shook his head.

"You should be damn thankful I did break up that fight,"

grunted Cohen, who was not best pleased to have had his talk with Arrowsmith interrupted. "Col. Leake would rip you apart if he learned what you'd been up to. He doesn't take kindly to people wasting their time on personal feuding when they've got important work to do."

Peveril's black rage suddenly died down as he realised that Cohen's words could apply to more than his supposed role as Capt. Thrigby. However, Cohen was not finished. "If it comes to that, you'll have an interesting time explaining those scratches away to Goodwin when you get back. I suppose you can come up with a decent excuse?"

Peveril raised his right hand and then regretted it as a shaft of pain shot through his arm. Dropping it back hastily to his side, he cautiously felt his cheek with his left hand. He had been too busy trying to throttle Arrowsmith to realise that his opponent had gouged his face in his attempt to free himself.

"What are you going to tell Goodwin?" demanded Cohen.

"That I had a spill in my motor, obviously."

"With no perceptible damage to your car? Most convincing."

Peveril's colour rose at Cohen's sarcastic tone. "I don't see why you should care. It's nothing to do with you."

"Yes, it is," retorted Cohen. "If Goodwin gets worked up about one of his chaps being attacked unfairly, he'll complain to Leake and I'll be the one left explaining what happened. I've got more than enough work to do without dealing with witness statements in triplicate – and so should you."

Peveril passed his hand wearily over his face again as he tried to think of some credible explanation of his marked state. Cohen watched his failure to provide one with sardonic contempt.

"Say you fell down the stairs. Say you had an accident with some barbed wire. Tell Goodwin anything you like as long as it keeps him – and you – off my back." He snorted derisively. "Tell him that you fought a rose-bush to give your girlfriend flowers. I don't care."

"*Roslein auf der heiden*," muttered Peveril, thinking of the song which Midge had been playing on the gramophone, and wishing that he was back in her snuggery.

"What the devil did you say?" demanded Cohen in a tone of

such authority that Peveril automatically snapped to attention.

"N… n… nothing, s…," he stammered, before cursing himself for behaving like a subaltern in the presence of a superior. After all, he – as Thrigby – was meant to outrank Cohen, whatever his actual rank as Peveril was.

"For goodness sake, pull yourself together, man," growled Cohen. "And don't go rowing with Arrowsmith – you could end up on a charge of assault if you can't control yourself."

Peveril nodded shakily, reflecting that it would have been disastrous if he really had hurt Arrowsmith. "Err… thanks," he added awkwardly.

"Discovered that Jew-boys have their uses after all?" enquired Cohen. "That's what you called me last time, wasn't it?"

Peveril's face flamed. Why had he been such a fool as to fall in with Midge's idiotic suggestion that he act like a Fascist? How could Jervis have passed on his comment to Cohen? And what the devil did he do now? If only he could think straight.

Cohen waited for a few moments, but when it became apparent that Peveril was not going to respond, he shrugged his shoulders and stalked off. Peveril stared after him unhappily, conscious that he had botched his opportunity. He slumped back against the wall heavily.

'Oh hell and blast and damnation,' he cursed. 'Either I should have behaved like my Thrigby character and come out with another offensive remark or I should have had the guts to apologise to Cohen and dealt with any complications for the mission later. I've behaved like neither Thrigby nor Ralph Peveril.'

The noise of someone approaching roused Peveril from his depressing introspection. He made for the Alfa, sensing that he had the greatest chance of avoiding embarrassing questions if he left camp until the scratches on his face looked less startlingly fresh. 'I suppose I'll have to come back in a bit to check whether Leake has any response to Goodwin's rot, but I'm not sticking around to be asked what I've been doing.' He flushed. 'I don't want to see Cohen again, either.'

An hour later, Peveril returned, only to be greeted by the

adjutant telling him that Col. Leake would attend to the despatch on the following day. Ralph drove off, suspecting that Poole had been proved correct about Goodwin inventing emergencies to teach juniors their place. If Goodwin claimed that it was his fault that Leake hadn't responded, that would strengthen Poole's interpretation further.

The harassed major did indeed seem to derive some pleasure from criticising Peveril.

"If there was no reply, why did you delay so long before returning to camp? And what the devil have you been doing to your face?"

"A trifling accident with some barbed wire, sir," explained Peveril. "Absolutely nothing to worry about. As to the delay, sir, Col. Leake couldn't deal with the despatch at once – I gather that he's got a problem with some incompetent record-keeping in the battalion. The adjutant was apologetic, but apparently there's a whole lot of war-stores missing – he said that all hell was going to break loose when they traced the man responsible."

"Haven't you yet learned to make a formal report?" snapped Goodwin, who was looking distinctly concerned.

"Sorry, sir. I was quoting the adjutant – I thought it would be helpful to keep to the exact words."

Goodwin grunted something under his breath, before saying, "I'll want you up there first thing tomorrow."

"Very well, sir," replied Peveril, before snapping off his best salute. His expression did not change until he was out of view; then it creased in a slight grin. Clearly, Goodwin didn't like being shown up as incompetent – and he'd certainly never have the nerve to check whether the adjutant, rather than Hetherley, had said anything.

Although Peveril had been momentarily amused by Goodwin's worry, by the time he strode upstairs to his quarters, his attention was devoted to his own concerns. In particular, he still didn't understand how someone could have adopted the identical plan which he had invented for getting Poole out of gaol. It was almost as if someone were reading his mind, which was a foul thought. But the only alternative was that Midge had been talking, which was an impossible thought.

Ralph sighed. Why had he been such a fool as to provoke Collingwood? If he'd handled things better he might have persuaded Collingwood to let Midge help. All he'd achieved was to annoy the major and receive a damned unpleasant reprimand. The fact that he deserved it hardly improved matters. And what if Collingwood decided that Midge was a security risk?

Contemplating Midge reminded Peveril that he ought to be trying to think intelligently about Poole's evidence. He looked longingly at his bed. He was desperately tired, but he daren't go to sleep. He couldn't endure another nightmare. Suddenly Ralph stiffened in shock. Oh God, surely that couldn't be what had happened? He couldn't have cried out in his sleep, could he? Had he given away the gaol plot in a nightmare, whimpering like a scared child? No wonder his exact self-same plan had been used – he'd presented it to a would-be murderer. Trying to stop shivering, Ralph attempted to test his theory. After that lecture at training about not leaving yourself vulnerable, he'd started keeping his window shut at night. So nobody could have heard him from below. And since he always locked his door, no-one could have sneaked in unnoticed. So whoever had heard him must have come close to the room. That implied an officer or one of the batmen – Trent, Ulph, and whoever was on guard. And one of them was the traitor.

After a moment's thought, Ralph corrected himself. Whoever had overheard him wasn't necessarily the traitor. It could have been a friend of Poole's who decided that the bomb plot was a good way of freeing him. But, to judge by Collingwood's reaction, whoever blew up the gaol was risking pretty severe trouble – after all, presumably the explosives had been stolen from a military store. Was there anyone sufficiently close to Poole in C Coy who would run those risks? He couldn't imagine Hetherley chancing gaol for Poole, while Snellgrove seemed a most unlikely candidate for a flagrant breech of military discipline. Was there any evidence that Trent liked Poole? Or might he have done it for money? If so, who had provided the cash? Or did all of this confirm the likelihood that someone had tried to kill Poole?

Wondering whether he really had narrowed things down much, Ralph tried to think rationally. He couldn't see any flaws in his logic, which left him with the problem of what to do next. If he told Collingwood his conclusions, the chances were that his C.O. wouldn't believe him – after all, he hadn't today. He'd probably think it was an invention to protect Midge. But if the major did believe him, then his C.O. would be an absolute fool to leave him in position, betraying military secrets every time he had a nightmare. Ralph shivered. It was abundantly obvious that, once his usefulness in Suffolk was finished, Collingwood would detain Midge and court-martial him. His sole chance of persuading Collingwood not to take vengeance on Midge was to solve Durrant's murder. But he couldn't do that if he were under close arrest somewhere in London. Hence it followed that he couldn't risk telling Collingwood how the bomb plot had leaked out. But if he didn't tell Collingwood, his C.O. wouldn't be given clear proof that criminal was located in C Coy.

Ralph bit his lip. According to his analysis, he had a choice of endangering the girl he loved or his country. And it didn't answer what he ought to do about himself. He had to face facts: if he'd given the bomb plot away, what else might he give away? Was it his duty to leave Suffolk and abandon his mission before he revealed more important things? But he'd just proved that the traitor was connected with C Coy, which meant that he was the person best placed to solve whatever was going on. He couldn't tamely run away, particularly when it would be impossible to infiltrate another operative into C Coy. In any case, if he hadn't been such a brute to Poole none of this would have happened, so he had to sort it out. But that still left the problem of Midge.

Chapter Thirty

The next morning, Peveril was up early. His excuse, should anyone ask, was that Goodwin had ordered him to visit HQ first thing, but the reality was that he was afraid to sleep. He had nodded off a couple of times, but on each occasion he had woken up, clawing the air in terror as he tried to fight off the flitting shapes which surrounded him, dragging him along with them to the banks of the Styx. There he had been faced with the sight of Charon, the boatman of the dead, poling his rust-coloured boat steadily towards the river-bank. As Charon came closer, the spectral shades swirled and twisted through the mist, each pleading to be transported to its new home. But Charon, dressed in filthy, stained robes, his elf-locks hanging down and streaked with dirt, ignored the imploring ghosts. Instead he walked straight through their midst, driving them back until he reached Peveril. He crooked his finger and Ralph followed, unable to resist him, even although the smell of death and corruption on the boatman's breath warned of what awaited him. It was only as Peveril was about to step into the boat that the silent wailing of those left behind turned into sound and he awoke to the blaring trumpets of the *Requiem*.

Unsurprisingly, Peveril was in no mood for conversation, but, as he was leaving his quarters, Snellgrove, who was the duty officer, stopped him.

"Woolf wants you to call in at the police-station."

Peveril tensed. Did that meant that the inspector had found out that he had visited Poole in hospital? He forced a bored yawn.

"Why does our local bluebottle require my presence?"

"I don't know. I'm merely passing on the message which, I may add, was endorsed by Major Goodwin." Snellgrove regarded him disapprovingly. "I am aware that you regard our local problems with contempt, Captain, but I cannot see that efficiency is going to be harmed by collaboration with the civilian authorities."

"I rather thought that collaboration was regarded as a very bad thing nowadays." Noticing that Snellgrove looked decidedly displeased, Peveril added, "And I can't see many signs of efficiency in C Coy." With that, he left.

Snellgrove glared after him. Considering how little work Thrigby appeared to do, he had a nerve in talking about efficiency. But that remark about collaboration was worrying. Did Thrigby know something? Damn. That was going make matters harder.

For his part, Ralph was tempted to go directly to HQ and ignore Woolf's request altogether. However, not only would that look highly suspicious, but it would enrage Goodwin if he found out. Thrigby might be an arrogant swine, but he was unlikely to disobey direct orders without a very good reason and Ralph didn't want Goodwin starting to wonder quite what he had been up to. Hence, soon afterwards, Ralph drew up the Alfa outside the police-station.

When he entered the inspector's office, it was soon apparent that Woolf was in the grip of extreme anger.

"I told you that nobody was to talk to Poole, but now I discover that you appeared at the hospital accompanied by some crippled girl. What were you doing there?"

Ralph's hands tightened into fists at this description of Midge, but he restrained his anger.

"I thought Poole might welcome a friendly visitor."

"I don't believe you. I want to know who the woman with you was and what you said. I may add that it would be advisable to co-operate."

"That sounds remarkably like a threat."

"It is. You'll tell me exactly what I want to know – or else."

Ralph summoned up a supercilious gaze. "I can't see what's so wrong with visiting an injured military colleague, but if there is, I might point out that army officers explain their actions to the Military Police, not country bobbies."

"Do they, by God!" Woolf swore. "You may not wish to explain why you took some girl in to see a dying man, but you'll damned well explain exactly what you said to him which made him kill himself!"

"Kill himself?"

"Yes, Captain, kill himself. It may, or may not, come as a surprise to you, but Poole died last night, which is why I intend to investigate exactly who spoke to him." Paying back Peveril's insults with one of his own, the inspector added, "Of course, you'll be very familiar with this sort of affair as an ex-gaol-bird yourself."

Ralph kept a tight control over himself. Woolf might be making a wild accusation, so he must react as Thrigby would. "What the devil do you mean?"

"I mean that you are Ralph Peveril, not Ernest Thrigby. One of my constables recognised you. And while army officers explain their military actions to the Military Police, some issues come under civilian jurisdiction." Woolf leant forward unpleasantly. "For example, you might explain why you are passing under an assumed name. Being from Eton and Cambridge doesn't give you the right to use false identity papers."

"Do you think that I wanted to spend the rest of my life watching everyone avoid me? I decided to use the army to create a new persona. Once the war's over, I'll settle down somewhere as the gallant Captain Thrigby."

"And your papers?"

"I bought them off a back-street spiv."

"Really? That doesn't explain how you became a captain when you've been in the army for less that a year."

Peveril hoped that he had not changed colour. If Woolf had spotted that point, it wouldn't take the inspector long to suspect his real role. And admitting that he was in Intelligence would leave him with no excuse not to reveal who Midge was. In any case, judging from the inspector's fury, it was quite likely that Woolf would not believe such a claim. What was left? Only to go on the offensive – in all senses of the word.

"Grow up, Woolf. I didn't go to all the effort and expense of being found not guilty only to be shot dead by some German peasant. I pulled strings at the War Office."

"I don't believe you."

Peveril shrugged. "If you've studied my trial in such detail that you know where I was at school, you'll have no difficulty in realising that I know a lot of useful people. This particular chap was my old Captain of Boats. I fagged for him, so he was happy to help out when I asked for a transfer."

"Captain of Boats?" Woolf snorted. "What sort of bloody silly title is that?"

Peveril forced himself to sound at his drawling, insufferable worst. "I don't suppose you'd understand. Round here people row boats for a living, don't they? So they wouldn't understand sport."

"And there's a lot you don't understand – such as the fact that you were seen in the vicinity of the police-station on the night when it was attacked and Poole freed. You'll find that rather hard to explain away."

Remembering how dark it had been that night, Peveril doubted that he could possibly have been recognised. Nonetheless, he avoided the trap of saying so and stuck to a generalised statement. "I was not there."

"You may deny it all you like, but I don't suppose that a jury will have much difficulty in believing that you blew up the gaol to let Poole out. Nobody else has shown any eagerness to speak to him, which is why you – and that woman – will have to explain your actions at the hospital."

"I have nothing to explain."

"Don't you, by God!"

"No." Peveril got up. "And, if you'll excuse me, I have an urgent appointment at HQ."

Woolf was practically spitting with rage. "Don't talk to me about appointments. You ought to have had an appointment with the public hangman once, and you may still face him for making Poole kill himself. But, if not, by God, I'll ensure that you – or that girl – face a good few years in gaol for attacking a police-station. You won't be half so sure of yourself when you're back in the dock."

Chapter Thirty-One

Although Peveril fully expected that Woolf would try to keep him at the police-station, the inspector made no attempt to stop Peveril when he walked out. As he reached the Alfa, Peveril wondered if he had handled Woolf correctly. Or had he merely antagonised him to no purpose? Ralph winced. He felt damned guilty about taking Cartwright's name in vain to prop up his story. As if Cartwright would ever have helped him to evade his duty – if he'd approached him with that sort of request, Cartwright would have harangued him about skulking away from danger, before literally booting him down the stairs. Peveril pushed away a memory of reading the notice that Major Rupert Vyvyan Cartwright, M.C., was 'missing, believed killed in action'. Cartwright might not have had a musical bone in his body, but he had stopped anyone from teasing his fag about singing solo in the chapel choir and Peveril had never forgotten his decency.

Ralph shrugged, trying to think like his supercilious alter ego. The fact that Cartwright was dead meant that the major could not deny anything which Woolf chose to investigate. There was no point feeling guilty about what he had said, any more than there had been any point the previous year in letting himself be consumed with guilt that he was hanging around Cambridge achieving nothing while others died. All that had led to was a filthy row with Hartismere.

Gunning the motor of the Alfa in his desire to escape, Peveril instinctively turned in the direction of Brandon. He felt desperately in need of Midge's cool sense and intelligence. However, as Peveril roared out of Newton, he was struck by second thoughts. Woolf sounded determined to speak to Midge. And Woolf had accused him of a crime; why hadn't he been arrested? What if Woolf had let him go in the hope that he would lead Woolf straight to Midge? Peveril glanced behind him. There was an Austin Seven which seemed to have a surprising turn of speed. Was it a souped-up police car? If he carried on to Brandon, he would show Woolf exactly where Midge lived.

'I can't betray Midge,' he swore, as he stamped on the brakes. 'She shouldn't have been wasting her time on my problems as it was. And if Woolf really thinks that we got Poole out of gaol and drove him to suicide, he's bound to arrest us. I can't expose Midge to that sort of treatment. She hasn't done anything wrong, and I'm damned if I'm going to let her suffer because of me.'

The result of Peveril's decision became apparent several hours later in Cambridge. Hartismere, as befitted the Vice-Master of Trinity, was making his way across Great Court towards the Library, where he intended to consult one of the many illuminated manuscripts held by the college. Although he was walking briskly because of the dank mist which was swirling around the court, he became aware of a voice in the general direction of the fountain. Something about the pitch and the cadences suggested that the voice was speaking in a foreign language and, as Hartismere drew closer, he realised that the unknown was reciting Latin verse. Since there were hardly any undergraduates in residence during the vacation, and since none of Hartismere's Classical colleagues were given to such outbreaks of spontaneous poetry-recitation, the Vice-Master was intrigued. However, his interest turned to macabre horror when a face loomed out of the mist and addressed him.

"Sir? No-one told me that you had died as well."

"Peveril? What are you doing here?"

"Charon won't let me cross. I thought he wanted me, but now he won't appear. I thought that you were Charon. You aren't, are you, sir?"

The hairs on the nape of Hartismere's neck prickled. If it had been term-time and Peveril had still been an undergraduate, he might have assumed that this was a rag, but the boy was in deadly earnest. What the devil had happened?

"I am not Charon," he replied, as calmly as he could.

"Are we going to be stuck here for a hundred years?" Peveril gazed round hopelessly. "I can't see any of the other souls. There has always been a multitude before. I've even touched Charon's boat."

"Perhaps," suggested Hartismere cunningly, "you have driven them off by waving that revolver around. Why don't you give it to me?"

Peveril's grasp on his weapon seemed to tighten. "No, I need it. How else can I blow my brains out? An arrow won't work, nor a sword-thrust."

The Vice-Master sidled closer to Peveril. "My dear boy, you must tell me what happened to you. How did you arrive here?"

"I don't know. Maybe I had a crash." Peveril stared into the mist unhappily. "I didn't want to die. There's no-one to warn Midge about Woolf and I ought to have gone to see Fletcher when he asked me to. If it comes to that, I wanted to apologise to you properly, sir. I don't suppose it counts now that we're both dead." Peveril broke off in a sudden gasp as Hartismere wrenched his gun from him. He turned an accusing stare on him. "You have far too much power for a wraith – when did you die?"

"I am still moving between the two worlds."

Ralph seemed disposed to dispute this statement. "You aren't Hermes. You don't have a caduceus, nor winged sandals."

Rapidly summoning up his memories of classical mythology, Hartismere attempted to provide a convincing explanation of his unexpected strength. "There have been many libations poured to my shade. Each sacrifice has given me potency. You are insubstantial because no-one has yet cast red wine over the ground which holds you. But I can pour a libation, which will re-animate your spirit for a few hours."

Peveril frowned. "If you do that you will be depriving yourself. I don't deserve it – not after insulting you as I did."

"You will be closer to Charon if you come with me."

Although Peveril seemed reluctant to agree to Hartismere's offer, he allowed the Vice-Master to shepherd him across Great Court, over Trinity Street and into Whewell's Court, where Hartismere's rooms lay. Once there, Hartismere sought a wine-glass with his right hand, while his left fumbled inside a thin drawer in his desk. Turning away from Peveril for a moment, he crossed to where he kept his decanters and poured a glass of red wine. Peveril took it from him and seemed about to cast it on the carpet, but Hartismere intervened.

"No, that would be correct if you were making an offering to someone else, but this is an offering from me to you. You must drink it."

Ralph hesitated and then, as if concerned lest he hurt Hartismere's feelings, he drained the wine.

"*How they would wish to be now in the upper air...,*" he quoted, "*But divine right stands in their way, and the sad marsh of hateful waves, and the Styx, with its nine-fold windings, enclose the captive souls.*"

"How true," agreed Hartismere, who was watching Peveril closely. Was it his imagination or was the boy beginning to waver to and fro? Suddenly, Peveril uttered a low moan. He cast a look upon Hartismere in which horror and an appeal for help were mixed.

"Sir, what have you given me?"

"Nothing which will harm you."

Ralph ran his tongue over lips which seemed blubbery and unresponsive. With a great effort he forced himself to speak. "I thought... you were going... to help... keep me... sentient. I feel... drugged. Now... I must be... truly dead." With that, he slumped onto a chair.

Chapter Thirty-Two

One day later, Hartismere was talking to a florid man who had bright, intelligent eyes and an intense manner.

"What do you make of him, Silberstein?"

"It would be easier to judge if he would talk. Even although he's under morphia, he refuses to speak to me." The doctor shrugged. "That's not entirely accurate. He asked me why I was with him, since I was a Jew."

Hartismere winced. Dr Silberstein had fled Germany when racial laws had made it impossible for him to practise as a psychiatrist. He would hardly relish having a patient object to his race. "I do apologise for the boy. If he genuinely thinks that he's in the Underworld, perhaps all he meant was that he was surprised to find someone who did not worship Jupiter there."

"I hardly suppose he worships Jupiter himself," commented Silberstein dryly. "In any case, he kept calling me Cohen, so he must have intended to insult me." The alienist shrugged again. "I've heard much worse, and he did mutter something about not knowing whether it mattered any more now that he was dead."

Hartismere's ears pricked up. "Did he, by God? In that case, my dear fellow, I think you may be mistaken if you assume that he actually wished to abuse you."

Silberstein looked affronted. "Don't worry, Hartismere, I'll still treat your young man even if he does mock me. I happen to believe in the Hippocratic oath."

"I know." Hartismere paused. "Do you think that the Hippocratic oath would allow me to see the boy?"

"First do no harm," quoted Silberstein. "I don't think that you would harm him and I cannot keep him under such heavy morphia for much longer. He has much on his mind, but I need him to speak. Perhaps he will speak to you." He grimaced. "Normally, morphia makes patients talk too much – last month a patient assured me with utter conviction of the fact that Hitler was hiding on the curtain-rail."

"I wish Herr Schicklgruber was so easy to capture," grunted Hartismere. "Then we could all get on with our real jobs, including that boy in there."

When Hartismere was ushered in to see Peveril, the younger man looked grey and drained. His eyes opened at the sound of footsteps and he cast a cursory glance over Hartismere's face. Then he drifted off again. The Vice-Master waited patiently. There was no point in forcibly rousing the boy; he would be of more use when he came to of his own accord.

An hour later, Peveril's eyes flickered open. They fastened upon Hartismere and seemed to recognise him. "I meant to apologise to you in person. I shouldn't have called you a coward. Now it's too late."

"But who's been calling *you* a coward?" asked Hartismere softly.

Ralph flinched. "Do you know the truth now, sir? That's why I sneered at you. I thought if I insulted people who scuttled off into Intelligence, no-one would realise that I was only too glad to do the same. I didn't want to go on active service. I just pretended I did." He laughed abruptly. "And now I'm dead all the same."

"And why did you insult Cohen?"

Ralph looked as if he were close to tears. "I didn't want to insult him, but I had to. I mustn't betray my identity. Now he's trying to trap me by changing his appearance." Peveril suddenly appeared frightened. "I oughtn't to be talking to you, sir. I haven't told you anything, have I?"

"No," replied Hartismere, soothingly. "In any case, anything you told me wouldn't count. After all, aren't I dead, too?"

Peveril glanced round the room uneasily. "I don't want to talk anymore. Anyone could be listening."

"There's no-one other than me present."

"You don't understand," argued Peveril agitatedly, "there are dictaphones and things." He suddenly beckoned the Vice-Master close to him and hissed, "You must warn Midge that Woolf is after her."

Hartismere was momentarily reassured by this concern for issues of the normal world, but Ralph's next remark depressed him.

"You're not Hermes; you're Rhadamanthus. That's why you

want me to tell you everything. *Here strict Rhadamanthus rules, he hears and judges each committed crime; enquires into the manner, place, and time. The conscious wretch must all his acts reveal – loth to confess, unable to conceal.*"

As Hartismere returned to the door, he heard Peveril's final whisper. "*Here are those who, whilst alive, hated their own brothers, or struck their parents.*"

Silberstein raised an eyebrow when Hartismere returned. "Did you discover anything useful?"

Hartismere sighed. "Frankly, if he hadn't quoted Virgil at me, I'd have said that the boy had religious mania."

"What makes you say that?"

"He accused me of being the judge of the dead."

Silberstein appeared amused by this. "Thus giving you rather more power than you have as Vice-Master?"

Hartismere gave a brief smile in acknowledgement of this sally. "Yes, but Pev…, that is, undergraduates never accord me a similar level of respect. Mind you, I was correct that he hadn't meant to insult you personally. I think that Cohen's a real person – the boy confused him with you." He sighed. "What are you going to do now? I don't know what terminology you use, but he's clearly lost his reason and I imagine the morphia is making things worse."

"A crude, but vivid, summary," agreed Silberstein. "Did you notice how exhausted he looks? I suspect he hasn't been sleeping – a shock on top of that may have been enough to precipitate this breakdown." He frowned. "Unfortunately, he resists every time he is given morphia, which undoes much of the value of the rest which the drug gives him." Recollecting the young officer's struggles, Silberstein grimaced. "Although he thinks that he is dead already, he doesn't want to lose what limited awareness he has."

Hartismere made a number of telephone calls that night. The first was to Collingwood to inform him that Hartismere had found his half-tame whelp and was looking after it until it was fit enough to be sent to London. Since Hartismere warned that this might take some time, Collingwood was able to infer that something had gone badly wrong. The second telephone call was to Midge. Whilst Hartismere had no reason to assume that anyone might be listening to their call, he mentioned no names and merely stated that the young man whom Midge had helped the previous year was ill and might benefit from a visit. Since Midge had started to worry why she had heard nothing from Ralph, she was only too happy to fall in with Hartismere's suggestion that she come to Cambridge the following day.

By the time that they reached the hospital, Hartismere had cautioned Midge that Peveril had been heavily drugged and was likely to say strange things. However, notwithstanding this warning, Midge was shocked at how grey and ill Ralph looked. For his part, Peveril stared at Midge without recognising her. It was only when Midge limped over to his bedside that his eyes took on a semblance of normality.

"What are you doing here? You can't be dead, too? Surely Woolf didn't manage to blame you for Poole's suicide and get you hanged?"

Despite Hartismere's warning, Midge shivered. Ralph sounded so rational and normal, but what he was saying was abnormal in the extreme. "I am not dead and nor are you."

"I am dead," protested Peveril. "*I have seen the deep pools of Cocytus and the Stygian marsh, by whose power the gods fear to swear falsely.*"

Fortunately, Midge recognised the reference. "Good, then you will have to answer my questions truthfully."

"I never tell the truth, let alone the whole truth and nothing but the truth."

"But you haven't been asked to swear by Cocytus before. You dare not lie."

Ralph scowled, dimly aware that he had been trapped.

"What colour is this scarf I'm wearing?"

"Sea-green. Why?"

"There are no colours in the Underworld. If you are in the Underworld, how can you tell me what colour my scarf is?"

"There was sunlight in the Elysian Fields."

"Are you a great-hearted hero, exercising your horses as you did in the upper world?"

Ralph gave a cackle of bitter laughter. "I am neither great-hearted, nor a hero. As for horses, I must have died chasing too much horse-power."

"Your Alfa is parked without a scratch in Trinity Street," remarked Midge prosaically. She dug around in her bag and held up a book which Hartismere had discovered in Peveril's greatcoat. "Was this what... err... killed you?"

Peveril gave a shuddering gasp, before slumping down in a dead faint. Shaking, Midge laid the book on the bed. Given what Ralph had previously told her, she was not surprised that a book entitled *'Cowards Die Many Deaths'* and inscribed *'From your loving Mother'* had upset him. Nevertheless, it was pretty grim to see at first hand the effect of such a gift.

When Ralph came round, he shook his head violently, as if to clear it.

"What's up?" murmured Midge.

"I can't hear," he protested angrily. "I can't hear and I can't think."

Noticing that his eyes were clouding over again, Midge grasped Ralph's arm. "Look here, Ralph, that book probably wasn't sent by your mother. If she wanted to send you a book why would she write an inscription on a separate piece of paper and glue it inside the front cover? And look at this wrapping – your address has been cut off an envelope and glued on to the brown paper. Is that the way your mother normally sends you parcels?"

Peveril stared at her sightlessly. In despair, Midge resorted to her conclusion. "Wake up, Ralph. Didn't I suggest that Robert was behind those anonymous letters? This book proves it. Your mother would never send an accusation of cowardice to you. Only someone who had access to your mother's letters could cut off the address and paste it onto a parcel to you. Who has access to her letters, other than your own family? And which of them would want to harm you, other than Robert?"

Much to Midge's relief, Ralph's eyes acquired an appearance of intelligence. "Leo wanted to destroy me, too."

"Leo is dead," pointed out Midge, wondering whether Ralph had forgotten that he had been put on trial for his father's murder. "Anyway, just because someone sends you poison-pen letters, it doesn't mean that they are true."

Peveril shuddered. "They are true. You shouldn't be talking to me." He frowned in concentration. Surely there was something it was vital to tell Midge? A haze of morphia overtook him and he drifted off again. When he woke up the next time, he looked and sounded much more alert.

"Has Woolf or Collingwood contacted you?"

"No."

"Poole's dead," Ralph explained bluntly. "Woolf accused me or you of having driven him to kill himself. He threatened to seek you out and question you."

"What happened to Poole?" demanded Midge, shock having temporarily driven away her inclination to treat Ralph gently.

"I think he was poisoned. I don't see how else he could have killed himself in hospital. He was on the ground floor, so he wouldn't have died if he threw himself out of a window." Ralph shivered. "Midge, promise me that you will ask for help from Hartismere – or even Collingwood – if Woolf does find out who you are. He's so furious that he may invent a case against you."

"Then," argued Midge, wondering if she should tell Ralph how much she had already revealed to the Vice-Master, "you ought to trust Hartismere, too. After all, it was he who brought me here."

Chapter Thirty-Three

Despite Midge's suggestion that Ralph confide in Hartismere, a glance at Peveril's face the next day would have shown that he was disinclined to take this advice. Silberstein had stopped the injections of morphia in the hope that the young officer would come round in a more coherent frame of mind. Whilst this was the case, if anything, Peveril appeared even more reserved than when Hartismere had first visited him. He fielded every question put to him and the only subject upon which he was prepared to discourse freely was his desire to apologise for having accused the Vice-Master of showing the white feather in the Great War.

"I really am devilish sorry about what I said in November. I know that you fought in the trenches, sir. I was vilely rude."

"You were vilely hung-over," retorted Hartismere unflatteringly. "I did take that into consideration at the time."

Peveril flushed, but Hartismere was not finished. "I might recommend that you resort to morphia next time you seek to banish black care – you have much nicer manners under its influence."

"Oh God," muttered Peveril, wondering what he must have said to have justified this remark.

Hartismere sighed. "What I am attempting to tell you, albeit in my own inimitable manner, is that you have already apologised to me at sufficient length, including in that letter you sent me several months ago. We can turn our attention to more urgent matters. You might, for example, indicate some level of trust in me and stop refusing to answer my questions."

"But, sir, I'm not meant to talk to anyone. Honestly, I'm not. My C.O. gave me hell for having talked out of turn – I don't want him to go for you as well." Ralph sounded unhappy. "He already thinks that my actions have called into question your judgement. I daren't make things worse."

At this response, Hartismere feigned anger. "If you are not prepared to trust me, then I would appreciate it if you would have the courtesy to tell me so outright. Then," he added acidly, "I could return to Trinity, instead of being dragged out here to help someone who doesn't appear to want to be helped."

Peveril shifted uncomfortably, some of his reticence fading. It was clear that Hartismere was going to be horribly hurt if he refused to speak, and he trusted Hartismere as much as he trusted anyone. He stated this latter fact rather baldly.

Hartismere sighed. "I suppose I can't entirely blame you for being suspicious, but it is infernally inconvenient at times."

Peveril saw no need to respond to this comment.

"I don't propose to ask for details of your assignment, but you might explain why you wanted to kill yourself."

"I didn't."

"Indeed?" remarked Hartismere astringently. "Why else would you be wanting – and I quote – to blow your brains out?"

Peveril's colour rose again. "I didn't want to kill myself. I thought that I was dead already."

"So what the blazes were you talking about?"

"I... I..., it sounds so stupid, sir."

"All the same, I should like to know."

"I wanted to stop the music."

"*Music?*" exclaimed the Vice-Master.

"Yes," snarled Peveril, wishing that Hartismere had not placed him in an impossible situation whereby he either explained and made a fool of himself, or refused to explain and implied that Hartismere was not to be trusted. "It's the *Dies Irae*. I can't stop it. Sometimes it grows so loud that I can't hear or think properly." He gave a bitter laugh. "Now do you understand why I wanted to put a bullet through my brain?"

"Entirely." Hartismere ran a thoughtful glance over Peveril. "Does that also explain the nightmares which you were having when you were still in college?"

Peveril froze. "What do you mean, nightmares?"

"My dear boy, every time I saw you, you looked half-asleep. It clearly wasn't dissipation and, ah... enquiries revealed that you probably weren't burning the midnight oil over your work. So what was left other than nightmares? There's nothing to be ashamed of in having them." A swift look in Peveril's direction suggested that the young officer was not convinced by this claim. The Vice-Master sighed, reflecting that it would hardly help the boy to be told that the Zoology Fellow who lived on Peveril's staircase had been woken by Peveril's screams several times and had compared it to living next door to a howler monkey. "People don't immediately recover after a time of great strain," he remarked briskly. "That was why I wanted you to stay here until you'd taken your degree."

"Because you'd guessed that I would crack up at the first hint of danger?" demanded Peveril in a voice which attempted, but failed, to sound matter-of-fact.

"Shall I put it this way?" compromised Hartismere. "I thought that your new independent and combative stance might not endear you to your superior officers. The Army tends to have high expectations concerning obedience and outward displays of respect – expectations which do not appeal to undergraduates."

"I know," muttered Ralph unhappily.

Since Hartismere had been privileged to hear Collingwood's unvarnished opinion of his latest recruit, Peveril's dejection required little explanation. The Vice-Master hesitated, before commenting. "I have informed Collingwood of your whereabouts."

Peveril turned green.

"Do I take it that you don't have permission to be in Cambridge?" When there was no reply, Hartismere sighed. "My dear boy, I had to tell Collingwood. He is the only one capable of making decisions concerning your assignment. You cannot just disappear."

"Will you visit me in the Tower as well as here, sir?" asked Peveril sarcastically.

"More usefully, you might explain in more detail why you ended up in Cambridge."

Peveril glanced at him. "This is a test, isn't it, sir? If I can't explain, you'll conclude that I'm still off my head; if I won't, then I can't be trusted."

"I shouldn't phrase it in quite that manner myself."

"And my help is needed?"

"It would be useful."

"So if I don't explain, and you send me back to London as unsuitable, the operation gets damaged, doesn't it?"

"In part, yes."

Ralph cursed inwardly. However much he loathed explaining himself, he could hardly put his feelings above his duty. "Sir, I don't want to make excuses for my actions."

"I'm not asking you to. I simply want to know what happened."

"It was Midge, that is, Miss Carrington."

"Go on."

"I had to get away before Woolf forced me to reveal who Miss Carrington was."

"Why Cambridge?"

"Well, sir, I couldn't think of anyone other than you who could help me to protect Midge. You see, sir," Ralph added uncomfortably, "even if I didn't think that I ought to protect a woman, Midge isn't anything like strong enough to be in gaol – and all her neighbours would cut her dead if she were even held on suspicion. It's all right for me. I don't care if the county cuts me. It's far harder for women; they've got no escape." Ralph glanced at Hartismere again. "Sir, I know I did the wrong thing, but what ought I to have done? Whatever I did, I was bound to let someone down."

"Trust your real C.O. a bit more in future."

"Yes, sir," replied Peveril in unconvinced tones.

"Why didn't you approach him?"

"He doesn't much like me – and it's my fault." Peveril's glance dropped. "You'd have every reason for not liking me either, sir, but you do like Midge, and you know that she's better at this sort of thing than I am. So I thought that you'd help, if only to make use of her brain."

"I'm glad that yours was working when you made that calculation."

Ralph fiddled with his watchstrap. "You could have accused me of cowardice, sir."

"In revenge for what you said? Well, Peveril, I don't happen to believe such an accusation."

Ralph looked acutely embarrassed. "I didn't believe what I said, sir, but that didn't stop me."

"True, but I am nearly three times your age." The Vice-

Master coughed, "Even I, when I was twenty, made the occasional remark which I later regretted, although those regrets tended to be that I had had shown confidence in another's scholarly judgement which was later shown to be flawed."

"Err... yes, sir."

The Vice-Master sounded amused. "My dear boy, do stop worrying about any temporary annoyance which I might have felt. More to the point, you will explain to your C.O. precisely what you have just told me."

"But, sir..."

"I am well aware that you do not wish to explain your motives, but Collingwood does not have time to waste trying to disentangle them."

"But..."

"That is a direct order."

Unconsciously, Peveril's eyes went to the Vice-Master's shoulders. Hartismere had been watching him. "I think you may safely assume, Lieutenant, that any war-substantive rank which I hold is superior to yours."

Peveril flushed. "I didn't... I wasn't..."

"You weren't challenging my authority and you didn't mean to appear offensive? You will also avoid those traits when you speak to Collingwood."

"Yes, sir." Peveril swallowed, aware that his father would have despised him for yielding so easily. And Robert had spent Christmas taunting him with the fact that murderers had no conscience. Nevertheless, Ralph added, "I beg your pardon, sir." Then a thought suddenly struck him.

"How did you know that Collingwood was my C.O.?"

Hartismere decided to risk the partial truth. "He spoke to me about you."

"Before or after I was seconded to him?"

"After."

"But why to you?" Peveril hastily attempted to explain his question, fearing that it sounded somewhat accusatory. "What I mean, sir, is that you recruited me into this me-"

"I recruited you into this mess," agreed the Vice-Master, as Peveril broke off too late to disguise his thoughts successfully.

"Yes," muttered Peveril, before continuing. "But, if he spoke to you recently, it must be because he's had second doubts about my recruitment. However, you were the person who first got me involved – will he really trust your judgement? After all, if you say that you got it wrong and I am unsuitable or untrustworthy, that'd be a black mark against you for having recruited me. Surely that will make you more inclined to say that I am reliable?"

"Good boy," applauded Hartismere. "You do appear to have grasped some essence of logic from your studies with the Dean." Then, seeing that Peveril appeared to be disinclined to allow this academic rivalry to distract him, Hartismere returned to more serious matters. "You are, of course, entirely correct, which is one reason why a recruiter ought never to be sent to investigate their recruit later on. For your part, I would strongly exhort you to be absolutely frank with Collingwood: no evasions and no equivocation, whether about your part or Miss Carrington's." He sighed, wondering whether he had made a dreadful mistake in practically forcing the boy into Intelligence. "At the very least you can expect a thundering reprimand from Collingwood, so don't lose your temper, either."

Peveril shrugged. "Doubtless I'll survive." Then his face contracted. "What about Midge? It's hardly fair if she gets dragged into this; the responsibility is entirely mine."

"Doubtless she'll survive, too."

Chapter Thirty-Four

The next day Collingwood arrived and went straight to Hartismere's rooms in Trinity, where Peveril was awaiting him. Collingwood's first thought when he entered was that it was damned casual of Peveril to be lolling up against the window-frame. 'I suppose he wants to indicate an insouciant contempt for what's likely to happen to him. Young fool.' With that, he spoke the officer's name sharply, causing Peveril to spin round from his unhappy scrutiny of the beauty of the creamy stone against a brilliantly blue sky.

"I suppose you know what you have done?" demanded Collingwood, in a tone of careful restraint.

Peveril could not bring himself to salute. There seemed no point when he was bound to be thrown out of Intelligence and, quite possibly, the army. However, a dim feeling that Hartismere would think it pretty poor form to ignore Collingwood's question led Peveril to reply in greater detail than he would normally have chosen.

"Yes. I've failed. I haven't discovered anything useful in the East Suffolks. I've probably alerted everyone to the fact that there's been an Intelligence agent loose in C Coy." He swallowed convulsively. "And I ran away."

Although Hartismere had warned Collingwood that Peveril was damnably unhappy, the major had not expected such bitter despondency – contemptuous arrogance had seemed a much more likely response. Moreover, the tremor in his voice suggested that Peveril was close to tears.

'If I push him,' calculated Collingwood, 'he'll break down and tell me what I want to know, but I'll destroy him in the process.' The major sighed, guiltily aware that it was not considerations of preserving a potentially useful agent which was stopping him from following the obvious course. Damn it, why the devil was he taking pity on a callous young hound like Peveril?

Making free with Hartismere's possessions, Collingwood poured a stiffish glass of brandy, then thrust it at Peveril. "Drink that," he commanded, before directing his attention to the nearest bookcase.

Peveril bent his head over the glass as he tried to regain control of himself. He toyed with the drink, swirling the amber liquid round and round, but not tasting it. Collingwood did not speak, apparently eagerly studying Hartismere's collection of works on early mediaeval French romances. Suddenly, Peveril stammered out a halting explanation.

"Woolf was furious because I wouldn't tell him who had been at the hospital with me. He called me a murderer. He said I ought to have been hanged. He said I could still be hanged over Poole's death. He threatened Miss Carrington. And when I got to Cambridge, I found an anonymous letter accusing me of being a murderer. I've... I've had them before. They all say that nobody believes I was innocent." Ralph forced himself to continue. "Woolf said that nobody would believe my excuses that I wasn't involved in getting Poole out of gaol. I... I lost my head."

Collingwood stiffened. He had no desire to have to prop up the boy's plummeting confidence – after all, had he wanted to spend his time wet-nursing callow subalterns, he could have stayed in a regular regiment. Nonetheless, he was prepared to admit that the police inspector had chosen a peculiarly insidious means to attack Peveril. "I should imagine that the jury at your trial followed the evidence with greater care than Woolf did, and you are hardly responsible for Poole's death."

Something about the quality of silence which greeted this remark led to Collingwood glancing more sharply at Peveril, before cursing under his breath. Ever since he had become sufficiently senior to command operatives, Collingwood had dreaded that a subordinate would go too far and leave him with a corpse on his hands. Surely Peveril, with his background, could not possibly have pushed Poole so hard that he killed himself?

"You aren't responsible, are you? Did you let Poole out after all?"

Peveril gave a harsh laugh. "Oh, I didn't kill him personally, if that's what you're worrying about, sir. Nor did I cause the explosion. But aren't I morally responsible? If I had acted a bit quicker when he got out of gaol, he wouldn't have ended up in hospital, where it was easier to get at him."

Collingwood leant back, apparently relaxing, but in actuality watching the younger man even more carefully. Acceptance of moral responsibility would be a damned good way of disguising the perturbation which Peveril might feel if he really did have blood on his hands. "You must forgive me," he remarked softly, "I was so surprised to hear you talking of morality that I naturally assumed that something was gravely amiss."

"I don't suppose ethics often enter into Intelligence deliberations – or police work," retorted Peveril. "Woolf seemed to think that it would be quite natural for an interrogator to end up croaking a witness."

"You tried your best with Denman, didn't you?" agreed Collingwood pleasantly.

Peveril's face turned so bloodless that Collingwood thought that he was going to faint. "Didn't you?" he repeated.

Clawing back some element of self-control, Peveril muttered, "I suppose Hall-Gordon told you."

"Yes. He was good enough to inform me of the details after you had left for Suffolk."

Recognising the implication that Collingwood might not have sent him to Newton if he had known the full history of his new recruit, Peveril glanced unconsciously at the doorway. Collingwood had no difficulty in interpreting this movement. "Hartismere doesn't think that you're inherently vicious. He was rather more concerned about your brother's sadistic tendencies."

This double shock deprived Ralph of speech. He became dimly aware that Collingwood was presenting him with a document. "Here is a copy of your brother's confession. He was behind those anonymous letters and, I gather, he arranged a few parcels." Collingwood's lip curled. "When put to the test, your brother didn't seem to have too much courage of his own. Whatever else you may have done, you haven't yet whined for mercy."

"But," Peveril stammered, "how did you…?"

"Your Miss Carrington had already asked Hartismere to look into the matter before you turned up out of the blue. Apparently, she had her suspicions concerning your plague of letters."

"She thought Robert wanted me dead."

"He didn't quite admit that," commented the major dryly, "but his confession makes for interesting reading. I shall leave you for a few minutes with it whilst I speak to Hartismere." He fished in his pocket, before adding casually, "And you may as well have your revolver back."

When Collingwood rejoined Hartismere, the Vice-Master raised his eyebrows interrogatively. "Well, what's he doing?"

"Awaiting sentencing," Collingwood growled. "I've given him the confession – and his revolver."

"Is that entirely wise?"

A grim smile crept over the major's face. "Don't worry, sir, I loaded it with blanks. And if he can't cope with waiting to hear what I'm going to do with him, he's not fit to be sent back to Suffolk."

"You reassure me, my dear fellow. I had feared that you had lost some of your cunning. And what, if I may enquire, do you intend to do with the boy?"

Collingwood looked harassed. "To be quite honest, I don't know. I can't risk him cracking up again if I send him back to Newton, but if he doesn't return, it will encourage all sorts of speculation as to what he was doing there. And he is very well-placed in C Coy – even if the local inspector seems to have done his best to threaten him with exposure." He frowned. "If I were judging the whelp as an individual, I'd feel sorry for him because he's in a cursed difficult situation."

"You shouldn't let sympathy for Peveril affect your decision." Hartismere gave a brief twist to his mouth, which might have been interpreted as a smile. "And if you are prompted by sympathy, bear in mind that the boy has hardly any self-respect left. If you take him off this assignment, he will have none."

"I agree; but is he robust enough to cope with a potentially dangerous situation?"

"If he isn't and he does crack up," commented Hartismere, "he may stir everything up so effectively that the truth is revealed. But he's got a much better chance of coping if he's not being driven half-mad by poisonous bilge. If he's been getting anonymous letters since the trial, I'm surprised he didn't crack up earlier."

"I wish I'd acted immediately you alerted me to the possibility," Collingwood admitted. "I was a bit too ready to assume that someone of Peveril's stamp wouldn't care."

"I don't suppose that you could have prevented Peveril's breakdown. Woolf's threats triggered his flight here and goodness knows when the letters he found at his solicitor's were posted." Hartismere glanced at the major appraisingly. "You might ignore the fact that Peveril visited his lawyer in order to draw out a fair amount of money."

"I'm not about to accuse him of attempting to desert," retorted Collingwood. "God knows what the young fool was planning to do, but I don't want a court martial for desertion any more than you do." He grunted forcefully. "Mind you, Robert Peveril can be thankful that he isn't already in khaki, because he definitely would have faced a court-martial for misusing His Majesty's Mails." He snorted. "At least I've wrecked his plans to adorn the Guards – he'll be damn lucky to get a commission of any sort."

Hartismere found it hard to care what happened to Robert Peveril, who sounded about as attractive as his late cousin. Ralph Peveril, however, was rather different.

"If you want to keep Peveril in position why don't you give him some support?"

"I can't send another man down – I've none spare."

"I wasn't thinking of a man."

Collingwood stared at Hartismere in horror. "You're not going to foist that Carrington woman on me."

"Why not? You've just said that you have no-one else. Everyone would suspect yet another outsider being posted to the East Suffolks, but no-one will suspect a girl who lives reasonably nearby. And Peveril trusts her. He will be far more open with her than with another operative."

Observing Collingwood's expression of distaste, Hartismere continued. "Don't forget that she's been instrumental in unravelling several murders and at least there's no question hanging over her loyalty. Not with her father in the army and her cousin serving – as I happen to know – in a rather discreet brigade in Alexandria."

"You get treason springing up in the most unlikely places," muttered Collingwood, who was starting to wonder whether there was a viper concealed in his own office, such was his lack of recent success. "And I don't approve of women in the Services."

"Nor do I, normally," agreed Hartismere calmly, "but we are not living in normal times and Miss Carrington is an able girl. It seems a mistake to let her brains lie idle, purely on the grounds of her sex, when she could be achieving something for her country."

"Damn it, Hartismere, the gel can't walk properly."

"I do not entirely see why her physical disability should imply that she does not have the mental capacity to contribute usefully to your current investigation."

Collingwood resumed pacing around the room. "You know perfectly well that I am not disparaging her brains. I never mixed much with Newnham gels when I was up, but I am aware of their reputation. But it would be deuced remiss of me to put a frail girl in the path of danger."

Hartismere suppressed the comment that Peveril wasn't exactly in tip-top condition either, and merely contented himself with his belief that Miss Carrington could be of significant use. "There isn't much point in cutting her out of something, the greater part of which she knows already. And if you're worried about security, she'll be a lot less likely to do something foolish if she thinks that she's part of a wider operation. If you don't involve her, she's perfectly capable of turning up in Newton on some exceedingly flimsy excuse which will merely alert anyone who has cause to be suspicious of newcomers." He shrugged. "Moreover, I would be prepared to risk a ten-pound note on the fact that Peveril will tell her what transpires today, no matter whether you order him not to speak to her. If you attempt to cut off all communication, either you will remove a possible additional source of ideas or you will force Peveril to break your standing orders."

"He doesn't seem to have found much difficulty in doing that so far," snorted Collingwood.

When Collingwood re-entered the room, Peveril had drunk the brandy, but was still looking very subdued. Robert's confession, fully admitting his loathing of Ralph and his desire to drive his brother into a breakdown, had shocked Ralph deeply. Moreover, Peveril cringed with embarrassment and humiliation at the thought of Collingwood reading Robert's accusations of cowardice. Indeed, the major's first words seemed to indicate that his thoughts were running on similar lines to Robert.

"Are you scared of being in danger if I send you back to Suffolk?" he demanded abruptly.

Peveril opened his mouth to say that he could not care less what happened to him when he suddenly remembered his promise to Hartismere to be open with Collingwood.

Collingwood was watching him closely. "I want the truth."

Peveril shrugged his shoulders, "I'm not exactly keen on the idea."

To Ralph's surprise, the major appeared pleased with this pusillanimous response. "Good, because I'm not inclined to employ death-or-glory boys. Their own lives may not be worth much, but they're all too inclined to throw away others'." Then, as if he regretted having implicitly shown any confidence in Peveril, he proceeded to issue very clear instructions as to what Peveril was to do and say when he returned to the East Suffolks.

At the end of the briefing, Peveril spoke hesitantly. "Sir, about the gaol being blown up…"

The major gave a grunt of displeasure. "The less said about that at the moment, the better."

"But…"

"Right now, Lieutenant, you need to concentrate on the deaths of Poole and Durrant, not whatever idiotic actions you and that girl have got up to. Do you understand?"

"Yes, sir, but…"

Collingwood smiled saturninely. "Oh, I shan't overlook it, Lieutenant. I shall go into the matter very fully when you return. Until then, I do not wish to discuss it."

Faced with such clear disapproval, and such a clear threat relating to the future, Ralph gave in.

"Yes, sir."

Chapter Thirty-Five

It was dark when Ralph approached Newton. Collingwood had insisted upon him waiting in Cambridge until certain confirmatory details of his alibi were established. Since this alibi consisted of Peveril having crashed his Alfa and ending up unconscious in hospital, Ralph was now driving an elderly Austin, which he was inclined to despise in comparison with his own motor. However, he was given an immediate demonstration of some unexpected benefits to the Austin when the corporal at the gate did not at once recognise who was behind the wheel. When he did, he seemed to have some difficulty in hiding his amusement as to Captain Thrigby's unglamorous new machine. Hetherley, on the other hand, made no effort to disguise his mirth.

"Dashed glad that you didn't write yourself off, Thrigby, but where did you dig up that ghastly contraption?"

"Beastly, isn't it," agreed Peveril, who had not enjoyed the Austin's lack of responsiveness on sharp corners. He glanced at his wrist-watch. "I'd better go and report. You might tell Trent to have some gin waiting for me."

"Goodwin got the wind up no end when you went missing."

"Why? Was Leake due to make another inspection and he didn't want to explain away a straying captain on top of Poole?"

Hetherley looked somewhat taken aback. "Steady on, old chap. Poole's dead."

Peveril angled for further reaction. "Sorry, but it can't have been much surprise. People don't tend to survive being shot at close range."

"Haven't you heard?" hissed Hetherley conspiratorially. "There's a rumour going round that he did himself in!"

"You can't believe rumour," scoffed Peveril.

"It's true! That inspector chappie haunted us for two days, wanting to check what else Poole could have been up to, other than killing Durrant." Hetherley shot a sly look at Peveril. "He seemed a bit worked up that you'd gone missing. We rather wondered what you'd been up to."

Peveril yawned. "How dull for him when he learns that I've

returned. He needs to understand that Survey Unit officers have better things to do than hang around waiting to talk to civilians."

Leaving Hetherley staring after him with raised eyebrows, Peveril presented himself at Goodwin's office. The major was looking distinctly harassed and had no time for Peveril's carefully prepared excuses.

"You shouldn't have been driving carelessly in the first place. Good God, man, you're meant to be carrying out important work, not lying around idle in hospital."

"Quite so, sir. That's what the police said."

"What? The police were involved?"

"Yes, sir. I gather I may have to answer a charge of dangerous driving."

"I suppose that means that you'll disappear off again – not that you've proved much use so far."

"The magistrate's court will demand my attendance, sir."

"Then I damned well hope that you get fined the maximum possible." Goodwin scowled angrily at him. "And you can damned well undertake some ordinary duties instead of playing around with your semaphores. Snellgrove will tell you what to do." He gave a sarcastic laugh. "Of course, you may feel that C Coy's needs are beneath the Survey Unit, but don't forget that we're currently down an officer – it won't harm you to help out."

Peveril saluted smartly and departed, wondering why Goodwin couldn't explain what he had to do. Was it because he wanted to teach the supposed Captain Thrigby his place by making him obey a lieutenant, or was it because only Snellgrove knew what had to be done?

When Peveril entered the mess, Chatham's tall presence soon revealed a third reason why Goodwin might be so eager to utilise his hypothetical experience.

"Hello, Thrigby, the grapevine said that you were in hospital."

"Car-smash. What are you doing here?"

Chatham grinned. "Waiting for my lord and master to finish gossiping with Snellgrove."

"Is Leake here? No wonder Goodwin seemed on edge."

A snigger greeted him. "Odds are being laid as to who'll be the new company commander."

"Why?"

"Lord, you C Coy types are dim. Haven't you noticed that Goodwin's useless?"

"Obviously I have. What I meant was, why do you expect a change now?"

"Leake's keen on paperwork being kept properly."

"Do you mean the missing rifles?"

"The missing rifles; the missing ammunition; the lack of records of decisions which were taken; the existing minutes of a meeting which can't have taken place." Chatham shrugged. "All that would have been bad enough, but three nights ago seven of us infiltrated the camp without being spotted by the guards."

Peveril's eyebrows rose. He had rather assumed that any slack attitudes towards guard-duty would have died with Poole. "Snellgrove's pretty hot on the importance of patrolling the perimeter."

"Not on Tuesday he wasn't. There either weren't any guards set on the section overlooking the Hart or they weren't doing their job properly."

"Perhaps they were bored and didn't spot you."

Chatham shot Peveril a contemptuous look. "You cannot possibly justify such incompetence. Do you suppose that's how the Wehrmacht operates?"

The following day, Peveril sought out Midge. "It's all right," he reassured her, "Collingwood authorised me to speak to you." Seeing Midge's surprise, he added, "He cursed me a bit, but Hartismere must have persuaded him not to throw me into the Tower."

"What about Goodwin?"

"Currently, I'm meant to be on my way to a planning session at HQ."

Midge regarded him anxiously. She could quite see that the imperatives of war meant that Ralph ought to be back in position, but he still looked far from well. "How are you?"

Peveril scowled. He had hoped that, with the discovery that Robert had deliberately co-ordinated the anonymous letters, he would no longer be troubled by nightmares. The previous night had proved his hopes wrong. However, he did not want to reveal his inadequacy to Midge, so he contented himself with passing on what he had discovered from conversations in the mess.

"Poole apparently killed himself. He died from an overdose of morphia and none of the nurses will admit to having administered it."

"That sounds like suicide," agreed Midge cautiously, "but I suppose it could have been an accident and the nurse is scared to own up."

A shudder ran through Ralph. "Her conscience will give her hell if that's the case."

"It isn't your fault."

"It is. I didn't stop Poole quickly enough to prevent him from being shot. And my exact plan was used to get him out of gaol. Someone else adopted it."

Midge stared at him, wondering what he meant. "But you told only me about it. How could anyone else have learned of it?"

Ralph sounded apologetic. "I'm not accusing you of telling anyone. It's my fault. I must have called out in a nightmare and given someone the idea. If I hadn't, Poole would still be snug in gaol with no access to morphia." His face twisted. "I suppose it narrows the traitor down to C Coy, but what a price to pay."

Midge winced. "Do you mean that only a C Coy member could have overheard you at night?"

"Yes." Ralph rapidly outlined his theory to Midge.

At the end of it, she nodded. "I think that you must be correct as to how the plan got out. But although C Coy may be the source of the leak, it doesn't mean that the traitor is there. What if someone simply talked about the strange thing he heard Capt Thrigby saying? That wouldn't make him a traitor."

"Trent gossips," admitted Peveril. "Blast. I thought I'd narrowed things down more."

"What did Collingwood think?"

Peveril sounded embarrassed. "I didn't tell him. At least, I tried to, but he shut me up."

"Why on earth did he do that?"

"At the time, I thought he was annoyed with me. Now I wonder if he suspected that I was about to confess to blowing up the gaol. You see, he couldn't ignore an admission of lawbreaking. He might be able to skate over misuse of military equipment since I'm actually in the army, but he'd have had to take action if one of his men admitted to blowing up a civilian building."

"But that means he doesn't know that there may be someone dubious at work in C Coy."

"Ye-es," agreed Peveril slowly, "but he did place me there. Maybe he has his suspicions. And you know, so the information won't be lost if..." His voice broke off as he realised that it would hardly be reassuring for Midge to suggest that he might be killed. "Look here, Midge, do you think that Poole's death was suicide? I know that the argument is that Poole realised that he was going to hang for the murder of Durrant and took the easy way out, but it seems a dashed sight too convenient."

"I think that you've got a point." Midge sighed. "It certainly makes sense that someone would prefer morphia to the noose, but Poole appeared to be an inveterate gambler. Surely he would take a chance that he'd be acquitted? And, from what he said to me, he didn't even seem to have realised that he'd go to gaol for smuggling."

"Maybe he later did realise, and that was why he killed himself."

Midge shook her head. "No. I'm sure he knew that he'd be gaoled for treason. Why would an additional charge make him kill himself?" She frowned. "I rather wish I'd asked Poole for more names of those who had gambled at Cosford's."

"But do you think that lots of people would have been put under pressure at the same time? It would be deuced risky – one of them might talk. Poole was probably chosen because he was the worst in debt." Suddenly Peveril frowned as a thought struck him. "Arrowsmith said that C Coy was useless because we had a Fascist in charge of guard duty and a murderer in charge of the armoury. Poole may not have been a murderer, but he could have been behind those missing rifles. And he could have acquired the ammunition as well."

"To pass on to Cosford to reduce his debt?" asked Midge. "It doesn't sound quite right to me."

245

"Because he couldn't possibly have pretended that selling guns in wartime was smuggling?"

"Not exactly." Midge made a gesture of frustration. "I don't know how to explain, but it doesn't sound wild enough. I'm sure he'd have contemplated a raid on HQ armoury for the excitement of it, but lifting rifles from the store which he was in charge of seems terribly tame." She shifted angrily. "If only I'd asked him more details."

"You couldn't have," stated Peveril abruptly. "The man was dashed ill. Of course you had to concentrate on the general outline. And you got him to talk, which was more than I did." A vision of what Poole had looked like in hospital, grey and ill, rose unwanted in Peveril's mind. "Poole must have gone through hell. Thank goodness he knew that you believed him." Ralph swallowed. "I ought to have. If anyone was in a position to understand, it was I, and I didn't. In fact, I wouldn't. He might still have been alive if I had been quicker to believe him."

"I don't think it would have made much difference."

"But it might have done." Ralph stared at the floor. He had never been so ashamed of himself and it didn't help that Midge was trying to find excuses for him. Nor would being ashamed bring Poole back to life. "I wish... Oh, what's the point?"

"Don't forget," Midge pointed out dryly, "that Poole was hardly a lily-white innocent. Think of what he admitted to me: he suspected that he was involved in espionage, but he continued to take money in return for failing to post guards. Do you think that a jury would have done anything other than convict him?"

"It's one thing a jury condemning him – and he'd probably have only been sentenced to imprisonment – it's quite another for me to interfere and cause his death."

"If you feel bad about it, think what the chap who actually shot him must feel," argued Midge hotly, before suddenly saying in a completely different voice. "I say, Ralph, what do you know about him?"

"About whom?"

"The LDV chap who shot Poole. Who was he?"

Peveril suddenly saw what Midge was thinking. "Do you mean that it may not have been an accident?"

"Precisely. You've said yourself that Poole was relatively safe in gaol – safer still if he had been transferred to a London prison. If you were involved in the supposed smuggling ring and you suddenly spotted the potential chief witness against you, what would you do – particularly if you were armed and Poole was not?"

"Assuming I was ruthless, I'd probably shoot him."

"It's reasonable to assume that a Nazi sympathiser is ruthless," commented Midge. "Tell me again what happened."

"I was face down in the shingle trying not to be spotted," protested Ralph. "I didn't see much. There were two of them, one called Dennis and another one who did the actual shooting. They asked Poole for his papers; he had none. Dennis shone his torch upon him and recognised him. Then the other chap shot him. It was all very quick." He shrugged. "The man who fired sounded quite pleased at hitting Poole, but you'd expect him to – he'd apparently just prevented a murderer from escaping."

"What about Dennis?"

"Equally natural, given the circumstances. The first chap said something like, 'Winged him, by God', and Dennis replied that he'd done more than wing him, he'd killed him. They certainly didn't break out into the Horst Wessel Leid."

"It certainly sounds quite plausible," Midge agreed. "All the same, don't you think it's worth checking up? Moreover, they didn't know that there was a witness, so they may have given a slightly different story to the police."

"I don't see why they should have," argued Peveril. "After all, they knew that Poole hadn't died and could thus contradict what they said. In any case, what they said seemed perfectly innocent – it certainly didn't arouse my suspicions at the time." He sighed. "But I'll look into it."

"I wish your C.O. had told you the name of the other operative. Then he could follow that lead while you concentrate on C Coy."

Ralph grimaced. "I can't say I entirely blame Collingwood. Look at it from his point of view. Here's a new, young recruit with no record in his favour. He doesn't achieve anything – unsuccessful; he shows off about his mission to a girl –

indiscreet; he may have Fascist sympathies – unreliable. What would you do in Collingwood's place? Risk exposing another operative's cover? Anyway, I'm not sure I want to know who it is. Imagine if I let that out in a nightmare as well."

"You didn't say anything about your mission when you were lying drugged in hospital," countered Midge. "The only thing you kept talking about was Charon and quoting from Virgil."

"I must have confused you with your cousin," suggested Ralph, attempting to change the subject. "He got fed up with me littering the courts of Trinity and doing no work – I must have wanted to impress you with my grasp of Book Six of the *Aeneid*."

Midge tried to follow Ralph's lead. "Just as well it was only me, then; Charon used a pole, not oars."

Peveril frowned as he tried to capture an elusive memory. "I know that, but where have I seen a boat with oars in it recently?"

"You can't have. All oars have to be stored safely away from boats."

"But I have, Midge, honestly I have. I can remember lifting the boat, seeing the oars underneath, and thinking it was a bit odd that they were there." Suddenly Peveril looked very downcast. "Maybe I imagined it all. After all," he added bitterly, "I'm a madman, aren't I? That's what you think, isn't it?"

"I don't, but it's what Robert wants you to think," agreed Midge cunningly.

Peveril sat up. "I'm damned if I'll let that bastard drive me mad." He suddenly recollected Midge's presence. "Sorry, Midge, I shouldn't have sworn in front of you."

Midge appeared unmoved. "You should have heard what Dr Hartismere said." She risked a slight grin. "I didn't understand him because he chose to express himself in mediaeval French, but his tone was unmistakable."

Peveril's expression suddenly cleared. "I *didn't* imagine it," he declared triumphantly. "I saw it on the banks of the Hart." He turned eagerly to Midge to explain. "I went to look at where Durrant's body was found, took a wrong turning and then decided to head upstream along the riverbank in the hope of striking the path. I saw the boat, and the oars were stashed underneath it." He gave an embarrassed laugh. "I got stuck in mist shortly after and I forgot about the boat – I was a bit too carried away thinking about the Underworld."

Midge ignored quite why Ralph had been contemplating Pluto's realms when he was supposedly investigating the site of Durrant's murder. The possibilities inherent to his discovery of the boat were much more valuable than speculations as to the effect of mist upon his mind. "I say, Ralph, that boat might have been used by the murderer. I can't think why else it would have its oars."

"I assumed that someone was lazy about putting them away – it must be quite some distance to carry them to the hamlet I saw."

Midge shook her head. "I doubt it. A man further south got fined a hefty sum for leaving his oars out for just one evening. Everyone has been extra careful since then, especially now that coast-watchers have been asked to check that sort of thing."

Peveril nibbled his lip thoughtfully. "I see what you mean. It's certainly rather odd. Do you think that one of the villagers had intended to go out in it that morning, noticed the mist coming in, and changed his mind?"

"The tides would be wrong for fishing. And the fisher-folk know all about mist – I don't suppose that any of them would have thought about going out with fog threatening."

There was a pause. Peveril knew what he ought to say next. He ought to volunteer to investigate whether the boat was still there and whether there were any traces of blood inside it – his original cursory glance had been dictated by mild curiosity, not investigative rigour. However, he shuddered at the thought of returning to the bleak mud and bleached reeds, so reminiscent of his nightmares.

Midge glanced at Ralph, noticing that he had resumed the pinched, white expression which he had worn in hospital. Clearly, something was disturbing him and, since she had no desire to precipitate another breakdown, she moved off the subject of the mysterious boat.

"Why have you got to go to HQ?" she asked. "Surely planning is Goodwin's job?"

"Goodwin doesn't know what the word means," grunted

Peveril contemptuously. "He thinks that waiting until things happen and then scurrying around trying to find a solution counts as planning."

"Even so, he's the company commander. Why has he sent you?"

Peveril gave a short laugh. "Presumably he expects Leake to deliver a reprimand for C Coy's incompetence and he'd rather that I had my knuckles rapped, not him." He shrugged. "At least it gives me the chance to sniff around HQ for a bit. Goodwin told me I didn't have to be back until four, so I'll have a bit of spare time."

Chapter Thirty-Six

Peveril's suspicions that C Coy was unpopular at HQ were confirmed when he reported to Col. Leake. However, before the colonel reached the matter of how unfit C Coy was to repel raids, he turned to the particular question of Thrigby's recent absence from duty. After having questioned Peveril in great detail, he administered a blistering rebuke on the subject of idiots who drove fast cars to the hazard of their own lives and others.

"An officer appearing in a police-court, indeed! You are a disgrace to the regiment."

Although Peveril might have been justified in pointing out that he was only on temporary secondment, so unlikely to bring the regiment into disrepute, his main concern was whether he had convinced Leake that his story was true. The colonel had sounded beastly suspicious. Did he suspect that 'Thrigby' had treated himself to some extra leave? Or did Leake think that Thrigby wasn't quite what he seemed? But if so, why draw attention to the fact by questioning him at such length? An unpleasant thought struck Peveril. If Leake investigated what had happened, that police contact of Collingwood's wouldn't be able to maintain his story – and the nurses at the hospital might let out that he wasn't brought in on a stretcher covered in blood. Peveril swore inwardly. He was going to have to be damned careful.

The meeting closed with Leake's caustic remark that he trusted that C Coy would prove to be more effective on this larger mock raid than they had on smaller events. Peveril swallowed this insult, hoping that he had taken sufficient notes to be able to explain to Goodwin – or, more likely, Snellgrove – exactly what the latest exercise entailed. In the meantime, he ought to attend to his real mission. Following the rest of the officers into the mess bar, he spotted Arrowsmith from B Coy. He groaned. Presumably this was where he ought to make a frank, manly apology and hope that he could get something out of Arrowsmith.

Unfortunately for Peveril, Arrowsmith did not seem to have read the sort of books in which frank, manly apologies were greeted with a hearty handshake and pledges of future goodwill. Instead, he looked Peveril up and down, before remarking with withering contempt, "If attempting to murder a chap for making a joke is the sort of behaviour which you normally favour, then I'd prefer you to seek the other end of the bar. You may think that leaping at people without warning is reasonable; I consider it treacherous and cowardly."

"And clawing at someone's face is to fight like a barbarian," retorted Peveril, furious at Arrowsmith's insult. Suddenly remembering that he was pompous Thrigby, he added, "So is refusing to accept an apology." With that, he swung round and stalked off, ignoring a thoughtful look from Chatham.

Although 'Capt. Thrigby' was meant to take luncheon at HQ, Peveril had no stomach for a meal, particularly not if he were going to have Arrowsmith and Chatham glaring at him all through it. In fact, he suspected that leaving was by far the safest course. Another fight with Arrowsmith would be disastrous – he couldn't possibly risk the sort of row which would occur if Col. Leake caught him striking a fellow-officer. But he had no desire to listen to anyone making jokes at Midge's expense.

As he started the Austin, Peveril looked rather disgustedly at it. After the Alfa, the Austin really was unimpressive. Then he reproached himself. 'I don't suppose there were many motors which Collingwood could impound at a moment's notice in Cambridge.' He suddenly grinned. 'I wonder which don I've left bereft at the loss of his cherished vehicle. I do hope it's the Dean.'

Although Peveril managed to keep his thoughts tolerably occupied on the way to Harting Magna, when he parked the Austin he was conscious that his hands were shaking in a way which could not be accounted for by a combination of an elderly motor and the jolting of the track.

'Arrowsmith's quite correct to call me cowardly,' he thought. 'What is so devilish dangerous about this little number? All I have to do is go down the track, seek out the wretched boat, look at it, and come away immediately. I don't even have to try to find where Durrant's body was found.' He glanced round him. 'Nor is there much more than a light sea haze.'

Despite such cheering observations, Ralph found that he could not move. Reminding himself that men in the trenches were shot for funking attacks, he forced himself out of the car. Trying to reassure himself that it would take him less than half an hour to investigate the rowing-boat and then return to the relative safety of the Austin, Ralph set off at a brisk trot down the path. He followed the track down towards the river, wondering whether it was a bad sign that he did not recognise any of the twists and turns.

'The problem is, all of this damned marsh looks the same to me,' he cursed. 'Nothing but reeds, mud, and stagnant water. That'll teach me to think that I'd be better off in France. I can't begin to imagine what it must have been like in the trenches last war with a load of high explosive going off round your ears.' He shuddered, conscious how little effort it took to snuff out life. Then he attempted to pull himself together. 'I think I've got to scramble down here and then follow the bank round.' He suited actions to words, looking with distaste at the grey stains which had appeared on his hands. 'Stop thinking about Charon, you fool, and get on with your job. Nobody made you come here today, so it's your own fault if you don't like it. And it's only mud, so it won't drive you mad.'

Since the tide appeared to be coming in, Peveril was forced to wade through ankle-deep water in order to round a bend in the river. Then with profound relief he spotted the dinghy, drawn up on the bank. 'At least it's still there,' he thought, unwilling to admit that he had started to wonder whether he had imagined the whole thing. 'A quick look to check the oars, and then I'd better hotfoot it back before the tide rises much further.'

For a second time, Peveril knelt down on the mud and raised the boat enough to look inside. "Oars!" he remarked triumphantly, before trying to fish them out. However, they were too far under for him to do so. He eyed the mud with revulsion, tightened his belt round his trench-coat, and then lay at full stretch, holding the boat up with one hand whilst he scrabbled for the oars with the other. He had just grasped the closer oar when he heard a sucking sound near his ear. Twisting round to check that the tide had not suddenly crept right up to the bank, he stared with shock at a pair of heavy sea-boots which were planted on the mud. As his eyes travelled upwards, he took in a weather-beaten figure and, much more ominously, a shotgun pointed straight at him.

"You take your hands slowly out of there and put 'em on the sand where I can be a-seein' 'em."

Ralph unwillingly obeyed. He momentarily considered trying to snatch up a handful of mud and throw it in the face of his assailant, but he had little doubt that he would be blown to pieces long before the mud would reach the target.

"No, don't you be a-tryin' to get up. You lie on that there mud whilst you be explainin' to me what you be up to."

Staring into the muzzles of the shotgun, Ralph wished that he were not lying splayed out like some sacrifice before an altar. It would be just as dangerous if he were to be standing up, but somehow it would feel less as if he were already dead. The icy damp was creeping through his clothing and it would be infernally easy for the stranger to snap his neck with one stamp of those heavy sea-boots.

"Right, mister, who be you, and what are you doin' a-spyin' round here?"

"I'm not spying."

"No? Then why be you a-crawlin' around in the mud like a swift?"

Ralph attempted to adopt an air of authority, although it hardly fitted with his current undignified position. "Dash it all, man, you must know perfectly well that there's an order about not leaving oars with boats. It's part of my duty to check up on things like that."

"Is it really, mister? Be you some kind of expert sent to teach us our trade?"

Sensing a contemptuous undercurrent to the man's tone, Peveril played safe. "No, of course I'm not, but I've no intention of leaving a boat lying around in a condition which might aid the enemy. Is it yours?"

"It can't be aidin' the enemy."

"What the devil do you mean?"

"Ever heard of rowlocks, mister? It be hard to row a boat

with nothin' to hold the oars."

Peveril's eyes flickered momentarily towards the dinghy. The man was quite correct. Nothing protruded over the rim of the boat. "I didn't notice that. I was concentrating on the oars."

"Now why were that? Were you a-plannin' to sail off to Germany?"

"Don't be ridiculous. I'm not a spy. I'm attached to the East Suffolks."

The sailor spat on the ground. "That for the East Suffolks." He spat again. "And I don't reckon you're in 'em. They don't speak Italian in the East Suffolks."

"*Italian?*" repeated Peveril in amazement. "Nor do I."

The unknown laughed. "I've seen you here afore. You were a-callin' out in Italian."

Ralph's face flamed in humiliation as he realised what else the man must have heard. Then it occurred to him that he was potentially in an extremely dangerous position. If this chap decided to shoot a spy, there was nothing to stop him – the river even presented an easy method of disposing of his body. "I wasn't calling out in Italian, I was singing to pass the time whilst I was lost in the mist."

"That weren't English."

"No, of course not. I was singing in Latin. Church Latin. That's what I learned to sing when I was young and in a chapel choir."

The frown on the sailor's face darkened. "Romish stuff? I don't hold with that."

Peveril rolled his eyes in exasperation. Of all damn silly ends, he was going to be shot because of bigoted religious superstition. "For God's sake let me get off this blasted mud and take you back to C Coy if you're so suspicious."

The sailor eyed him thoughtfully. "Roll onto your front and hold your hands behind your back." When Peveril made no move, he gestured with his shotgun. "You heard me."

With the utmost reluctance, Peveril obeyed. Glancing sideways he saw the sea-boots approach. Wondering if he were about to have his head blown off, Ralph was momentarily relieved by the sight of a piece of rope dangling down to the mud. Surely that meant that the stranger wanted to tie his hands together and prevent him from fighting back? As Ralph's wrists were wrenched behind him, the stranger thrust his knee into the small of his captive's back. The man's weight drove Ralph's head down into the mud and he jerked instinctively upwards, but in vain. The burly seaman was heavier and stronger than he was, and Ralph had no chance of throwing off his assailant. He struggled desperately, but the last thing Ralph felt was his head being thrust back into the thick, choking mud.

Chapter Thirty-Seven

After Ralph left, Midge tried to get on with her work. She was conscious that she was falling behind in what she needed to cover, but it was difficult to concentrate when she was worrying about both Ralph and John. If it came to that, she wished she knew how to comfort her aunt. It was John's birthday soon, and she had surprised Alice with tears in her eyes that morning. It seemed heartless to be entertaining Ralph when Alice must be worried sick about her son – presumably the sight of a young man in uniform merely reminded Alice of the dangers which John faced.

After lunch, Midge decided that it would do her good to have an afternoon nap. However, she had hardly lain down when her aunt tapped at her door and entered.

"Midge, are you fit to see Mrs Serring? She's turned up and seems determined to speak to you."

Midge groaned.

"You shouldn't have encouraged her," stated Alice, before taking pity on Midge's obvious tiredness. "I did try to put her off, but she started muttering about attempts to prevent her from talking. It seemed unfeeling to send her away without letting her speak and she insisted it had to be to you." She shrugged. "I suppose it may make her feel better if she can talk about her husband – she was clearly devoted to him, and it was such a tragic death."

When Midge entered the drawing-room Mrs Serring was pacing backwards and forwards.

"Ah, you have come. Good. I have information for you."

"About the dates you gave me? Have you remembered something else?"

"No. I have seen something else."

"Seen?"

Mrs Serring looked round stealthily, before drawing close to Midge. "Yes," she hissed in Midge's ear. "I have seen lights."

"Where?"

"Where there should be no lights." Mrs Serring glanced round again, as if trying to reassure herself that no-one else was listening. "There was a light flashing near Harting Magna."

"Harting Magna?" exclaimed Midge.

"Ssh. It is not good to speak of it."

"When did you see it?"

"Yesterday, late at night."

Midge made a rapid calculation. In a country district, everyone would be asleep by this point, unless they were coast-watchers or a soldier on guard. "Are you sure it didn't come from the camp?"

"Quite." Mrs Serring leaned closer again. "It was at the wrong angle. It could not have come from the camp."

"And in any case they ought to be observing a strict blackout," commented Midge thoughtfully. "Have you seen it before?"

"No." Suddenly Mrs Serring's face crumpled. "My Dickie saw lights where there should be none. Since he died I look for his murderers. I, too, look for lights where there should be none."

'And,' thought Midge to herself, 'I bet you don't much care whether you get killed, either.' Trying not to appear patronising in the face of grief, she answered rapidly. "Your discovery sounds very important. Did you take an exact note of where and when you saw it?"

"It was exactly at five minutes before twenty-four o'clock, but I do not know precisely where." She sounded upset. "The signal lasted less than three minutes and I cannot take compass bearings in the dark. I could not work out where, but it was nearer the sea than Harting Magna."

"How could you tell?"

"I could see the surf where the sea meets the shore. The light was beyond that, but not much beyond."

"Where were you?"

"I have a rowing-boat."

Midge was shocked. "But, Mrs Serring, the tide is treacherous by the bluff. You might get caught in it. If the boat capsized, you would drown."

The widow shrugged fatalistically. "That is where my Dickie died. If I die there, then I shall die in his arms."

Midge swallowed. "Err... have you told the police what you

have seen?"

"Pah! When I tried to tell them that my Dickie was murdered, they took no interest. They say that I am the foreigner, the Jew. If Hitler were in my front room they would still not believe me."

Midge thought rapidly. "You mustn't keep going out in your boat."

Mrs Serring shot her a look of angry despair. "You are trying to stop me. I trusted you. I thought that you would warn the right people.

"Honestly, Mrs Serring, I'm not trying to stop you. And I will pass on your warning."

"You do not mean it. You are just the same as the rest – you think I am mad. Do you know what the policeman said? 'Your sufferings have turned your brain.' You think the same. But if I am mad why do I not see the lights every night? Why have I seen them only once?"

Midge made a gesture of protest. "I don't think that you are mad. But if there is someone signalling to the enemy, it is vital that they don't realise that they've been spotted. I'd be terribly suspicious if I saw you sculling around down-river of my signalling point. In fact, I'd be so suspicious that I'd either start signalling from somewhere else or I'd stop altogether. We can't trap the signaller if we don't know where he is."

There was silence as Mrs Serring considered Midge's argument. "You have ten days," she eventually replied. "Then I begin my watch again."

When Mrs Serring had left, Midge stared out across the garden. 'Unless she really is off her head and is imagining things, those lights must be suspicious. I cannot think of any innocent explanation. Everyone knows that they're not meant to show any light at all by night, and flashes suggest signalling. It must be a pre-arranged agreement.' Suddenly she cursed. 'What an idiot I am. Why didn't I ask her whether the flashes were in Morse? Mind you, I suppose it would be in some sort of code, so it would be impossible to read.' Midge shivered. 'If someone's signalling out to sea, they must be trying to contact a U-boat. It's vile to think of one lying off-shore.' She shivered again at the thought of how much more vile it would be if there were an entire invasion force silently approaching the coastline. 'Is Mrs Serring's news sufficiently important to justify alerting Major Collingwood? Or should I wait until I can tell Ralph? I haven't any actual proof and nothing may happen.' She gulped. 'But what if I'm wrong and something happens much sooner?'

Suddenly deciding to take action, Midge found her purse and went downstairs. Fortunately, Evans was in the kitchen and agreed immediately when Midge asked him to drive her to the train station. Guiltily conscious that she was going to use up petrol on something which might prove a waste of time, Midge sought out Mrs Carrington.

"I need to go into Ipswich, Aunt Alice."

"Am I to assume that this desire is connected with Mrs Serring's visit?"

"Not exactly." Midge hesitated. "I want to go to the hospital."

Alice sounded concerned. "My dear, are you in pain? Shall I ask the doctor to call in?"

Midge blushed. "No, it's not me. You don't need to worry."

"I think I do. I don't like you travelling after dusk on your own and it's bound to be dark by the time you return." Alice sighed. "I suppose you'd rather I didn't come with you?"

Midge realised with surprise that the idea of company was reassuring. She didn't think that anyone would guess what she was up to, but somehow it was all too easy to imagine what might happen in an empty railway carriage if someone did suspect her actions. "It would be terribly dull for you," she pointed out, "and, I'm afraid, I might have to abandon you at the hospital."

"Would your uncle approve if he knew what you were doing?"

Thinking about her uncle's early days as an investigative reporter, Midge nodded. "He'd do exactly the same thing." She smiled gratefully at her aunt. "You're jolly decent not asking what I'm doing."

"Frankly, Midge, I can think of so many awful possibilities that I'd rather not know. Occasionally, ignorance is both bliss and useful."

By the time that they reached the hospital, Midge was rather concerned. The journey had been tiring and now she had to change a very vague plan into a useful operation. Moreover, it was a plan which depended almost entirely upon her powers of persuasion – and what mood Matron Roberts was in.

No-one paid any attention to Midge as she made her way through the hospital and it occurred to Midge that her crutches gave her the perfect excuse to be in the place. It was only as she approached Ward F that anyone spoke to her.

"You must have come the wrong way. The consulting rooms are at the other end of the building."

Midge smiled at the speaker – an unhappy-looking nurse probationer, whom she thought she recognised from her previous visit. "This is Ward F, isn't it?"

"Yes."

"May I speak to Matron Roberts, please?"

The probationer glanced nervously behind her. "Well, I don't know, miss. She's busy and I'm not really sure."

A commanding voice came from behind a curtain. "What is the problem, Nurse?"

"Someone wants to speak to you, Matron."

There was a rustle and Matron Roberts appeared, clearly displeased at being disturbed in this manner. Then she saw who was waiting and her expression changed to one of slightly menacing interest. "Ah. I think I might find time for you. Come this way."

Midge observed the probationer staring at her in stupefaction. Clearly, Matron Roberts did not normally react to interruptions in this manner. However, the senior nurse showed Midge into a small room, before closing the door firmly and turning to Midge.

"Well?"

Midge tried to sound confident. "You will have recognised me from my last visit, Matron, and thus you will know that I had authorisation from London to speak to your patient."

"And?"

"Since he died in rather strange circumstances, I was very

much hoping that you might spare me a little time to discuss the matter."

"That is a very odd request."

"I know it probably seems like that, but I shouldn't be wasting your time unless I thought it was important." Midge sighed, unsure what else she could say without giving too much away.

Unexpectedly, the nurse gestured towards Midge's walking-sticks. "What's behind those?"

"Infantile paralysis."

A flicker of what could have been sympathy crossed the older woman's face. "I thought it might have been. We saw quite a lot of it at St Jude's, where I trained. Poverty made it worse."

Midge winced, unsure whether the nurse disapproved of her clothes and her accent. "I was lucky. My aunt and uncle were very good to me."

"We had children in from Hoxton and Bow who ended up in iron lungs."

"And some," added Midge softly, "will have died."

"Yes. So why are you here?"

"Poole died."

"Yes."

"I gather it may have been suicide."

The matron bristled. "A very selfish act, I call it, after all the effort Mr Taphill put into saving him!"

Midge recognised a note of admiration in the nurse's voice. "Is Mr Taphill a very fine surgeon?"

"Outstanding. He's gives everything to his work. Why, he operated on Mr Poole in the middle of the night and stayed by him until he was sure that he would recover. The patient would have died if it hadn't been for Mr Taphill's skill."

"So Mr Taphill must have been disappointed that Mr Poole decided to take his own life?"

Matron Roberts nodded. "He said it just went to show that you could never tell what a man was thinking, and that he was glad he'd never wanted to be a psychiatrist."

"What made him say that?"

"I gather that the patient had made a joke that he'd stand a better chance of avoiding the hangman now that he'd been shot. Mr Taphill thought that he was in reasonable spirits."

Midge frowned. "The police think that your patient killed himself because he knew he was going to be hanged for murder. Those words don't sound as if he were certain that he'd hang."

"Perhaps not."

Midge risked a direct question. "You're a nurse; you'll have dealt with people who wanted to take their own lives. Did you think that Mr Poole was so low and depressed that he had decided to kill himself?"

The matron hesitated. Then she shrugged. "He didn't have the air of gloom I'd have expected. In fact, I'd mentally marked him down as one to cause trouble with the nurses when he got a bit better. Some of our young girls are far too impressionable."

Midge suddenly made a connection. "Like the probationer I was talking to?"

"Yes."

"I thought that she had been crying."

"Why people cannot keep their emotions separate from their work is beyond me," snapped Matron Roberts. "If those silly girls knew what men were really like they wouldn't be so ready to fall for them."

Diagnosing a failed love affair in the past, Midge continued to fish for information. "Of course, men behave differently in hospital when they are in pain and in need of comfort. That would be why Poole managed to seem attractive, despite the fact that he was accused of a very serious crime."

"Glamour," declared the nurse, with a snort. "Girls pay far too much attention to glamour and not enough to solid virtues which would lead to a happy marriage. And with all these young men in uniform it simply makes matters much worse. Any scoundrel can appear a hero."

Midge nodded sympathetically, before inventing an outright lie. "The police say that someone must have been very careless and left a syringe of morphia by the bed where Poole could get hold of it."

Matron Roberts stiffened. "Do they indeed? Well, the police are wrong. Whatever happens in other hospitals, in my ward all drugs are kept under lock and key until they have to be administered."

"Then how did Poole get hold of the morphia?"

The nurse suddenly looked very drawn and worried. "He was given the appropriate injections at 7 a.m. and noon – they were recorded in his notes. He was due for another injection at 5 o'clock."

Midge frowned in thought. "He was tired and in pain when I left him just after three. Could he have persuaded someone to give him an injection?"

"Not without access to the supplies, and only I – and the evening matron – have the keys."

It didn't seem terribly credible to Midge that a nurse would have acquired the morphia the previous evening. Nor did she think it likely that a nurse had the necessary knowledge to pick a lock, but she asked all the same. "Had the lock of the drugs cabinet been tampered with?"

"There was no sign of it and the amount of morphia was as it should have been, less a dose which that silly girl dropped on the floor and had to dispose of because the syringe broke."

"Did you tell the inspector that?"

"Yes, but he was so full of the note he'd found that he wouldn't listen to what I was saying. He seemed to think that a hospital was awash with drugs, available for anyone to help themselves."

"What note?"

"It said 'I wish I hadn't done it'."

"In the patient's handwriting?"

"I don't know. Presumably, or the inspector would have come back to ask more questions."

"Did Poole have any other visitors that day?"

"No."

"Could Poole walk by himself?"

"No."

Midge frowned. "Forgive me for saying this, but if Poole couldn't walk, someone must have brought him the morphia. If he didn't have a visitor, then it must have been a nurse – or someone dressed as a nurse."

"I'm sure a strange nurse would have been spotted."

Midge summoned up her courage. "Matron, you are obviously extremely conscientious in regard to any drugs on the ward. Is every ward as well-run as yours?"

The nurse stared at Midge unhappily. It was one thing knowing that Robina Smith was careless and that old Mr Tasker occasionally slipped into the dispensary and helped himself when his arthritis was playing up, but it was quite another thing to tell an outsider who couldn't possibly understand the closeness of a hospital and how you had to support each other. But that young man had died. And if one of her nurses had helped him to die – whether accidentally or deliberately – then the sooner the woman was discovered the better. But it would be simply awful if it did turn out to be Probationer Rivers; and who else was likely? None of the others was so upset – and none of the others had known Poole. Only someone who had cared for him would have helped him to cheat the gallows.

Midge tried again. "It could be important. It's a question of professionalism, as well as justice."

Matron Roberts winced inwardly. She knew about questions of professionalism. All those years ago, Archie had wanted to know about the influential Member of Parliament she'd been nursing. When she'd said she couldn't talk about the man, that had been the end of her relationship with Archie. She'd been stupid leaving London over it, but she'd never wanted to see or hear of Fleet Street again. She gave a mental shrug. Goodness knows what organisation this woman belonged to, but truth must out. A nurse who began to make judgements of life or death was a danger.

"It might be possible to acquire morphia in another ward, but Mr Poole could not have walked there."

"Thank you." Midge hesitated. "I don't suppose I could speak to any of the nurses who were on duty when Mr Poole died?"

"No, absolutely not."

The nurse's reaction was so strong that Midge immediately realised that she suspected somebody. Was it the tearful probationer? And, if she couldn't talk to her, was there anything else she could persuade Matron Roberts to tell her?

"Why didn't the Ipswich police do the investigation?"

"When I showed Mr Woolf in to question the patient just before five, I realised that the patient was dead. With Mr Woolf there in his uniform, nobody thought about calling the Ipswich police. In fact, there was no reason to call in the police to begin with – we all thought that the patient had died from the effect of his wound. It was only the autopsy which revealed that morphia was the cause of death." The nurse shrugged. "Then I overheard the Ipswich inspector telling Mr Woolf that Ipswich had more than enough on their hands and that, since he knew all the background, he could investigate Poole's death."

"Pass the parcel," suggested Midge.

"Yes." Matron Roberts stared at Midge combatively. "Normally, I shouldn't dream of talking about a patient to an outsider."

"I am sure that you wouldn't and I am very grateful that you have been so accommodating. My people in London will be very pleased to have this information." Feeling awful at having misrepresented herself so much, Midge added impulsively, "I can see it's a perfectly ghastly situation for you, and it must have upset you no end."

"Yes."

Suddenly a thought struck Midge. "Don't forget, morphia ampoules are kept in army camps as well as hospitals."

A wave of relief washed over the matron's face. "If only it could be that." She suddenly sounded much more confident. "I'm afraid that you will have to go now. I need to get back to the ward."

As Matron Roberts shepherded Midge away, it was obvious that she did not want to run the risk of Midge talking to any of the nurses. Midge consoled herself that she might be able to track the probationer down later; there was no point in antagonising anyone at this point.

While Midge was slowly making her way down the corridor, she observed a man going into a ward and frowned. Surely he looked familiar, but how could Cosford be wheeling a trolley in Ipswich Hospital? Deciding to wait, Midge sank down onto a convenient bench. Five minutes later, the man came out of the ward and started walking towards her. As he came close, their eyes met.

"Good afternoon, miss. I didn't expect to see you again so soon."

Midge cursed. It was annoying being so recognisable. "I have to come to the hospital for check-ups."

"Mmm."

Unsure what this noise meant, Midge glanced at Cosford's trolley. "You've got a good selection of books there."

"Wednesday's early-closing day at Newton, so I come down here. It helps people in pain to have something to distract them."

"The children must be particularly glad to see you."

For a moment, the bookseller seemed to stiffen. "I can't visit them, miss. The little ones have no money. It wouldn't be fair."

"Of course. How silly of me." Midge pointed to one volume. "I'll take that book on archaeology, if you're allowed to sell things in the corridors."

"Yes, miss. Plenty of people get bored waiting around."

Once the transaction was finished, Cosford nodded politely, before pushing his trolley along the corridor. Midge watched in fascination as he entered Ward F. Wednesdays were early-closing at Newton and Cosford came every week. That meant that he had been in the hospital on the day when Poole had died. And, judging from the way in which he walked in and out of wards, he was so well-known that nobody took any notice of him. Had she just been talking to Poole's killer?

Chapter Thirty-Eight

Slowly, Ralph became aware of two things. First, that he could breathe again, and, secondly, that someone was thumping him on the back. He coughed and spat out a lump of mud. He tried to wipe his mouth, but discovered that his hands were tied behind his back. His captor pulled him upright and unceremoniously dragged him over to the dinghy.

"You sit on that there boat and answer my questions."

Ralph opened his mouth to protest, but ended up coughing again. The sailor laughed.

"Netted fishes always make life worse for theirselves by strugglin'."

"I'm not a fish. I'm an officer in His Majesty's Forces and you will suffer unless you release me immediately."

This threat seemed to have no effect on the stranger. "Not a fish? Then you be tellin' me what I want to know or I'll knock you on the head and throw you into the sea to drown."

"Look, if you don't believe me, why don't you hand me over to Col. Leake at battalion HQ? He knows who I am."

"He do, do he? But he's not heard you a-singin' in Italian. I have. You need to prove to me who you might be. You can start by tellin' me about the East Suffolks."

Peveril stared at him for a moment. The man's accent was obviously local, and both officers and men regularly fraternised with the locals. Surely it wouldn't be giving away important information if he stated who commanded various sections? It might even help to prove that he wasn't some strange Italian spy.

"Col. Durrant was in command, but it's now Col. Leake."

"And who be the other officers?"

"In C Coy there are Snellgrove, Hetherley and myself. Major Goodwin is the Company Commander."

"What about Lt. Poole?" demanded the sailor.

Peveril groaned inwardly. He would much prefer to break the news of someone's death when he didn't have a shotgun directed at his stomach. But maybe the man knew already and was testing him. "Err... Poole... well..."

"Go on."

"He died last week in hospital."

"How?"

"He was shot."

The shotgun wavered momentarily. "So you don't be an escaped prisoner?"

"No. I've told you what I am. It's time this farce ended."

"An' what if I told you that I be a German spy?"

"You hardly sound German," snapped Ralph.

"Ah, but maybe I be a-takin' their gold."

Realising that in this case he had no chance of escaping, Peveril felt a onrush of blinding fury. He had achieved absolutely nothing and his drowned body would probably be attributed to an accident. Midge would assume that he was a fool who had been trapped by the tide. Without allowing himself to think further, Peveril lunged up from the keel of the boat and charged at the sailor. Shotgun pellets would require a bit more explanation than mere drowning and at least it would be quicker.

For one so burly, the sailor moved remarkably swiftly. He jinked to one side and stuck out his boot. Peveril went flying down onto the mud. Determined to meet death face to face, he rolled his body over, wishing that he had his hands free to try to strangle his opponent.

"Go on, shoot, damn you," he snarled.

Much to Peveril's surprise, his captor did not immediately blaze away at him. Instead, he dragged out his clasp knife and cut the tarry rope which imprisoned Peveril's wrists, laughing as he did so.

"You be over-young for a-tacklin' of Germans, but I reckon you be English."

Peveril struggled to his feet, humiliated at being mocked by this ruffianly pirate. About to curse him in no uncertain terms, he was suddenly visited by a brilliant inspiration. "I say, you're not Abel, are you?"

"Abel?"

"Poole told me about a friend of his who took him shooting. He called him Abel, but I thought that might have been a false name."

A brief smile flickered over the rough-hewn face. "My name's

Caine." Then, so softly that Peveril almost missed the words, he added, "Young Master Edwin was always a clever rogue, that he was."

"Yes," agreed Peveril, wondering how much information he could risk giving away. Even if this chap were thoroughly reliable, it was probably far too dangerous to reveal that Poole might have been murdered. "He used to win money off me at poker. Mind you, I don't know why he had to – he told me about his other source of income."

"And what might that be?"

Peveril forced himself to look conspiratorial. "He said he didn't like the Revenue too much. I gather you feel the same."

"Oh?"

"I prefer my brandy to be a bit stronger and a bit cheaper than I can buy in the mess."

A grunt greeted this remark.

"Poole said that he'd let me in on his game to make up for how much I'd lost to him." Peveril coughed in an embarrassed fashion. "I'd be prepared to give a cut to anyone else who helped to introduce me."

Caine gripped his shotgun. "You be off afore I change my mind."

"But why? Poole…"

A snarl of rage interrupted Peveril. "Be off with you. He that toucheth pitch shall be defiled therewith."

Peveril retreated rapidly. When he reached the point where the river-bank twisted sharply, he glanced back. The sailor gesticulated angrily and raised his shotgun. Without waiting to see whether Caine intended to carry out his threat, Peveril splashed through the water and scrambled round the other side of the protruding bank. When he reached the hamlet, he was glad to see the Austin still there unharmed. He drove off rapidly, but once he judged that he was sufficiently far away, he pulled up and buried his head in his hands.

'Oh God, I can't take this. I thought he was going to kill me.' Ralph bit back a sob. 'I didn't even achieve anything. I ought to have tried to talk him over. At the very least I ought to have waited to see what he did. Perhaps there was something hidden in the boat.' He shivered uncontrollably. 'I can't go back there. I simply can't. If only I could go and see Midge.'

Glancing down at his watch in case there was miraculously enough time to return to Brandon, Ralph was shocked to see weals from the rope round his wrist. 'Glory, those'll take some explaining away. I supposed I wrenched my hands when I fell.' He became conscious of the rest of his appearance. 'What a mess. I'll have to say I fell into the sea. Even if I leave the Austin and try to slip in through the wire, I'll be bound to be spotted going into my quarters. Blast.'

When Ralph drove into C Coy, he was relieved to be informed that there had been an officers' briefing timed for three o'clock. Since it was now ten past, he had every chance of reaching his quarters unobserved. There was no-one in sight when he approached the building and his hopes began to rise. He had just mounted the stairs when he heard Goodwin's voice.

"I had assumed, Capt. Thrigby, that you would have been back before this."

Reluctantly, Peveril turned round.

"Good God, man, what the devil have you been doing?"

"I slipped, sir."

"Slipped? What do you mean, slipped?"

"I mean I fell into the sea, sir."

"Fell into the sea? You were meant to be reporting back from HQ."

Ralph momentarily wondered how Goodwin would respond if he answered that he had been chatting to a smuggler who had turned violent. The major, however, was not finished.

"I ordered you to come back immediately after the meeting."

"Actually, sir, you didn't."

"I most certainly did. Why would I have sent you if it weren't important to hear what was discussed?"

Realising that it would not be politic to answer that Goodwin had feared Leake's wrath, Peveril resorted to facts. "You told me to report back by sixteen hundred hours, sir."

Goodwin ignored this. "Our entire meeting has been delayed because of you." He looked at Peveril with distaste. "I can't have you appearing like that. Go and clean yourself up. You should provide an example to the men. Leadership by example is what we look for here."

"Indeed we do, sir."

Goodwin shot Peveril a suspicious glance, but he had already saluted and gone upstairs.

Chapter Thirty-Nine

Ralph had not expected to sleep well that night, nor did he. Every time he closed his eyes, he visualised the muzzles of Caine's shotgun. Nor could he push away a guilty awareness that he ought to try to investigate the smuggler's obvious suspicion of Poole's unknown acquaintances.

'He must think that Poole was in with a really bad crowd. After all, he's a smuggler himself, so he wouldn't regard ordinary crime as defilement. The trouble is, Poole admitted as much to Midge, so I haven't found out anything new.' He swallowed at the thought of meeting Caine in a lonely place again. 'Caine's about the only real lead that I've got. I can't ignore it just because I'm afraid.'

Peveril tried to think about other matters, without much success. When morning came, he had little appetite for breakfast, not helped by the fact that he feared lifting his hands lest the weals round his wrists show.

Trent, the mess-waiter, raised his eyes when Peveril refused bacon or eggs. Hetherley was also surprised.

"Are you suffering from a guilty conscience because you enjoyed the delights of an extended lunch at HQ yesterday, while we were all waiting with baited breath for your return?"

Peveril scowled. "Considering the fact that Col. Leake repeatedly aired his views on our state of efficiency, I would hardly describe the atmosphere at HQ as delightful."

Hetherley laughed. "The benefits of seniority, Captain. You get it from the horse's mouth, whilst we have to rely on your summary. No wonder we can't improve our performance. You don't give us enough information."

Thrusting back his chair, Peveril left abruptly. Hetherley's words were far too apposite for the situation. In fact, they were so apposite that he had an unpleasant suspicion that they were deliberate. 'Is Hetherley Collingwood's other operative? I suppose that was a coded warning that I'm not achieving enough. Well, I know I'm not, but I don't know what else to do.' Peveril kicked a tussock of grass. 'Who am I fooling? I need to speak to Caine. And not knowing where he lives is not a good enough excuse to avoid talking to him.'

Spotting Goodwin making his way back from inspecting the men, Peveril hurried towards the barn where the Austin was garaged. Even although his Survey Unit cover supposedly allowed him complete freedom of movement, he strongly suspected that, if Goodwin saw him, the major would invent something to tie him to C Coy all day.

Once he was a safe distance from camp, Peveril pulled over to think. 'Poole mentioned meeting Caine in a pub, but which one? I can't go round all the pubs in Newton in the hope of finding him. Nor can I ask about him in them – the chances are that his friends would be suspicious and close their mouths.' A faint grin crossed Ralph's face at the thought of demanding a Kelly's Directory and looking for Caine under Poachers and Smugglers. 'I don't suppose he's a telephone subscriber either.'

A thought struck Peveril. 'Caine said he'd seen me before. Surely that suggests that he lives in Harting Magna – unless he was keeping an eye on the rowing-boat.' Peveril swallowed. What would happen if he did find Caine and the smuggler pulled his shotgun on him? The place was beastly remote. Caine might be the only person there. If Caine forced him out into the marsh, no-one would pay any attention to shots – they'd assume that someone was out hunting ducks. And if someone did investigate, they were probably all horribly inbred and wouldn't care about a stranger being murdered. Ralph shrugged. He didn't have time to concoct coded messages to his C.O., but he could telephone Midge. And he'd have his revolver out.

After telephoning Midge, Ralph parked his car some distance from Harting Magna. Then he worked his way round through the sedge and tussock grass, rather than risk being observed on the track which led through the hamlet. His intention was to wait in the hope of seeing Caine and he had pinned his trust on the furthest cottage, since its situation seemed ideal for a man who would wish to conceal his comings and goings.

Once in position, time seemed to pass very slowly. To make matters worse, mist was beginning to creep in from the saltings.

'I am not afraid of water droplets,' Ralph told himself. 'If I must be afraid, it should be of something which can actually harm me, such as shotgun barrels.' He shuddered, wishing that he hadn't chosen that example to bolster his morale. 'Serves me right for resorting to bravado,' he growled inwardly. 'I'll recite Greek verbs instead.'

By the time that Peveril had run out of various forms of the optative and subjunctive, he was conscious that he was both cold and damp. He was also increasingly aware that not only might Caine not appear, but he might not even live in the hamlet. Ralph glanced at his watch. He was just wasting time. He'd give it half an hour and then he'd go back to camp.

Suddenly, Peveril became aware of movement as a black shadow seemed to float along the path. Surely that was a man? Then the mist swirled back and he caught a glimpse of the face. It was Caine, and he was indeed going towards the furthest cottage. Peveril counted the seconds. He had to give Caine enough time to get inside. On a filthy day like this, he was probably taking off his boots. If he were armed, he probably wouldn't put the gun down until he was inside the house.

After five minutes, Ralph decided to move. Ignoring the path to the front door, he circled round to the back, wishing that the mist would evaporate. It might have made it easier to approach the cottage unseen, but it was devilish eerie and it was damned difficult to discern the path. The last thing he needed to do was blunder over a pile of stones or fishing nets.

Once he had reached the back door, he hesitated momentarily, listening to the sounds of running water within. Did Caine's neighbours knock at the door? Or would that alert Caine to the presence of a stranger and send him straight out the front? Maybe he should barge in, as he had been taught at training. On the whole, perhaps not. It would justifiably enrage Caine. Nonetheless, he would draw his revolver, just in case.

Peveril carefully turned the door-handle and slipped inside. As he edged into the kitchen, gun in hand, he was greeted by a terrified shriek and the smash of a broken plate. Taken aback at the sight of a frightened woman, Peveril half-lowered his gun and attempted to reassure her.

"I'm very sorry; I didn't mean to startle you. I was looking for someone else."

The menacing sound of a gun being cocked came from the hallway behind him. "And who were that?"

Peveril slowly turned round to face Caine. The smuggler looked furiously angry.

"Why might you be a-threatenin' my woman?"

"I thought she was you. I wanted to talk to you."

"You did? Then you be droppin' that gun."

Ralph swallowed. He doubted whether his revolver was of much use in the present situation, but if he lost it, he would be utterly defenceless. "I didn't come here to threaten anyone. I only drew it because I didn't want you waving a shotgun in my face. I didn't realise that your wife was here or I wouldn't have drawn it."

"Drop that there gun or I be shootin' you."

Peveril's eyes were bright with fear as he stared at Caine. Every instinct told him to give in, but his training ordered him to stand firm. Then, out of the corner of his eye, he saw Mrs Caine approaching. The obvious thing to do was to grab her and use her as a human shield, placed between him and her husband's shotgun. But that would mean hurting her, and he had vowed long ago never to use masculine strength to harm a woman. With a vicious snarl, he thrust his revolver onto the table.

"I don't hit women, no matter the circumstances."

However, Peveril had little time for reflection as Caine loomed over him, forcing him back against the wall.

"I'll be teachin' you to come a-threatenin' my woman."

Mrs Caine now spoke for the first time. "No, Ezekiel. He be too young."

Praying that she might soften her husband's desire for revenge, Peveril tried to excuse his actions. "I honestly didn't mean to scare you. I'm very sorry. I didn't think that a woman might be in the house. I wouldn't have rushed in like that if I'd known."

Caine cast him a baleful look, but lowered his shotgun and placed it on the kitchen table. He turned to his wife. "Go and keep a lookout."

"Yes, Ezekiel, but remember he be young."

Caine turned his attention back to Peveril. "You be tellin' me what you be wantin' and then I'll l'arn you your manners."

Thinking that being beaten up, whilst exceedingly unpleasant, would not be half as bad as being filled with shot-gun pellets, Ralph attempted to explain. "I'm investigating Poole's death. He didn't die from being shot. I think someone poisoned him and I need to find out who it was. I know he had some very peculiar contacts. He said that they were smugglers."

"Why be you a-carin' about his death?"

Peveril temporised somewhat. "Well, you see, I knew him. And there's something very odd going on."

"Indeed there be."

"So I wanted your help because you were a friend of his and I thought that you might be able to tell me about his contacts." Peveril hesitated, wondering whether it was safe to remind Caine of his anger yesterday. "I'm not really trying to get involved in smuggling. I want to find out who gave Poole that money, because I think that his killer is one of them."

"I don't know who they be," retorted Caine flatly. "If I were knowin', then I'd be dealin' with them myself."

Peveril's face fell. He'd put himself in a rotten position for nothing. He'd been sure that Caine must know something or why had he been so suspicious the previous day?

"Didn't Poole say anything about them when he met you? He told me that he'd talked to you about trade and how you'd said that there was nothing doing, what with mines and the men being conscripted into the navy."

"No, he were as close as a whelk."

More out of a sense of frustration than because he expected a useful answer, Peveril asked the only thing he could think of. "Did you see him at all after that?"

"I did."

"What did he say to you?" When there was no reply, Peveril tried to sound more persuasive. "Look, I know you must be furious with me, and I know that you were suspicious of my loyalties yesterday, but, honestly, I am trying to clear up Poole's death – and I'm not a traitor."

Caine's eyes travelled to the shotgun. Then, as he heard Peveril swallow, a grim smile crossed his face. "As well for you that you be loyal. And you be determined, too." There was a pause as the smuggler appeared to be making up his mind. "I be seein' Master Edwin the night the colonel be killed. I be in the marsh."

Ralph had no difficulty in realising that Caine must have been out poaching. "Did you see anyone else?"

"There were another soldier."

"Was he an officer?"

"He were too far away for me to be seein' who he be. But he weren't the colonel. The colonel do come over the river."

Peveril was confused. "Do you mean that Colonel Durrant came from the north and had to cross the river, whilst Poole and the other man came from this side of the river?"

"That be so."

Peveril tensed. This was the first proper confirmation of his suspicions that the killer had come from C Coy. "Are you quite certain that the other man didn't go back across the river after the shooting?"

"That I be. There were no boat unless he used the colonel's. And it be still a-lyin' where he left it, upstream of here."

"Do you mean the dinghy I was looking at yesterday?"

"I do. When I be seein' you a-spyin' round it, I were mighty suspicious. Them as shot the colonel be the most like to be a-searchin' for his boat."

"But why hasn't anyone noticed that it's missing and come looking for it before? Surely someone at battalion HQ must have seen that it had gone."

"It were a private boat of the colonel's. He were keepin' it upstream on the river. He be keen on watchin' birds."

Peveril considered that this tranquil occupation sounded most inappropriate for the fire-eater whom he had met. However, it certainly explained why Durrant had had easy access to a craft on the night of his murder. "Was there anything else you noticed that night?"

"Be you investigatin' the colonel's death, too?"

Thinking that Caine was far too sharp to be fooled by an outright lie, Peveril demurred. "Since Poole was out that night, I thought that anything odd might tie in to his own death."

"I heard the shooting, but I weren't seeing anythin' else."

"Not even the colonel's body?"

"No."

Peveril was sure that Caine was lying, but he was disinclined to push him much further. There were already some important deductions to be drawn from what the man had said. "That's very useful information," Peveril stated rather awkwardly. "Thank you."

"Be you l'arnin' your manners?" enquired the smuggler with grim humour. "You come back here when you be knowin' who killed Master Edwin." His voice grew harsh. "Yes, you be tellin' me, and then I be a-dealin' with he."

With that he yanked open the door and gestured for Peveril to leave. To his surprise, Peveril noted the glint of tears in the man's eyes. Poole must have had hidden depths to have engendered that sort of regret in so fierce a man. Or perhaps grief explained his ferocity. Whatever the cause, Peveril was relieved that the smuggler no longer seemed inclined to vent his ferocity in violence.

As he went down the path, Peveril met Mrs Caine. He stopped and raised his service cap. "I really am terribly sorry for frightening you, Mrs Caine. I ought to have thought that there might have been someone else in the house. I wouldn't have dreamt of scaring you." He swallowed in embarrassment. "And I caused you to break some of your dishes. Err... please, will you take this to buy some new ones?"

Much to his surprise, Mrs Caine patted him on the hand as she took the notes. "You be a nice boy to think of an old woman's feelings. Don't you be a-worritin' yourself. Ezekiel, he be hasty-like. And he be a-grievin' for Master Edwin."

"Did you know him well?"

"When he be younger, he be out with my man night after night. His father called him a scapegrace, but he be naught but wild. He loved the excitement and now the poor boy be dead."

Chapter Forty

Deciding that he might as well be hung for a sheep as for a lamb, Peveril headed for Brandon, rather than back to C Coy. Moreover, he wanted to see if Midge would draw the same conclusions about Caine's information as he had. However, Midge's look of relief when she saw that he was safe left him feeling distinctly guilty.

"I'm sorry if I scared you earlier, Midge. I didn't think properly."

"You sounded a little het-up," agreed Midge cautiously. "I wondered what was happening."

Ralph bit his lip. "I oughtn't to have said anything at all, but Caine pulled a shotgun on me yesterday." He smiled ruefully. "And today, although that was my own fault."

Once Ralph had finished narrating what had occurred, Midge sucked in her breath. "I think that confirms that Poole wasn't the killer, but, Ralph, you'll have to be terribly careful. You're right that the murderer must have come from C Coy."

"Because of the boat?"

"Precisely. He clearly couldn't have followed Durrant, since Durrant rowed across to meet Poole. I suppose the third man could have been lurking well in advance, but it sounds from what Caine said as if he had followed Poole. And as the unknown didn't row back across the river, he must have returned to C Coy."

"Unless he lives locally," suggested Ralph, who was keen to explore all possibilities, in case he had made a mistake in his own deductions.

"But he was in uniform. The coast-watchers only have armbands. Anyone in uniform must have belonged to one of the camps, and it would require an enormous detour to go upstream and back round to get to HQ, let alone B Coy."

Ralph nodded. "That's rather what I thought, although he might just have had some transport stashed away to get back to camp before the body was found."

"I doubt it. Your smuggler chap seemed pretty certain that he didn't go north or west, and I should imagine Caine was listening very carefully. In any case, Mrs Serring came to see me yesterday and what she said points to C Coy."

Midge swiftly filled Ralph in, before admitting her concerns of the previous day. "It doesn't sound as if the signalling is happening very frequently, but what if I'm wrong? Mrs Serring hasn't been keeping watch every night. There may be some sort of regular arrangement. If we don't act immediately, anything could happen."

Peveril frowned. "I don't imagine that the signaller would dare signal too frequently. And I don't suppose that the German navy would risk having a U-boat off-shore in much the same place every week. If the Nazis really believed that their man was going to supply them with so much information, wouldn't they have given him a wireless transmitter?"

"Surely it would be dangerous to hide a transmitter in camp?"

"No more dangerous than constantly signalling out to sea. Anyway, it could be hidden out in the marshes – that would avoid any chance of it being accidentally spotted."

Midge frowned. "Are you sure about that? It's an odd sort of place to be going to regularly without any reason. Moreover, wouldn't the damp affect the machine's workings – particularly in winter? And rain or lashing wind might affect transmission."

"I suppose so," agreed Ralph uncertainly. He sighed. "I don't normally care about having practically no scientific knowledge, but this may be an exception." He furrowed his brow as he tried to remember what he had been told during training. "You need to have something to earth a wireless, and something to act as an aerial. Chimneys are good for supporting an aerial, because they give height."

"But it must be possible to transmit without using a chimney," argued Midge. "Our spies use wireless sets, too." Suddenly her eyes lit up. "I say, Ralph, if Cosford is as dubious as he seems, maybe he's hiding the transmitter. Do you think that Woolf would raid his house if you asked?"

"Or his shop – it could be hidden in that cupboard you spotted." Then Peveril grimaced. "Actually, I don't think that's very likely. I know Cosford didn't realise that you could see his reflection in the mirror, but he'd have to be an absolute fool to open up wherever he was concealing a wireless. It would be asking for trouble."

"Trouble which could lead to him being shot," agreed Midge sombrely. "In any case, we've no proof that he possesses a transmitter. In fact, it's probably a bad idea to ask Woolf to search his premises. We don't have enough evidence for a search warrant and, if nothing were found, it would simply warn off whoever does have it."

"If anyone has a transmitter at all," Ralph pointed out.

"Ye-es, but we can't ignore the possibility. Something vital might be passed on."

Wishing that he were in a position to reassure Midge that her fears were unnecessary, Ralph grimaced. "Maybe I ought to ask Hetherley; I think he's Collingwood's other operative."

Midge looked startled. "He told you who he was? I thought that Collingwood didn't want you to know."

"He didn't actually identify himself to me, but he made a sharp remark this morning about my never handing over information."

"But that doesn't prove anything. You told me that Goodwin had made similar remarks. And Trent's always listening in when he's serving you. It's far too great a risk."

Peveril sighed. "I know, but I'd like to talk to someone about things. Neither of us has sufficient experience and matters are getting far too serious." He added hastily, "Obviously, your experience of murders is highly relevant, but Intelligence is different."

Midge attempted to reassure him. "It's all right; I'm not going to take offence. But since Collingwood authorised my involvement, why not make use of it? I can let Dr Hartismere know that we've got something to pass on. Even if he can't come down to speak to me, I'll only have to get to Cambridge and back." She added rather edgily, "You'd better tell me what your plans are for investigating C Coy."

"So that you can report what I was doing if I disappear?" asked Peveril. Noticing Midge's shiver, he apologised. "Sorry, not the best joke." He frowned. "The problem is, everyone was accounted for on the night of the murder."

"Then one of the alibis was a fake."

"How could it be? The police went through everyone's stories."

Midge ran her hands through her hair. "Either the police didn't pick up a lie or there was an accomplice who provided an alibi, just as there may have been an accomplice who poisoned Poole in the hospital. And I think that it was Cosford." She explained what she had discovered from Matron Roberts and how she had seen the bookseller in the hospital.

Ralph blinked. "That sounds beastly suspicious about Cosford, but if you're correct that the matron suspects one of the nurses, does that mean that it really was suicide?"

Midge sighed. "It could be, but apparently Poole's surgeon was a bit surprised that he'd killed himself. And the matron didn't think he seemed sufficiently miserable to have done it."

"At least it sounds as if you can rule her out – why on earth would she draw attention to her suspicions if she had killed Poole and wanted to pass it off as suicide?"

"I agree with you, but I suppose we'd better not be too hasty." Midge frowned. "Cosford is the obvious suspect, but how did he get hold of the morphia?"

"You could be correct about it coming from army supplies. So I'd better concentrate on a possible link to Durrant's killer at C Coy." Peveril gave a sigh of relief. "At least we know when Poole returned to camp – that narrows down when Durrant was killed."

"Mmm," agreed Midge. "All the same, it might be worth checking up on Trent. I know he told the police that he spotted Poole at 1.50, but what if he wasn't absolutely certain? He might have felt forced to give a definite time to satisfy Woolf."

"Yes, I don't imagine that Woolf has much sympathy with imprecision." Peveril shrugged. "Not that I suppose that ten minutes either way would make much difference to anyone's alibi, but starting with Trent is better than flailing around questioning the entire company."

"Don't forget that you can't necessarily trust what Trent says. What better way of providing himself with an alibi for the murder than saying that he was in camp, observing Poole?"

"Rather than being out in the marsh murdering Durrant?"

"Precisely."

Peveril grimaced. "I take the point. And Trent did seem rather interested in learning where I came from and exactly what could be achieved with semaphores. Equally, are we foolish to trust Caine's version of events? What if he were making up a load of lies about a third man to protect Poole's name? If he were so sure that Master Edwin was innocent, why didn't he come forward when Poole was arrested?"

"Perhaps he didn't think that he'd be believed. Most countrymen are suspicious of the law, but he's also a poacher and a smuggler. He must have known that he'd hardly make a credible witness, although I imagine he would have eventually come forward." Midge glanced at Peveril. "You won't do anything rash, will you? I know you were very brave to tackle Caine, but you can't take risks with a murderer."

Peveril gave a humourless bark of laughter. "I wasn't in the slightest bit brave. I was petrified, and the last thing I want to do is to fool around with a killer." He suddenly frowned. "And I'm pretty sure Caine's lying about whether he went over to look at Durrant's body. I mean, the man's a poacher. He'd seen or heard three men in the marshes; don't you think he would be a bit suspicious when he heard shooting and only two men leave?"

"Yes." Midge sighed. "I suppose that makes his evidence a bit less reliable, but I can't say I'm surprised that he's suppressing having been near Durrant – he probably doesn't want to be blamed for the killing."

"Do you think that he went and dragged the coast-watcher out of bed and made him say that he'd found it? I imagine all of Harting Magna knows what Caine's like."

"Bowdyke isn't from Harting Magna," replied Midge absently. "He's from Fytton."

Ralph looked startled. "Are you sure?"

"Yes, he's Ellen's cousin. He's a reed-cutter by profession and Fytton's in the midst of the reed-beds."

Peveril frowned. "But that doesn't make sense. I was told that the coast-watcher found Durrant's body as he took a short-cut home. Why would he take a short-cut via Harting Magna? It's completely in the wrong direction." He crossed over to the bookcase and brought back the map which Midge had shown him once before. "Look – do you see what I mean?"

Midge poured over the map. "Yes. It's like one of those beastly geometry problems. The watcher's post, Harting Magna and Fytton make up the three points of a triangle. It would be far quicker to go directly from the post to Fytton rather than to take a detour via Harting Magna."

"Exactly." Ralph traced a route with his finger. "This track to Fytton branches off before you reach Harting Magna." He swallowed. "I know it's pretty easy to get lost, but if this chap is a reed-cutter he must know the area extremely well."

"It's probably as you said. Caine can't have wanted to get involved with the police."

Ralph grimaced in thought. "If Bowdyke is your housekeeper's cousin, do you think that you could persuade her to find out from him whether Caine did ask him to go and 'discover' the body?"

"I could ask, and he might even tell her, but I don't think that she'd pass it on." Midge spread her hands apologetically. "Ellen's not stupid. She'd know immediately that it was more than idle curiosity on my part and she wouldn't want her cousin to get in trouble with the police." She shrugged. "They probably have their suspicions that he's not told the whole truth, but they're also probably grateful that at least the body was reported."

Ralph paced around in irritation. "How on earth is it going to be possible to track down who killed Durrant if even perfectly innocent people lie all the time?"

Chapter Forty-One

When Peveril returned to C Coy, his overriding wish was to be left alone. He knew that it would be easier to track him down in the officers' quarters than outside, but he doubted his ability to consider alibis intelligently in the rain. Slipping past the mess, he overheard raised voices in Goodwin's office. He grinned momentarily – it sounded as if Goodwin were annoyed with someone other than him for a change. In fact, he reflected, if Goodwin had spoken to him in that tone, he would have wanted to hit him. He listened to see who had earned the company commander's displeasure.

"My dear Snellgrove, all I am doing is offering you friendly advice, which you ought to take in a constructive manner. After all, I am much more experienced that you are."

When there was no response, Goodwin added, "I am in no way reprimanding you, but the episode did not reflect well upon you. So you must accept my criticism in the spirit in which it is meant."

Noises which suggested that Goodwin was getting up forced Peveril to dart swiftly back down the corridor. He had no intention of being caught eavesdropping – he doubted that Goodwin would treat such an action with the same level of unctuous goodwill which he was currently displaying towards Snellgrove. Once outside, Peveril positioned himself where he could observe Snellgrove's departure. The lieutenant soon appeared, his back rigid with anger and his face a mask of hatred.

'Glory,' Peveril thought to himself, 'he loathes Goodwin. If the major suddenly disappears, I'll have a prime suspect in Snellgrove. I wonder if he's sufficiently angry to let something slip?'

Snellgrove glanced at Peveril in an unfriendly manner when he approached. What did Thrigby want? The man was an idle hound – even worse than Poole had been. Snellgrove's mouth tensed involuntarily. If he were the C.O., he'd demand a damned sight more discipline, including from the officers. In fact, particularly from the officers. But until his brother was somehow released from Wandsworth, there was no chance of that happening.

"Well?"

"I say, Snellgrove, do you think you could help me?"

"I doubt it."

"I'd rather ask you than Goodwin; I don't think that he'd take it seriously."

A flash of anger appeared in the older man's eyes. "Go on, although if it's about gambling debts I'm not interested."

"No, no, I've plenty of money." Peveril glanced round conspiratorially. "The thing is, I suspect that the manoeuvres are going to be another excuse to try to trip us up."

"The orders are very straightforward."

Peveril waved away the orders. "They're not what I'm worrying about. Chatham let out something which makes me suspect that Leake may be planning an additional reconnaissance."

"Against us?"

"Yes. I wondered if they might come over with a platoon to test our readiness on the night before the manoeuvres. We ought to be prepared in case they do."

"Why should you care?" demanded Snellgrove. "It's not like you to be concerned about duty. You use the Survey Unit as an excuse to avoid practically everything, even although you know that we are short-staffed."

"I'm sick of being laughed at by Chatham and Jervis each time they see me. Everyone in A Coy regards us as a joke. Apparently something happened on Tuesday night – Chatham said it wouldn't occur in the Wehrmacht."

Snellgrove flushed angrily. "What happened was that my orders were countermanded. There ought to have been a patrol on the north section of the eastern perimeter. It was not set, so we were infiltrated just before dawn."

"I've never understood why the camp isn't actually out on the bluff. Surely that would be easier to guard – and of more benefit for protecting the coast?"

"When we moved here in January, Goodwin sited it," retorted Snellgrove, in a voice heavy with contempt. "He thought that the men would suffer if they camped out right next to the sea. He

287

was advised as to other possible positions, but he has more experience than we do."

Recognising a phrase from Goodwin's conversation, Peveril made sympathetic noises, whilst busily wondering what else Goodwin had said to have driven Snellgrove to such open avowal of his disdain for the company commander.

"His choice wouldn't have had anything to do with the fact that the farmhouse isn't on the bluff, would it?" he suggested mischievously.

Snellgrove gave a snort of disgust. "I don't much fancy sleeping in a tent, either, but personal convenience is not the point. Wars rarely lead to comfort."

By the time that Snellgrove had walked Peveril round the entire perimeter of both the camp and the alternative position where he would have preferred to site the camp, Peveril was very much inclined to agree that wars did not bring comfort. The rain had continued to pour down and it was only the desire to maintain Snellgrove's new-found approval which enabled Ralph to counterfeit an interest in where his invented raid might take place.

When they eventually retired to the mess, Snellgrove commented approvingly on Peveril's swift realisation that the bluff was a weak spot in the general defences. Nonetheless, he still had a complaint. "Why didn't you say anything before? Between us we might have been able to persuade Goodwin to take action to improve the camp."

Peveril shrugged. "You've heard what he says about semaphores. He wouldn't listen to me." He shrugged again. "Sorry if I didn't pay attention to your fears earlier, but I was told that this was the slackest company in a slack battalion."

"You mean you assumed that I was covering up idleness with a load of talk?"

"Err…"

Snellgrove snorted. "I can't say I entirely blame you. To hear Goodwin speak, you'd think that he was working himself to the bone and that all we do is hinder him."

"Don't you believe that he leads by example?" suggested

Peveril maliciously.

"Pah! Don't talk to me about examples, Thrigby. When we were in the old camp…"

Just as Peveril was leaning forward in the hope of gaining a vital new revelation, Trent appeared with their beer.

"The police inspector's been looking for you, Capt. Thrigby."

"Has he?"

Trent's eyes glittered. "Oh, yes, sir. Very interested to know where you'd been, sir."

Peveril feigned indifference. "You can tell me all about it later, although I can't imagine what's so surprising about my visiting HQ."

"That's not what he was interested in, sir. He kept asking questions about your car-smash."

"Indeed?" intervened Snellgrove coldly. "Capt. Thrigby and Maj. Goodwin are both perfectly capable of dealing with the police without your intervention, Trent."

As the mess-waiter wandered off, Snellgrove glared after him. "That man is far too familiar."

"Goodwin seems inclined to encourage him."

"Perhaps. Now, about this raid."

Peveril sighed as he realised that Snellgrove's moment of loquacity about the company commander was over.

Later that evening, Peveril found himself unable to decide about Snellgrove. If he were the traitor, why had he agreed that the bluff was badly guarded? Was it a cunning attempt to throw Peveril off the scent? Had he decided that, once Thrigby had spotted what was obvious, it would be dangerous to claim that the precautions were acceptable? But if so, why had he drawn attention to the insecurity of that section of the camp by insisting on dragging him round the perimeter and beyond? The rain would have been a good excuse not to go so far. On the other hand, Snellgrove was the man assigned to posting guards. Surely that made him the most obvious suspect for whatever lapses of security there had been? And he was the only person with known Fascist connections. It wasn't pleasant to suspect a man just because he possessed a dubious brother, but it would be stupid not to take that into consideration.

While Peveril was trying to make up his mind about Snellgrove, Midge was being interrogated by Hartismere. Her coded telephone call, informing him that she had discovered the book of Petrarch sonnets which John had borrowed, had worked on the Vice-Master to such effect that he promised to arrive in time for dinner. Mrs Carrington had made a mild protest about the difficulties of suddenly providing for an extra guest, before realising that Midge was not being inconsiderate.

"I hope that Peveril boy knows what he's doing," she remarked irritably. "It's all very well for him; he doesn't have to get a degree."

Midge shrugged. "Nor do I, according to most people."

"Don't be ridiculous, Midge. In any case, degree or no degree, I won't have you tiring yourself out like this. Let Ralph Peveril solve his own problems."

When Midge made no reply, Alice gave a wry laugh. "I'm sure you think that you're doing whatever you're doing out of a desire to serve your country, but, if you ask me, you're as inquisitive as your uncle."

Midge grinned. "If you think I'm inquisitive, then I can't begin to imagine what you'd make of Dr Hartismere."

"In that case, I shall warn Ellen to delay dinner."

Mrs Carrington's fears that dinner would be delayed by Hartismere's questioning were entirely justified. The Vice-Master went through every piece of information in considerable detail, paying particular attention to what Caine had said.

"The boy did well," he remarked eventually. "He must have been looking particularly innocent and vulnerable to get some old reprobate to trust him."

Midge found her hackles rising in defence of Ralph. "I think it was more a matter of good manners to Mrs Caine."

"I doubt it, my dear. Fisher-folk don't trust the slinking ways of the gentry – with good reason. More to the point, is the boy bearing up?"

"Yes."

"So he's expressed no fears at all about men who turn shotguns on him? Now that is remarkable."

Midge flushed at Hartismere's tone, but said nothing. The Vice-Master was not so easily put off.

"I ask because it may be important."

"I don't see why."

"Really? I had never before thought that you were lacking in imagination." There was a short pause, before Hartismere sighed. "Come, come, Miss Carrington, I'm not accusing the boy of cowardice – not am I going to pass on any such wild accusations to his commanding officer. But if he is likely to panic if he has to spend twenty-four hours in a misty marsh waiting to trap a spy, then I'd rather know before an operation is launched with him at the heart of it."

"Is that what's going to happen?"

"It's a possibility." Hartismere spread out his hands in a gesture of distaste. "The pair of you appear to have been working on the assumption that whoever is signalling is sending out information. Has it not occurred to you that they may be preparing to land – or send back – agents?"

Midge turned white. "How many have we missed?"

"Since Mrs Serring only told you two days ago I doubt that you can hold yourself responsible for whatever was going on this week. Moreover, I find it very hard to believe that strangers are being landed on a regular basis at the same spot. It would be asking for trouble."

"So the signalling may be infrequent after all?"

"Let us hope so. And since confirming that may involve Peveril, let me ask again, how is the boy bearing up?"

Reluctantly, Midge admitted that Ralph had said that he was scared by Caine. She hesitated, before adding her own suspicion. "I don't think he much enjoyed hanging around in the mist, either."

"I'm not surprised," stated Hartismere. Noticing Midge's reaction, he laughed dryly. "The boy may be overly-imaginative, but even one as worldly as I can remember the sensation of watching curling mists as I waited to go over the top at dawn." Suppressing a more tormented vision of wreaths of gas snaking across a pitted landscape, he added as unemotionally as he could, "If Peveril does show signs of cracking up, get him out. He was only sent back from Cambridge because his sudden disappearance might have alerted people as to his true role. There are others who can lay traps."

"Collingwood's original operative?"

"He – and the others who will be sent in if necessary."

Chapter Forty-Two

Since Hartismere had decided that Midge's information was sufficiently important for him to set off for London straight away, Midge was spared trying to make polite conversation with him and her aunt. Peveril, on the other hand, was faced with the full glories of a guest-night dinner at C Coy's mess. Judging by his position next to two 2nd lieutenants, it was obvious that he was still out of favour with Goodwin. However, whilst O'Connor had only joined B Coy a week ago and thus posed no difficulty, Peveril had found it hard to suppress a groan when he read that his left-hand neighbour was to be Cohen of A Coy. Whatever else had been covered in training, it hadn't included how to spend an evening mouthing platitudes to someone who justifiably loathed the sight of you.

The evening proved to be as profoundly embarrassing as Peveril had feared. O'Connor was a very young subaltern, straight from grammar school and with nothing to say for himself. Peveril toyed with the idea of patronising him horribly, before deciding that it would be both unkind and unproductive. When the main course was served, he found that it was his turn to have nothing to say. Instead he addressed himself to his wine-glass, drinking two glasses in quick succession until he caught sight of Cohen's contemptuous expression. Swearing under his breath, he glanced surreptitiously at his watch, hoping that more time had passed than he feared.

"Boring you?" enquired Cohen politely.

Wondering what would happen if he ordered Cohen to call him 'sir', Peveril muttered something about being on duty later.

"You surprise me," returned Cohen. "C Coy don't seem very devoted to duty, generally speaking."

"What do you mean?"

Cohen waved his hand airily. "Chasing girls, car-smashes, fighting, gambling – none of those paints the picture of a dedicated officer in any branch of the army." He took a delicate sip of wine. "Of course, I realise that normal rules may not apply as you enjoy your unregulated life here in C Coy."

"Do you normally insult your dinner-hosts?"

"Naturally; it's a Jewish trait to go with the others which you have observed."

Peveril flushed. "I never said that."

Cohen regarded him with interest. "Ah, I must have misunderstood your comment to Jervis about parasites feeding off hosts. I didn't realise that you were referring to host *nations*."

Peveril dug around for a suitable response. "I'm rather too busy to worry about private quarrels. But if I weren't, I'd happily demand satisfaction for what occurred at HQ."

"Satisfaction?" repeated Cohen. "If I remember correctly, my action was taken to recall you to your duty – the duty which C Coy are so keen on."

"Oh, shut up and stop being so damned superior."

A surprised look from the other side of the table suggested that Hetherley had overheard Peveril. Ralph glanced at Cohen, unsure what to say, but the reappearance of Trent signalled the welcome fact that dessert was now approaching. Unless Goodwin decided to maunder on forever, there couldn't be more than about half-an-hour before he could leave.

Peveril's estimate was only out by ten minutes, but he had passed most of those ten minutes cursing his company commander, Cohen, and whoever had made the seating-plan for the evening. He then proceeded to spend five minutes talking conspicuously to Hetherley, before escaping to his quarters. Glancing in the mirror to check that he had not suddenly grown a pair of horns, he flung himself down on the iron bedstead. 'I'm a fool. If I'd provoked Cohen a bit more, I could have established myself as Uncle Adolf's favourite Fascist.' He shivered. 'Ugh, it must be beastly having to listen to that sort of bilge. I wonder how Cohen stands it. If I ever go undercover again, I'll pretend to be a Bolshevik; then I can be equally rude about all races and creeds. I'll even be allowed to be vile about Trotskyites.'

When the noise from the mess died down, Peveril slipped downstairs quietly. Trent was bound to have a lot of clearing up to do and this would be the perfect opportunity to get him on his own and find out what – if anything – Woolf actually had said. Somewhat to his surprise, he found Ulph polishing the table.

"Trent not around?" drawled Peveril. "What a bore; I wanted a brandy and soda."

"The corporal be a-lyin' down, sir."

"Been finishing off our port, has he?"

Ulph appeared shocked at this suggestion. "No, sir. It's one of Lt. Snellgrove's ideas, sir. He said we be getting too set in our ways. So I be tidyin' up and Trent he be keepin' my post for me." A slow smile spread over the private's face. "I were down for the dawn patrol, so the corporal went off to be a-catchin' his sleep."

Although mildly amused by Snellgrove's swift attempt to punish Trent's gossipy nature, Peveril cursed the fact that he, too, would now have to be up at dawn. After acquiring an unwanted drink, he sauntered off to check the duty roster. Ulph's name had indeed been scored through, but Peveril could see that he had been originally posted to patrol on the eastern perimeter which overlooked the river. 'At least that will be quiet,' thought Ralph. 'Mind you, I bet I'll drag myself over there on a fool's errand. Hetherley said that Trent invents gossip – goodness knows what he'll make of my sudden arrival. I'll have to go round all of the various guards. How dull.' He grinned suddenly. 'Snellgrove really will believe that he's made a sudden convert. I've never shown such keenness since trying to distract that ghastly sergeant-major during training.'

When Peveril's alarm-clock shrilled out the next morning at the unearthly hour of half-past four, he was immensely tempted to bury his head under the blankets and go back to sleep. Eventually, he dragged himself out of his bed, shivering at the unexpected chill.

Five minutes later, he made his way quietly along the corridor of the farmhouse. Having slipped unnoticed past Tompkins, who appeared to have decided that guarding the officers' quarters was best achieved while comatose, Ralph set off at a jog-trot towards the edge of the camp. 'If I were a mess-waiter who likes an easy life,' he mused, 'would I march up and down a cold path, or would I edge into the gorse and enjoy a few cigarettes? I suppose it depends on how often I'd been ordered to rendezvous with the other guards and whether they'd all agreed to ignore those orders.'

When Peveril reached the perimeter of the camp, he strode forward, reminding himself of his cover-story that he was checking up on the possibility of raiders sneaking through unnoticed. Somewhat to his disgust, he reached the end of Trent's section without meeting the corporal. That meant he'd have to retrace his steps. More to the point, if Trent was gossiping with the guard on the next section, he'd have no chance of questioning him on his own.

As Peveril returned, he was conscious that the rising sun made it much easier to see. He could even spot where the tussock grass appeared to have lost its struggle with gravity and had fallen away from the raised path. Odd that the drop should be much higher here than round the rest of the camp. No wonder Snellgrove thought that the camp should have been moved right out onto the bluff. Ralph carried on walking, wondering where the devil Trent was. If the corporal had sneaked back to get a hot breakfast whilst he was stuck wandering around, then Trent would live to regret it.

Eventually, Peveril spotted another figure in the distance, but it was too tall to be Trent. He paused, wondering whether to hail the unknown and ask him when he had last seen Trent. He shrugged. There was no point. Whoever was on guard-duty with Trent would lie and say that he had fulfilled the various rendezvous times. Moreover, judging by the sunrise, the guards would soon be relieved – if he did want to catch Trent alone, there was little time to be wasted.

As Peveril passed the gap in the tussock grass for a second time, something made him pause. Surely it was odd that such tough vegetation should suddenly fail to hold on to its parent earth? It almost looked as if it had been wrenched away. With a sense of foreboding, he approached the gap. As he reluctantly peered over, he caught sight of an army boot. Craning further, he saw a leg bent in an angle which must have been very uncomfortable if its owner were still alive.

"Oh God," breathed Peveril, "it's Trent. What's happened?"

Trying desperately not to think about what might await him, Ralph edged forward. The drop to the ground did not worry him, since he possessed more than enough skill to climb down the twenty feet of sandstone, but he had no idea how to nurse a dying man. However, when he reached the ground, Peveril realised that he would not be faced with that eventuality. The sightless eyes and the twisted neck showed all too clearly that Trent was dead. Hurriedly turning his back on the corpse, Ralph stared up at the escarpment, trying to work out what had happened. Had Trent blundered over the edge in the dark, then frantically grabbed at the tussock grass in a desperate attempt to save himself? Had he hung on and on, calling for help, until the grass parted and he plunged to his doom? Ralph shivered at the thought. The poor devil must have been petrified. Why hadn't someone heard him and come to his aid?

Suddenly, Peveril recollected that he was meant to be an Intelligence agent. It was far too late to get Trent to speak, but he ought to do something. Couldn't doctors tell when a man died by testing his body temperature? Fighting down revulsion, he edged back towards Trent's corpse. He tentatively touched the back of Trent's hand, before snatching his own away.

'Don't be so feeble,' he cursed. 'Wouldn't dear brother Robert sneer if he could see you now!' Having thus adjured himself, he felt Trent's hand again, unsure whether the clamminess he could feel was due to the dew, Trent's cold skin, or his own sweat. His gorge rose and he withdrew rapidly to behind a convenient rock. He had just finished vomiting when he became aware that he was being hailed from above. Pulling himself together, he stepped back onto the sand and looked up at Hetherley's distorted face.

"What's going on?"

"I've just found Trent. He's dead. Can you get some help?"

"Good God." Hetherley glanced up and down the track. "Are you alone there? How did he die?"

Disinclined to announce that Trent might have been murdered, Peveril stuck to facts. "He seems to have broken his neck. Do hurry up, Hetherley. I don't want to be stuck here guarding his corpse."

"I thought you were meant to be a cool specimen," retorted the subaltern, before setting off back in the direction of camp.

Left alone again with the body, Peveril shuddered. Somehow, it seemed eminently probable that Trent's shade was haunting the place where he died. Did the sea-mist, which was rolling off-shore, know the secret of his death? Or did the brave sea-swallows? Even if they did, they were not going to reveal the truth about his end.

Ralph grimaced. If Trent had been killed, presumably there must be a reason for killing him. It was too late to question him, but might he have concealed some important evidence on his person? Somehow it seemed peculiarly vile to search through Trent's pockets, but Peveril suspected that if Midge were in his position she would possess the necessary determination. Swallowing his distaste, Peveril returned to Trent's corpse and slipped his hand inside the tunic. The sensation of solid, but lifeless, flesh nearly defeated Peveril's resolution, but he continued to delve against all his instincts.

A few moments later, Peveril looked at his finds. Cigarettes and matches were only to be expected, but Ralph checked to see that there was nothing hidden inside either box. Then he turned his attention to the worn brown wallet which Trent had kept in his shirt pocket. There was a ten-shilling note and a small snapshot of two elderly people – presumably Trent's parents. Wondering whether there might be any names on the back, Ralph reluctantly eased the photograph out from the wallet. As he did so, a folded treasury note came with it. Peveril blinked in some surprise. Five pounds? That didn't suggest murder for gain, although the killer could have missed it, just as he nearly had. Mind you, it was quite a sum for Trent to have – surely it would take a long time to save that on a corporal's pay?

Peveril glanced at the corpse again and shuddered. When the man lay splayed out lifeless on the sand, it was beastly to be speculating whether he had been filching from the mess accounts. All the same, the possibility had to be considered. Ralph dug around in his own tunic until he found pencil and paper. He scrawled down the number of the note, before glancing at the back of the snapshot. His pleasure at seeing writing faded when he realised that it was only a date – and one which was hard to read, given the crabbed handwriting and the cross-bars through the two figure sevens. Just as he was considering whether there was anything noticeably significant about the seventeenth of July, he heard the sound of someone approaching. He quickly thrust the money and photograph back into Trent's wallet, before attempting to replace the wallet in Trent's shirt-pocket. He had no time to do up the button on the pocket, but he had little desire to be caught apparently robbing a corpse.

On this occasion, Hetherley did not stay on top of the path, but clambered down in a somewhat ungainly fashion to join Peveril.

"I sent Catchpole back to report," he informed Peveril. "I thought I might be able to help."

"You can raise the dead?" enquired Peveril sarcastically. He ignored Hetherley's scowl and stared moodily out to sea. "And on that note, I hope you told Catchpole to bring something to help get Trent's corpse up from here. I don't know how high up the tide comes."

"How did you discover him? You weren't down in the orders to check up on the sentries."

Ralph assumed an omniscient air. "No, but not everything is put in orders."

By the time that Trent's corpse had been taken back to the farm-house, Peveril was more in command of himself. Moreover, he knew that either the Medical Officer or the police would be bound to want to know exactly what he had seen. Hence it came as no surprise when Goodwin ordered him to stay in the mess. However, he could not face the smell of the cooked breakfast and he moodily took himself outside into a less stale atmosphere. Just as he was wishing that he smoked, since it would, at least, give him something to do, he heard Goodwin's voice. The major, who was something of a fresh-air fiend when he remembered that this was the correct attitude to adopt, had left his window open and it was easy to hear most of his conversation.

"Yes, I'll hold him until you come. The motors are all under guard, so he can't escape that way."

There was a pause and then Goodwin's voice came again. "Good God. Why didn't you tell me before?" There was another pause and Peveril realised that the company commander must be speaking on the telephone.

"For God's sake, Woolf, you've left me harbouring him for weeks and only now do you tell me that he's a murderer. Oh, very well, has been accused of murder. I can't see the difference myself."

Peveril swallowed in horror. Woolf must have just revealed who he was. If he had, that must mean that the inspector believed that he was involved in Trent's death. Suddenly aware that he had missed part of the conversation, Ralph forced himself to concentrate.

"Oh, yes, there's plenty of evidence. Hetherley saw him searching the body. And Catchpole spotted him on the path. Don't worry, Woolf, I'll not prevent you from doing your duty."

Realising that once Goodwin emerged from his office he would have no chance of escape, Ralph pulled himself together. Assuming an air of casual unconcern, he lounged away from the window. It was clearly too dangerous to aim directly for the camp exit, but there was a chance that he could loop round behind the farmhouse and make his way along the perimeter until he reached the bluff. Then he could climb down and make his way upriver. However, behind the farmhouse lay the garages, and Goodwin's words had made it clear that the guards had been warned about him. Praying that the guards only had orders to stop him if he attempted to drive off, Peveril strolled past in his usual languid manner. To his strained nerves, it appeared that Pte. Wetherill cast him an unusually searching glance, but the soldier made no attempt to intercept him.

Wondering whether a shot would ring out at any moment, Peveril moved rapidly away from the buildings. The camp seemed remarkably quiet, and he could not decide whether this was because everyone was inside discussing Trent's unexpected death, or whether an edict had been issued to keep the men close at hand for the arrival of the police. He smiled bitterly.

'Collingwood told me to contact him if I ended up in trouble with the local police. Even if I can reach him, why should he believe me? He suspects that I blew up the gaol; he may think I was doing something equally stupid to Trent and it went wrong. Or he may be like Woolf and think that I really am a killer who can't control his actions.' Ralph bit his lip. 'I suppose Midge will learn what's happened through local gossip. Please don't let her lose faith in me.' He shivered. 'She'd have every reason for disbelieving me. I don't think I'd believe anyone who was in a similar position. And I didn't believe Poole.'

Chapter Forty-Three

At noon, Alice sought out Midge.

"I take it that you are interested in news from the East Suffolks?"

Midge looked up, surprised and somewhat worried. "Yes."

"One of their corporals was found dead on the sands this morning. He'd broken his neck."

"Good grief. What had happened?"

"The rumour is that one of the officers is responsible. He was seen rifling the body and the police want to interview him. Apparently he's been living under a false name, following a spell in gaol." Alice eyed Midge closely. "I'm well aware how things can get distorted on the village grapevine, but perhaps you might tell me whether young Ralph Peveril has been going under his real name or not whilst he's been serving with the regiment."

Midge stared at her aunt in horror. Her response seemed to confirm Mrs Carrington's worst suspicions.

"My dear, I know very well that he wasn't guilty of murder in Cambridge…"

"But he was tainted by the trial so that makes him more likely to be guilty of murder now?"

"I wouldn't suggest anything so illogical," retorted Alice. "However, I have a duty both to your parents and your uncle – quite apart from my own concerns – not to let you get mixed up in anything."

A number of ripostes rose to Midge's lips, but she choked them off. Getting angry with Aunt Alice was hardly fair, nor would it achieve anything. "Has anyone been arrested?"

"No. Apparently, the officer under suspicion disappeared this morning just before the police arrived." Mrs Carrington glanced at Midge doubtfully. "Now look here, Midge, I can quite understand that you want to help the Peveril boy, but I am not going to stand back and wait for you to be arrested for harbouring a fugitive. If Dr Hartismere wants to get himself involved in whatever's going on, that's up to him. But it's not your place."

"Because I'm a girl?" enquired Midge silkily. "Or because I'm crippled?"

Mrs Carrington sighed. She felt that both points applied, but knew that Midge would respond badly to either suggestion. "Because even if Ralph Peveril has been sent in undercover, you have not. Nor can you afford to annoy Newnham any more."

"Sometimes," growled Midge, "I wonder whether it would make much difference if I committed a murder myself."

"Women hang too, you know," pointed out Alice dryly. "And for goodness sake, if that wretched boy does turn up here, don't tell me or Ellen. I don't want to have to lie to the police."

"Quite," murmured Midge, before surprising her aunt with a sudden hug.

Midge was, naturally, worried sick by her aunt's news. Even although the details were somewhat hazy, she had even less faith than Mrs Carrington that Ralph was not involved in whatever had occurred. And if he had fled, that would be taken as an indication of guilt. Why on earth hadn't he waited until he saw Woolf? Goodwin might have assumed that Ralph had killed the corporal, but Woolf was a trained policeman. Midge bit her lip nervously. She wished now that she'd told Dr Hartismere how tense Ralph seems. She buried her head in her cat Bertie's fur and murmured, "I hope he does come here, whatever Aunt Alice says."

Midge's fears would have been even greater if she had known precisely what had happened to Peveril. After escaping from the camp, he had plunged upstream, with the full intention of joining a road as soon as possible in the hope of finding a telephone box. However, when he finally sighted telephone wires marching across country, he retained enough caution to wait motionless behind a thick crop of sedge. He could hear nothing suspicious, nor could he see far, but still he waited. Suddenly, there was a low whistle.

"That you, Bob? Where the blazes have you been?"

Peveril shivered. Had someone seen him?

A second voice replied. "Getting orders. You're to guard the telephone box."

"What about my relief?"

"I've got to go all the way to Easton and warn them there."

After some further grumbling, the owner of the first voice could be heard marching down the road. Peveril remained, hugging the damp earth. It might be coincidence. It might be some exercise. But he strongly doubted whether it was. In any case, it would clearly be impossible for him to ring up Midge and warn her as to what had occurred. That left him with the prospect of trying to reach Brandon. It only took him half an hour to drive from camp, but he had no idea how long it would take on foot – especially since he dared not be seen, which ruled out ordinary roads.

'I must think,' he told himself. 'I don't know what's going on, but I'm damned if I'm going to let myself be caught.' He scowled inwardly. 'Fletcher may trust the law, but I've no intention of risking summary justice at a court martial. And it may be cowardly to flee, but surely even Collingwood would accept that my body riddled with bullets won't help anything?'

By eleven o'clock, Peveril was becoming increasingly worried. When he had finished his military training he had been relieved at the thought that he would no longer have to crawl through mud on his stomach. However, he had spent most of the previous three hours doing precisely that. Worse than the physical discomfort was the fear that he might fail to spot a soldier on the look-out for him – after all, he'd had to sneak past at least four sets of patrols. It was all very well saying to himself that he'd manage because Goodwin was too incompetent to think of sending out all available troops, but Snellgrove might, and Col. Leake seemed all too capable of mounting a well-planned exercise.

'In fact,' cursed Peveril, 'he'd probably relish hunting me as opposed to his mock raids. Good for the troops to have a real purpose for a change.' He swallowed. 'Why did I trust Snellgrove? Why didn't I carry on pretending to be some rich, lazy ass? He must have had his suspicions raised by my new-found enthusiasm for military duties. I'm a fool. I even heard him telling Trent to be quiet and thought nothing of it. He must have decided to silence him forever. It would have been so easy for him – post Trent to an isolated part of camp, and then go and kill him before dawn. And how the hell am I going to prove that he did it – and I didn't?'

As Peveril gazed round, he spotted smoke rising slowly into the air. 'Houses? Surely I can't have reached Newton?' He shook his head violently, as if to clear it. 'Of course,' he breathed. 'I've reached Harting Magna. I must have gone a bit too far when crossing that cornfield.'

He paused in thought. 'Poole was keen on gambling, wasn't he? Perhaps this is where I take a gamble of my own. I don't have much to lose. At this rate of progress, I won't reach Brandon before tomorrow evening – even if I don't get nabbed on the way.'

Despite these words, Peveril waited for some time before he headed towards where the smoke lay drifting in the sky. Even when the sight of cottages confirmed his supposition that he had reached Harting Magna, Ralph still slipped round the edge of the hamlet before sidling towards Caine's house. Having knocked on the back door, he lifted the latch and entered softly.

"Caine? Are you there?"

A low rumbling greeted him and a great brindled dog appeared, hackles raised high.

"Good boy," murmured Peveril, hoping that the animal would let him come in out of sight. "I've come to see your master. I'm not a thief."

The dog seemed unconvinced by such reassurances. It bared its teeth and the rumbling grew louder. Ralph backed towards the door, then stopped when it became clear that the creature was readying itself to leap at him.

"You know, old chap," Peveril remarked in conversational tones, "normally I should enjoy the irony of a smuggler's dog being so keen on law and order, but currently I'm in rather too much of a rush to want to hang around."

"And who be you a-callin' a smuggler?"

Peveril groaned as he swivelled round. "Sorry, I wasn't trying to be offensive."

"And why be you here?"

"The fact is…"

"Yes?"

"The fact is, I'm on the run from the police and you're the only person I can think of who might help me. And I wanted to ask you something about the night of Durrant's murder."

"Murder," repeated Caine softly. "I be a-hearin' of a murder today. Is that what you be fleein'?"

"Yes, but I didn't do it. I found the body; I didn't kill him."

Caine spat. "And if you were bein' found with a cask of brandy, would the magistrates believe that you weren't a-smugglin' that brandy?"

Peveril swallowed at the hostility in the man's voice.

"Well?"

"I don't know. I'm not a magistrate. But I didn't kill Trent."

"They be sayin' in Newton that you sneaked out of your quarters past the watch. That be mighty suspicious to the likes of I."

"Tompkins was asleep. I wasn't trying to evade him. I had no idea what had happened to Trent."

"If you be a-killin' Trent, then you be a-killin' young Master Edwin."

"I didn't. I swear I didn't. I wanted him alive. I wanted both of them alive."

"Why?"

"Because both of them could tell me things I need to know."

"What could Trent be a-tellin' you?"

"When Poole returned to camp." Ralph hesitated momentarily, wondering how safe it was to explain further. However, a dangerous gleam in the smuggler's eye convinced him that he needed to provide more details. "Trent told Woolf that Poole returned at ten to two. But I don't know if that was correct."

"Why do the time matter?"

"If the time was wrong, other things could be wrong."

"Be you meanin' that if Trent lied then Master Edwin were innocent?"

Peveril nodded, before adding hastily, "I don't know whether Trent did get the time wrong. And if he did, I don't know whether he was deliberately lying or whether he made a mistake."

"And be you suggestin' I hide you until you find that out?"

"Not exactly. I thought… I thought you might help me get out of this area."

A suspicious frown settled on Caine's forehead. "Would you be thinkin' of the likes of France, then?"

"Good God, no. There's someone I want to talk to who lives about twenty miles away."

"And why can't he come to you if I was a-takin' he a letter?"

"It would be hard for them; they don't know the area."

"A foreigner? Then I think I be accompanyin' you to see that he's not a German."

Peveril bit his lip. He had no desire to reveal Midge's identity, but he did not see how else he could convince Caine to help him. "It's not a man; it's a girl."

Caine gave a throaty chuckle. "You be sweetheartin'? My lass were a loyal wench too." Then his face changed. "But if you be a-lyin' to me, then I be throttlin' you with my own hands."

"I'm not lying. You'll see that she exists if we reach her house. But I've no chance of getting through the police cordon on my own, and I don't want the police picking up my trail and then questioning her."

Caine spat. "Police? Pah. They be town-folk. They know naught of the marshlands."

Peveril shivered involuntarily, a fact which did not escape Caine's eyes.

"Be you one of those who see the wraiths dancin' over the marsh? They do say that the wraiths call them to a bad end if they cheat and lie."

Chapter Forty-Four

Seven hours later, Peveril felt as if he had come to a bad end already. Caine's contempt for the local police's knowledge of the extent of sedge and mud which surrounded Harting Magna had been justified, since he and Peveril had reached his boat without seeing any sign of either the police or the army. The tortuous route which the smuggler had followed had certainly aided this escape, but Ralph had been deeply relieved that no-one had been placed to watch over Caine's vessel.

The next stage had been singularly more unpleasant. Lying in a tiny, hidden compartment built into the bottom of the fishing-boat, and warned not to attempt to emerge, no matter what happened, Ralph had started to wonder whether he had made a terrible mistake. After all, Caine was a known criminal – it would be very easy for the smuggler to take him out to sea, kill him, and then dispose of his body. No-one would ever know what had become of him. Ralph cursed himself. What was the point of thinking about the danger when he was already trapped? If Caine were the murderer, it was far too late to take action. And if Caine were innocent, it was vital not to ruin the whole enterprise by calling out in some feeble funk and alerting the real enemy. He had to keep his head; he simply had to.

When the vessel had eventually anchored in an isolated cove, Caine made no move to open the compartment until dusk fell. Even then, he only relented sufficiently to allow fresh air in. When the smuggler finally decreed that it was dark enough to prevent anyone from observing the presence of a second man, Ralph emerged, only to be told to wait while Caine went on reconnaissance.

"You be a-stayin' here while I go ashore. Bess, on guard!"

Bess nuzzled her master, before showing her teeth in Peveril's direction. Ralph suspected that the dog was there to prevent him from leaving, rather than to guard the boat, but he was grateful that his fears as to the smuggler's intentions appeared to be wrong. When Caine reappeared soundlessly out of the darkness, Ralph attempted to thank Caine for his efforts, the smuggler brushed the words away.

"That be nothin' if you be provin' that young Master Edwin be no murderer."

"It would help me enormously," suggested Peveril cunningly, "if you could tell me when you heard the shooting on the night of Durrant's death?"

The smuggler spat over the side of the boat. "'Tis time we left. You be a-followin' me and don't talk."

As they made their way across country, Ralph blessed the fact that his early training had left him with the ability to sneak unseen through the night. A sudden memory of the hollow tree where he used to hide his music sprang into Ralph's mind. That subterfuge had worked for weeks, until his cousin had lain in wait for him one evening and had then promptly revealed that he'd found Ralph studying music in secret, against his father's orders. Peveril shuddered as he recalled his father's retribution. God, it had hurt; Leo must have been drunk to have hit him quite as hard as he had. And Leo's savage mockery had gone on for days afterwards in front of Robert and the others. Ralph thrust away the memory. Leo was dead, and he had to concentrate on more important threats to the free world.

After what Peveril judged to be the best part of three hours, Caine murmured that they had arrived at Brandon. The moon was full enough to allow Ralph to pick out the crossroads, but, when he had given directions to the Grange, progress slowed to a crawl. Caine appeared to expect an ambush at every moment, while Peveril, able to see the tantalising outline of the house, fidgeted impatiently.

Once they had reached a clump of bushes close to the rear of the house, Caine halted.

"There do be a guard," he muttered.

Peveril could see nothing suspicious, but he was ready to believe the smuggler's warning.

"If I be a-callin' off the guard, do you be climbin' in?"

"Where?"

"There, where the music do sound."

Relieved that he was not imagining the music which drifted across the lawn, Peveril nodded. Midge must be in her snuggery, and he knew that there was a conveniently placed drainpipe which passed next to the window.

"Remember, I be takin' vengeance if you be a-cheatin' me." With that final warning, Caine stepped forward onto the path and walked briskly towards the house.

"Who goes there?"

"Be you the householder?"

"No. Who are you, and what are you doing?"

Peveril started in surprise as he recognised the voice of the guard. What the devil was Cohen doing at Midge's house? He was so taken aback that he nearly missed Caine's next statement.

"There be two armed men in the wood."

"Are there, by God?"

"They be up to no good, I'll be bound. They speak like foreigners."

"Indeed? Well, I'll just warn my man guarding the front of the house, and then I'll come and see what you've found."

Recovering from the shock of recognising Cohen's voice, Peveril forced himself to inch forward towards the house. It sounded very improbable that there was anyone else at the rear of the building, but he knew perfectly well that a sudden movement was much more likely to attract attention than a stealthy crawl. Nevertheless, it required considerable determination not to race across the grass to safety. However, once he reached the house, it took him seconds to shin up the drainpipe. After he was on a level with the open window, he hissed, "Midge, are you there?"

"Ralph? Thank goodness you've come. I've been worried sick about you. Can you manage to scramble across?"

Feeling that he could manage anything now that Midge had said that she had been worried about him, Ralph negotiated the awkward traverse sideways and slipped into the room.

"Thank goodness you were still up, Midge. I don't know how I'd have got in if you hadn't been. Cohen was on guard below."

Midge blushed in the darkness. "I thought that you might aim for Brandon, so I decided to stay up a bit longer than normal. That's why I was playing the gramophone – so that you would realise that I was here."

"You're an angel," breathed Ralph, aware that he wanted to seize Midge and smother her with kisses. "Do you know what's happened?"

"Do you mean Trent's death? We heard on the village grapevine, and then your Lt. Cohen turned up, wanting to check whether you had been here."

"He's not my Lt. Cohen, and hopefully Caine's distracted him sufficiently that he'll lose interest in here for a bit."

"Caine? The smuggler?"

"Yes. He's taken me on trust for the moment, although I don't much fancy my chances if he decides that I did kill Trent." Peveril suddenly thought of a further danger. "I say, Midge, hadn't we better close the window in case anyone hears us talking?"

"No. We'll leave it open with the gramophone playing, but we'll go elsewhere. That way, nothing will appear to have changed if Cohen does reappear."

Ralph followed Midge across the darkened room into the passage and then into another room. The slight scent of perfume suggested that it was her bedroom and Ralph was overwhelmed by an image of himself there for rather different ends. Reminding himself fiercely that only a cad would take advantage of a girl in such circumstances, he fought off the temptation to take her in his arms. Just as he was trying to thrust away the thought of Midge in a lace negligee, she turned on a bedside lamp to reveal herself prosaically dressed in a skirt and sweater. Ralph suddenly became aware of the fact that he was filthy and smelled of a mixture of oil and fish. Lust died, and he found himself stammering out an apology for his appearance.

"Don't be silly," Midge replied. "I can't imagine how you got away from camp, but I'm very relieved that you did." She hesitated, before adding in an embarrassed fashion, "I was terribly worried when Cohen showed up. It wasn't just that he seemed to think that you were in trouble, it was the fact that he wouldn't go away, even when he'd been inside the house."

"He searched the house? How dared he!"

"Given that you weren't there, it seemed safe enough to let him poke around."

"I suppose so," admitted Peveril grudgingly, "but he's got a damned nerve doing so, and I wish to goodness I knew how he'd tracked you down." Then a thought struck him. "What if he doesn't believe Caine's story? He might insist on searching the house again."

Midge nodded. "I know, but there's an odd little cupboard in the attic tucked away under the eaves. It wouldn't defy a professional searcher, but Cohen didn't notice it this afternoon. At the very least you'll have somewhere to sleep tonight."

Ralph shook his head. "No. If I'm caught inside, you'll never be able to deny knowing about me. I'm not having you placed in danger."

"Danger?"

Ralph gave a harsh laugh. "I don't know how many years incarceration you can get for harbouring a fugitive from justice – you'd have to check with Fletcher. And, since I'm meant to be a murderer, they could claim that you were an accessory after the fact."

"That would be very hard to prove, not least because you didn't kill Trent."

"I don't care. I'm not taking the risk. I'll go up onto the roof – it's warm enough tonight, and I could have hidden there without your knowledge. Anyway, a searcher wouldn't expect anyone to climb up there."

Knowing that Ralph was an expert night-climber, Midge reluctantly agreed. "I'd rather you were in the house, but I can see that you might be safer outside. If I give you a blanket, you could hide it in a chimney if anyone came."

"No. I don't want anything which could prove that you were involved. I'm sorry, Midge. I should never have dragged you into this. And I'd better tell you what's happened. Then you can decide whether I'm worth hiding or not."

When Peveril had finished narrating what had happened and how Caine had helped him, he gazed at Midge unhappily. "I can see why I'm under suspicion, but I don't understand why Trent was killed."

"Do you think he could have seen something he wasn't meant to? After all, he was on guard duty. Could he have spotted someone signalling?"

"I don't see how. He was on the wrong side of the bluff."

"Unless the signaller has shifted position."

"That wouldn't work – if there is a boat lying out to sea, it will be looking for a signal in the same position as before. And if Mrs Serring saw a signal a few nights ago, would someone risk signalling again so soon?"

Midge frowned. "It doesn't seem very likely. Maybe his death was nothing to do with anything he saw last night. Maybe he was killed because of something he saw on the night of Durrant's murder."

"Are you still wondering about Trent's statement?"

Midge nodded. "Yes. Nothing else Trent appears to have done seems especially important."

"He gossiped a lot; maybe he'd picked up something incriminating we don't know about."

"Possibly, but we do know for certain that he said that Poole returned to camp at 1.50. Poole thought that he took around half an hour to return, so that places the shooting at 1.20. But if Trent were mistaken, that would change the time of the shooting."

Peveril grimaced. "I wish I knew whether Caine actually could fix the time of the shot, but he's so infernally cagey that I can't get anything out of him." He paced round the room angrily. "Why didn't I question Trent when I had the opportunity? If there was something fishy about Poole's return to camp, I've lost the chance to ask him. Why didn't I think of it before?"

"I didn't think of it either."

"You're not meant to. I'm the supposed Intelligence expert, not you."

Midge gave a swift intake of breath as a thought occurred to her. "Ralph, could Trent have been Collingwood's other operative? If so, no wonder he was killed."

"I don't know, and I've no way of finding out."

"You could ask Collingwood when you tell him what's happened."

"No, I want you to summon Hartismere."

Midge frowned. "Wouldn't it be better to alert Collingwood?

After all, it will take time for Dr Hartismere to pass the information on to Collingwood."

"Hartismere is less busy than Collingwood."

"Really?"

Ralph flushed. "Look, if you want the truth, I'm scared of what Collingwood could do to you. He was furious when he found out that I'd told you anything. I should never have involved you and this is the only way in which I can report vital information while being sure that you won't suffer."

"But what about you?"

Ralph shrugged. "What matters is finding out what's going on. I'm valueless as an operative now that I've been accused of murder, but I must pass on all my information in case I get caught by the police." He tried to sound encouraging. "Nothing much will happen to me."

Midge eyed him shrewdly. "You don't believe that, do you?"

Since Ralph had not forgotten Collingwood's threat that he would be under close arrest but for the fact that he was needed in Suffolk, it was difficult for him to sound convincing. However, even if he were about to hand himself over to a court-martial, he couldn't let Midge realise the truth. "You don't need to worry. I'll probably be sent back to London." Seeing that Midge looked unpersuaded, he added, "I'll get it in the neck from Collingwood for having talked out of turn, but I deserve that. So please don't worry. And please don't cover up for me – Hartismere knows that you only got involved because I told you things." Peveril sighed. "The one thing I regret is that I've let him down. He was dashed supportive after the trial."

"Is that why you joined Intelligence?" asked Midge, who had never quite understood how Ralph had ended up there when he had wanted to go on active service.

Ralph shifted uncomfortably. "Hartismere said that it was my duty."

"But you were going to join up anyway."

"I know, but he seemed to think that I'd be more use to my country pretending to be other people, rather than shooting at Germans."

Midge was unconvinced. "I bet there was more to it than

that."

Ralph made a deprecatory noise, but otherwise remained silent.

"There was, wasn't there?" demanded Midge.

Swallowing in embarrassment, Ralph muttered, "After the trial, he told m'mother that he'd keep an eye on me. I didn't know that for some time, but it made her much happier – she said so. So how could I fail to repay him when he asked me to do something for him?" Peveril shrugged. "I obeyed orders for a change and did what I was told. But I've not succeeded, so Hartismere'll get a black mark against him for recruiting me."

Midge was shaken by this prediction, but attempted to encourage Ralph. "I'm sure that Dr Hartismere is sufficiently experienced not to blame you if we don't discover who killed Trent."

"I don't care if I am blamed," snarled Peveril. "In fact, I am to blame. Don't you see? Woolf has assumed that I'm a killer because I've been in the dock once before. So he won't investigate Trent's death properly and he'll leave a traitor loose to undermine the war effort. If Collingwood had sent someone else in, rather than me, Woolf would be forced to take things seriously."

"Then it's just as well if Dr Hartismere does come."

Chapter Forty-Five

The next day, the guard was lowered to one soldier. Midge decided not to tell her aunt that Ralph was carefully hidden on top of the roof, but Alice drew her own conclusions when Midge quite clearly jibbed at going to the inquest on Trent.

"My dear, Maria Gregory insists upon having an escort to the inquest. You are much more suited to that affair than I am, whilst I am far more capable of driving away invaders from our midst."

"Yes, but…"

"I shouldn't imagine that Capt. Peveril will be tactless enough to draw attention to himself by knocking on the scullery door, but if he is, doubtless Ellen will direct him towards me."

"I know, but…"

"And if you are determined to help that rather tiresome young man, you will do better by scrutinising the evidence presented at the inquest than hanging around here fretting."

After that conclusive remark, Midge gave in. If Ralph were half as exhausted as she was, he was likely to sleep during the afternoon, and it was certainly true that the inquest might present evidence of which Ralph was unaware. Moreover, since Cohen had already searched the house, it was not as if her presence at the inquest would give away her link with Ralph.

Mrs Gregory subjected Midge to a keen examination both before and after the inquest, when she aired her considerable surprise that the coroner had adjourned the inquest, rather than immediately returning a judgement against the mysterious captain who had gone missing. Since the inquests into Durrant and Poole had been similarly adjourned, Midge was not particularly surprised at the delay. However, she had no intention of revealing to Mrs Gregory that there were several points which she had found odd. It was only later that evening, when Ralph had been summoned down from the roof by the agreed signal of Elgar's *Sea Pictures*, that Midge was able to explain what she had noted.

"Didn't you say that Trent had a five-pound note in his wallet?"

Ralph nodded.

"Well, the police evidence was that he only had ten shillings."

"Maybe they didn't check behind the photograph."

"There was no mention of any photograph either. The evidence was quite categorical – the wallet was empty apart from a ten-shilling note."

"Are you sure?"

"Yes. That young lieutenant said that he'd seen you returning the wallet to Trent's pocket, so the coroner insisted on knowing whether there was anything in it. The police sergeant produced it in court and showed everyone what it contained."

"But that's ridiculous." Ralph shivered. "Midge, I did see it, honestly. It was a snap of an elderly couple outside a house and there was a date on the back."

Midge stared at him in some surprise. "I'm not suggesting that you made it up. Why on earth would you?"

Peveril shrugged. He had no desire to explain to Midge that he no longer trusted his own eyes.

When there was no response, Midge continued, "I can see why a five-pound note might disappear, but why would anyone steal a photograph?"

"Perhaps someone grabbed the contents of the wallet and didn't stop to check what they were?"

"I suppose that could have been the case," admitted Midge grudgingly, "but it seems a terrible risk to run. No-one could prove that the note belonged to Trent, but the photograph might have been recognised."

"The number on the note would be traceable."

"But we haven't got it – nor do the police."

"I have got it."

"You have? Gosh, Ralph, that's terribly important. If we can trace it, we might trace the thief."

"I know; that's one of the reasons I want to speak to Hartismere. I wish he'd hurry up."

Midge glanced at Ralph's face. He did not look as if he had had much rest whilst she had been at the inquest. "In the meantime, perhaps we ought to consider who might have killed Trent."

Ralph ran his fingers through his hair. "It would have been a lot easier if he'd been killed in the mess. That way I'd have been sure it was one of C Coy who were responsible. But, given what Jervis said about how some of A Coy infiltrated the camp only a few days ago, how can I be sure that someone didn't come in from outside?"

"At least the medical evidence ensures that time of death is pretty clear-cut. If we could check up who's got alibis, that would narrow things down somewhat."

"Impossible," grunted Peveril. "How can you provide an alibi for 3 a.m. when you're meant to be asleep? Take my case. I slipped out just before 5 a.m. without Tompkins spotting me – what is there to prove that I wasn't out murdering Trent two hours earlier? There was no-one in my quarters to know otherwise." Realising that he was staring at Midge hungrily, Ralph added hastily, "In any case, I still think that it was dashed fishy that Snellgrove changed the duty-roster immediately after he'd said that Trent talked too much."

Midge sighed. "Everything's fishy, if you ask me. So much so that I'm starting to wonder whether there is some vengeful local at work, rather than someone in the army. It's such a pity that Cosford had an alibi for the night of Durrant's death."

A trace of wry amusement crossed Peveril's face. "So much for studying logic at Newnham, Midge. You just want to affix blame on whoever's convenient."

Since Midge wished to avoid drawing attention to herself, she observed her normal routine after luncheon. However, instead of sleeping, she found herself wondering whether Ralph was correct that his presence was damaging the investigation. It seemed so unfair that his trial was being held against him. It had been proved categorically that he was not guilty; why should the fact that he had been wrongly arrested make him an obvious suspect now? Why did such small-minded attitudes thrive in country districts? Or would Ralph have faced similar prejudice even in Cambridge? Midge growled angrily to herself. It wasn't fair; no wonder Ralph was so sensitive about matters. At least Aunt Alice had greeted him warmly the first time he had visited, whatever she might think about him at the moment.

In the late afternoon, Alice declared that she intended to attend Evensong. As the walk to church was beyond Midge, there was nothing surprising about Midge staying behind. What was surprising was that Midge did not then return upstairs, but instead chose to position herself in the drawing room, where she had an excellent view of the path to the front door. When the village taxi-driver – now reduced in status to a pony and trap – drew up in front of the door, Midge opened it before there was any danger of a door-bell summoning Ellen from the kitchen.

"Leave your bag there in the corner," she hissed. "Can you come upstairs with me now?"

Apparently unsurprised by this cloak-and-dagger approach, the visitor followed Midge's slow steps upstairs. Once the stairs had been conquered, Midge pushed open the door to her snuggery. "He's on the roof. Let me turn on the gramophone to signal that it's safe to come down."

Five minutes later, Ralph climbed in through the open window. "Thank God you're here, sir."

After Midge left to keep a watch over the approach to the front of the house, Peveril briefly explained the situation. At the end of it, Hartismere glanced at him thoughtfully.

"May I enquire why you did not report directly to Collingwood?"

"I thought you'd get here more swiftly, sir."

"And was that the only reason?"

Peveril looked embarrassed and muttered something meaningless.

"Do I take it you feared that Collingwood might think that you were a murderer? Or did you believe that Miss Carrington was in danger?"

Peveril had a sudden fear that his erstwhile tutor thought that he was playing the self-sacrificing hero. Well, he might have brought Hartismere in to protect Midge, but he was damned if he were going to say so.

"Everyone else seems to think that I'm a murderer – why shouldn't Collingwood?"

"Hasn't it occurred to you that the medical evidence indicates that Trent had been dead for some time before you discovered him?"

"I know that. At least, Midge – Miss Carrington – pointed it out to me. But Collingwood might have thought that I killed Trent earlier and then returned to the body to rifle it. After all, Woolf is a policeman, and he thinks that I'm guilty."

Hartismere snorted. "You might do Collingwood the justice of acknowledging that he has a brain and knows how to use it."

Peveril flushed, but the Vice-Master was not finished. "Nor is Collingwood suddenly going to arrest Miss Carrington because she has the misfortune to know you."

"But he thinks that I let Poole out and am lying about it."

"Does he, by God?"

"Yes. At least, he's pretty suspicious." Peveril hesitated, before deciding that he might as well raise his real fear. "Anyway, what if he decides that Midge might talk?" He grimaced. "I know you'll hand me over to him, sir, but I wanted someone else to know what was happening."

Hartismere sighed. "I did tell you to trust your C.O. more, did I not?"

"Yes, sir."

Hartismere sighed for a second time. "I suppose at least you had the sense to summon me."

"And now you want me to be a good boy and redeem myself?"

"You needn't become quite so dull, but your co-operation would be appreciated. And don't forget that Collingwood didn't abandon you when you turned up in Cambridge, even although he might quite reasonably have assumed that you intended to desert."

This suggestion shocked Peveril horribly. "I didn't, sir; I swear I didn't."

"I don't suppose you did. More to the point, nor did Collingwood, although he has far less cause than I to trust you."

The implication that trust might run both ways hit Peveril hard. "I… that is…. oh, hell!"

Hartismere regarded him with tolerant pity. "I can make allowances for your past, you know. But what exactly did you see? Miss Carrington mentioned a photograph."

Keen to avoid the subject of Midge, Peveril briefly explained how he had found a five-pound note tucked behind a photograph in Trent's wallet and how both had since gone missing.

"I don't suppose you have the number of the note?"

"Yes, sir." Peveril scrabbled inside his own wallet and held out the paper on which he had jotted it down.

Hartismere looked relieved. "Good. Of course, nothing may come of it, but it's certainly worth following up. Now, what did the photograph show?"

"Just an elderly couple outside a house – nothing special."

"How old were they?"

"Around fifty, I suppose." Suddenly realising that describing fifty as elderly was not especially flattering to Hartismere, Peveril began to apologise, but the Vice-Master waved him to be quiet.

"Never mind that. What made you think that they were around fifty?"

"He looked a bit stooped and his hair was quite lightish."

"And hers?"

"You couldn't see it, sir. It was done up in a sort of wrap affair."

"What do you mean?"

"Well, like one of those silk handkerchiefs girls sometimes wear when they're driving."

"Did it look like silk?"

Peveril frowned in recollection. "N-o, I don't think so, sir."

"Why not?"

"It wasn't very silky. I mean, it didn't gleam or anything. It looked sort of flattish. More like linen."

"And did it match her skirt?"

"In colour?"

"In colour or pattern."

"It was quite pale and so was her blouse. But I got the impression that the blouse was quite fancy."

"Why?"

Peveril ran his hand through his hair. "I don't know, sir. I just did."

"Was it the sort of thing that Miss Carrington would wear?"

"Gosh, no."

"Or your sister?"

A momentary grin crossed Peveril's face. "Far too fussy for Honor."

"What makes you think that?"

"She doesn't like bits of lace and…" He suddenly stopped and stared at Hartismere. "I say, sir, how did you get me to remember that there was lace on the blouse?"

"It's a matter of asking intelligent questions. Most people are hopeless when describing a photograph. Now, what about the rest of her clothes?"

Hartismere proceeded to subject Peveril to a similarly exhaustive process on the man, the house, the garden and the general backdrop to the photograph, By the end of it, Ralph was dejectedly conscious that, had their positions been reversed, he would never have extracted one-tenth of the information which Hartismere had, not least because he lacked sufficient patience to keep probing away at the imperfect recollections of an unobservant witness. Somewhat to his surprise, however, Hartismere appeared pleased with him.

"Just as well I did come here in person, or I shouldn't have got all of the necessary information." Since Peveril looked uncertain whether this was an implied criticism of the need for his journey, the Viçe-Master added, "That photograph may prove vital, as may the number of note. If you hadn't kept your head you wouldn't have spotted either."

Peveril gave a brief nod.

Hartismere shot him a searching look. "I shouldn't worry too much about Miss Carrington, if I were you. Collingwood won't arrest her."

Fearing that he had made another wrong move, Peveril attempted to make amends. "I'm sorry if I've dragged you down here unnecessarily, sir."

The Vice-Master decided that there was no purpose in lecturing the boy – doubtless his C.O. would make his views clear enough later on.

"The important point is the information which you have

passed on, not to whom you have conveyed it." Hartismere coughed. "In any case, it is never easy going undercover, particularly when you are surrounded by enemies. Now, if you'll excuse me, I shall fetch Miss Carrington back – it would hardly do for you to be seen wandering around the house, and I want to talk to both of you."

Chapter Forty-Six

When Midge returned, Hartismere immediately asked her about the photograph.

"If I were to ask you to imagine a woman in quite smart clothes with a handkerchief round her hair, standing in front of a wooden house, what would you think of?"

Midge frowned. "It sounds a bit like one of those old Dutch masters."

"Now why do you say that?"

"She can't have tied her hair back to do cleaning if she were in smart clothes, and a wooden house doesn't suggest that she was about to go for a drive."

"Very good, my dear," purred Hartismere. "I particularly like the suggestion of Teutonic influence, but I am slightly at a loss as to why neither of you thought of that before, particularly since the numbers 7 on the back of the photograph were crossed in the continental manner."

"But Ralph didn't say that," protested Midge.

"That's because Ralph didn't remember," admitted Peveril. "It was extracted from him."

The Vice-Master smirked. "The, ah, Socratic method, you know. Years of interrogating undergraduates in an attempt to encourage them to use such brains as they possess does give me a certain advantage when it comes to this sort of affair."

Midge brushed away this attempt to prevent her from feeling that she ought to have discovered the same information earlier. "Do you think that Trent was actually a German agent? Surely it was very silly of him to carry around something which exposed his identity?"

Hartismere shook his head. "He wouldn't have been carrying that photograph if he'd been flown in from Germany – they search agents before they're sent overseas."

This statement of the dangers of being an operative chilled Peveril, but he pressed on. "Does that mean, sir, that Trent had been here since before the war broke out?"

"Oh, he wasn't German; he was English, all right. Most of C Coy's antecedents have been checked already. But," Hartismere added, "it looks like we'll have to look into Trent's in greater detail. Either he'd acquired false papers which happened to match with a man who'd joined the army before the war began, or he'd got some relative in Germany about whom he'd kept quiet. The latter is much more plausible. However, until we can discover the truth of that, we need to consider why he was killed."

Midge glanced at Ralph. "We wondered whether he was another British agent. That would explain the need to kill him."

"You may rule that out," declared Hartismere. "Whatever else, Trent had not been sent down to investigate the East Suffolks."

"In that case," continued Midge, "we thought that he'd perhaps seen something on the night of Durrant's death."

"Do go on."

"Well, given that Poole was the one who sought the interview with Durrant, it seems unlikely that he'd be late for it. Poole maintained that it took him around half an hour to get back to camp after the shooting broke out. Since he was meant to meet Durrant at 12.45, that would have him back in camp at around a quarter past one, but Trent said that he saw Poole returning at 1.50. The times don't make sense."

"So you are postulating that Trent was lying?"

"Yes."

"Have you considered the fact that Poole might have been lying. Or, alternatively, he could have genuinely underestimated how long it took him to return."

"Exactly," agreed Peveril. "Poole admitted that he never looked at his watch. If I'd been racing around trying to escape from a killer, I'm unsure how accurate my grasp of timing would be."

Midge frowned. "Don't you think that you'd be inclined to overestimate how long it took, rather than underestimate it? Surely terrifying moments seem to last much longer than pleasant moments?"

"That may be convincing in psychological terms," agreed Hartismere, "but what is the purpose of any lie which Trent uttered?"

"One of the soldiers reported hearing shooting at 1.20," Peveril reminded them. "Maybe Trent guessed that it would take around half an hour to return from where Durrant died, and decided to link Poole directly to the shooting. He might have wanted a quick conviction to avoid anyone sniffing around and discovering whatever connection he had with Germany."

"And," suggested Midge, "at least we've now got a reason for why Trent might want to help the killer. He may have known that the killer is on the side of the Nazis. What's more, even if Poole protested that he came back earlier than 1.50, no-one would pay attention to him since he was meant to be guilty."

"Everyone accepted his guilt very easily," commented Peveril. "All the same, Trent was taking rather a risk that someone might have believed Poole."

"But," pointed out the Vice-Master, "Poole didn't speak out and then he was killed. In fact, I suspect that the only reason he wasn't killed earlier was that it was hard to get at him in the police-station."

Midge noticed Ralph flinching at this reminder what had happened. She cast around for something to distract him. "Who was the soldier who reported hearing shooting? Do you consider him to be reliable? Or was he the sort of man who'd make something up to appear important?"

"I don't know," admitted Ralph apologetically. "Woolf's notes only referred to a soldier; his name wasn't given – and I can't exactly go and ask Woolf, now that he's convinced I'm a murderer."

Hartismere was unmoved by Peveril's bitter conclusion. "Perhaps not, but I can."

"You, sir?"

A sardonic smile crossed the Vice-Master's visage. "My dear boy, such lack of trust! I no longer have the circumference to pass myself off as a brass hat, but I have in my possession papers which prove that I am a chief inspector at Scotland Yard, currently seconded to the Military Police. They ought to have been called in before, so it's a perfectly credible cover." He grew serious. "More to the point, if need be, the Yard will back up my claim, whereas there could be any number of tedious officers who would question the veracity of my regimental position." He cast a sideways glance at Peveril. "Also, I have powers of arrest. If necessary, you will become my prisoner until I get you out of here."

Peveril licked his lips. "In other words, sir, you expect a raid."

"Precisely. So I suggest that we continue to explore the various possibilities which you and Miss Carrington have considered."

"Well," suggested Midge with a bravado she did not feel, "if you are going to arrest Ralph and demand papers, I think you ought to impound Poole's diary. Everyone has said that it had an entry for 1.15 on the night of Durrant's death, but, if the appointment really were for 12.45, why would Poole write down the wrong time. If it comes to that, why did he write down a time at all? He said that he was too scared to speak openly to Durrant in case he was overheard – would he then go and carefully note down when he was due to meet the man?"

"The only problem with that," argued Peveril, "is that by the time I returned to camp on the morning of Durrant's death, the diary entry was being talked about quite openly. Would there have been time to alter it?"

"It rather depends who was doing the altering," pointed out Hartismere. "Assuming it was the killer, he must have had around six hours. That's quite a lot of time and, if the killer is an officer, he would have been in the same building."

"I shouldn't think it would be very hard for other ranks to get into the farmhouse, judging by the usual standard of guard-duty," Peveril grunted. "More importantly, Poole must have been in his room for most of those six hours. I don't see how someone could have got back from committing the murder and gone straight onto forging diaries. Furthermore, how did he recognise Poole in the dark? If it comes to that, how did he learn that Poole had an appointment with Durrant? I know that Poole suspected that someone must have overheard him at HQ, but we're postulating a murderer in C Coy."

"There are such things as conspirators."

Midge ignored this remark, since she had suddenly been seized with an idea of her own. "I say, what if Durrant wasn't meant to be the victim. Maybe the killer actually wanted to get Poole. After all, Poole said that he hadn't told Durrant what was going on. Surely it would be far safer to kill Poole before he had the chance to spill the beans to Durrant? I agree that Durrant was dangerous, because he'd have had no hesitation in acting on Poole's information. However, murdering Durrant wouldn't actually solve the problem that Poole had reached the stage where he was ready to squeal."

Peveril whistled. "You're right, Midge. Golly, the assassin must have got a bit of a shock when he discovered that he'd killed someone else."

"And if you are correct," added Hartismere, "we may be able to remove the troubling issue of who passed on the information from A Coy that Durrant had a meeting with Poole. It could be that no-one noticed anything odd at all about Poole being at HQ."

"I've been there on pointless errands lots of times," stated Peveril. "Why shouldn't Poole? All the same, sir, why wasn't Poole killed earlier? Why not shoot him in camp?"

"He was known to have disreputable friends, wasn't he?" replied Hartismere. "Doubtless his murderer waited until he saw him apparently going off on a poaching expedition. That way he could guarantee that there would be no witnesses."

"Except for Caine," pointed out Peveril.

"Except for Caine," agreed the Vice-Master. "I am increasingly of the opinion, my dear boy, that you must have further detailed speech with the man. I don't suppose that he trusts you very much, but the fact that he trusts you at all makes you a far better potential interrogator than anyone else – particularly Chief Inspector Thomas of the Yard."

Having raised that possibility, Hartismere returned to the discrepancy between the two estimates as to when Poole had arrived back at camp.

"How many of the alibis for Durrant's death can you remember?"

"Some of them, sir, but not all. Twenty of the men are definitely ruled out, because they were up at B Coy."

"I suppose it would be unreasonable of me to expect you to

remember a detailed list of what the remaining thirty had been doing," agreed the Vice-Master. "However, I think that we might concentrate on some new times."

"Do you mean that the alibis for 1.20 are worthless?"

"On the contrary, my dear boy, they may prove to be highly significant."

"Exactly," confirmed Midge enthusiastically. "If someone's got a rock-solid alibi for the supposed time of death, but a very weak alibi – or none at all – for the real time of death, then they're going to look very suspicious."

"I am glad," remarked the Vice-Master to the air, "that I have always supported the admission of women to the University. It means I can enjoy the fruits of their brains without any lowering sense of having been proved wrong in my arguments."

Ralph shifted uneasily. "Err... quite." He became conscious that Hartismere was scrutinising him, and he rushed into speech. "Some chaps talk a lot of rot." Then, realising how this could be misinterpreted, he stammered, "I don't mean you do, sir."

"And with that graceful apology to all concerned now concluded, shall we return to our alibis?"

Peveril subsided, aware that he was blushing, and wishing that Hartismere would remember that he was no longer at Trinity. For her part, Midge guessed that Ralph had been trying to make amends for his earlier remark about girls being afraid of explosives, and shot a friendly grin at him.

"If we accept Poole's claim that his appointment was for 12.45," she stated, "then the murder must have taken place around then."

"Yes," admitted Peveril slowly. "The trouble is, while I think that everyone was questioned pretty closely about what they were doing at 1.20, I don't think that there was much discussion about what happened before one o'clock."

"Don't forget," Hartismere pointed out, "that it would take some time for the killer to get back to camp. I think that you can consider any alibis – or lack of them – for just after one."

"I'll try," replied Peveril doubtfully, "but I honestly don't know how much I can remember."

While this discussion was going on, Midge had kept checking

her watch. Eventually, she explained her concern. "I'm terribly sorry, but I'm sure that my aunt will be back shortly."

Ralph got to his feet immediately. "I'd better disappear, then."

"I really am sorry."

"Don't be silly. You've already put yourself at risk to give me shelter." He paused. It would be a lot easier to say what he wanted to say if Hartismere weren't there. He attempted a joke. "I've got plenty to think about with all those alibis." He turned to the Vice-Master. "I'm extremely grateful to you for coming, sir. Err... will you look after Miss Carrington?"

"Of course, my dear boy."

At this point the gravel crunched. Ralph turned white.

"Go on," hissed Midge. "I'll delay her."

"And," murmured Hartismere, after Peveril had left, "if it is not your aunt, I shall do my best to delay him or them."

Chapter Forty-Seven

Fortunately, the gravel had announced Alice Carrington's return, rather than an incursion by hostile forces. However, when Midge informed her that the Vice-Master was upstairs in her snuggery, Alice's eyebrows rose.

"How much does that man know?"

"About…?"

"Don't waste time, Midge. How much does he know about what Ralph Peveril has been up to?"

Midge took in her aunt's unusually fierce countenance. "Everything."

"Including the fact that the boy is here?"

Midge gave a sharp intake of breath. Her aunt sighed. "My dear child, immediately you didn't fly at me for calling him tiresome, I was sure that he was here. It was a test. If he'd been safely elsewhere you'd have leapt to his defence."

Thinking that she had underestimated her aunt, Midge admitted that Ralph was currently concealed on the roof.

"In some ways that simplifies things. At least I don't have to worry that you'll go racing off to Newton to pass on my news. Go and fetch him – I suppose we'd better go to your snuggery, rather than risk someone looking in through the drawing-room windows and recognising him."

When Ralph reappeared, he attempted both to apologise and to thank Alice. She gave him the kind of look which suggested that she would like the chance to speak frankly to him on the subject of the appropriate manners to be shown during courtship. However, she contained herself, instead explaining where she had been.

"After Evensong, Col. Gregory asked me to drop by and inspect his roses, which he suspected were being attacked by a new form of blight. I thought nothing of it, until he told me that young Baldock had been to see him."

"The constable at Newton, Mrs Carrington?"

"Precisely, Mr Peveril. Now I don't know whether Midge has told you, but Baldock's aunt and uncle work for the Gregorys. So when Baldock was faced with a conundrum, he promptly sought Col. Gregory's advice."

Midge swallowed. It was clear that Baldock had not brought good news.

"Somehow, it has come to the attention of the police that you, Mr Peveril, have been hidden here." Despite herself, Alice could not keep the outrage from her voice. "They propose to raid this house late tonight. My husband employed young Baldock in the garden before he was old enough to join the police. Baldock was, therefore, appalled to be told that he was 'to invade Mr Geoffrey's house and arrest his lady'. Apparently, Woolf is too inclined to jump to conclusions and stick to them, no matter what, so Baldock knew that he had no chance of persuading Woolf to change his mind. Hence he asked Col. Gregory what to do, and the colonel said that he would see to it." Mrs Carrington regarded the assembled company. Had Midge been alone, she would have been very tempted to quote the colonel's precise words – 'inexperienced gels fall for wrong 'uns, m'dear. I've never understood why, but I saw enough of it in India…'. However, she had no intention of humiliating her niece and, in any case, she knew perfectly well that there was no surer method of interesting a girl in a man than by suggesting that everyone misunderstood him.

"Is that the only matter which your friend raised?"

"No, Dr Hartismere, it was not. Last night someone tried to kill the inspector in charge of the case."

"What?" exclaimed Midge. "How?"

"A grenade was thrown into the police-station at Newton. The inspector was lucky not to be killed."

Ralph felt Hartismere's eyes on him. "It wasn't me, sir. I know I..."

The Vice-Master cut short his protestations. "Be quiet. Now, Mrs Carrington, let me get this quite clear. The police-station was attacked?"

"Yes."

"With one grenade, or a string of them?"

"Col. Gregory mentioned only one, but I don't know whether there were others."

"Where exactly was the attack? In the front or back of the

station?"

"I don't know. All I know was that a whole lot of papers went on fire and the sergeant's furious because he's lost practically all his evidence against a jeweller who's under suspicion of buying stolen goods."

"And, finally, if I may, when did the attack take place?"

"Around nine o'clock." Alice's eyes travelled again towards Peveril.

"I'm surprised that we haven't already heard about it on the village grapevine," commented Midge.

"I suppose that the police don't want to advertise the fact that they've been attacked again – it might encourage the local rogues to think that they can do what they like. However, they are determined to track down the man responsible."

In the face of her aunt's obvious distrust, Midge leapt to Ralph's defence. "It wasn't Ralph, and he can prove it."

"Was he here already?" demanded Alice, hoping that Midge was correct.

"No, but there was someone with him."

"Then the sooner you produce that someone the better."

There was an uncomfortable silence as both Midge and Ralph contemplated how Alice would be likely to respond to the information that Ralph's alibi was provided by an acknowledged smuggler. Hartismere intervened.

"Is it known when this raid by the police is to take place?"

"After ten, according to Baldock."

"In that case, I should prefer to have you out of here by eight at the absolute latest, Peveril." The Vice-Master frowned. "It will still be light – anyone in army uniform will attract attention. Do you have any clothes suitable for a disguise, Mrs Carrington?"

Alice inspected Peveril carefully. "With a hat on, he might just be able to pass for a girl. That would fool any searchers."

"I rather fear that his voice would give him away," pointed out Hartismere.

"Try to sound like a girl," Alice ordered.

Feeling a fool, Ralph attempted to speak in higher tones than usual. "Will this do?"

The other three looked at each other.

"No," admitted Alice. "Midge, come and help me look through some clothes."

When the two women had left, Hartismere motioned to Peveril to sit down. "Do you know anything about this attack on the police-station?"

"Just because I was going to attack it before doesn't mean I attacked it last night, sir."

The Vice-Master sighed. "My dear boy, I do have a reasonably secure grasp of basic logic. More to the point, if you had blown it up last night, I am quite prepared to believe that you had a reason for doing so."

"I was with Caine."

"And he never left you?"

"I don't know, sir. Half the time I was inside a hatch in his boat. He could have cleared off without my noticing."

Hartismere doubted whether Peveril was lying, but he produced a large-scale map of the area. "Before we plan your route back, you might indicate to me your route here."

"Route back?" Peveril sounded surprised. "Sir, everybody's hunting for me. If I spoke to anyone, they'd summon a policeman straight away."

"Not the particular gentleman I had in mind. Caine is not precisely on the side of law and order, is he?"

"You mean I could be of use?"

"Of course. I need you to question Caine about the time of Durrant's death, and you also need somewhere to hide for the moment. Do you have any other proposal?"

Peveril shook his head.

When Peveril had traced how he had reached Brandon, Hartismere concluded that the boy must have been miles away from Newton when the police-station was attacked. With that problem dealt with, he concentrated on how to extricate Peveril from his current position. Eventually, Hartismere decided that the safest route involved Peveril heading north out of Brandon, before curling round to the west.

"They'll either expect you to head north-east to the railway-line, or south-west with the ultimate aim of reaching Ipswich and London. There's no apparent shelter in the marshes, other than a few isolated hamlets. If the police know their job, the inhabitants will all be warned, so don't risk going near them. Stick as much as possible to the reed-beds until you reach Harting Magna."

"Yes, sir," agreed Peveril, trying not to think what it would be like spending days and – worse – nights in the wastelands of his nightmares.

The Vice-Master cast a sharp glance at him. "Now listen to me, Peveril. I need that information from Caine, but his probable confirmation of the time of the shooting is less important than keeping this operation secret."

"You mean, am I going to crack up again and give the show away?"

"Put bluntly, yes."

Ralph stared at his hands, conscious that any half-decent chap would have laughed away the suggestion. "I don't think so, sir. I mean, I know what to expect. And," he added bitterly, "no-one's called me a coward recently, so perhaps I shan't be one."

Hartismere sighed. If the boy had been a few years younger, he could have patted him on the shoulder and tried to reassure him with glib words. However, time was very limited and he had to cover all eventualities. "Will you be able to maintain an even equilibrium if the police or the army get their hands on you?"

"If I'm copped, I'll keep my mouth shut." Peveril suddenly glanced up at Hartismere. "Sir, could I have chucked that grenade at the police-station without knowing it? Midge's aunt clearly thinks I was responsible."

The Vice-Master winced. The boy must be very unsure of himself if he were starting to wonder about this sort of thing. "My dear chap, don't you think that Caine might have noticed and remonstrated with you? Even smugglers don't normally resort to such public outbursts of violence."

"No, of course not. Sorry."

"Last term," continued Hartismere smoothly, "I had the experience of attempting to explain to an undergraduate that his desire to, as he put it, 'whang a missile' into his friend's set was insufficient excuse for breaking a Fellow's window with a bottle of ale. Your youthful follies never involved brainless hooliganism, so I cannot imagine that you have resorted to it now."

A brief grin travelled over Peveril's face. "Just as well I didn't get nabbed chalking the fountain in college colours the night our boat bumped Corpus. You might have had to revise your opinion of me."

"Oh quite. I should have been shocked – Corpus doesn't merit such ostentatious celebration. Now had you been doing it to celebrate bumping John's or King's, I should have let you off with a caution."

Shortly afterwards, Alice and Midge returned, carrying some clothing.

"You're to be a travelling sweep," announced Midge baldly. "Not only does it get you out of army kit, but it gives you a reason to be wandering around. It's less obvious than becoming a tramp."

"And soot over your face might deceive someone who doesn't know you well," added Alice. "You're slighter in build than my son, so the clothes won't fit very well, but I don't suppose anyone expects a sweep to be well-dressed."

Midge noticed Alice's acerbic tone. She was fairly sure that it was due to her aunt's concern for John, rather than hostility to Ralph, but she hastened to intervene. "You'll have an old coat of Evans', too. Mrs Evans has been trying to get him to throw it out for years, so she'll be delighted if it disappears."

"What about brushes, Mrs Carrington?" enquired Hartismere.

"We've a few which Evans keeps in case of emergencies. They aren't good enough to fool a real sweep, so don't fall into conversation with one."

Peveril thanked Midge's aunt, whilst wondering how he was meant to know whom to avoid. Midge, however, was more concerned with another problem.

"I don't know your route, and I suppose I had better not know, but do be careful if you go anywhere near the coast. It's not just the police you need to watch out for, there are the coast-watchers as well."

"I'll be careful," promised Ralph, before suddenly remembering something important. "Caine knows where you live – he might possibly bring you a message. I'll use 'Bertie' as a code-word, so that you know it really is from me."

Midge was mildly amused by Ralph adopting her cat's name as a signal, but Mrs Carrington reacted very differently. "Caine? The smuggler? Have you involved Midge with *him*?"

"No," protested Peveril. "Midge has never met him."

Alice's eyes narrowed. "I suppose he's the man who can provide you with an alibi for last night. If so, I suggest that you don't get caught – the magistrates round here take a very dim view of that sort of activity."

Chapter Forty-Eight

Half an hour later, after a brief conversation with Mrs Carrington, Ralph slipped out of the back of the house. Hartismere had been very unhappy about the exposed nature of the graceful sweep of the lawn at the front of the house and had insisted that the kitchen-garden was a much safer exit. In theory, Ralph agreed with him, but as he squirmed in and out of the tall fruit poles, he felt unpleasantly as if he were already caught in a trap. Eventually, he reached the stone wall which bounded the grounds. He could hear nothing on the other side.

'As well now as at any other time,' he thought, before pulling himself onto the top of the wall. The lane was empty, so he jumped down. As he had been told, there was a gate into the fields practically opposite and it only took seconds to climb in. 'I don't suppose that the hedge will give me much protection from being seen from the road, but it's better than nothing. I'll risk the lanes when I've got a bit further from Midge's house.'

Peveril scowled. Midge had looked worried and upset when he had left. If there had ever been a time to kiss her, it had been then. But Alice Carrington had made that impossible. 'Why did her aunt have to warn me off? I mean, I can see her point that she doesn't want Midge involved with me until all of this is cleared up. And she did say that she doesn't think that I'm a murderer. But she's very suspicious about the arson attempt.' A cynical smile crossed his face. 'Just as well she's concentrating on the second attack – I can plead Not Guilty to that – but if she knew that I'd planned to involve Midge in an earlier one, I'd have been thrown out of the house.' He kicked a clod of earth savagely. 'Thank God Hartismere's there to look after them. I'd like to wring Woolf's damned neck. How dare he raid their home?'

Just after nine o'clock, it became apparent that Woolf had very little difficulty in daring to raid the Grange. Not only did he push past Ellen when she answered the door, but he was openly carrying his revolver.

"I am a police officer," he informed Mrs Carrington when she appeared from the drawing-room. "According to information received, you are harbouring a fugitive from justice. I would advise you to give him up. The house is surrounded."

Alice looked him up and down regally. "Are you drunk? How dare you behave in this manner!"

In the drawing-room, Midge was feeling – and looking – terrified. Hartismere gave her a brief, encouraging smile, before emerging into the hall. The presence of a man clearly surprised Woolf.

"Who might you be? You can't be Peveril's father because he killed him."

Alice spoke in a voice so glacial that the room seemed to have turned chilly. "This person is a detective from Scotland Yard, seconded to the Military Police."

Midge blinked in shock. She had never heard her aunt being 'county' before. 'Golly,' she thought, 'thank goodness Aunt Alice isn't really like that; I'd have had a dreadful time.'

Hartismere had, by this point, produced his documents. "I am Chief Inspector Thomas. Do I take it that you are the officer in charge of this case?"

"Yes."

"Then I suggest that we discuss the matter out of the way of the ladies."

Woolf looked unconvinced. "Well, I don't mind doing you a favour, but my men need to get on searching the house. The suspect is a dangerous character and the sooner he's under lock and key the better."

"Have you got a search-warrant?" demanded Midge.

Woolf smiled unpleasantly. "Oh, yes, my dear young lady, I have a search-warrant. There'll be no getting out of this on some sort of legal quibble."

Hartismere wished that Midge had kept quiet. Her question suggested rather too much awareness of police procedure. To distract Woolf from this, he began his prepared lies. "I have already conducted an extensive interrogation and I see no reason to believe that the ladies know where the man is. However, if you have your constables here, you may as well make sure of it."

Mrs Carrington drew in her breath sharply. "Disgraceful! I

shall make sure that the Chief Constable gets to hear of this!"

"Madam, if you please," remarked Woolf. "It will make things much easier if you don't protest."

Alice looked him up and down with superb disdain, before stating distantly, "Come, niece, we shall retire to the morning-room until these creatures have concluded their work. Doubtless they will tell us when they are finished – or when they want to check that we are not hiding some unfortunate renegade under the table."

With this Parthian shot, she swept passed Woolf. He, after giving directions to his men, followed Hartismere into the drawing-room.

"Bit of a Tartar, that one," Woolf complained. "She'll regret taking that tone once we find some evidence to Peveril's presence."

"Peveril?" repeated Hartismere.

This question brought a satisfied smile onto Woolf's face – or as much of it as could be seen behind some plasters. "Ah, so Scotland Yard doesn't know everything. I recognised him from reading about his trial. He attacked the police station with a grenade last night."

"Last night?"

"Yes."

"You are referring to a second attack?"

Woolf looked puzzled. "Yes. How did you know about the first?"

"We had a tip-off."

"From whom?

"Information received, in the shape of an anonymous letter. We were told that explosives had gone missing from the local regiment." Hartismere coughed. "And I gather there have been some military personnel killed."

Woolf's voice hardened. "I cannot see what additional local knowledge an urban policeman can bring to a rural crime."

Hartismere pretended not to notice the man's anger. "It is a matter of jurisdiction, as much as anything. Crimes involving military personnel are to be investigated, where possible, by Military Police. However, there is no reason why we cannot collaborate. Perhaps you would be good enough to bring me up to date."

When Woolf had finished, Hartismere asked a number of unimportant questions, before leading up to the one in which he was really interested. "Who was it who heard the shots on the night of Durrant's death?"

"I haven't the faintest idea – one of the privates, I think."

"Presumably you wrote it down in your notes?"

Woolf gave a sarcastic laugh. "I suppose you Scotland Yard types think that county constabularies are staffed by fools. Of course we noted down the evidence – and a whole lot of other evidence from other interrogations – but it's rather hard to read ashes."

"Ashes?"

"Yes. When Peveril tried to kill me, he set the police-station on fire."

"He tried to kill you?"

"Oh yes – where do you think I got these burns? That gaol-bird threw a grenade in the window of my office. I was damned lucky to escape."

"My dear chap, are you sure you should be working?"

Woolf shrugged. "If the furniture hadn't taken most of the blast I wouldn't be working in any meaning of the word. Just wait until I get my hands on that man – he won't be so damned supercilious when he feels the bracelets round his wrists."

Ralph, meanwhile, was not feeling in the slightest supercilious. Instead he was tired and more than a little apprehensive. On the map, it had not looked such an intolerably long distance from Brandon to Harting Magna, but by midnight he had made very little progress. He had been forced to make a diversion northwards to avoid a road-block on the other side of Brandon. That had wasted well over an hour. Then, as he was approaching Brandon St Nicholas, some sixth sense had warned him to beware. He had never intended to go into the village itself – only to make use of the ford downstream of it. But when he reached the point where the road curved round to begin its slow approach to the ford, he stopped, certain that there was someone on guard.

After fifteen minutes, there was still no sign of a human presence and he told himself that he was a fool to waste time. Nevertheless, instinct overrode all arguments to the contrary and he remained motionless, listening intently. After another ten minutes, Ralph heard the crunch of a pebble underfoot. At that point, he had retreated soundlessly, shocked by how easily he could have been caught. Whoever had laid that trap had planted it well. Any fugitive would have been alert at the ford itself, but the soldier had been posted several hundred yards off, hidden by the curve.

Going downstream and swimming across the Gip had taken Peveril out of his planned route, and he had been forced to walk through a plantation, rather than along roads. It was certainly safer, but it was much slower. It was also much harder to see where he was going and, by three o'clock, Ralph decided to halt for an hour or so. He would be able to move more swiftly when there was a bit more light – it was devilish dark under the trees and he didn't want to go further off course. He had a nasty suspicion that he was getting too far away from the road leading southwards.

Although Ralph fully intended to stay awake until sunrise, the events of the past few days caught up with him and he nodded off. The next thing he knew was when his arm was seized and he heard a voice proclaiming in his ear, "Got you, my lad."

"Wh… what?"

"Playing the innocent, are you? Turn out your pockets!"

Peveril stared vacantly up at the man. It seemed a strange sort of command to give a suspected murderer.

"Come on, you heard me. Turn out your pockets."

Wishing that his revolver was not strapped to his inside leg, where he had hidden it to avoid it being found by a casual search, Peveril meekly did as he was told. The stranger regarded the motley collection of wallet, handkerchief and bar of chocolate with disdain, whilst his two dogs snuffled excitedly at them.

"Now your coat."

The sandwiches which Mrs Carrington had given Ralph aroused nothing more than a snort. However, when the map failed to excite interest, Peveril wondered whether he was dealing with an idiot. The man then ran his hands over the coat himself, before dropping it in disgust.

"You may not have poached anything so far, but I'll have you know that you are on preserved ground."

Realising that offended anger would do no good, Peveril adopted a whine. "I be honest, I be." He gesticulated towards his brushes. "I be going up Norfolk way for work."

"More like smoking and setting fire to haystacks. Now be off with you before I have you up in court."

Peveril scrambled to his feet. The aggrieved landowner watched him collect his brushes and then, as Peveril set off towards an open ride, barked at him impatiently. "Not that way. I don't want you on my land a moment longer than is necessary. You go this way, my lad, and stay on the road or I'll set my dogs on you. They bite."

Encouraged by the dogs, Ralph made his way as quickly as possible to the lane. When he looked back as he scrambled over the estate wall, the man was watching him with steady hostility.

A quick glance at the sun enabled Ralph to work out that the lane ran from east to west. If he headed east until he was out of sight, the landowner wouldn't be able to give his position away if he had second thoughts about what he might have captured. Ralph suddenly grinned. When he'd been speaking to Midge's aunt, he'd regretted refusing the loan of Carrington's razor – being dishevelled hadn't increased her approval of him. But his desire to have no obvious links with the Carrington household had paid unexpected dividends just then. Not only was he less recognisable, but being scruffy fitted in with his late interlocutor's prejudices about tramps. Ralph's grin widened. He could tease Midge horribly about how Plato would have characterised the ideal tramp. Then his grin disappeared. It was all very well making stupid jokes, but what if Hartismere hadn't been able to look after Midge? What if Mrs Carrington hadn't disposed of his uniform and Woolf had been able to prove that Midge had been hiding him?

Chapter Forty-Nine

In his own way, Hartismere was to have an equally exciting time. He had had a useful discussion with Midge whilst they were waiting for the raid and Midge had suggested to him that, if he were going to look at the police evidence, he might also investigate Cosford.

"Poole claimed that he was involved in the smuggling racket which we think is linked to espionage. Admittedly, Poole could have been lying, but Cosford definitely holds vehemently anti-Soviet views and he sold me a book which suggests he could be a Fascist. Also, he sells books at the hospital every Wednesday, which is when Poole was killed." Midge suddenly looked embarrassed. "We didn't get much further than that. I'm afraid. I... well, I can't really follow him around and Ralph has had too much else to do."

"Without official authority you would have got no further," Hartismere stated emphatically. "For a start, you cannot gain access to a list which exists of dangerous Fascists. Moreover, if you will forgive me for saying so, there are some advantages to the fact that you are clearly not a member of the Master Race. For one thing, it makes you much less likely to be suspected of being an investigator than I would have been." Hartismere attempted to lighten the atmosphere with a joke. "The term Master Race always makes me think of the struggle to be elected to lead a Cambridge college. Mind you, most of the candidates are literate, unlike Hitler's baboons."

Midge had frowned, as a memory flickered. "Gen. Whitlock said that he'd reported Cosford. Is Cosford on that list?"

"Apparently not, but it is mainly restricted to those who are actively involved in recruitment to various organisations. If Cosford had the sense to keep clear of the BUF, then he may well have escaped notice – particularly if there has been only one complaint. The Security Services do suffer somewhat from letters from choleric retired army officers."

Notwithstanding his comments on the likelihood that Cosford had been overlooked in a whirl of wider activity,

Hartismere was determined to have an interview with the man. However, he led up to the possibility gradually, with a series of tantalising lies. The first move was to question Woolf as to why he was so certain that Peveril had been behind the grenade-attack the previous night.

"Who else was loose?" Woolf demanded. "If he'd killed me, that would have stopped the hunt for him."

"I rather doubt that. Surely, if anything, the hunt would have intensified? After all, this was not the first such attack which you had suffered. Has it occurred to you that perhaps the two bombing incidents were linked?"

"What do you mean?"

"The first incident resulted in the escape of a murder-suspect. Now, I don't know what your suspicions are about the killing of Durrant, but I had wondered whether his death was part of a plot to damage the command-structure of an important coastal area."

"And Poole…?"

"If my suspicion is correct, then Poole must have been a Fifth Columnist. Other sympathisers tried to get him out of gaol before he was put on trial, and it was only thanks to your security precautions that he was recaptured. Similarly, last night may have been undertaken by Fifth Columnists, rather than this Peveril character."

"Unless he is one of them," grunted Woolf. "Still, I see what you mean. Such an attack would – did – destroy most of the evidence against Poole." He gave a grim laugh. "If Poole had known that, he might not have been so quick to kill himself."

"Are you quite sure it was suicide?"

"It must have been – he left a note. The way I see it is that Peveril, who was a friend of his, told him that he hadn't a hope, and he took the easy route out."

"There was no sign of Fascist sympathisers at the hospital?"

"Not that we've uncovered so far."

"And, of course, you are a small force and fully-stretched at the moment."

"Quite."

"Well, I don't want to neglect the Fascist angle. It would be useful to consider those already under suspicion."

"You've got someone in mind," remarked Woolf. "Who is it?"

Awarding the inspector full marks for perspicacity, Hartismere nodded. "I gather that Basil Cosford may have some interesting political views. What is known about him?"

Woolf gave a hollow laugh. "My files are ruined. How can I show you anything about him?"

Hartismere decided that the Military Police would have been unimpressed with this answer. "That's all very well, Woolf, but you must have some local knowledge."

Woolf shrugged. "Off hand, I don't remember anything, other than that he was once fined for being in licensed premises after hours."

"Politically?"

"He certainly wasn't a socialist. I think he'd lost a bit of money in the Revolution. But there was never any suggestion that he did more than curse the Soviets." A brief grin traversed the inspector's face. "Quite a few of the gentry round here curse the Soviets – but most of the time they're referring to their own government."

Hartismere laughed. "Not quite recovered from the shock of seeing Ramsay MacDonald in Number 10? There are plenty similar in London. Nevertheless, I suppose I'd better have a look at this Cosford specimen."

"If you get him to admit to arson I'll eat my hat," Woolf declared. "Cosford is no bold highwayman figure."

While Hartismere was perfectly happy to accept Woolf's estimate of Cosford, he still requested that the inspector accompany him to Cosford's shop.

"The presence of two of us may help to overawe him," he explained.

Woolf looked aggrieved by this addition to his duties, but he did not demur, other than to point out that there was no point in arriving before ten o'clock since, in these provincial parts, there was no call for a bookseller to open any earlier.

When the two men arrived at half past ten, Hartismere felt

moved to comment on the fact that there appeared to be no call upon booksellers at any hour of the clock. "The blinds are still down," he pointed out, "but there isn't any appreciable queue at the door."

"Things are always a bit slow on Tuesday mornings," argued Woolf, dimly sensing that the detective from London was laughing at him. "He'll be here by eleven."

However, eleven o'clock came and went with no sign of Cosford. Hartismere's countenance lost all trace of amusement. "Where does Cosford live?"

"Err, on the shore road, I think."

"Once you have confirmed that, then I suggest that we go there in search of him."

At Cosford's house, the two men rang the doorbell in vain.

"Ask the neighbours," urged Hartismere.

Enquiries produced a harassed maid at no. 59, who could not remember anything about anyone, and a middle-aged woman at no. 63, who appeared grimly pleased that the police were interested in Cosford.

"Who was she?" asked Hartismere, when the door had closed with a bang. "Foreign, wasn't she?"

Woolf groaned. "That was Mrs Serring, our resident madwoman. Mind you, I feel sorry for her, losing her husband a few months ago and all that, but she's always down at the police-station. My sergeant reckons she's lonely, but I wish she'd join the W.I. and be done with it."

"Given that no-one has seen Cosford since Sunday morning, don't you think that we ought to try his shop again?"

"What do you suspect?"

"Put bluntly, Woolf, that he's either done a runner or he's dead."

The inspector screwed up his face in thought. "The regulations don't allow me to break into his house without much greater reason than that."

"Peace-time regulations don't," countered Hartismere. "But this is war-time." He gave a derisive laugh. "Furthermore, this isn't London. In this half-dead place, no-one would notice if we slipped into the front, let alone the back of his shop."

Entering Cosford's shop proved to be as easy as Hartismere had suggested. No-one, either outside or inside the shop, protested at their actions. Woolf seemed rather uncertain when 'Thomas' insisted on raising one of the blinds, but Hartismere overrode him.

"I'm not an owl and I can't see in the dark. Anyway, this window doesn't look out onto the street, so nobody will notice."

There was no-one in the shop and Woolf reported that there was no sign of anyone upstairs. Nor did the large stock cupboard reveal anything untoward.

"I suppose we'd better go back to his house again."

Hartismere shook his head. He doubted whether he could persuade the inspector to break into Cosford's house, and this was his best chance of discovering what less orthodox literature the bookseller stocked.

"Pull up another blind, will you, Woolf?"

When this order had been obeyed, Hartismere smiled with satisfaction. The improved light enabled him to see something which had been hidden before – a faint line round one of the panels on the back wall. So the Carrington gel had been correct; there was a further store cupboard. He crossed to it and pushed gently. The panel creaked. He pushed again, this time with more force. The panel resisted and then moved three inches, blocked by something on the other side. Hartismere put his eye to the gap and then drew in his breath.

"Good God."

Woolf appeared beside him. "It's Cosford. But what the hell has happened?"

Chapter Fifty

It took some time for Hartismere to edge his bulky frame into the cupboard. He surveyed the dead body, splayed on the floor in its final spasm, and a broken glass and bottle which lay beside it. Everything pointed to poison, although it was unclear whether it had been self-administered or not. The Vice-Master lifted Cosford's hand and let it fall limply back onto the floor.

"Hmm, he's been here some time – rigor's passed off." He cast a brief glance round and spotted a folded letter on one of the shelves. "*To the Coroner*," he read out loud. "I think that might provide the answer to some of our questions." He pulled on his gloves and unfolded the letter.

"What does it say?" demanded Woolf.

"I'll read it. *I have decided to end everything. I cannot go on. I should never have got involved.*" Hartismere frowned. "Hardly enlightening. I wonder why he thought it necessary to type such a short note?"

"He was a businessman. Perhaps he was more used to typing."

"Or maybe his handwriting was poor," agreed Hartismere. "I should like to see samples of it – and to check this against his typewriter."

Woolf's eyebrows rose. "Do you suspect something?"

"I am attempting to check things now, rather than leave them until it is too late."

The inspector grunted, sensing a rebuke. "Perhaps you might care to hazard a guess as to why he killed himself?"

"You're the local expert, Inspector. Why don't you?"

"Maybe he was worried about the course of the war."

"He wasn't 'involved' in that."

"No, I suppose not." Woolf appeared to be computing some complicated calculation. "I wonder," he breathed. "I wonder."

"Wonder what?"

"It's a bit early for theorising, but suppose he'd helped this Peveril character to free Poole from gaol? Maybe Peveril then started blackmailing him and he realised that he was in a very difficult position. After all, Peveril is a killer."

"Ye-es," agreed Hartismere slowly. "But there may be another explanation. We don't know for certain that it's suicide."

"How many other people knew of the entrance to this cupboard?" demanded Woolf, offended at having his theory queried. "You only found it by accident. I didn't spot it."

Since Woolf was keen to have medical confirmation of the time of Cosford's death, he lost no time in summoning the police-surgeon. Dr Fellowes, with the gallows humour of his tribe, complimented Woolf on the cause of death.

"You're running quite a refresher course for me, aren't you, Inspector? You've presented me with a shooting, a drugs overdose, a broken neck, and now another poisoning. Cyanide, by the looks of it, poor beggar. When I choose to do away with myself, I'll select something a bit less painful."

"Was it definitely suicide?"

"Hard to be certain with poison. Haven't you found a note?"

"Yes, but it's rather short," admitted Woolf.

Fellowes shrugged. "That's better than nothing. Mind you, I've known suicides without notes." He gave a cynical grunt. "Sometimes it's better for the poor devils who are left if there isn't a note. I don't suppose old Foley up at the Gip Arms enjoyed learning why his wife had done herself in."

Hartismere joined in the conversation. "Do you know of any reason why Cosford might have killed himself? You don't seem terribly surprised that he has."

"I gave up being surprised by anything after I qualified. Nonetheless, he'd looked pretty fed-up recently. Once told me that if we'd declared war on the Nazis we should have followed it up with declaring war on their allies, the Soviets."

"And how did you respond?"

"Said that whilst we might have been fool enough not to back the Czechs in '38, we weren't yet fools enough to fight a war on three fronts." Fellowes frowned. "If I'd known that something like this might result, I'd have been a bit more tactful."

"Hard words break no bones," declared Hartismere sententiously. He wondered quite how thin-skinned Cosford had been, or whether he had simply found the whole political situation profoundly depressing.

Once Fellowes had left, Hartismere insisted on making a very thorough search of the rest of the shop. In particular, he directed his attention to the small scullery and lavatory which were at the back of the shop. Woolf gave a dry laugh when 'Thomas' climbed up to lift the lid off the cistern.

"We may be a country force, but we do know to search there."

"Quite so, my dear fellow, but it never does to neglect anything." As he spoke, Hartismere ran his fingers down behind the pipe which led to cistern. As he encountered a wire, he breathed a sigh of relief. It looked as if the Carrington gel's suspicions about a wireless were accurate. He turned to Woolf.

"Find me a jemmy or a screwdriver. Even a knife from the scullery will do."

"Why?"

"There's a wire attached to this pipe. I want to see what's behind the skirting-board."

Woolf disappeared. A few moments later, he returned with two knives of different sizes. Bending down, he helped his Scotland Yard colleague to prise off the skirting-board.

"That came away rather too easily," he observed.

"Quite." Hartismere pulled on his gloves and scrabbled around in the gap which had been opened up. Then he withdrew a small black suitcase. Opening the lid, he revealed the contents.

"Good God," breathed Woolf. "It's a transmitter. Is that why Cosford killed himself?"

"It would appear so."

When Woolf took himself off to the police-station to write up his notes, Hartismere sought out Cosford's bank-manager. Smithson was elderly, fussy, and – in Hartismere's judgement – almost certainly easily overawed. However, to begin with, the Vice-Master stuck to orthodox lines, presenting the bank-manager with his warrant-card and explaining that Cosford had just been found dead from unknown causes. The interview swiftly ruled out one possible reason for suicide, since the bookseller had possessed a very healthy bank-balance at the time of his death. In fact, Smithson admitted that he had wondered how Cosford had managed to achieve it, what with trade regulations and the current state of taxation.

Hartismere coughed. "I have heard of cases where people manage to supplement their income by judicious bets. Was Cosford inclined to frequent the races or bookmakers?"

The bank-manager paused, clearly undecided as to whether to say anything or not.

Hartismere leaned forward persuasively. "Naturally, I quite understand that you would not wish to talk about your customers. But Cosford is dead, and we want to establish the cause of his death as quickly as possible. In any case, I have no intention of telling anyone where I acquired any information which you might be able to provide."

Smithson continued to hesitate, before asking, "Is it definitely suicide? I mean, if it might be murder…"

"It might be; which makes it even more imperative that you help me. You see, I can trust information which comes from a respectable professional man like yourself. If I have to dig around in some of the lower class of public houses, I would undoubtedly discover the same information, but it would be tarnished by potential unreliability. You know how that type of person loves notoriety, whereas a professional man despises it."

Faced with both flattery and an appeal to his duty, Smithson yielded.

"I did hear that Mr Cosford enjoyed playing for rather high stakes." The interest on Hartismere's face caused the bank-manager to retreat somewhat. "Oh, I don't mean anything illegal. He certainly wasn't running a roulette wheel or anything like that. It's just that one of my customers complained about losing money to him. It made me wonder whether there were other people who went to his house to play poker with him and how their luck fared."

"People other than Lt. Poole?" suggested Hartismere smoothly.

"Precis…, that is, what do you mean, Poole?"

"He had an account here, didn't he? And he ran through his money and became heavily overdrawn."

Smithson regarded Hartismere unhappily. "I cannot talk

about my customers in this manner."

"How many others were in Poole's unfortunate position?"

"That is not something which I am prepared to discuss."

"Let me put the question in another way. Has anyone else among your customers mentioned gambling to you?"

Smithson shook his head in relief. "Of course, if there were regular gamblers, they may have their accounts at the Commercial and Provincial Bank."

Hartismere ignored this tantalising red herring. "And are there any amongst your customers who have unexplained heavy debts?" When Smithson did not speak, Hartismere feigned anger. "Good God, man, this may become a murder investigation. Can't you see that anyone who owed Cosford a large sum of money might be delighted to kill him? Do you want to aid and abet a murderer?"

Frightened by this, Smithson rang for his confidential clerk and asked for a series of account ledgers. From these he proceeded to extract a number of names, which he gave to Hartismere. The Vice-Master scanned them, whilst listening to Smithson's babbled commentary. It sounded improbable that Eliza Spooner, spinster, had been gambling away her patrimony in Cosford's company, while elderly Mr Jacobs' unfortunate investment in an Alsatian vineyard could certainly explain his current problems. Another six appeared to have equally good reasons for their financial woes. However, if these too could be dismissed, one name stood out: Lieutenant Nigel Reginald Hetherley.

"And why is Lt. Hetherley in difficulties?" enquired Hartismere with interest.

Smithson fidgeted. "I'm not entirely sure. However, I made it quite clear to him that he had to clear his overdraft."

Hartismere repressed a grim smile. Had he been inclined to gamble, he would have wagered that Hetherley had told the bank-manager to go to blazes when questioned about his account.

"He doesn't appear to have had much success in doing so."

"No. Quite."

Hartismere toyed with the idea of asking Smithson if he could trace the number of the five-pound note which Peveril had found in Trent's wallet. Then he rejected it. That sort of enquiry would be bound to involve the tellers and while, for all he knew, they might be paragons of discretion, there would be speculation enough as to his visit. An enquiry from Scotland Yard itself would be less obviously connected with Cosford's death – or other recent deaths. After a warning to Smithson not to let slip any hint of what had been discussed, Hartismere left the bank and wandered down to the shingle beach. Listening to the raucous squawking of the seagulls might not be as useful as taking witness statements, but it brought back memories of childhood excursions to the Norfolk coast. Moreover, it gave him time to plan his next move.

Hartismere spent the afternoon digging around in Cosford's shop and home. He had not expected to find anything as startling as the earlier discovery of the wireless transmitter, nor did he. All the same, he found food for thought in the books which Cosford kept in his tiny study. 'Plekhanov, Marx, Lenin?' he queried. 'I thought that the man was meant to hate the Soviets.' He tugged out another book. 'More Lenin? I can't bear it if our local Fascist turns out to be a Hero of the Soviet Motherland. Who else would choose to relax with *The Taxonomy of the Class Enemy*?' He prowled around further, reassuring himself that the books had actually been read, rather than merely put on display. 'I wonder what he reads in bed – or does he merely sing The Red Flag?'

Acting on this thought, Hartismere went upstairs. 'Pretty Spartan,' he observed, as he took in the iron bedstead and the dark blankets. 'No photographs. Did Comrade Cosford spring into the world unfathered and unmothered?' He glanced under the bed. 'Aha! A man who keeps books under his bed cannot be all bad. What have we here? *The Memoirs of Wrangel; Denikin, Fighter for Justice; The Soviet Orgy; The International Jewish Conspiracy and the Destruction of Imperial Russia; The True Hell of Russia Today.*' He dragged out another pile with similar titles. 'Well, well, well. Definitely not a little Marxist in the making. And, with the exception of one of them, not the reading matter of a little

Fascist in the making, either.'

The drawer in the bedside table revealed nothing more exciting than a pile of handkerchiefs. Hartismere eyed it thoughtfully. 'I don't quite trust you, my friend. You're a bit too shallow. Let's see what happens when we pull you out.' Suiting action to word, he carefully extracted the drawer and laid it on the bed. He prodded at it, before deciding that a peculiar-looking crack was probably part of its secret. Sure enough, when pressure was applied, the crack rose, revealing an inner compartment. Wrapping a handkerchief round his fingers in case he left prints, Hartismere pulled out the contents – a rather beautiful icon and a shabby leather case. Reluctantly, he opened the latter, suspecting what he would find. Inside was a photograph of a dark-eyed woman seated on a chair, with her arms around a little girl who stood next to her. Hartismere grimaced. How old was the child? Four? Five? He turned over the photograph and read the inscription – Elga and little Elga, Petrograd, 1917.

"That explains a lot," he muttered. Then, aware that his hand was shaking, he wrapped the icon and case up, before thrusting them inside his jacket. "Twenty years of hate must have destroyed him. Thank God I had Cambridge."

Chapter Fifty-One

By the evening, Hartismere was ensconced at C Coy, where he was endeavouring to collect alibis for both the evening of Durrant's death and the evening of the grenade-attack on the police-station. He had few hopes that he would discover some glaring inaccuracy, not least since those being questioned could justifiably claim that they had given much of the information already and had now forgotten the details. Nonetheless, it was clear that the Newton police had enough on their hands without having to reproduce the work which had been destroyed in the fire. More importantly, it meant that he would be on hand if Peveril were captured.

For his part, Peveril was rather too conscious of the likelihood of his capture. He had made good progress early in the morning and, although he had been forced to lie up during much of the day, he was now south of the River Hart. In theory, this meant that all he needed to do was to cross the road which divided the marshes from the inland farms and then make his way through the sedge and mud until he reached Harting Magna. However, like many theories, there were unexpected snags. In particular, the presence of a patrol along the road caused Peveril considerable alarm. Now that he was back in C Coy territory, there was no chance of him being able to bluff his way through a roadblock. Furthermore, the presence of the troops suggested that he was believed to be in the area, and that someone was determined to have him under lock and key. He lay quite still as he watched the patrol.

'They're not here by luck. The road serves as a perfect cut-off point. You can't get to or from C Coy without crossing it, unless you go round by sea or along the headland. I can't go by sea and if someone's had the sense to pick this as one of the best crossing-points, there's no point attempting the headland; it's bound to be stiff with troops.' Ralph tried to estimate how long the stretch of road under guard was. 'What did Midge say about geometry problems? Well, this is another one. If Guard A, walking at four miles an hour and keeping a close watch on the locality, traverses Road R for eight minutes in a south-westerly direction, and Guard B walks at four and a half miles per hour in a north-easterly direction until the road bends round in direction C, at which point he turns back, how the devil is Fugitive F supposed to get across the road? Particularly when Road R is straight at this point.' Peveril supplied his own answer. 'Either Fugitive F investigates the bend at point C or he waits until nightfall. And he wishes he'd paid a bit more attention in training.'

Cautious exploration suggested that moving further along the road was not going to improve matters. Peveril glanced at his watch. Surely they couldn't have kept this up all day? Were they expecting to be relieved and didn't want some inconvenient NCO to appear and notice them being slack? Ralph grimaced. 'If so, I wish he'd hurry up. Apart from anything else, I don't much fancy my chances of finding my way through the reed-beds in the dark.'

After another half hour, Peveril suddenly realised that he could not see as well as before. A quick look round confirmed his suspicion. There was a sea-mist rolling in. 'This,' he told himself, 'is my opportunity. Only funks would waste another three hours waiting for dusk.'

Perhaps if Peveril had devoted less attention to his potential cowardice, he might have noticed that the mist was decidedly patchy. As it was, just as he had reached the centre of the road, the mist parted, leaving him visible to both guards. Without hesitation, one of them aimed his rifle at Peveril and fired. Peveril raced forward, jinking across the tussock-grass like a startled snipe. Confused shouts behind him suggested that the guards intended to intercept him before he reached another patch of mist. A second shot came whistling past his ears and instinct took over. Diving flat onto the ground, he stayed motionless, watching the mist roll towards him.

'Once that reaches me, I'll be invisible. And if they think that I was trying to break out from the marshes, they may go back to guarding the road. At the very least, one of them will have to go back to report.'

Although Ralph had intended to move rapidly once he was hidden from view, he soon made the disconcerting discovery that the mud made glutinous sucking noises unless he moved extremely cautiously. Moreover, rather than one, or both, of the soldiers going back to report what had happened, the pair had continued to beat the marsh for him. At one point they came sufficiently close for Peveril to overhear a conversation which helped to explain such exceptional enthusiasm.

"Do you go and report, Longy."

"I be wantin' that ten pound, too."

"You be gettin' nothin' if he escape again. Or if he shoot at you."

"Be you sure it were he?"

"Who else be a-dartin' across the road in secret?"

Longy laughed sarcastically. "Better hope he not be dead."

"Why? Weren't orders a-tellin' we to shoot if needful?"

"When you be a few more years in the army, Catchpole, you be l'arnin' that shootin' an officer, even be he a murderer, be a-causin' a great deal of enquiry and trouble. Happen it may be more trouble than be worth ten pound."

The rest of the argument became lost as the soldiers moved off, but Peveril was left staring into the mist in horror: there was a price upon his head.

Since it was clearly only a matter of time before Catchpole alerted the rest of the guard to his presence, Peveril realised that he had to get out of the immediate vicinity of the road. For all he knew, the tracks to Fytton and Harting Magna might also be under guard, so there was no point in aiming for them. That left the reed-beds. If he stuck to a north-easterly route, he ought to end up in the correct general area, but the first thing was to put some distance from those men.

Although Peveril achieved the latter relatively quickly, sticking to a defined direction proved to be significantly harder. The problem lay in the fact that the sedge did not lie in one vast reed-bed. Instead, it was intersected by numerous small creeks and streams, some of which were hard to spot. After plunging through apparently firm ground into brackish water several times, Peveril grew much more wary. Drowning suddenly seemed unpleasantly possible – particularly with a heavy coat dragging him down.

'Even if the whole of C Coy search this damn lagoon, they won't find me if I've gone under,' he thought. 'I wish my map showed tracks through the reed-beds. From the sludge I've been trailing through, you'd think I was practically in the river and Midge warned me that it's tidal. What if this lot gets covered by water?' Trying to check his compass, Peveril slipped again. As he extracted himself from the mud, he was assailed by a repulsive smell. He shuddered. His father had enjoyed regaling company with the fact that in the Great War he had learned to tell how many days a German had lain dead by the squelch the corpse made when you stood on it. Leo had thought the story uproariously funny, but it had always made Peveril feel sick. 'There aren't any corpses here,' he told himself firmly. 'It's just some gas or other from rotting vegetation. If the mist would clear off, everything would smell a bit fresher.'

An hour later, Peveril was forced to admit that the mist, rather than clearing, had thickened. Worse, it absorbed all sound. Instead of reassuring him that no-one was close to finding him, Peveril found the silence so ominous and intense that he began to wonder whether there really were two hamlets buried in the marsh. He bit his lip, aware that he was starting to lose his nerve. If only he could see something other than this filthy mud he might be able to work out where he was.

Thinking that he might feel a bit better if he rested for a while, Peveril squatted on a more substantial pile of reeds. Even if he had felt like eating, the sandwiches which Mrs Carrington had given him were ruined. He eyed the hip-flask which Hartismere had given him. True, brandy would warm him up, but would it have other effects?

'Just because this hole looks exactly like my nightmares doesn't mean that they've happened. It serves me right for being overly imaginative; I've been criticised enough for that. *equidem merui nec deprecor* – "I have deserved it, nor do I ask for mercy". And what the blazes am I doing quoting Virgil when the last thing I need to start thinking about is the Underworld?'

With this bracing comment, Peveril began to get up, only to freeze in motionless terror as he took in the scene which faced him. 'Oh Christ, it was true. I am dead. It is the Underworld.' He started to shake uncontrollably. 'I saw it – the punt, the muffled figure with its pole. I should never have come back in here; never.'

While Peveril was convinced that he had just seen Charon gliding past in a punt, Midge was growing increasingly frustrated.

"If I were a man, I could pretend to be from Scotland Yard, too," she growled to her aunt. "But nobody would believe me if I turned up at C Coy and started questioning everyone."

Alice attempted to register sympathy. "You've done as much as you could do – and you've saved me from having to listen to Mrs Serring talking about the habits of Greater Black-Headed gulls."

"What, here in Suffolk?"

"Yes. The first time she came here, when you were in Cambridge, she was full of how poor Mr Serring had been watching a colony of them."

"Are you sure she didn't say Greater Black-Backed?"

Alice looked puzzled. "I don't think so. She talked about Black Terns as well. I remember thinking that it was better for her to talk about them than about Black Shirts. Does it matter?"

"Whatever Mr Serring was watching it wasn't Black Terns and Greater Black-Headed gulls."

"What do you mean?"

"They don't exist. Or rather, they don't exist round here."

"Are you sure?"

Midge nodded and disappeared into her uncle's library, before returning with a fat green book. "Look what it says here: the Black Tern nested in the fens and broads a century ago. They don't any longer."

"Couldn't she have muddled up the name? Isn't there a Sooty Tern?"

"She was married to an ornithologist; do you really think that she would have got the names wrong? Anyway, the Sooty Tern is a very rare visitor – it wouldn't have a colony here."

Alice sighed. "You're meant to be working for your exams, not worrying about birds."

"These birds might turn out to be condors. I can hardly

ignore them."

Alice stared at her niece in perplexity. She had little interest in ornithology, but she was dimly aware that condors were not native birds of prey. "Condors?"

"I mean Germans. They had a Condor Legion in Spain." Midge bit her lip. "Look, I honestly think that I need to speak to Mrs Serring. I can't risk the telephone, because if the police have any sense, they'll have tapped it. I can't ask her to come here, but I don't want to leave you if you won't feel safe."

The thought that Midge could protect her raised a slight smile on her aunt's face. "My dear child, you are running far more risk than I shall. If that inspector discovers you on your own in Newton, he may decide to take you in for questioning. How do you propose to alert me if that transpires?"

Chapter Fifty-Two

Back in the marsh, Peveril had spent several minutes retching in shock. Exhausted, he had then collapsed back onto the mud. At last, it occurred to him that he had never read of the dead being sick in the Underworld. He stared at his hands miserably. 'If I'm not dead, then I've lost my reason. Oh gods, what a choice. I wish I hadn't come. I wish I were with Midge. I wish…' This time, he did unscrew the hip-flask, and the fiery liquid within served to provide some warmth.

'I mustn't let Hartismere down,' he told himself. 'I simply mustn't. He gave me the opportunity to draw back. He didn't suggest that I would be a skulking hound if I did. So I can't let him down now. All I have to do is talk to Caine and then I can give myself up. I don't have to stay in this beastly place any further than that.' He gulped at the thought of having to get to Harting Magna, fighting mirages all the way. 'If I have another slug of brandy then I can blame anything I see on alcoholic delirium. And when I get back, I can write a tremendously learned article for the Journal of Roman Studies, after which they'll bung me in an asylum. At least Robert won't be able to come and gloat over me there.'

Eventually, Peveril forced himself to get up. Much to his relief, he did not immediately encounter another vision of Charon, but the bleak, empty landscape offered little encouragement. Moreover, the sections of open water were growing deeper and he was several times forced to retrace his steps. He knew perfectly well that, without a fixed point from which to take a bearing, his compass was increasingly useless, but he kept glancing down at it as the only proof of rational existence in his mist-enshrouded world.

After what felt like an eternity of aimless meandering, Ralph became aware that the sedge was giving way to tussock grass and that the ground was much firmer. A few more minutes and he was on an actual path.

'Just as well,' he thought. 'It's getting dark and the idea of trying to find my way in that…' He broke off, unwilling to risk conjuring up the possibility.

Careful exploration convinced him that he had reached the track to Fytton. If he kept on it, he would reach the turn-off to Harting Magna. For a moment, he deliberated whether to wait until it was completely dark, but, in the end, he decided to press on.

Fortunately for Ralph, there was no-one guarding the Harting Magna turn-off and Peveril blessed the fact that he knew this particular area. 'I can be inside Caine's cottage within ten minutes,' he promised himself. 'Warmth, shelter, and, above all, light.'

Although Peveril was, by this point, both mentally and physically exhausted, instinct told him to approach the house cautiously and to wait before knocking on the back door. As he waited, he heard the low murmur of voices; then the front door opened. Peveril shrank into the protection of the lee of the house, praying that it was only Caine. Instead, in horror he recognised Snellgrove's voice.

"You remember what I said. There's a reward for anyone who turns him in – and a nasty bit of explaining to do for anyone who shelters him."

"Don't you be a-worritin' yourself, sir. I be as keen on money as the next man."

"Good."

With that, the door closed and Snellgrove strode off down the track. At the back of the cottage, Peveril sank down into the grass in despair. If he hadn't spent so long in those cursed reed-beds, he would have arrived in time to question Caine. It was too late now; Caine would betray him. Hartismere had asked him to do just one thing and he had failed – utterly.

As Ralph slumped on the ground, trying to decide what to do next, he heard a panting nearby. He stared in the direction of the sound, too exhausted even to be frightened. The panting came closer, until Ralph could feel hot breath in his cheek. He closed his eyes. First Charon, now Cerberus. That might solve everything.

Soft footsteps padded after the panting. Then the hot breath disappeared.

"What be you findin', girl?"

Ralph opened his eyes and peered into the gloom, resentful that Fate was teasing him in this way. It wasn't fair to move his mind in and out of the Underworld like this. Caine didn't belong with Cerberus. Then a fumbling hand touched his shoulder.

"Who be there?"

"Go away."

The hand tightened as Caine recognised Peveril's voice. "You be a-comin' inside afore you be seen."

"So you can sell me to the authorities?" challenged Peveril. "Has the reward for betrayal reached thirty pieces of silver yet?"

"You be eavesdroppin'? Then you be a-hearin' naught but lies. Be I a-wishin' money, I be handin' you over afore."

With that, Caine hauled Peveril upright. Knowing that he had no chance of escaping the smuggler, Peveril accompanied him inside the cottage. Caine took one look at him and pushed him in the direction of the fire.

"You sit there," he ordered, before forcing him to drink a glass of rum.

The rum and the flames brought some warmth, and Peveril found himself having to fight sleep just when he most needed to be awake to plan his escape. Mrs Caine appeared briefly and exclaimed at his filthy, sodden clothes and the cuts which the reeds had made on his hands and face. She then disappeared to fetch a basin, before proceeding to bathe his wounds and clean them with some sort of neat spirit. The pain of this operation revived Peveril enough to let him protest when she presented him with a clean shirt and trousers.

"I can't take your husband's clothes."

"They be my son's – he be in the Navy."

Caine seemed to realise that Peveril was embarrassed at stripping off in front of a woman. "You be feedin' Bess, Kezia, and I be a-lookin' after the officer."

Once clad in clean clothes, Peveril felt more able to face Caine. Despite Caine's remarks to Snellgrove, he had a dim suspicion that referring to money would cause offence, so he resisted the temptation to offer a counter-bribe. Instead, he decided to refer to Hartismere. "I know that Lt. Snellgrove is trying to get hold of me, but there's a new police officer in charge of the case. He doesn't believe I'm guilty."

"And how be you knowin' that?"

"Because I talked to him the night that you smuggled me out of here."

"Be he from Ipswich, then?"

"No, absolutely not. He's a chief inspector from Scotland Yard, now in the Military Police, and he's taken over the whole investigation."

Caine laughed. "Woolf won't be likin' that."

"You mean not being in charge?"

"That – and the man a-comin' from Scotland Yard. Mr Woolf took hisself up to London to be a fine detective."

Peveril was sure this was not the end of the tale. "And?"

"He be a-failin' some examination and he be comin' back. Some ten or twelve years ago that be. Mortal cross he were, too."

"Well, yes, failing exams is always rather irritating," agreed Peveril with feeling. "But I didn't come to talk to you about that. I wanted to ask you a few more questions about the night of Durrant's death." He looked at the fisherman's face, which had turned closed and expressionless. "Look, I realise that you must be sick of being asked questions, but I honestly am trying to find out who killed Durrant and I honestly don't think that it was Poole." He paused, wondering how safe it was to tell Caine that he thought that Poole had been the intended victim. He compromised "I suspect that someone wanted to make Poole look guilty right from the start. That's where you could help."

"Help provin' that young Master Edwin be no murderer?"

"Exactly. It's a matter of timings. It's critical to know precisely when Durrant was killed. I thought that you might be able to tell me when you heard the shooting on the night of Durrant's death."

There was a long silence. Peveril had just decided that Caine would not answer him when the smuggler cursed, before adding, " 'Twere some twenty minutes before one o'clock."

"Are you sure of that?"

"Be you thinkin' as I cannot read a watch?"

"No, no, not at all. It's just that everyone thinks that the shooting took place later."

"That's as may be."

"Did you notice anything else?" enquired Peveril. "I mean, you might have stumbled over the body and noticed something about it."

"What be you meanin'?" enquired Caine dangerously. "That I be a-stealing from the dead?"

"Good God, no, absolutely not." Peveril hastened to explain. "The coast-watcher lives in Fytton. He shouldn't have come anywhere near here – particularly if he were hurrying home to look after a sick cow. The only reason he could have found the body was if you told him to go and look for it."

"Be that so? And why might I be tellin' him such things?"

Peveril shrugged. "I don't know. Maybe you realised that the body would be washed away by the early morning tide. Maybe you didn't like the thought of it not being buried. But I still think that you saw the body. And you could prevent Poole from being blamed for Durrant's death if you tell me what you saw."

"And why be I trustin' you – a boy out of school?"

At this insult, Peveril's temper snapped. "Damn you, I've spent the last four days on the run. I've had no sleep, no food, and I don't know whether the girl I love has been arrested for helping me. And if that's not enough to convince you, try this. You asked me if I could see wraiths dancing over the marsh. The answer is yes, I can. And I spent the whole of today fighting your beastly wraiths. Do you think I did that for a joke?"

As Peveril's voice cracked, Caine gave a short laugh. "There aren't many as fight wraiths and survive. They be comin' out drownded or mad." He poured Peveril more rum and took some himself. "Respect the marshland and it be respectin' you."

Peveril nodded, suddenly too tired to talk. After about five minutes, Caine spoke again.

"Be you certain that the new inspector be from London?"

"Yes."

"Why be he not a-comin' from Ipswich-way?"

"I understand that they're already short-staffed. There's been an outbreak of arson in Harwich and a murder at Felixstowe docks." Peveril shrugged. "We're quite a long way north, so we've probably been forgotten about."

366

Caine seemed to be trying to make up his mind. Then he reached inside his tobacco pouch and withdrew something very small. "This be for the man from London."

"A bullet? From Durrant's body?"

Caine nodded.

"Good God. It is enormously important. It might be possible to trace the revolver which fired this." Peveril winced, thinking how awful it would be for Caine if the bullet proved to have been fired from Poole's gun after all.

Caine appeared to have read his mind. "That be from a lighter revolver. Master Edwin, he be usin' his father's gun from the last war – a good, heavy gun, that."

Peveril frowned in concentration. Snellgrove had bored him with his complaints about the need to keep two stocks of ammunition because there were two different calibres of Webley automatic in service. Presumably, Poole must have used the .455 calibre Webley. In that case, Poole couldn't have shot Durrant, since the fatal bullet was a .38. However, had Snellgrove mentioned what the other officers used? He thought not. If it came to that, he wasn't absolutely certain what calibre his own revolver was. He fished it out from under his chair and cracked it open. The bullets appeared to match.

"That be a .38," remarked Caine. "And he be choked with mud, so don't be a-firin' of he."

"Err... no," agreed Peveril, who had heard horrendous tales of revolvers exploding in men's faces. "And I'll certainly make sure that this bullet goes to the Scotland Yard man. At least, I will if I can get out of here without being caught."

Chapter Fifty-Three

While Ralph had fallen into an exhausted sleep on a makeshift bed tucked under the rafters of Caine's cottage, Midge was staring at Serring's ornithological notes. To begin with, Mrs Serring had seemed positively aggrieved at the suggestion that her husband might have noted down birds which were not there.

"My Dickie was an expert. How can you suggest that he made mistakes?"

"I don't think he made a mistake. I think he did it deliberately."

"To claim that he could see what others did not? He would not do so; he was honourable."

"I'm sure he was," agreed Midge tactfully. "But he was out in the marshes at unusual times. If he saw things which were suspicious, he may have used code-words to record what he saw."

"Do you mean lights?"

Midge shook her head. "No. The times in this notebook are wrong. This sighting of a Black Tern is after dawn."

"Then what do they record?"

"Perhaps it was a boat – or a person." Midge sighed at the thought of the task which lay ahead of them. "The only way forward is to check which birds aren't local, and then note down every occurrence of the birds in these diaries."

After three hours, it became obvious that there were three prime suspects: the Black Tern, the Greater Black-Headed Gull, and the avocet.

"I must say," remarked Midge wearily, "that I know rather more about seabird distribution than I did previously. And the birds were cleverly chosen. The first two are close enough to the names of ordinary seabirds not to attract attention, and the avocet does visit here, it just doesn't nest."

"Do you think that every reference to an avocet is important, or just those which refer to an avocet on a nest?"

"I don't know. I suppose we should concentrate on the references to nests." Midge laughed darkly. "If there really is something in all of this, then we've discovered a nest of vipers."

"You mean traitors?"

"Exactly. I wonder what made your husband suspect them."

"The Nazis invaded my country."

"Err... yes. What I meant was, what was it about these three people which attracted his attention?"

Mrs Serring shrugged. "Why would three men meet at such strange times unless they were plotting?"

"I suppose so," agreed Midge, suddenly hoping that Serring had not merely stumbled upon some smuggling or – still worse – poaching. It would be dreadful for his widow to learn that he had died for something so trivial.

"What do you intend to do now?"

"The dates can be used to rule out suspects." Midge pulled one of the diaries towards her. "Look at this reference to a Black Tern on February 20th. Any soldier who was posted here after that date can be ruled out."

Mrs Serring appeared unconvinced. "How can you be sure that these codes refer to soldiers?"

"I can't, but it's much easier to trace their movements and we have to start somewhere."

"And what if Black Tern refers to a group of people, rather than a single individual?"

Midge groaned. "Then I give up. It's bad enough having to trace three people; unknown quantities would be impossible." She frowned thoughtfully. "Actually, it's very important to know that three people are involved. Until now, there was no definite proof that there were more than two."

"And one was Cosford."

"Why do you say that?" demanded Midge, hoping that she had not given away any important information to someone who appeared perfectly careful of storming round to accuse the bookseller in person.

"Cosford calls me a Russian Jew. Cosford encourages officers to lose money. And Cosford is dead."

"What?"

A vengeful smile flickered over Mrs Serring's face. "Yes. Two police inspectors came to ask if I had heard anything suspicious. They said that he had been found dead in his shop."

"Golly," murmured Midge, wishing that she could speak to Dr Hartismere. "Did they say whether it was murder or suicide?"

"No."

"Are you sure there were two inspectors?"

Mrs Serring nodded. "There was that Woolf, who calls me mad, and an older man. He was in charge."

"He's not there now, is he?" asked Midge, thinking that she could pass on her idea to Hartismere if he were.

The widow misunderstood Midge's question. "No. There is no-one there; not even a constable to guard the property, although he will return." She looked at Midge speculatively. "Do you wish to search it? To search the nest of a Black-Hearted Gull?"

Midge was startled by the suggestion. Breaking into property was not a normal undergraduate activity and she attempted to explain this. Mrs Serring, however, waved away her protests.

"The key of my back door is the same as the key of Cosford's back door."

"How on earth do you know that?"

"The cleaning-woman who comes twice a week to Cosford's often forgets her key." Mrs Serring smiled coldly. "When she first asked to borrow mine, I had further locks fitted. And bolts. But I kept the key."

Midge licked her lips. Her aunt had suggested that Woolf might question her if he saw her in Newton, but if she were caught entering Cosford's house, she was sure to be arrested. Despising herself for doing so, she entered a protest. "What can I discover that the police cannot?"

"Discover whether Cosford killed my Dickie." When Midge still hesitated, Mrs Serring turned on her. "I let you stay here when you waited to spy on Cosford. Now you can spy much more. You ask me to let your friend take refuge here. You tell me a password he will give. But if you do not search, then I shall send him away to be taken off and shot."

"You wouldn't."

"You are wrong. To bring my Dickie back, I would let your friend die in front of me. But my Dickie is dead and I can never bring him back. All that is left is to trace his killers and see them die, too."

Badly shaken, Midge gave in. "All right. I'll do it, but I don't know why you haven't gone in already."

Mrs Serring gestured with her hands. "You have family to protect you. How can I have revenge if I am locked up in a camp for Jews?"

Although Midge feared that Mrs Serring was distinctly exaggerating the ability of her family to get her out of gaol if she were apprehended for entering enclosed premises without the owner's consent, she gave a resigned shrug. "Give me the key and a torch. I think it's highly unlikely that I shall find anything, but I'll do my best."

In the event, Mrs Serring insisted on Midge waiting until nearly three o'clock before she tackled Cosford's house. Not only did that allow the widow to check that there was no-one watching the house, but it was much less likely that there would be any police patrols so late at night. As Midge cautiously made her way towards the back door of Cosford's house, she could hear the waves crashing on the shingle. Was Hartismere correct? Were agents really being landed at night?

'Just my luck if I run into one tonight,' she thought. 'Maybe he'll have a door-key, too.' As she paused to listen for the signs of any human presence, she regretted her joke. It was all too easy to conjure up the possibility of someone lying in wait on the other side of the door. The very black-out which made it impossible for anyone to see her would make it easy for a malefactor to attack her before she had sensed their presence. Telling herself that Ralph was facing far greater dangers with considerably more courage, Midge forced herself to unlock the back door and to ease it open. She waited. She could hear nothing. She had no preternatural sense of another presence. There was nothing for it but to inch her way inside and to begin her task.

Since Midge was unsure what, exactly, she was looking for, she had no real idea of where to start. Moreover, it was hard to gain an impression of the house by torchlight. Dare she turn on the lights? The blackout curtains ought to prevent any light from showing, but if anything did show, it would attract suspicion immediately. Only a burglar or a policeman would be inside a dead man's house. Midge shivered, before trying to apply her mind to the problem in front of her. 'I don't suppose that Cosford kept any papers which would obviously condemn him, but I might as well start with his desk. Thank goodness Aunt Alice insisted on my wearing a decent pair of gloves for my friendly visit; at least I shan't leave my fingerprints everywhere.'

The few documents in the desk seemed innocent enough. Somewhat discouraged, Midge turned to an inspection of the books in Cosford's study. Like Hartismere, she was struck by the political nature of the volumes. She checked inside the front covers in case the books were different from those described on the wrappers. However, there was no incongruity. Nor were there any letters hidden inside.

'What does Mrs Serring expect me to find?' queried Midge irritably. 'A signed confession of the murder of her husband? Cosford doesn't even seem to have kept a diary, or we could attempt to match up his movements with Serring's bird-code. In any case, if there were any worthwhile evidence, those two police officers have probably already impounded it. If so, I do hope that one of them was Dr Hartismere.'

Midge shone her torch onto her wrist-watch. She had told Mrs Serring that she would be back before dawn broke, and one hour had already passed. 'I suppose I'd better have a look upstairs,' she thought. 'After all, I thought about hiding Ralph under the eaves."

More to calm her nerves than because she expected to find anything, Midge leafed through the pile of books which Hartismere had discovered under Cosford's bed. Several were printed on an unusually thin, creamy paper. Wondering which publishing house used this paper, Midge flicked idly to the frontispiece, where she discovered that the books were printed under the auspices of the Movement for the Freedom of the Suppressed People of Latvia. 'I must ask Uncle Geoffrey if he's ever heard of it, but I can't see anything suspicious about these titles.'

Midge had just finished tucking the books neatly back under

the bed when she heard a noise. She froze. There couldn't be anyone inside the house. She had locked the door. It must be the house creaking. Houses did. It was nothing.

Despite these reassuring thoughts, Midge found herself unable to move. Then, just as she was telling herself that she must have been imagining the noise, she heard another creak, this time louder. Struggling to move silently, Midge lowered herself onto the ground and crawled under the bed. 'Please don't let him come upstairs,' she prayed. 'Let him stay downstairs. And if he does come up, please don't let him look under the bed.'

For what felt like hours, Midge lay concealed under the bed. She could hear more noises from downstairs. Indeed, so loud seemed one crack that she could not understand why the intruder did not flee. 'Surely Mrs Serring will hear that,' Midge calculated, relief washing over her. 'She's got a gun. She'll come and scare off whoever it is downstairs and save me in the process.' Then Midge's hopes sank. 'She'll think that I made the noise. She won't realise that there is someone else inside. I'm trapped. I don't know what to do.'

Fatalistically sure that she was about to be discovered, dragged out and killed, Midge tried to trace the movements downstairs. It sounded as if someone were pulling the furniture around, but that made no sense. There had been nothing concealed behind the sofa and chairs, and to check behind the cushions would not require the suite to be moved. Eventually, the noises appeared to die away, but Midge continued to lie hidden. Not for anything was she going to run the risk of going downstairs to fall into the hands of an assassin.

Chapter Fifty-Four

Shortly after two o'clock, Ralph was wakened from his sleep by Caine shaking him. He shot upright, banging his head on the roof, briefly wondering why his rooms in Trinity appeared to have shrunk so much.

"Be you ready to move?"

Ralph nodded, grateful that the smuggler did not seem to have changed his mind about helping him.

Accompanied by Bess, the pair slipped out of the back door. Despite the dark, it seemed to Peveril that it took much less time to reach Caine's boat than on the previous occasion. Had Caine taken a direct path because he trusted him more, or did Caine think that he had no chance of picking out the route if he returned in the daytime?

Whether or not the smuggler did trust Peveril more, he still insisted on the officer entering the hidden compartment below deck, overriding Peveril's protest that it was dark and nobody would be able to see him.

"And if we be stopped? I be a-foolin' the Revenue all my born days but they do see and hear. There be no call for foolish risks."

Once the boat was underway, Ralph started to wonder whether it was he who was taking a foolish risk. Ought he to have tried to report directly to Collingwood? But Hartismere had said that the railways would be under observation. If they were, he'd never reach London and he simply had to hand over that bullet. Ralph gasped as the boat rocked unexpectedly. If only he'd managed to persuade Caine to take the bullet to Brandon, then he'd have been sure that it would reach Collingwood.

Shortly afterwards, Caine summoned Peveril on deck, murmuring that they were close enough to Newton to attempt the approach to Mrs Serring's house. Peveril had expected all manner of guards on the beaches, backed up by patrols in the town. However, from the moment when Caine's dinghy grated upon the shingle of a deserted inlet to the point at which the smuggler showed him which house was Mrs Serring's, Peveril saw no sign of any guard, whether police or Local Defence

Volunteers. Muttering to himself that this serendipity was all too easy, he knocked gently on the widow's door. Almost immediately, it opened as far as the chain would allow.

"What delayed you?" whispered a voice, followed by a sharp intake of breath. "Who… who are you?"

"Ralph Peveril, Mrs Serring. Didn't Midge, that is, Miss Carrington, warn you that I might appear?"

"Who is she?"

"She is my friend."

"Indeed? Who is anyone these days? Who is Ralph Peveril? Who is Pallas?"

At this last question, Peveril sighed in relief. "Pallas was the son of King Evander."

"Not Pallas Athene?"

"No. Turnus killed Pallas, and Aeneas killed Turnus."

Now that sign and countersign had been given, Mrs Serring removed the chain and opened the door fully. Ralph entered, hoping that Midge was waiting indoors.

"Where's Miss Carrington? I need to speak to her urgently."

"She is inside Cosford's house. She went there to search it."

Ralph's mouth turned unpleasantly dry. "But if Cosford catches her…"

"Cosford cannot catch anything other than justice now."

"You mean he's been arrested?"

"I mean he is dead."

"Dead?"

"Ssh. Yes. The police say that it is suicide." There came a noise indicative of great contempt on Mrs Serring's part. "If it was suicide, why was there someone in his kitchen on the night he died?"

Peveril's voice sharpened in anxiety. "When did he die? And where?"

"Last night, in his shop."

"Before or after you saw this person?"

"I do not know. The police have not said when he died."

"Don't you understand?" demanded Ralph furiously. "If there was someone prowling around his house last night, it may have been a murderer – and you've let Midge go in there tonight!

How could you?"

Mrs Serring shrugged. "She wishes to search. Why should I stop her if it helps to find my Dickie's killers?"

Peveril glared at her. "She is alone and unarmed. If she's been harmed…" His voice tailed off at the thought of what might have happened. "How did she get in?"

"The back door. I have a spare key."

"Do you have another?"

"Yes." By some sort of sleight of hand, a key appeared in Mrs Serring's hand. Ralph snatched it and made for the door. Then he paused. Every instinct told him to rush to check that Midge was safe, but there was also his own information to consider. He fished out the bullet which Caine had given him. "This is vital evidence," he explained. "You must hide it until I, or Miss Carrington, or Chief Inspector Thomas, ask for it. You mustn't let anyone else take it. And if you've let Midge go into danger alone I shall… I shall…"

With that, he left, forcing himself to approach Cosford's house slowly. Nevertheless, despite his realisation that he ought not to rush up to his objective, he made only a cursory survey of the garden. He wasn't going to waste time when Midge could be in danger. If something had happened to her, he would never forgive himself.

When Hartismere arrived at Mrs Serring's house the next morning, he found Peveril, half out of his mind with worry.

"I don't know where Midge is. Mrs Serring said that she went over to Cosford's house, but I've been in it and I couldn't find her, either inside or nearby."

Hartismere frowned. "Your orders were to stay hidden. You had no business running unnecessary risks."

"Damn my orders. Midge has gone missing. Don't you care?"

"Caring – or even loving – does not make for effective Intelligence investigations, and the sooner you learn that the better. As for Miss Carrington, she is currently at Newton police-station, where she will remain for at least the next few hours."

Ralph made a move towards the door. "Then I'm going to check that she is all right."

The Vice-Master planted himself in front of the door. "You are not. One, because you are under my orders and I do not intend to have my – or Miss Carrington's – cover blown. And two, because immediately you walk in there you will be arrested – or had you forgotten that you are accused of killing Trent? How do you expect to help Miss Carrington from inside a cell?"

Ralph's face took on a pinched look. "But what are we going to do?"

"I am going to visit the branch manager of the Commercial and Provincial Bank, while you will remain here until further notice."

"I'm damned if I will. And how can you be worrying about money while Midge is under lock and key?"

"Do use your brain, Peveril. This morning I was informed that Trent's five-pound note was one of a number sent to the Newton branch of the Commercial and Provincial. I am going to ask questions regarding it and I cannot afford to have you arrested – or shot – whilst I am engaged in doing so." Hartismere glanced at Peveril's face and his tone softened. "I may seem unduly unfeeling to you, but I can assure you that I have no intention of abandoning Miss Carrington. I may also say that your information about the photograph has raised some interesting points about Trent's antecedents. His mother is not dead, as he claimed on his next-of-kin form. Or," Hartismere corrected himself, "if she has died, Somerset House has no record of it. However, there is a record of Terence Trent's divorce from her on the grounds of her misconduct with one Lauritz Falkenberg."

"A German?"

"Or a man of Germanic ancestry."

"Then that photograph which Trent was carrying may have been of his mother and step-father. Do you think he visited them and was indoctrinated?"

"Given his eventual end, I should think it is more probable that he was told that if he didn't co-operate his mother would suffer." Hartismere gesticulated towards the hall. "Do you think that Mrs Serring trusts our authorities? Imagine what Frau Falkenberg's position is like – and Trent must have known it, poor devil. Alternatively, he could have been threatened with arrest for having German relatives and having lied about them. Quite a convincing case could have been made against him."

"But treason…"

"I don't suppose it was ever put as brutally as that to him. More a case of say this, or don't say that."

"Do you mean the time of the shooting on the night of Durrant's death?"

"Exactly. Would you be willing to hazard someone's life, or your own liberty, in order to give a precise time in a police investigation?"

Peveril grimaced. "Probably not. I'd persuade myself that I might have got it wrong. Or I'd say that I could always clear it up later."

"Which may have been the point at which someone decided to do away with him. And Trent's antecedents are another reason why I need to investigate that bank-note." Hartismere eyed Peveril thoughtfully. "I may not be able to secure Miss Carrington's release, but I want your word of honour that you will not leave here except in an emergency – and some hare-brained attempt to free Miss Carrington is not an emergency." When there was no immediate response, he added. "If you are not prepared to give me your word, I shall ensure that you cannot leave." He nodded towards the door. "Mrs Serring would be more than willing to help me if she thought that you were endangering the chance of tracking down her husband's killers."

"If you're ready to lock me up, then I'm surprised you'd trust my word of honour."

"You haven't let me down before."

Peveril flushed. He thought he preferred Hartismere snapping at him than being kind – it made it much easier to respond in a like fashion. "Oh, all right."

Hartismere ignored the ungracious nature of Peveril's response. "Very well; I shall be off. I gather from Mrs Serring that Miss Carrington had compiled a schedule of dates when Serring observed suspicious behaviour. You might run your eye over it and see whom you can rule out because they were not yet posted here."

Peveril nodded. It seemed a feeble sort of thing to be doing whilst Midge was arrested, but it might help to pass the time. Then a sudden look of horror crossed his face. "Sir, wait!" He hurried over to the mantelpiece, lifted off the stuffed avocet and dug around in its innards. Hartismere watched this activity in some surprise, although surprise changed to sharp interest as Peveril presented him with a small lump of lead.

"A bullet? Where did you get this?"

"Caine gave it to me. He said he found it near Durrant's body. I should have given it to you immediately, sir. I... I forgot."

Hartismere forbore from pointing out how serious this lapse might have been. Judging from the boy's tone of voice, he was fully aware of it. "This could be very useful."

A thought struck Peveril. "When I learned about weapons going missing from C Coy, I wondered whether they were being stockpiled for invading troops or spies – even if ten rifles seemed very small beer."

"Go on."

"Maybe the rifles were a blind, sir. Maybe the point was to throw away the revolver used to kill Durrant lest the bullet ever be found."

"I think that that is quite credible."

Ralph looked downcast. "Then we won't be able to prove anything with this."

"Don't forget that if the bullet doesn't match Poole's gun, that casts considerable doubt upon the case against Poole. It is negative evidence – and, of course, it could be argued that Poole had several weapons on him that night – but it is important evidence all the same."

Peveril said nothing. He had felt that getting the bullet had made his return to the marsh worthwhile, but if there was no gun to match the bullet to, then he had achieved practically nothing. Hartismere's voice recalled him to the present.

"Have you anything else to report, no matter how minor?"

"Just that Snellgrove was prowling around looking for me. There's a price on my head and Snellgrove offered Caine a reward if he turned me in. I don't understand why he's so keen to lay his hands upon me."

"Snellgrove? That's interesting." Hartismere glanced at his watch. "You must forgive me, Peveril, but the bank will be opening and I don't want to lose any time."

"Yes, sir. Sorry, sir."

Meanwhile, Midge was sitting in a chair in Woolf's office. It still stank of burnt wood and sodden paper, but she was thankful that she was not in an actual cell. Admittedly, this appeared to have occurred not out of kindness, but because the inspector had moved his papers to a more secure location than his bombed-out office. Nevertheless, it made the experience one degree less frightening.

'Thank goodness I managed to hide the key to Cosford's house before Woolf found me,' Midge thought to herself. 'I'm sure he didn't believe my story of seeing a light and wanting to enforce blackout precautions.' She shivered. 'And he certainly can't have believed my act of offended dignity at having my word disbelieved. It gave me an excuse to refuse to answer any further questions, but it can't last much longer – any sane person would tell their story just to get out of here.'

To distract herself from the thought of what might happen next, Midge stared round the room. 'I suppose being incarcerated here enables me to inspect the effects of a grenade at close quarters.' She forced a laugh. 'This chap can't have been much good. The attack on Poole's cell blew out a wall. This man only managed to burn out Woolf's desk.'

She craned round to look into the main part of the room, which ran, like the long leg of an L, at a right angle to where the desk was placed. 'I know I was lousy at games, but I don't see how anyone could have reached the desk from the window, unless the grenade bounced off a wall. If it comes to that, the main burns are on this side of the desk, by the chair. Surely Woolf ought to have died if that was where the grenade struck?' Her frown deepened as she took in further details. 'Wasn't the filing-cabinet supposedly burned and all the files lost? But it's by the window. How could one grenade start two fires far apart?'

Midge stared in confusion round the room. Woolf must have lied about what happened. But why? Was he trying to cover up an accident? Did he think that a murderous attack on him sounded better than a drunken subordinate setting fire to the curtains? Midge shook her head slowly; Woolf didn't sound the sort to hide up his subordinates' mistakes. Midge shivered as she reached her conclusion. 'He's lying because he's implicated in Durrant's murder. In fact, he *is* the murderer. He deliberately set fire to the filing-cabinet to destroy all the statements. By this stage no-one will be able to remember exactly when they were doing things that night, so it'll be impossible for anyone to check all the alibis. Any defence counsel would have a wonderful time picking holes in the prosecution case.'

A thought struck Midge. She had assumed that whoever killed Poole had been in the army. But Woolf had been at the hospital soon after Poole's death. What if he had been there earlier and it had been he, rather than a nurse, who had given Poole the lethal dose of morphia? Poole had been in a room on his own and too weak to put up much resistance. Moreover, Matron Roberts had referred to Woolf having been in uniform. No-one would have connected a man out of uniform with Woolf. Midge corrected herself. Perhaps Woolf had been in uniform – that of a doctor. It wouldn't have been difficult to pick up a surgical coat, while a stethoscope would serve as a badge of office. No-one would have thought of challenging him – particularly if the ward had been short-staffed that day. And, even if anyone had noticed a stray doctor wandering around, Woolf could have suppressed the information, while at the same time destroying any other leads. It was hardly surprising that the suicide theory had been accepted with so little fuss.

As she considered the implications, Midge shivered. No wonder Poole had been terrified – he *had* been trying to assure Ralph he wouldn't talk; he must have been desperate for Ralph to pass news of his silence back to Woolf. And it wasn't particularly consoling to reflect that Poole, too, had once been locked up in Newton police-station. Nor did she know whether Dr Hartismere or Ralph would be able to help her if Woolf decided that she, too, was a danger to his safety.

When Hartismere reappeared at the police-station some time

later, Woolf was absent, leaving only Baldock in place. After exchanging greetings, Hartismere informed the constable that, once he had spoken to both Miss Carrington and Woolf, he would see about taking Miss Carrington home.

"Yes, sir," replied Baldock, scrutinising Hartismere intently.

Hoping that his statement had helped to make the constable trust him, the Vice-Master asked whether there was somewhere less official where he could question the suspect. "She's hardly going to run away and, if I play the friendly, fatherly figure, she might trust me and talk. It would help enormously if I didn't have to question her here."

Baldock scratched his head thoughtfully. "Well, sir, there be my cottage, but it be something of a walk. Or there be the police house. Sergeant isn't married, so it's not very tidy-like, but he be a fair hand in the garden and you might sit there."

"That would be ideal," agreed Hartismere, reflecting that it was highly unlikely that the sergeant's currant bushes would contain listening apparatus.

Once he had escorted Midge to a sheltered spot, the Vice-Master turned to Midge. "I haven't much time. Peveril is safely at the Serring woman's house. Is she reliable?"

Disconcerted by the Vice-Master's brisk, no-nonsense approach – one which was most unlike his normal loquacious and mellifluous manner – Midge could only nod. Then she pulled herself together. "I think so. She certainly hated Cosford. He sneered at her and called her a Russian Jew – even although she's Polish."

"I doubt that such details as the Miracle on the Vistula count for much when you're eaten up with hate," commented Hartismere. "If I am correct, then Cosford's wife and child died in the Revolution. I shouldn't imagine that it was a pleasant death."

Midge winced. "Do you think that that is why he got involved with Fascists?"

"Most probably. His reading material suggests far greater interest in attacking Bolshevism than in supporting anti-Semitism. Presumably he saw Fascism as a means to destroy those who destroyed his family."

"My enemy's enemy is my friend?

"Precisely. The current truce between Germany and Russia won't last and, presumably, Cosford was attracted by earlier attacks on German Communists."

Suddenly a thought struck Midge. "I noticed that quite a few of his books were published by the Movement for the Freedom of the Suppressed People of Latvia. Could that be some sort of a front organisation for the Nazis? It was registered in London; perhaps it's being used to fund the Fifth Column."

"I didn't spot that," admitted the Vice-Master. "It will certainly bear looking into."

"Woolf must be suspicious of Cosford, too," added Midge. "He was in Cosford's house last night, moving the furniture about."

"Are you sure?"

"Yes. I was upstairs – I thought that he was a burglar. I was terrified that he'd find me." Midge twisted uneasily at the memory.

"And he did find you."

Midge nodded. "I don't actually think he suspected I was there, because he didn't look under the bed immediately. Then he pulled out some books and he caught sight of me."

"Indeed."

Midge glanced at the Vice-Master before adding hesitantly, "I... well, I rather wondered whether Woolf was involved."

"And what makes you say that?"

After Midge had explained her theories about Poole's death and the pattern of burns in Woolf's office, Hartismere thought for a few moments, before scribbling rapidly on a piece of paper. "I need you to go to the post-office and send this wire. You will then lurk inconspicuously – I suggest a tea-room – for at least an hour before collecting the reply. It may take longer. Only when you have got the reply can you return to Mrs Serring's house – again, inconspicuously. Do not, on any account, return here."

"Are you trying to get me out of the way?"

"My dear girl, I don't know what I have done to make you and young Peveril so suspicious of my actions, but I can assure that I need that telegram sent urgently and I have no desire for it, or the reply, to be intercepted."

Chapter Fifty-Five

With Midge safely bundled off out of the way, Hartismere waited for Woolf's return. The inspector was furious that Chief Inspector Thomas had overridden him and released Midge.

"What the devil were you playing at? Cosford was a civilian, so you have no right to interfere on my patch."

"You can't prosecute the girl."

"Why not? She was on enclosed premises."

"She said that the back door was unlocked, and I fail to see how you can prove otherwise. If she saw a light and came in to investigate, then there is no case to answer."

"But…"

"I grant you that she was most foolhardy, given that there is a murderer on the loose, but I cannot see anything criminal in her actions. Nor will the Bench."

"Her presence is deeply suspicious."

"Overly zealous and mischief-making, perhaps, but you'd have half of the Bench locked up, too, if those were criminal charges. Mind you, it was fortunate that you were passing by and caught her."

Woolf attempted a more emollient tone. "You know what it's like, work never stops. I thought I'd have another search of Cosford's house in the hope of finding something we overlooked."

"And did you?"

"Not unless you count that girl, no."

"I apologise for not being around earlier to help question her. I was looking into a rather odd fact. A five-pound note which was seen in Trent's possession was issued to you."

"I imagine a great number of notes have been issued to me over the years."

"Indeed, but this was issued to you the day before Trent's death. How did it end up in his wallet?"

Woolf shrugged. "I have no idea – assuming it ever did. As I remember the evidence at the inquest, nothing of that nature was found upon him."

"Perhaps it was not spoken of publicly, but I have implicit

faith in my information. Can you explain how Trent ended up with that note in his wallet?"

"I probably spent it at the mess and he filched it."

"Does mess etiquette allow guests to buy drinks?"

"I'd rather have a drink than be ruled by some hidebound tradition."

"So are you now saying that you did spend the note in the mess?"

"I don't remember getting any specific five-pound note, and I don't remember spending it. And I may say, Thomas, that I don't like your tone."

"You'll like this even less. I strongly suspect that your story of the grenade attack on your office is inaccurate. Perhaps you might favour me with the truth."

Woolf stood up abruptly. "See here, Thomas, I'm damned if you are going to come in here and sneer at me. Just because you're from the Yard doesn't give you the right to treat me like this. You can get out."

"I think not."

"Then you needn't think that I'm going to stay here any longer, listening to your insinuations."

Hartismere rose. "Baldock!" The constable entered. "Arrest that man!"

Baldock's jaw dropped. "Sir?"

"You heard me. Arrest that man."

"You'll do nothing of the sort, Baldock. I've had enough of this tomfoolery. Thomas hasn't even said on what charge."

"On a charge of arson."

Baldock looked even more surprised. "*Arson*, sir?"

"Indeed. Of course, if there is a reasonable explanation for how Inspector Woolf came to set fire to his office in two different places, I am prepared to listen to it, but, so far, I have met with nothing other than lies and obfuscation."

"By God, if you obey him, Baldock, you can forget about any prospects in the police," swore Woolf vengefully.

"I been thinkin' that my duty lies with the Army, not in a cushy job with no real crime, barrin' poachin'." With this statement, Baldock stepped forward and grasped Woolf. For a moment, it looked as if Woolf would hit him, then the inspector submitted, muttering maledictions upon his subordinate.

After Woolf was locked up, Hartismere turned to Baldock. "Thank you, constable. Not an easy task for you."

"No, sir." There was a pause. "Beggin' your pardon, Professor, but be you sure that Miss Carrington won't be charged with anythin'?"

"What did you call me?"

"Professor, sir. I followed the Peveril case, sir, what with it being Mr John who got hurt. That was how I recognised Peveril when he came in here. And you were the professor from Mr John's college."

"I don't recollect any photographs of any professors being in the press," stated Hartismere, who had taken considerable care to avoid any such contingency.

"Maybe not in the big London papers, sir, but your photograph was in the *East Anglian*. It was a group photograph, which is why I didn't recognise you immediately."

Hartismere evaded an outright admission of his identity. "I have no intention of charging Miss Carrington with anything, but on no account must you mention your speculations to anyone."

Baldock grinned happily. "No, sir. This be much better than spendin' nights tryin' to catch Arthur Abbots a-sellin' unlicensed game."

"And keep an eye on Woolf, there's a good chap. I don't want him to escape."

Despite the urgency of the situation, Hartismere took care to approach Mrs Serring's house via a circuitous route. He had no desire to expose Peveril's hiding-place, not least because his own credibility would suffer if he were observed hobnobbing with a murder suspect. Ten minutes after he had arrived, Midge appeared, apologising for the delay.

"I'm sorry I took so long. Everyone seemed to want to visit the post-office and I decided it was safer to collect the reply when no-one was looking."

Hartismere thought that Midge looked exhausted. "I am sorry

that you had to wait, but I commend your discretion." He opened the telegram and deciphered the contents. "Good." He thrust the paper into the fire, before turning to Peveril.

"Woolf is currently locked up in Newton police-station. This wire confirms that two reliable men will arrive shortly to remove him to a less vulnerable location. Since I have not much time, let me summarise the case against Woolf. The scorch-marks in his office suggest that fires were started deliberately to destroy the filing-cabinet, rather than being caused by a grenade, as Woolf claimed. Moreover, the five-pound note which you found on Trent's body was issued to Woolf the day before Trent died. Miss Carrington suggests that Woolf, rather than Cosford, killed Poole – he was in the hospital when Poole was found to be dead, and Woolf would have become practically invisible if he shed his uniform." The Vice-Master gave a brief shrug. "The police doctor has confirmed that cyanide killed Cosford, but I suspect that Woolf may have given it to him. The apparent suicide note is not entirely convincing."

After Hartismere had quoted the note, Peveril glanced at him uncertainly. "I say, sir..."

"Yes?"

"I don't want to appear rude, but surely your grounds for arresting Woolf are rather weak. I mean, even if he had given Trent the fiver, that doesn't prove he killed him. I don't understand why he submitted."

"You're quite correct. It is a weak case, which is why he submitted. He expects to have it dismissed, whereas to have attempted flight would have been tantamount to admitting guilt."

Midge frowned, conscious that she was not thinking straight. "Then why did you arrest him? Was it because otherwise he would have the chance to destroy any evidence in relation to Cosford's death?"

"Partly – I should dearly love to know what he was up to last night – and partly in the hope of scaring his confederates into making a false move."

"Are we sure that he had confederates?" enquired Peveril. "I know Mrs Serring thinks her birds suggest three separate people, but they could easily be Woolf, Cosford and Poole – particularly now that we know that Cosford had a transmitter."

"Do you think that Poole was so fully involved?" queried Midge. "And, even if Poole were, perhaps Cosford doesn't count as one of Serring's birds. After all, anyone could visit Cosford in his shop without sparking suspicion. I don't see why he had to go out to obscure creeks to talk to people."

"Not if he only needed to speak to one man," pointed out Hartismere. "Individuals could easily slip in to buy a book, but I strongly doubt whether three people would have taken the risk of regularly meeting together at Cosford's shop. Don't forget that some of these discussions must have lasted for some time. If anyone noticed the coincidence that two of them always went to the shop at the same time it would start talk."

"Why did Woolf kill Cosford?" asked Midge. "Was Cosford having second thoughts? That suicide note of his sounds as if it could have been from part of a letter telling his co-conspirators that he no longer wanted to be involved."

"Quite so. And the superscription '*To the Coroner*' was typed, which struck me as odd."

Midge was visualising Cosford's shop. "I think it's even more odd that Cosford would choose to do away with himself in that cupboard. I know it goes back a certain amount, but surely it would be an uncomfortable place to kill yourself? After all, cyanide is pretty much instantaneous – it wasn't as if he had to ensure that nobody found him and saved him."

"Indeed," agreed the Vice-Master. "However, it was certainly in Woolf's interests to have some delay before the body was found. If any suspicion had fallen upon him, he might not have had a suitable alibi for the time of the killing."

"Ye-es." A thought struck Midge. "I suppose if that was where Cosford kept his propaganda, it was fairly natural for him to open it up if Woolf was talking to him. Perhaps Woolf asked him to have a drink with him while they discussed whatever was making Cosford unsure."

"It is certainly possible, although it is most likely that my interest in Cosford aroused Woolf's suspicions. He probably feared that Cosford wouldn't stand up to interrogation."

Hartismere shrugged. "However, my main concern at present is discovering the identity of the third conspirator whom Serring saw."

Ralph had an objection. "Since Serring was a birdwatcher, isn't there a danger that the same names might not mean the same individuals? One of these gulls could stand for one particular type of visitor."

"You mean, like sailors, or something?"

"Exactly, Midge." Peveril sighed. "Not that I can see how Serring could recognise everyone – he'd only been back in Britain for a few months."

"Or, indeed, how he could discriminate between types by their dress or appearance," pointed out Hartismere. "If there were a specific plumage adopted by traitors it would simplify the job considerably."

Ralph gave him a sidelong glance. Hartismere didn't appear to be jeering at him, but he didn't want another ticking off, this time in front of Midge.

For her part, Midge was frowning. "Assuming that there is a third man, what do you expect him to do? If he perceives that the case against Woolf is weak, he'll keep his mouth shut, too."

"I sincerely trust," declared Hartismere grimly, "that he will have no opportunity to discover what the case against Woolf is. Only we three know the precise details of the arrest. Baldock, should he talk, will only be able to refer to a charge of arson. Moreover, since Woolf will be removed unseen via the back entrance of the police-station, no-one ought to discover what has happened to him. How would you feel if you heard Woolf had disappeared?"

Midge grimaced. "I suppose I'd probably think that he'd fled because the net was closing in. Depending on how good my nerve was, I'd be tempted to flee, too."

"*He flees now this way and now that, like the hind with the Umbrian hound hot on her heels.*"

The Vice-Master shot Peveril a swift look, but made no comment on this literary addition to the discussion. "And how would you flee?"

Ralph, who appeared to have retreated into his own world

again, gave no reply, but Midge answered for him. "Do you mean, if I were a traitor?"

"Yes."

"I think, given the circumstances of being on the coast, and given that we suspect that he may be in communication with an enemy ship, I'd ask to be taken off in a U-boat. Is that what you think will happen?"

"It might. Don't forget that it's a new moon – ideal conditions for making an unobserved landing. Hence tonight we launch Operation Bellerophon."

Midge grinned. "I did wonder if the wire was from Major Collingwood." Noticing that Ralph looked blank, she added, "*Bellerophon* was the Napoleonic Collingwood's ship."

Peveril, who did not number naval history among his interests, merely grunted. Right at the moment, he didn't relish any reminder of his C.O.; moreover, he had a suspicion as to what the plan would entail.

"I shall suggest to Collingwood that he adopts less obvious code-words in future," remarked Hartismere, amused by Midge's response. "However, the plan is fairly straightforward. Indeed, it has to be, since it was created to cover various contingencies. Currently, thanks to Mrs Serring, we know that signalling has been taking place and we have a rough idea in what area. The aim is to lie up to trap the signaller and to prevent him from escaping by boat." Hartismere sighed. "Ideally, any boat would also be intercepted, but we have a fairly wide area to cover and a lack of manpower."

"If you can summon up men to take care of Woolf, can't they be placed in the marsh?" asked Peveril.

The Vice-Master shook his head. "It's too risky. Remember, we want our traitor to signal, but he won't if he learns that a whole lot of men who have no business there – and don't know the district well enough to remain hidden – have been infiltrated into the area."

"What about A Coy?"

"And have them spread the word round all of their friends? This may not be a one-night operation. We may have to be on the lookout for several days."

Midge intervened. "If the other Intelligence operative is involved, how is he going to prove himself to Ralph?"

"The code-word is Bellerophon."

For his part, Ralph was uninterested in code-words, or in finally meeting the other Intelligence operative. He knew he ought to volunteer eagerly to lie in wait for a signaller. And the fact that Hartismere had said that he hadn't let him down so far made it harder still. But all he could think about was what it would be like lying there in the dark, knowing that something was going to come closer and closer, and that he mustn't cry out, that he mustn't allow even one whimper of terror to escape him. And he would have to do that night after night, even although he knew that Charon was gliding through the reed-beds seeking him out to hang him. Suddenly, Ralph found himself speaking.

"I don't think there's much point in doing this – the third man *must* have been Poole."

Hartismere eyed him thoughtfully. There was something in the boy's voice which did not hold conviction – that, and the fact that Peveril would not meet his gaze.

"Miss Carrington, would you mind leaving us to check through those times again with Mrs Serring? It is vital that they are entirely accurate."

Midge started to protest, then stopped. Peveril remained frozen. Hartismere must have guessed.

Once alone with the Vice-Master, Peveril showed no inclination to speak. Mentally, he was back in the grey marsh of his nightmares, peopled by flitting wraiths and spectral shades of things. Slowly, he became aware that Hartismere was still there and that he would have to say something. Why had he been such a fool as to make such an obvious protest? Why had he drawn attention to himself? Now Midge knew that something was up and he could only explain his actions by admitting to further shameful cowardice. But why wouldn't Hartismere get on with whatever he intended to do to him?

Suddenly, out of desperation, Peveril broke the silence. "Sir, I can't go back there."

"Why?" enquired Hartismere, in not unsympathetic tones.

"You said I didn't have to."

"Yes, and I am prepared to honour that agreement. However, in return, I should like to know what has changed."

"I can't go back night after night."

"But you could go back for one night?"

Ralph stared at the floor, trapped by the Vice-Master's logic. How could he possibly explain?

"Look me in the face and tell me why you can't go."

Still unwilling to meet Hartismere's gaze and read the contempt which was bound to follow his statement, Peveril muttered, "You don't understand, sir. I'm unreliable. I see things."

"And what have you seen?"

"Charon."

"Have you, by God?"

Assuming that Hartismere was sneering at him, Peveril lashed back. "Yes, so either I'm so feeble that I can't invent a better excuse to evade my duty, or I'm mad and imagining things."

"Describe him."

"*An untamed beard grows from his chin, grey and matted, fire-lit eyes glaring and ablaze.*"

"In your own words, please, and thinking about what you actually saw, not what Virgil wrote."

Peveril shrugged. "Tallish, propelling the boat with a pole. I couldn't see his face properly because there was something swathed round it."

"What colour were his clothes?"

"I don't know. And it looked like a shroud, not normal clothes."

"Bright or dark?"

"Dark, I think. It didn't stand out against the mud."

"What was the shape of the boat?"

"Flattish. Like a punt, really."

"What colour?"

"Brownish, I suppose."

"Where did you see it, and when?"

"I don't know."

"Then think, boy. Was it still fully light, or was it getting darker?"

"I don't know. There was a mist."

"Was it dark when you reached Caine's place?"

"Yes. At least, it had just turned dark."

"And how long did it take you to reach Caine's from when you saw this image?"

Peveril scowled. "I don't know. Gibbering cowards don't notice the time."

"I would not describe you as a gibbering coward. Rather, I would describe you as someone who had singularly failed to obey his orders to pass on all important information."

Ralph gasped in surprise at the reprimand, which had been delivered in Hartismere's coldest tone. The Vice-Master noticed Peveril's reaction with relief – a rebuke might bring the whole incident out of a world of shadows and ghosts, and into the realm of normal things.

"The only thing which redeems you somewhat is that you have finally had the sense to tell me what you observed." Hartismere produced a detailed map. "You will indicate to me, as far as possible, your route."

Bending over the map in the hope of hiding his embarrassment, Peveril endeavoured to trace where he had been.

"I think I must have been about there when I saw... when I saw it, sir."

"Are you absolutely sure?"

Peveril shook his head unhappily. "No, sir. But I was most of the way to Caine's place and the water must have been deep enough to take a punt. There's a creek shown here and I think that might have been it."

"So you do know how to use your brain."

Peveril glanced up suspiciously.

"No, I'm not laughing at you, Peveril. I am extremely relieved to have this additional piece of information." Hartismere pointed to the map. "Just beyond where you were is a wide meander; after that the creek winds round into the area where Mrs Serring said she saw lights."

For a moment the implications of this failed to strike Peveril. Then he asked hesitantly. "Do you mean that I saw...?"

"A real person? Yes. And if I were a fool, I should have

dismissed your story, just as fools dismissed hers. I may add that, given that you probably saw a murderer, you had every reason to be scared."

Peveril turned away abruptly. "It's very decent of you to say that, sir, but hardly anyone would agree with you. The point is, I was too afraid to do anything other than cower in the sludge. It never occurred to me that he was real. I didn't even watch where he went."

"Just as well. If you had attracted his attention you would probably have ended up dead in the sludge which, apart from any other considerations, would have deprived me of this potentially vital information."

"But..."

"I am interested in trapping a traitor, not in heroics. '*Stand in the trench, Achilles, flame-capped, and shout for me*' is all very well in hand-to-hand warfare, but Intelligence has no use for men who leap in head-first. If you must resort to Classical analogies, take Odysseus as your model, not Achilles."

"He didn't bring any of his men back with him."

"If memory serves me right, that was because they disobeyed orders."

"Err... yes, sir."

Chapter Fifty-Six

Eight hours later, Peveril was lying hidden in a patch of reeds, cursing the cold which was already creeping through his limbs. Carrington's things were far too thin for this sort of lunatic adventure. The only vaguely consoling point was how decent Hartismere had been about it.

'He could have told me it was my duty to be here. He could have paid me back for my stupid insults by calling me a coward. Instead he let me volunteer. So I mustn't let him down. And,' Ralph added, guiltily conscious that this ought to be his priority, 'the traitor must be caught.' He scowled angrily at the thought of what Midge had undergone. She must have been terrified, locked up in that office, realising that she'd been arrested by a murderer. And he had not been there to protect her.

Back in Newton, Midge was feeling equally fed-up. With a mixture of trepidation and frustration, she had watched Ralph and the Vice-Master slip out of the house. Ralph looked exhausted, Dr Hartismere had admitted that they didn't have enough men, and what was she doing? Sitting around here like some early Victorian swooning miss. If her stupid leg worked, she could have been a fourth watcher. Even Mrs Serring had been drafted in to smuggle the men along the coast. For a moment, Midge allowed herself to be side-tracked by admiration for how the Vice-Master had solved the problem of entering the marsh without being seen.

'Goodness knows how he managed to persuade Caine to come and meet Mrs Serring's boat, but it's much the safest option. Chief Inspector Thomas might be able to talk his way past a patrol, but if they stopped Mrs Serring, they'd be bound to find Ralph under the tarpaulin. Then the balloon would go up. At least he'll be properly hidden in Caine's boat. It's bigger, too, so there's less danger navigating the entrance to the Hart.'

Then Midge's resentment resurfaced. 'Useless,' she muttered angrily to herself. 'You couldn't even scramble ashore. So what are you going to do?'

Wishing that she could work off her irritation by pacing

round the room, Midge ran through all the things she couldn't do. 'I can't look out for signals in the saltings. I can't lurk in C Coy, watching who leaves camp. I can't even go through Woolf's files, or the sergeant will question why 'Thomas' let me. Anyhow, I don't have the keys to the filing-cabinet.' A thought struck her. 'But I do have a key to Cosford's house.' She nibbled her lip. 'Is there any point? I know that Woolf seemed to be searching for something, but he may have been searching on the off-chance that Cosford had left something compromising lying around. There may be nothing there.'

Pushing to the back of her mind the lowering suspicion that she was frightened to re-enter the house, Midge tried to think things through logically. 'If Woolf moved the furniture around, then whatever he wanted to find isn't very big. He may have thought that it was tucked behind a bookcase, or something. And, presumably, he would have spotted any hidden trap-doors under the rugs, so I don't need to go looking for an agent secreted under the floorboards.'

Eventually deciding that, if Woolf had been searching for something, most likely it had been papers, Midge reluctantly made her way into the kitchen. Trix, the dog, lay in her basket and whined as Midge approached the door.

"Sorry, old girl, I'm not taking you out for a run." Trix whined again. Midge eyed her thoughtfully. "Look here, would you stay with me if I took you outside? I'm unused to dogs and I can't manage your lead, but I shouldn't be half as scared if I knew that you were there, ready to growl if someone came near." Trix got up and moved to the door. "God forgive me," muttered Midge, "if you run off and don't come back. I should imagine that would finally break your owner's heart."

Having carefully left a note for Mrs Serring under Trix's blanket, Midge set off, unsure if her precautions were adequate. 'I hope to goodness that Mrs Serring will understand what I mean by "I have used your key". I couldn't exactly say "I've gone to burgle Cosford's house. Please come and look for my dead body if I've not returned".'

Trix seemed delighted to be outside and frisked around happily as Midge slowly made her way down the garden path. 'At least Trix provides me with an excuse for being out,' reflected Midge. 'Moreover, even small dogs can bite hard.' Midge's steps grew even slower once she reached the back gate. 'I do wish it were possible to see the back quarters from Mrs Serring's house. That would at least have given me the chance to observe whether anyone had entered that way.'

Much to Midge's relief, no-one accosted her when she entered Cosford's garden, nor when she made her way to the back door. Summoning her courage, she unlocked it and pushed it forward very gently. There was a low growl from Trix. Midge glanced at her. Was there someone lying in wait in the kitchen? Trix growled again, before darting forward. A tiny shape shot out of the house and into a hedge, closely followed by the terrier.

"Trix!" hissed Midge in as commanding a whisper as she dared. The dog stopped scrabbling at the earth and returned unwillingly. Midge felt that she could have started cackling from sheer relief. Here she was fearing assassins and Trix wanted to chase rodents. "Fine protection you are," she muttered. The dog cocked her head, before prancing into the house. Trix ignored the door to the kitchen and scullery, and instead followed the passage all the way to the front door. Then, after sniffing at the wainscoting, Trix bent down and nuzzled something. She lifted it up and returned to Midge, wagging her tail proudly.

"Is that your party-trick?" asked Midge, as Trix pushed the letters into her hand. "How beastly to be presented with a dead man's mail. The world goes on while he lies in a morgue." She shivered. About to replace the envelopes on the mat, lest anyone realise that they had been moved, she paused. Wouldn't it be worth seeing what was in the letters? It was highly unlikely that there would be anything important, but surely it was silly to ignore the possibility, just because she was squeamish about opening mail addressed to a corpse? 'Mail addressed to a traitor,' she corrected herself fiercely. 'But if I do read it, I'll have to steam open the envelopes and I'm going to do that at Mrs Serring's. I'm not messing around with kettles whilst wondering if a killer is about to come in. Anyway, the gas has probably been cut off by now.'

Once back at the widow's house, with the door carefully

locked and bolted, Midge turned her attention to steaming open the envelopes. The process was much more time consuming and complicated than it appeared in books and, when Midge eventually succeeded in opening the first two, the results were disappointing. A gas bill and a circular about rationing held out no promise of high treason. "I suppose they could be in code," Midge informed Trix, "but I'm damned if I can see how." She looked at the third envelope in disgust. "This one is only addressed 'to the occupier'. I don't suppose it's even worth opening – it's probably information on the rates, or something equally dull."

A few minutes later, Midge had extracted the letter. Reading the beginning Midge blinked, then turned to the envelope. No, the number was quite correct for Cosford's house. Then why did it start 'Dear Mr Pelgard'? Was Pelgard an alias? There was no suggestion that anyone else lived with – or even visited – Cosford. She carried on reading.

Rothstein, Kuhn and Silver
146 Old Chancery
EC1

Dear Mr Pelgard,

In accordance with your instructions, we have sold 80 per cent of your holdings in both Tobacco Internationale and Municipal Iron Corporation, which we purchased for you on 21/10/39. Acting on a firm understanding of the market, by delaying the sale until Tuesday of this week, we were able to take advantage of a rise in the share price, which means that the total moneys accrued amount to £1036 10s 7d. These funds have been sent via telegraphic transfer to Aleksandrs Cimze et Cie., as per your instructions.

May we take the opportunity of advising you that Imperial Manganese Preferential Shares are performing particularly strongly in the current climate? Bauxite Consolidated (Deferred Shares), which you asked us to consider, do not appear to be holding up well, and we should not advise investing in the company.

Thank you for your esteemed custom,

There followed an illegible squiggle. Midge's eyes flicked back up to the engraved heading. So, Cosford, who sneered at Mrs

Serring as a Russian Jew, was quite happy to employ a Jewish-sounding firm of stockbrokers. She reread the letter. It all seemed perfectly innocent, even if a large sum were involved. But it looked as if there had been an unexpected delay in selling the shares whilst the stockbrokers waited for the price to rise. Could this letter have been what Woolf was looking for and it simply hadn't arrived? What did he want it for? He couldn't have hoped to steal the money, because it had already been sent to another company.

Midge regarded the second name thoughtfully. 'I refuse to believe that Mssrs Cimze et Cie are dubious purely because they possess a foreign name. However, I do wonder who Aleksandrs Cimze is. A White Russian exiled in Paris? Do Russians spell Alexander with an 's' at the end?' Midge felt a temporary burst of excitement. 'Could it be Latvian?' Then she sighed. 'Why would that be significant? We already know he buys anti-Soviet books from that Latvian freedom movement – assuming that it isn't a German front organisation.' Midge paused. 'Hang on, I've got that the wrong way round. Why would Cosford be giving a German front organisation money? Surely it would be sending money to him to pay for his services? If it comes to that, £1000 is a devil of a lot of money for a bookseller in a quiet country town to be speculating with. And Dr Hartismere said that he had a lot in his own bank account – enough to surprise his own bank manager. Where did he get it all?'

Wishing that she had instant access to Companies House to look up Cimze et Cie, Midge tried to decide what to do next. Somehow, with this new information to pass on, it felt foolhardy to return to Cosford's house.

Since Hartismere had foreseen the possibility of Midge having to communicate directly with Collingwood's department, he had made her memorise a telephone number which was manned day and night. Moreover, he had taught her a code based on the position of letters in the alphabet. However, unlike a simple substitution code, where each letter was moved forward the same amount, this code was based on a 5-digit number, and the individual digits of each were alternately added or subtracted. This meant that the code could not be broken by looking at letter frequency, since the same letter ended up coded in a different way. Thus C, C, C, C, C combined with 52798 became 3+5, 3-2, 3+7, 3-9, 3+8, or H, A, J, U, I. As an additional precaution, three random letters were then inserted and the process was repeated, this time with 5 subtracted, 2 added, and so on.

"It's not perfect," Hartismere had warned her, "but it's a lot safer than open speech."

At the time, Midge had agreed with the Vice-Master, but faced with the strain of transcribing a summary of the Pelgard letter into code, Midge wished that a less secure, but more straightforward, code had been chosen. 'We don't have time to waste,' she growled, as she checked through her transcription for the second time. 'Why can't it have been based on words; you don't have to count those. This is too long; I'm bound to have made a mistake. And some of the words may cause confusion at the other end. What if Cimze comes out garbled, or someone thinks that it has? It'll spoil everything.'

Eventually, Midge dialled the number which Hartismere had given her. As she waited for the telephone to be answered, her anxiety increased. Why wouldn't they answer? Had she got the wrong number? What if some enemy answered? Or if someone laughed at her and refused to believe that her message was important? Just as Midge was convincing herself that she must have made a mistake, a male voice informed her that she was through to Archibald Green Associates.

"Miranda Lewis here.

"Did you say Amanda?"

Midge sighed with relief. One countersign had been given. "No, Miranda, as in miracle."

"We all need those at the moment."

As the second countersign was given, Midge launched into her cover-story of dealings on Wall Street, and the information which she was relaying from there. When she finished, the voice thanked her emotionlessly and she was left staring stupidly at the receiver. 'Was that all?' she wondered. 'He sounded so matter-of-fact.' A burring noise recalled her to her senses and she slowly replaced the receiver. 'I suppose that's the point. If he'd got worked up, anyone listening in might have questioned what was going on. All the same, it doesn't feel normal.'

Chapter Fifty-Seven

The following day, Midge had cause to bless the complexity of her code, since deciphering a return message gave her something to do after lunch. Although Mrs Serring had told her that she had heard no disturbance on the marsh the previous night, Midge wished she could be sure that this meant that Ralph and the Vice-Master were all right. When Hartismere finally appeared, looking tired, Midge immediately asked where Ralph was.

"In hiding." Hartismere turned to greet Mrs Serring, before asking whether she had a fire burning.

For the first time, Midge noticed that the don was not wearing a coat, despite the heavy rain. Hartismere took in her horrified expression. "Don't worry, my dear, I've been indoors most of the day. I merely thought that Peveril would welcome the extra protection if he couldn't take refuge."

Noticing the Vice-Master's deliberate failure to refer to Caine, Midge decided to wait until they were alone before producing her new information. Fortunately, Mrs Serring did not appear to take offence at being banished from her own front parlour and Midge was able to brief Hartismere as to what she had discovered.

"Hmm. I think you are probably correct that Pelgard is an alias for Cosford. It sounds faintly Cornish, but I wonder whether it's invented."

"Why?"

Hartismere ran his finger under four letters. "It's rather convenient that 'Elga' comes in the middle of it – the name on the photograph."

Midge frowned. "I ought to have spotted that."

"It's more important that you suspected the significance of the letter." Hartismere tapped the reply which Midge had received earlier that day. "Look at the information those stockbrokers gave – 'Pelgard' had been a regular investor with them for several years. In each case, he followed the same procedure of buying stocks, selling them a few months later, and sending the proceeds to your friend Cimze the timber importer.

Now why do you think he did that?"

Feeling as if she were back in Cambridge, Midge forced herself to think. "Because he didn't want to give the money directly to Cimze et Cie.?"

"Yes. Why?"

"Maybe he didn't trust them completely. Or maybe he didn't trust his stockbrokers."

Hartismere laughed. "Rothstein's would be deeply aggrieved to hear that suggestion. They take their reputation very seriously. No, Miss Carrington, I suspect that Cosford didn't want to take the risk of the tax-man discovering that he had significant additional resources to those which he declared."

"You mean, he'd have faced questions as to how he'd made his money?"

"Precisely. Whilst I, as a maltreated taxpayer, might relish the irony of expecting a smuggler to pay income tax upon his illicit earnings, I doubt if the Chancellor would regard an appreciation of irony as sufficient excuse for bilking the Revenue." The Vice-Master's face hardened. "Treason, on the other hand, I do not relish."

Midge stared down at the information which had arrived that morning. "I know we suspect treason, but do we have proof?"

"No actual proof as yet, but some very suggestive information. Look at the dates. Rothstein's put through a big purchase for Cosford in late October – they'd only ever handled small transactions before then, three hundred pounds at best. And there was another investment of nine hundred pounds in March. Clearly friend Cosford had either trebled his smuggling or found something more valuable to smuggle."

Midge frowns. "But that suggests that he turned traitor very late on – quite possibly after the war started. Isn't that the wrong way round? I mean, lots of Communists tore up their party cards and joined the Army once war was declared, even although they'd vowed previously not to. Surely it's easier – and safer – to be a peacetime traitor?"

"Indeed it is, but, on the 5th of October, Russia imposed a Mutual Assistance Pact across the Baltic States. I suspect that that may have been a powerful stimulus to a man who loathed

Bolshevism."

"Didn't the Pact force the Latvians to accept thousands of Soviet soldiers based in their country?"

"Yes. Cosford must have feared worse to come – and I cannot blame him in that respect. He will have remembered how the Letts were treated in the Red Terror, when they were blamed for an attempt to overthrow the Bolsheviks. Moreover, look at Finland."

Midge grimaced, remembering the aggressive invasion and the resultant deaths in the Winter War. "Imagine being caught between the Nazi jackal and the Russian bear."

"Quite. But Cosford wasn't."

"Do you think that Cimze et Cie really are timber importers, Dr Hartismere?"

"I should imagine that they certainly dabble in timber at the very least. Import-export companies are the ideal front for nefarious activities because you can explain away any number of dubious characters or items as 'representatives' or 'samples of goods'."

Wondering if the Vice-Master was speaking from personal experience, Midge continued. "Then Cimze may have links with the Baltic because of the trade in fir."

"More knowledge culled from Napoleonic history, Miss Carrington?" Then, as Midge looked embarrassed, Hartismere apologised. "I am not laughing at you, my dear. I mistrust students who wish to learn only what is supposedly relevant. They regularly prove themselves to have second-class minds. And once Collingwood's man has dug around, I shall be very much surprised if Messrs Cimze do not prove to have Baltic links."

"Perhaps even links to the Movement for the Freedom of the Suppressed People of Latvia?"

"Quite possibly."

Midge sighed. "I wonder if Cosford's wife was Latvian. It must be unbearably awful to lose your wife and child violently – maybe that explains why he cared enough about another country to betray his own."

"Indeed," agreed Hartismere in so expressionless a voice that

Midge was left wondering what she had said wrong.

Back at Harting Magna, Ralph was drowsily wakening. 'Thank God Caine let me come back here,' he thought. 'Was it because he thinks I'll lead him to Poole's killer? Or was it because of the money Hartismere gave him for services rendered?' He wriggled further down under the blankets, reluctant to get up. 'At least some spot cash may put Caine off handing me over to Snellgrove.' The thought of his erstwhile colleague made Ralph shiver. 'I wish I knew why Snellgrove came back here this morning. Does he have some definite evidence to make him suspect Caine? Why else would he have raided the hamlet at dawn today? It's just as well I listened to Hartismere and didn't barge in here immediately he left me. I'd have been well and truly caught. Plus it would have landed Caine in a devilish unpleasant position.'

Ralph turned to more personal matters. 'I did make it through last night. Whatever else, I didn't beg my way out. And Charon didn't appear. I know Hartismere treated him like a living, breathing human, but perhaps the real explanation is that he doesn't actually exist. I told a rational audience what I thought I saw, and now my imagination can't conjure it up in the face of Hartismere's scepticism.' He scowled. 'That doesn't say much for the state I'd let myself get into, but maybe now I can cease behaving like a lily-livered poltroon.' His expression lightened momentarily. 'And if I stop seeing Charon, surely I'd be normal enough to ask Midge to be my girlfriend?'

In the light and warmth of the afternoon, Peveril found it possible to convince himself that – notwithstanding various accusations of murder – he might soon be in a position to tell Midge how much he cared for her. However, by the time that the sun had set he was much less sanguine. As per instructions, Caine had led him to a carefully-chosen hide near where Peveril had first observed the figure in a punt. There the smuggler had left him. Cautiously parting the reeds, Ralph had ensured that he had a good view of the water, before settling down to wait. He knew perfectly well that there was little chance of any action for some hours, but since the plan was to intercept any signallers, it was essential to be in position before darkness fell. Even if it was difficult to see far, it ought to be possible to hear anyone coming upstream. The trouble was that noises seemed much louder and more frequent in the dark and, as they grew, so too did the music in Peveril's head. Telling himself fiercely that the rustling and slithering was merely the local creatures pursuing their avocations in the marsh, Peveril nearly cried out when something touched his hand. Shrinking back, he heard the reeds quiver as the animal scurried away.

'A rat,' he informed himself angrily. 'Are you about to make a complete fool of yourself over a water-rat? How can you tell Midge that you love her if you bungle catching a traitor because you're afraid of a mouse? And why the blazes has that Verdi returned? I thought I'd got rid of it this afternoon.'

Aware that attempting to remember other music would merely result in a jangling cacophony of sound inside his head, Peveril tried to concentrate on the lapping of the water. Slowly, the soft lilt of water caressing the reeds exercised a soothing influence, and Peveril found himself able to think more intelligently.

'I can see that signalling from the marsh is safer than signalling from the river-bank, where someone might intercept you. And I can see that it's quicker and quieter to make your way through the reed-beds by boat, rather than struggling on foot. So it probably is worthwhile concentrating our forces on this particular stream. All the same, I hope that Hartismere's correct and there actually is a third man.' Ralph scowled angrily. 'I know I suggested that Poole was it just to get out of this lark, but it seems as good an explanation as any other. After all, Poole was a smuggler and a pretty convincing liar. And he admitted that he'd wondered what was going on.' He snorted. 'I bet he wouldn't have admitted that if he hadn't realised that we had our suspicious. It was a mighty clever way of distracting attention from him.'

As he was wondering about Poole's guilt, Peveril suddenly became aware that the rhythm of the lapping water had changed. The suck and hiss on the banks had grown stronger, as if propelled by an external force. Ralph licked his lips. It was ridiculous to become uneasy just because the tide had turned downstream. There was nothing sinister in it. It was quite normal. Then he caught a whiff of decay. 'It's the mud,' he told himself. 'The tide's driving the water higher onto fresh mud.' Despite this rational explanation, Peveril's unease grew. 'I'm not going to crack up,' he swore feverishly. 'I'm not. I'm not.'

Then he saw it: a dark silhouette against the grey marsh, coming closer and closer. By now, the music inside Ralph's head was so strong that he could not hear anything else. The craft gliding past appeared noiseless, even although he could see the pole being raised and lowered into the water. Charon had reappeared. Hartismere's rational scepticism had not worked. Scepticism could not explain away sulphur and choirs of demons. Scepticism could not create a live man out of a wraith.

Almost as if in a dream, Peveril recalled Midge telling him that Robert wanted to drive him mad. Perhaps Robert had already succeeded. Robert liked destroying things. And so had his father. Midge had spoken of terns. Well, he had learned, aged eight, what could happen to them. He had admired one, effortlessly wheeling in the sky; Leo had blasted it with shotgun pellets. Moments later it lay on the ground, a blot of crimson blood marring its snow-white breast. He had exclaimed in guilt and grief at beauty destroyed – and Leo had struck him to give him a real cause to cry.

So Robert and Leo liked destroying things. They would have gloated that he had gone mad. But Hartismere didn't like destruction and he had told him that he wasn't mad. The choice was clear. He could lie cowering, destroyed by Robert and Robert's anonymous letters, or he could trust Hartismere. And Hartismere was out in the marsh, unaware that evil had entered it.

It was just after Ralph had forced himself to stand up and look in the direction of Charon that he became aware of a thin pencil of light. He gave a momentary shudder of relief as he recognised what had caused it. Classical gods didn't possess electric torches, and he wasn't mad. But if he hadn't stood up, he'd never have seen the light and had that reassurance.

Ralph kept watching the light, trying to trace its route.

Suddenly he stiffened. Hartismere had expected that the signaller would follow the meander of the main waterway, but surely the light wasn't in the correct position for that? Nor did it seem to be flashing on and off. Goodness knows why it hadn't appeared in the same area as where Mrs Serring had seen it, but whoever was holding it was going to escape being ambushed by Collingwood's other operative.

Ralph hesitated. His orders were to observe the route taken and, in the event of the traitor not being intercepted, to cut off his retreat. But, if he was correct as to where the man had gone, there was an alternative route back. If the traitor took that, then he would escape. Ralph tried to think. He couldn't tamely ignore the stranger, but if he disobeyed orders and followed the boatman he might lose him amongst the reed-beds. Wondering what the blazes he ought to do, Peveril picked up his own punt-pole and pushed off. If he got this wrong, he'd have wrecked the best chance of trapping the traitor – and it wasn't as if he knew the reed-beds particularly well.

Blessing the fact that Caine had lent him a punt, rather than a rowing-boat, Peveril slid swiftly through watery dark. A rowing-boat would never have crossed such shallow water and it was essential that he saved time by going by the most direct route possible, rather than sticking to the main meander. All the same, he had a couple of horrible moments when he thought that the punt had ground to a halt. An extra-fierce thrust with the punt pole got him off on both occasions and a curious exhilaration visited him. He had no doubt that the traitor was armed and dangerous, but, by God, he wouldn't be battling with Charon this time. Even if he did get shot, he wouldn't die insane.

Once Peveril had reached further into the marsh, the torchlight suddenly disappeared. Was that because the traitor had finished signalling – if, indeed, he had been signalling? Or had the man used it because he was afraid of missing the necessary turn-off which led into the narrower waterway – and had he then kept it on to check that he had taken the correct route? Thinking carefully, Ralph decided that it was probably the latter. After all, the traitor's punt was larger than Caine's, so that cut down considerably the number of possible routes through the reeds.

Ralph frantically recalled Hartismere's map, trying to decide where the man was going. Now that the main waterway had definitely been ruled out, there were three probable routes to the area where signals had been seen before. How the deuce was he to know which was the right one?

Just as Ralph was hesitating, the angry quacking of a flock of ducks arose, which suggested that the traitor was going by the middle route. Ralph swallowed, suddenly aware that his palms were sweating. What would happen if he got it wrong? It was devilish hard to trace the direction of sound at night, and the stakes were damnably high.

Poling feverishly, Peveril raced to outstrip the traitor. If his calculations were correct, then he would be able to lie in wait and observe exactly what happened. But he mustn't mistake the correct waterway – and estimating the comparative sizes of tracts of water in the pitch dark was going to be vilely difficult.

After another five minutes of frantic punting, Peveril thought that he had reached the intersection with a broader and deeper stretch of water. He retreated backwater for a few yards, before hunching down in the punt, trying to hear anything above the sound of his own breathing. Finally, he thought he heard the noise of water being broken by a pole. Was he imagining it? Or was the splash just the sound of the water lapping against the reeds – or a duck diving? Then, quite unexpectedly, Ralph saw light shine out above the reeds very close to him. Blast. That meant that the traitor wasn't coming past him. He'd hoped that he'd be able to intercept him from the rear and stop him from signalling. But at least he knew where the man was; he'd be able to follow him whether he went up or downstream of his current hiding-place.

Watching the Morse code flashing out, Peveril wondered why it jerked about so. Then the reason occurred to him. Of course, the punt was probably swaying a bit. And since the light wasn't flashing in his direction, he could probably risk trying to get a glimpse of the figure – an identification was vital.

Quietly ramming his own pole into the mud and tying up the punt to it, Peveril let himself over the edge and scrambled onto the mess of mud and reeds which lay between him and the traitor. Then he crawled in the direction of the light. When he had got near enough to the water's edge, he cautiously parted the reeds and stared forward. Damn. He could only see a dark figure. The sole light was cast by the torch. And it merely lit up the sky. Suddenly the torchlight dipped. Hearing the water lap against the bank, Peveril congratulated himself on having correctly deduced the cause of the variable heights. Then he froze in horror. Surely he'd just seen the face of a man on the opposite bank. Oh God, what was Hartismere doing here? Why had the Vice-Master let himself come into danger, attracted by the light like a moth?

Even as he was thinking this, Peveril saw the signaller crouch down in his punt and drop his left hand to his side. The traitor must have seen Hartismere; he was going to shoot him. Almost without thinking, Peveril rocketed upright and charged forward.

"It's me you want," he hissed, before leaping at the figure in the punt. The impetus of his attack rocked the punt badly and knocked the signaller off his feet. The torch went out and the pair were left struggling in the dark. The other man was heavier, and Peveril realised that if the traitor got on top of him, he would be able to hold him under until he drowned. As his assailant strove to get his hands round his neck, Ralph desperately struck out. His fist hit home and he followed this up by clawing at the man's face. A sharp hiss of pain rewarded him, and Ralph realised how easily the traitor could call out and warn his allies. Remembering the bitterly humiliating way in which he had choked on mud when overpowered by Caine, Peveril scrabbled with one hand over the side of the punt. Rewarded with a lump of marsh mud, he thrust it into the traitor's mouth. The yell which the man had been about to make was cut off in a strangled splutter and his struggles for an instant ceased.

It was at this point that Hartismere appeared. The writhing of the two men had driven the punt over to his side of the waterway, and the Vice-Master seized the mooring rope, before helping Peveril to subdue his captive. When the man was bound and gagged, Hartismere turned his torch upon the prisoner. Peveril stared incredulously. "Him, sir? But it can't be."

"I'm afraid so, Peveril. I need you to get him to C Coy – it's closest. Can you manage that? You aren't injured?"

"No, sir."

"And you can, ah, negotiate your way through the reed-beds?"

"Yes, sir." Realising that Hartismere was wondering whether he was going to keep his head, Peveril added, "Especially now that I know that you were right about things, sir."

The Vice-Master restricted himself to a brisk "Good boy," before adding further orders. "You will go via the second lookout post and collect your colleague. Obey his orders – he outranks you and has experience of this sort of thing."

"Yes, sir." Peveril paused. "How are you going to get back, sir? Will you be safe?"

The Vice-Master gave a brief laugh. "Don't worry about me. I have Caine to provide me with maritime assistance."

"Oh. I didn't know."

Hartismere sighed. "My dear boy, it was a wise precaution, rather than a lack of trust. You ran the greatest risk of being captured. I had no desire for you to be burdened with unnecessary information."

"Yes, sir," agreed Peveril, attempting not to sound hurt. "I'd better get going. Thank you for your help, sir."

It was at that point that the screaming began.

Chapter Fifty-Eight

Earlier that evening, Midge had been surprised when Mrs Serring had informed her that she intended to row round to the entrance to the Hart.

"You will accompany me."

"But I can't row."

"I don't need a rower," retorted the widow. "I need a witness. If there are lights, I wish an Englishwoman to say she saw them. I am a Jew. I am not trusted."

Unwilling to hurt the woman's feelings by an outright refusal, Midge tried to argue. "Why is it so important to have a witness tonight?"

"There may be lights."

"I don't see how you can possibly know that. Nothing happened yesterday."

Mrs Serring smiled coldly. "Not on the Hart, no."

For a moment Midge panicked, wondering if something had happened to Ralph and Dr Hartismere hadn't told her. "What do you mean?"

"Today there is talk that the inspector is missing from his post. He was not seen after yesterday morning. So everyone wonders   what   has   happened."

"Maybe he's investigating something elsewhere," suggested Midge weakly, certain that she was not meant to reveal that Woolf was under arrest.

"And he does not tell his sergeant where he has gone? Oh no. The man has fled. And he will wish to flee further. So that is why I say that we shall see lights tonight." She muttered something which Midge did not understand. "You will come with me, Miss Carrington. Have I not helped you?"

Feeling horribly ungrateful, Midge entered a protest. "Yes, you have, and I am very thankful that you did so. But I can't possibly clamber into a rowing-boat."

"So you do not care for that boy, then? I would have done anything for my Dickie. Anything."

Midge blushed fierily. Now was not the place to decide what she felt about Ralph Peveril. More to the point was that she had been co-opted to help Intelligence – that meant she ought to try to go. Apart from anything else, if Mrs Serring spotted a surfaced U-boat, she was perfectly capable of attacking it single-handed and spoiling the trap. "All right," she agreed grudgingly, "but don't blame me if someone hears us and decides that we're up to no good."

Midge's fears that someone would hear them proved to be well-founded. As they crunched over the shingle, a challenge came through the still night air. "Halt! Who goes there?"

Mrs Serring nudged Midge, who realised that accented English might arouse suspicion. "I'm going fishing," she replied, unable to think of any better excuse.

"Don't move."

All too aware of how Poole had been shot nearby, Midge stayed frozen. A slight movement, hastily averted, from Mrs Serring suggested that she also perceived the danger.

Footsteps approached rapidly, and then a thin line of light flashed onto the women.

"What be you a-doin' here, Miss? I thought you be back in Brandon."

Midge recognised Baldock's voice with relief. "I had to stay here. I need to go out in a boat."

"Alone with Mrs Serring?" queried the constable in a voice of considerable surprise.

"Yes. She's helping me."

"Well, Miss, I hope you be knowin' what you be a-doin'."

"Honestly, Baldock, it's all right. The chief inspector knows."

A low laugh greeted this remark. "The chief inspector? Well, I be happy to be helpin' the chief inspector. Perhaps I be a-carryin' you out to your boat?"

"Oh, thank you."

"And if you see the chief inspector, you might be a-tellin' him that sergeant, he be right worried because of Mr Woolf's absence."

"I shall. Err, you don't need to add to the sergeant's worries by telling him about us."

"Don't you be a-frettin' yourself, Miss."

Once the boat was launched, Mrs Serring rowed strongly until they had left the shore behind them. Then she addressed Midge. "How do you know that policeman?"

"He worked for my uncle until he was old enough to join the force."

"Can he be trusted not to talk?"

"I think so. If he talked, he'd get into trouble himself for helping us."

"It may not matter after tonight," replied Mrs Serring delphically, before whispering something in Trix's ears.

"I still don't understand exactly what you want to do."

"We shall row to where the Hart meets the sea. There is a place where we can wait, out of sight. There we shall watch."

Midge sighed. The prospect was unattractive and she wished she had not yielded to the widow's demands. Apart from anything else, if Ralph tried to seek shelter in Newton, there would be no-one there to help him. Nor would Collingwood be able to send a wire. 'I've made the wrong decision,' she thought, 'but Mrs Serring will never agree to row me back. Blast, blast, blast.'

As Midge was busy cursing herself, an alternative reason for Mrs Serring's eagerness to stay out on the water presented itself to her. What if the widow had been hand in glove with Woolf and Cosford? Pretending to hate Cosford – but retaining a key to visit him at night – would have been very convincing, while claiming to be a refugee was a typical cover for spies. Maybe Mrs Serring had killed her husband when he found out. Or maybe Serring had also been a spy – after all, he might have become enamoured of Fascism while living in Central Europe. Or perhaps the man who had returned wasn't Serring at all – it had been years since the ornithologist had been in England, so a bold spy could have adopted his identity.

Crouched in the boat, Midge wondered what on earth to do. She could hardly seek reassurance – that would warn Mrs Serring that her identity had been uncovered. Equally, if the woman weren't a spy, she would undoubtedly be highly suspicious of any attempts to question her. In fact, it was perfectly possible that Mrs Serring's grief had driven her mad – that would explain much of her behaviour, including tonight. Midge swallowed at the thought of what the widow would do if she decided that Midge was in league with those who had killed her husband. Wishing that she were strong enough to seize control of the boat and return to Newton, Midge forced herself to stay calm. She must not rouse any suspicions until she was sure what was going on.

It felt as if hours had passed before Mrs Serring eventually shook Midge.

"Look," hissed the widow, pointing into the darkness.

Midge stared obediently, but could see nothing. Then she saw a flicker of light. Then another. "Good grief," she whispered. "The signal!"

"Now do you believe?"

"Yes."

Midge felt something pushed into her hand. "Take a compass bearing," Mrs Serring ordered. "I must keep the boat steady."

Struggling with a torch and a tiny compass, Midge realised quite why Mrs Serring had failed to get an exact plot on the previous occasion when she had seen signalling. If it was hard enough with two hands, how much more difficult must it have been whilst also trying to keep the boat under control? Panicking that the signaller might finish before she had taken the reading, Midge managed at last to align the compass with the flickering light.

"I think I've got it," she murmured. "Is that what you wanted?"

"Do you wish to go home now? Revenge does not come as easily as that. We wait here."

Wondering again whose side Mrs Serring was on, Midge huddled back on her thwart. If only it weren't so beastly cold. Then she would be able to consider things sensibly. Currently, all she could think was how stupid it would be if they got caught up in the tidal race where the Hart met the sea. Her confirmation that signalling was taking place was hardly worth two deaths – particularly if the signalling were associated with some army exercise.

Just as Midge was about to attempt to persuade Mrs Serring

to turn back, Trix growled. Mrs Serring murmured something in Polish and the dog quietened. Then an icy hand was laid upon Midge's and she heard a faint whisper. "They come. Do not speak."

Midge stared into the darkness. Was that the creak of an oar? Could she see something moving in the blackness? Trix growled again. Yes, there must be something. The dog had been trained not to bark at seabirds. Another minute passed. Then another. Now Midge could distinctly see movement. Even the dark night could not fully disguise the rising and falling of oars, or the curve of the boat ploughing through the water. Midge hesitated. She knew perfectly well that any noise might warn the intruders, nor did she know whether she could trust Mrs Serring. However, any attempt to intercept the boat would ruin Dr Hartismere's plan. She had to take a risk. Leaning over, Midge whispered as quietly as she could, "We must let them pass upstream. There is a trap."

A slight stiffening of the widow's frame was the only response.

Now followed a nerve-wracking period. It was obvious to Midge that those in the approaching boat would be armed. If they spotted another boat apparently lying in wait for them, the likelihood was that they would turn to violence. The timber strakes of the rowing-boat would prove little protection from machine-gun bullets. 'Don't be so feeble,' she told herself. 'You chose to go on this expedition. Chaps in the Navy don't get to choose.'

Fortunately, the newcomers chose a route on the other side of the channel. 'Someone must have warned them about the tidal race,' Midge speculated. 'I wish I could see better and then I could work out whether they were landing someone, or coming to pick someone up.' She shivered. It was horrible to think that this same scene had been repeated several times earlier. Why had no-one spotted the boat before? Were all of Britain's shores as badly guarded as these?

Once the boat had made its way sufficiently far up the Hart to have faded out of sight, Mrs Serring began to row after them. Midge was momentarily reassured. Surely this meant that the widow planned to lie in wait for the sailors, rather than to help them? Moreover, it was essential to try to intercept the boat if the trap onshore failed. Otherwise, the strangers would beat a hasty retreat, perhaps with a traitor or a spy on board, back to the U-boat which had brought them.

As Midge waited, she saw the signalling recommence. Now that she was not trying to get a compass bearing, she was able to follow the pattern. 'Long, very long, long,' she thought. 'Then the same again, followed by six shorts. He must be trying to attract them to the correct landing spot. It would be horribly hard trying to navigate by compass.' The light flashed again, showing the same pattern.

Just as Midge was trying to decide where the flashes were coming from, the pattern was broken. The light seemed to be turned in a different direction, and then it disappeared altogether. Midge strained her eyes, scanning the land intently. Nothing. But why had the signalling stopped? Surely the plan had been to intercept the signaller and anyone who came to meet him. Or had something gone wrong? Midge found that her hands were clammy, and this time not with sea-spray. What if the signaller had spotted he was being watched? He might have attacked Ralph or Dr Hartismere. And even if she hadn't heard gun-shots, the signaller could have a silencer, or a knife.

Suddenly, Mrs Serring shifted position and began to row more strongly. Midge transferred her gaze to the water and gulped. Was she imagining things? Could she see movement? Trix certainly suspected something, because she was growling again. Midge cursed. Perhaps the widow had deliberately waited until the men returned in case they were caught and she was caught with them. Perhaps this was the moment when Mrs Serring would join forces. 'Why didn't I ask for a revolver?' she groaned inwardly. Almost as if Mrs Serring had read her thoughts, the widow leaned forward and whispered, 'There is an axe under the thwart. Be ready to use it.'

Encouraged by this instruction, Midge turned her eyes back to the river. The boat was now clearly visible. Two figures were rowing vigorously and Midge prayed that they would keep their eyes firmly fixed on the riverbank, rather than looking seaward. 'Why can't they hear us?' Midge wondered. 'I can hear them over our oars. Once they hear us... What use is an axe against a gun?'

As the two boats grew closer, Mrs Serring turned hers on a collision course. Still the other boat seemed unaware of their presence. Midge gripped the axe tightly. Submarines often had collapsible canvas boats. If this boat were made of canvas, there was just a chance that a lucky hit would fill the boat with water before the men had time to do anything. It was a very frail hope. However, since there was no avoiding the encounter, that hope was all that was left.

When the boats were within a few lengths of each other, Mrs Serring suddenly started calling in German. Midge understood enough to realise that she was demanding to know where they had been when she had been waiting for them to pick her up. Her tone was sufficiently imperious that the two men were confused. They stopped rowing, and one began to explain that they had tried to follow the signal. Mrs Serring snorted in disgust and ordered him to help her into the boat. He leaned over to do so, whilst the other held the boat steady.

All of Midge's fears came flooding back. She had been right. Why had she been such a fool as to persuade Baldock to let them go out in the boat? Mrs Serring was a German spy. And now Mrs Serring was going to flee. But the widow had another plan in mind. Seizing the axe from Midge, she crossed into the dinghy. She appeared to stumble and Midge assumed that she had been hurt. However, it was a ruse to let her grab the gun which the first man had laid down. There was a splash as it landed in the sea. The second man released his hold on Midge's boat but, before he could tackle Mrs Serring, Midge snatched up a walking stick and hit him with all her might. He collapsed. Now Mrs Serring wielded the axe, attacking both men with savage ferocity, all the while screaming a litany of hate. For a moment, Midge cowered back in shock. Then she forced herself to intervene. She managed to grab the second boat before it drifted completely out of reach. Holding on to it with all her strength, she shouted at Mrs Serring. "You must leave them alive to be interrogated. Take their guns. Leave them alive."

The widow turned on Midge with an expression of such blazing fury that Midge wondered if she, too, were about to be attacked. "They are snakes. You must kill snakes outright before they kill others. They killed my Dickie and you tell me to spare them."

"Take their guns and leave them," urged Midge desperately. "You must come back. I can't control this boat and Trix will drown in the tidal race."

This argument seemed to penetrate, because Mrs Serring rapidly ran her hands over the two men, one of whom was now lying unconscious on the bottom of his boat. Then, just as Midge feared that she could no longer hold the two boats together, Mrs Serring climbed over the side, bringing the mooring-rope of the second boat with her.

"If they live, I hope that they will hang as spies," she hissed.

Unsure whether she ought to point out that the men were probably ordinary sailors, Midge remained silent.

"You English are too soft. My country is overrun with snakes and you wish me to be kind to them. It is softness which lets such evil grow until it eats everything in its path." Mrs Serring patted the axe. "Iron is not soft."

Chapter Fifty-Nine

When Peveril heard the screaming, he promptly forgot any need for caution. All he could think was that Midge was in danger. His captive and the other operative, out in the marsh, were irrelevant in the face of Midge's peril. What was essential was to protect Midge. He jumped down from the punt.

"Where's the rowing-boat, sir? I can't go out on the Hart in this."

"What do you mean?"

"Can't you hear the screaming? I must help Midge. She's in danger."

"Those sound more like the screams of a triumphant goddess than a scared girl. In any case, Miss Carrington is still in Newton."

"She isn't. I know she's out there."

Hartismere's voice grew cold. "Did you make an additional arrangement without informing me?"

"No."

"Then how do you know she's there?"

Peveril swore. This was not the time for arguing about the niceties of English. "I don't know precisely, but who else could be screaming?" He attempted to sound less hostile. "Sir, is Caine's boat up or downstream from here?"

"You are going back to C Coy with the prisoner, not out on the Hart."

"Sir, please."

"Don't waste time."

For a moment, Peveril was tempted to reply that he would damn well do as he chose. Then it occurred to him that Hartismere had been proved correct so far. And if Hartismere and Caine refused to let him on the smuggler's boat, he wouldn't achieve anything by his protest.

The Vice-Master spoke again, with a note in his voice which Peveril had never heard before.

"Are you going to disobey a direct order, Lieutenant?"

"No," growled Ralph. "I'll do what you want. But, sir, look after Miss Carrington. Please." Then he saluted and re-embarked.

As he thrust the punt-pole into the black waters, Peveril was tormented by the thought that he had betrayed Midge. It was all very well calculating that Hartismere knew what he was doing, but the Vice-Master was quite old. Was he really capable of fighting off Nazis? Yes, he had Caine to help him, but who was going to help Midge? She couldn't fight anyone. His own job – if he really cared for her – was to protect her. And at the first test, he had failed.

Despite Ralph's fears, part of his mind was on where he was going. It would be disastrous to get lost and spend hours trying to find Collingwood's other operative. Also, he had an unpleasant suspicion as to who that man would prove to be. As he reached the second observation post, he slowed down. He mustn't be captured – whether by another traitor, or by soldiers out hunting for Trent's murderer.

As he glided cautiously towards the far bank, he decided that he would have to take a risk. Snapping on the torch, he held it so that the stream of light illuminated his face. That ought to show his colleague that he wasn't the traitor, even if it did leave him an open target for anyone searching for him. There was a rustle from the reed-beds, and then a man emerged from the sedge.

"Thrigby?"

Peveril suppressed a groan. His fears were correct.

"Cohen? Is that you?"

"Of course it's me. Whom else did you expect? Mr Chamberlain?"

"Hardly, but..."

"Good God, man, didn't you guess even after I supposedly believed that very unlikely story from your smuggler friend about foreigners in the wood?

"I need the code-word," muttered Peveril.

Cohen gave a short laugh. "Hoping I'm not on your side after all? The code-word's Bellerophon, courtesy of our mutual C.O., Collingwood."

Nothing was said on the rest of the journey. Peveril was full of his fears for Midge, while Cohen appeared to be checking that the captive was still breathing. When they arrived, Cohen issued orders to the surprised guards who, fortunately, seemed disinclined to query them. Once inside the main building, Cohen turned to Peveril.

"I want to get as much information as possible out of him now. I gather that you have some experience in questioning men."

"Yes, sir. May I make a telephone call first?"

Cohen sounded annoyed. "Don't you understand how important it is to interrogate a suspect while he is still in shock from being captured?"

"Yes, sir, but I want to ring a doctor."

Cohen looked at him with contempt. "For that little scratch?"

Since Peveril's face and neck were marred by several deep gouges, this response was perhaps somewhat unfair. However, Peveril ignored the issue. He absolutely mustn't antagonise Cohen at this point. "No, sir. I heard a woman screaming. It sounded out on the water. She may be hurt."

"A woman? Are you sure it wasn't a man?"

"It was too high-pitched, sir." A sudden suspicion occurred to Peveril. "I didn't scream, sir, if that's what you mean. The last thing I wanted was any noise alerting whoever had come to pick up the traitor. But if a woman has been injured, it may be important to have medical aid." Ralph thrust away an image of Midge hurt and in pain. Appealing to that wouldn't convince Cohen to agree. "We might require her evidence to help any prosecution, sir. She may have seen the German rescue-party."

Cohen regarded him thoughtfully for a moment. "Very well; you have ten minutes."

"Yes, sir. Thank you, sir."

Cohen raised his eyebrows at this unexpected response. Doubtless Peveril was trying to ingratiate himself now that he'd discovered that he was outranked. Well, it was far too late for that tactic to work.

When Peveril reappeared, Cohen turned straight to business. "The prisoner doesn't like you, does he?"

"No, sir."

"Then go in there and stir him up."

"Do you mean deliberately annoy him, sir?"

"Yes. I shouldn't imagine you'll have much difficulty in doing that."

Peveril swallowed the insult. "Do you think he might let something slip if he loses his temper?"

"Yes. People can give a remarkable amount away when they do that, can't they, Lieutenant?"

"Yes, sir." Peveril hesitated. "How far do you want me to go?"

"You can be as unpleasant as is necessary to get the information out of him."

"Do you mean hit him, sir?"

Cohen raised his eyebrows. "Is that the way you prefer to operate?"

"Of course not."

Cohen gave a disbelieving snort. "Then why ask? For God's sake, man, you've been at C Coy for weeks. You're meant to have been observing everyone, so you ought to be the best person to know exactly how he thinks and acts."

"Yes, sir," replied Peveril, wishing that Cohen did not so clearly doubt his capacity to carry out his job. And now, just when he was trying to eradicate all traces of Leo, he would have to go back to behaving like Leo. Peveril paused. No, not like Leo, he should never have made Thrigby like him in the first place. He'd behave like some anonymous interrogator. But perhaps the interrogator might be allowed to adopt some of Leo's tactics. Violence was obviously out of the question, but humiliation wasn't. Ralph swallowed. His father's humiliation of him had always worked best with an audience, but if he copied that approach, Cohen would observe everything. Oh God.

"Well?" demanded Cohen. "Are you going to do it or not?"

Peveril managed a nod. He was an officer, which meant he was supposedly fit to take command, and he had been at Cambridge, which meant he was supposedly able to think. And if he didn't get the information, his country might be in danger from another set of traitors. So his duty was clear.

"Yes, sir, but will you indicate when I've provoked him enough?"

Cohen sounded incredulous. "Are you trying to pretend that you have some sort of moral objection to being offensive?"

"No, sir. But I don't want to waste time, or annoy him so much that he refuses to talk." Peveril hesitated. "Sir, some of the things I said to you..."

"I have neither the time nor the inclination to discuss that at the moment."

"Very well, sir."

"Your role is to break him. To that end, you will go in there and be as arrogant, as sneering, and as unpleasant as is needed to extract the necessary information. Is that quite clear?"

"Yes, sir."

Cohen gave him a contemptuous look. "And don't start pretending that you aren't capable of doing it. I know exactly what you're like and I shan't be fooled by some spurious attack of conscience. Nor will Collingwood."

Realising that there was no point in trying to explain, Peveril saluted and followed Cohen into the room which held his captive.

Chapter Sixty

Once Hartismere had seen Peveril set off, he had rapidly returned to where Caine was waiting upriver in a rowing-boat. The smuggler's news that a second boat had intercepted the original craft surprised Hartismere, but he correctly surmised that Mrs Serring had been involved. At least, if she were in a boat, she had probably had more chance of escape than if she had been caught lurking on the riverbank.

Pulling strongly, Caine drove the boat through the water, Hartismere steering at the tiller. Before long, Midge was aware of the sound of oars. She glanced at Mrs Serring, who had done little more than guide their boat away from the banks since she had finished running amok.

"Someone's approaching."

Mrs Serring gave a fatalistic shrug. "Then we shall die. I have told you, I do not care. I have nothing to live for. And if they do not kill us, we shall be swept out to sea. That would be better, because then I can lie with Dickie forever."

Midge gulped. The thought of drowning appalled her, and it didn't sound as if Mrs Serring would make much effort to avoid the boat being capsized. On the other hand, if she hailed their pursuers, she might end up in a submarine on the way to Germany. What a choice.

Just as Midge had decided that it was better to risk being drowned, a low hail came across the water.

"Mrs Serring, are you there?"

"Dr Hartismere?" Midge exclaimed. "Thank goodness." A movement to the side caught her eye. "Put the axe down, Mrs Serring! They're friends."

"I have no friends. I can trust nobody. How can I trust you?" The widow gave a low laugh. "If these people are German, I shall kill you. Or perhaps I shall let you live long enough to allow you to hear the sound of Trix lapping your blood. I wish the ducks could fly overhead at the same time to take the news to my Dickie."

"Neither Dr Hartismere nor I are Nazis," replied Midge, as firmly as she could, given these unnerving threats, "so there is no need for you to risk hanging by making a blood-offering of my corpse."

"Hanging? Do you think that I care whether I die by hanging or by a soft bullet from a gun – a last, sweet caress? What have I to live for now?"

Reflecting grimly that, if she wrote a book entitled 'Murderers I have Known', it was likely to stop short at the fourth chapter, Midge appealed to sentiment. "If you don't trust me, you'll never be able to prove that your husband was correct and did see lights."

The axe wavered, and then was lowered.

Once the boats met, Hartismere took charge. The wounded men were clearly in need of urgent medical attention, and he wanted to find out exactly what the women had seen. On top of that, it was essential to speak to Cohen. Tying the painter of Mrs Serring's boat to his own, he told Caine to head for the bank as close to C Coy as possible.

"C Coy?" queried Midge.

"It may be a hornets' nest," agreed Hartismere, "but it's very close. In any case, someone must have heard the screaming and I have no desire to get shot because some over-excited yokel thinks that I am attempting to row out to a U-boat. We shall hail them as soon as we are within distance."

Hartismere's precaution not only prevented them from being accidentally shot; it also meant that there were a number of men able to help carry the wounded sailors into the camp. Once they had been deposited, Caine muttered something to Hartismere and rowed off. Midge surmised that he did not like being so conspicuously on show, but her main concern was Mrs Serring, who was in a terrible state. Clearly, the sailors were in much more urgent need of medical attention, but Midge couldn't help hoping that someone would soon give the widow a sedative. One of the soldiers had tentatively suggested fetching some brandy, but Midge had refused this offer. She had no idea whether you could mix brandy and sedatives, and she had no wish to take risks when Mrs Serring was in such a precarious way. Mind you, she rather felt that she wouldn't have minded some brandy herself. Thank goodness Ralph was safe. She had had a horrible feeling that something might go wrong. But Dr Hartismere had sworn that he was unharmed. Midge shook herself. It was quite wrong to be wishing that Ralph would come and talk to her when he was busy dealing with treason, but she did wish that she could see him.

Chapter Sixty-One

For his part, as Ralph entered Snellgrove's room, which was functioning as a temporary cell, he was conscious of a feeling of dread. He simply mustn't get this interrogation wrong, but he didn't even know where to start. In the end, his prisoner took the initiative.

"What the hell do you think that you are doing, Thrigby? I'll have you on a charge for your behaviour."

"When I caught you signalling out to sea? The one on a charge is you – and the charge is treason."

"Are you trying to distract everyone from the fact that you're a murderer?"

Unconsciously, Peveril glanced in Cohen's direction. The prisoner noticed this and laughed. "You're not a reliable witness. No-one will believe anything you say – Peveril."

"I'm not a murderer. I'm an Intelligence agent."

"Intelligence agent? Christ, they must be digging down low if they've started to recruit murderers." At Peveril's twitch of annoyance, the prisoner laughed again. "Woolf told me all about you – you murdered your father and used your connections to escape the consequences. So clearly you murdered Trent."

"I killed neither."

"You boasted to Woolf that you hadn't gone to all the trouble and expense of getting away with murder only to be shot by a German peasant. You should have been hanged. But you Eton and Oxford types think you can do anything you like. Immediately Woolf told me, I realised that you were just the same. Arrogant. Putting on side. When you got that puncture, you thought you were too important to change a tyre. All you university men are the same – you think you own the world just because you've studied some pointless subject. What you don't know is that everyone else thinks that you are weak, spineless, despicable cowards. A real man doesn't waste his youth in a library."

Peveril fought down the spurt of rage which assailed him, and forced himself to think coherently. For all Goodwin's bluster, the man looked in shock. His hands were shaking and his eyes had a disbelieving expression, as if he had never thought that things could end like this. So could Goodwin's knowledge of his true identity be turned to good use? Perhaps, even if it was going to be horribly like what he had done to Poole – and horribly like his nightmares.

"So you know I stood my trial for murder?"

"Yes."

Peveril lent forward, smiling unpleasantly. "Then, Goodwin, I can give you some useful advice. You'll start dreaming of the noose and the walk to the scaffold. Do you like the idea of waiting there on the platform, Goodwin? Waiting whilst the hangman puts the noose round your neck; waiting for the trapdoor to be loosened; waiting for your neck to snap as you drop through the floor?"

"Go to hell."

"Oh, I shall, but you'll go there first. You'll go there with a noose hanging round your neck – thick and strong. They use the best manila, Goodwin, so the rope won't snap – but your neck will. You can't struggle, because the gaolers will stop you. And you can't claw the noose off because your hands are tied behind your back. All you can do is wait for the long, long drop. And since you've no explanation, nor anyone else to blame apart from yourself, you will hang."

"What do you mean, no explanation?"

"It's not just treason you have to explain away; it's also murder."

"I don't know what you mean. Whose murder?"

"Trent's, for a start."

"I had nothing to do with that. You killed him."

"And you didn't kill Durrant either?"

"Of course not. You're useless, Peveril. You're just inventing things."

"I'm not inventing the fact that your accomplice is under arrest."

"What accomplice?"

"Woolf." Dimly remembering that the police weren't supposed to use made-up confessions from one accomplice to implicate another, Ralph turned to the one bit of firm evidence he did possess. "More to the point, I've got the bullet which killed Durrant. It'll hang you, Goodwin. Once the scientific types match it up with your gun, you won't have a chance."

Goodwin gave a harsh laugh. "Christ, you're stupid. Do you think I've still got the same gun?"

Peveril pounced. "If you didn't kill him, why did you get rid of your gun? The 'same gun' which you used to kill him."

"That wasn't what I meant at all."

"It is what you meant and, what's more, I've got a witness to the fact that you said it."

"You are twisting my words."

"Any jury will see their significance – as will the judge directing them."

"You lie."

"No, Goodwin, it's you who is lying. It's obvious that you or Woolf killed him – do you think that Woolf is going to admit to it? And do you think that Woolf is going to confess to killing Poole?"

For the first time, Goodwin was clearly shaken. "I had nothing to do with that."

"Prove it."

"Of course I wasn't involved. How could I have blown up his cell when I was on duty here? Anyway, it was your fault entirely that Poole escaped." Goodwin gave a harsh laugh. "Did you never wonder why Poole escaped on the same night you'd chosen?"

Hoping desperately that Goodwin wasn't about to betray his nightmares to Cohen, Ralph shook his head. "No."

"Fine agent you make. Woolf overheard you telling Poole about how you'd planned to get him out of gaol."

"How did Woolf hear that?"

Goodwin shrugged. "There was a ventilation grate in Poole's cell. If it was open, and the one in Woolf's office was open, he could hear what was being said. He found it damned useful for catching out the local villains."

A wave of relief flooded over Ralph. He hadn't given away the plot in his nightmares, and he could prove that Midge hadn't given anything away either. Then a much less pleasant thought occurred to him. Perhaps there had been a similar set-up in Hampstead; perhaps that was how Hall-Gordon had discovered that he had hit Denman. Had he been blaming Fletcher all the time when the barrister hadn't reported him? Oh God.

Goodwin was uninterested in why his interrogator hadn't responded. Instead, he gave a sarcastic snort. "Woolf found out rather a lot about you – he certainly hadn't expected to hear an officer and a gentleman declaring that he was the devil himself."

Conscious that Cohen's eyes were on him, Peveril struggled to find something to say. "So Woolf intended to kill Poole by blowing in the cell?"

"I suppose so. I knew nothing about it."

"And you didn't visit Ipswich Hospital to kill him later?"

"No – and don't believe Woolf if he says I did."

"Then we return to Durrant and the fact that your gun killed him."

"It didn't."

"I may say that Poole gave me a full description of what happened that night."

"He'd have said anything."

"Poole's gun was a .455 calibre. The fatal bullet was a .38."

There was a strained silence. Then Goodwin spoke slowly. "Well, if you know that, then perhaps I'd better explain. I didn't really want to reveal that Poole was a traitor, but I suppose it's now necessary after all."

"Go on."

"I'd noticed that Poole had unexpected amounts of money in his possession, and I knew that he was inclined to disappear off at night. Durrant had made a point of tightening up security in January, which made me start to wonder whether Poole could be trusted. Some of my papers had been moved, and I knew that Poole had access to them. So I followed him that night. I didn't really believe that he was a traitor, but then I spotted him shining a torch. I thought that he was signalling. I was worried that he might be about to send something very important to Germany. I shot at him." Goodwin made a dramatic gesture with his hands. "It was all I could do to stop him before it was too late."

"But you shot Durrant instead."

"That came as a terrible shock to me."

"Indeed. Do tell me why you didn't denounce Poole at that point."

"I wasn't sure whom to trust and Woolf had arrested Poole for murder. I thought that would prevent any more secrets being leaked."

"Then why were you signalling tonight?"

"That was different."

"How?"

At this most opportune moment, there came a soft knock on the door and an orderly passed in a slip of paper. Peveril unfolded it and breathed a sigh of relief as he read that both Midge and Hartismere were safe. Then he smiled unpleasantly. "Goodwin, I have to tell you that two German sailors were observed rowing upstream towards your signal. They have been apprehended."

Goodwin turned white.

"Would you care to explain what those sailors were doing on the Hart?"

Goodwin's eyes shifted from Peveril to Cohen. Finding no help there, he turned back to Peveril. "I had always been worried that there was espionage going on. I decided to try to discover what was happening by getting in contact with the Germans. I hoped that, if I approached them and offered information, they would give me the names of local agents."

"And they accepted this offer?"

"Yes." His voice gathering confidence as he spoke, Goodwin added, "Naturally, I didn't give them anything important. It was all out-of-date or wrong. And they asked me to undermine morale, although I did nothing other than leave a few leaflets lying around."

"How did you communicate with them?" Remembering Mrs Serring's remark about the boat which her husband had seen, Peveril commented, "This isn't the first time that a German ship has been off the coast."

"Well, they had to hand over a wireless."

"And the other times?"

Very reluctantly, Goodwin added, "Twice to pick up valueless information about coastal defences. And then we needed spare valves for the wireless."

"What about the man?" demanded Peveril, making his accusation as vague as possible, in the hope of tricking Goodwin.

"I didn't know about the agent until after he had landed. Then I sent a tip-off to London."

Peveril strongly doubted the last statement and the claims that Goodwin had handed over nothing of value. However, he thought that the rest of the information was probably true – Goodwin clearly suspected that he knew more than he did. Perhaps he could build on that fear.

"You referred to 'we' – I presume you mean that Woolf was involved in this?"

"Of course he was, and if he says otherwise he is lying to you."

"Where did you store the wireless?"

"At Co-, that is, at the coast."

"Cosford's. Which of you killed him?"

"Woolf said it was suicide. Wasn't it?"

"You know better than me. Why was Woolf involved with him? Was it the gambling?"

"Yes. No. Why are you asking me?"

"Because Poole named Cosford as the one running a gambling-ring and the one who persuaded him to get involved in smuggling."

Goodwin breathed a sigh of relief. "If you know that it was just smuggling, then I don't see why you're making such a fuss about it."

"Why was Cosford smuggling? He had plenty of money."

"Yes, but he wanted more." Goodwin sounded incredulous. "He didn't even keep it himself."

"What did he want it for?"

"To fight against the Soviets."

"Have you any proof of that?"

"Of course I do. It was only when they took control of one of those tin-pot Baltic countries that he got involved."

"Was that when you got him to hide the wireless?"

"A bit after."

"Where was it before?"

"On the bluff – Woolf refused to have it in the police-station or his house. But the bluff became impossible after C Coy was moved here."

The length of time involved sounded damning to Ralph, but he did not want to neglect anything.

"What about Serring?"

Goodwin tensed in shock. "What do you know about him?"

"That he was murdered."

"He wasn't. It was an accident. He appeared one morning while we were signalling and Woolf hit him. He fell back into the water and drowned before we could save him."

Ralph thought this a most unlikely excuse. "Did you threaten Mrs Serring at all?"

"No. Cosford swore that he'd checked up on her and that she knew nothing. Do you mean to say that she did?"

Peveril made a non-committal noise, wondering how Cosford had investigated the widow. Pushing this aside for later consideration, he turned to the last point he wanted to clear up – one which was vital to him.

"Did you know that Trent had a German step-father?"

At this display of omniscience, Goodwin's hands shook. "Yes, but I tried to prevent anyone else learning about it. I didn't want Trent to suffer for it."

"So it was sheer coincidence that Trent gave you an alibi for the night when Durrant died?"

"Yes."

"Even although that alibi was clearly false, since you have just admitted to shooting Durrant?"

"Maybe Trent made a mistake."

"A mistake aided by a substantial bribe. A five-pound note was found in his possession when he died."

"I don't know what you're talking about."

"He lied for you and then had second thoughts. Is that why you killed him?"

"I know nothing about Trent's death. Nothing, do you hear?"

"Better to confess everything – judges don't like men who are proved to have lied."

"Go to hell. Your judge was fool enough to believe you – even if nobody else did."

"Are you afraid, Goodwin? It's going to get much worse."

"Leave me alone. I didn't do anything really wrong. I only did what everybody else would have done."

"Everybody?"

"Yes, everybody who has to work – unlike you. You were born with a silver spoon in your mouth and you've had it easy your entire life."

"I haven't."

"You damn well have. Do you think that I, or Woolf, could afford an Alfa, even if we murdered every one of our relatives?"

"Is that why Woolf committed treason?" asked Ralph, unable to hide his disapproval.

"Don't look down your nose at me like that. What do you know about how the rest of the world lives? You killed for money – why shouldn't others sell a few worthless plans?" Goodwin gave a grunt. "Anyway, Woolf got fed-up with the magistrates round here being so unreasonable. Of course he sympathised with the Germans. At least they possess the sense to have law and order properly enforced by professionals. They aren't dependent upon the whims of lay magistrates who owe their places on the Bench to the fact that they've got useful connections."

"Then I am sure that both you and Woolf will be relieved that it will be a proper High Court judge who will hear your trials for treason."

"I'm not going to be bullied by you."

"It's hardly bullying to point out facts. And since you regard me as an expert in murder, you'd do well to take my advice about coming clean."

"Leave me alone. I'm not going to talk any more. I know what you did to Poole. No wonder he killed himself. Leave me alone, I tell you; leave me alone."

Chapter Sixty-Two

The two officers left Goodwin shortly after this point. When they were beyond earshot of the armed guard outside the makeshift cell, Cohen turned to Peveril.

"Enjoy yourself, did you?"

Peveril scowled. Cohen could hardly be more wrong. He might have taken a certain warped relish in being vile to Poole, because punishing Poole for cowardice meant that he could punish himself at the same time, but there had been nothing at all amusing about watching Goodwin come apart. He desperately wanted to find Midge and seek her reassurance that he wasn't some demon in human form, but he couldn't burden her with his problems after whatever she had been through. So he was left with Cohen, who despised him.

"I hope I acquired all the information you need, sir."

"No wonder he didn't like you. Do you mean to tell me that you deliberately set out to annoy him, even when you had no suspicions about him?"

Peveril hesitated. Was there any point in trying to explain that Goodwin had taken a dislike to him, or that Poole had been treated in a similar way by Goodwin? "I didn't change the tyre slowly on purpose, sir."

Cohen snorted. "You know perfectly well that that's not what I mean. And what the devil was all that about your Eton connections?"

"I had to protect my identity, sir. Woolf asked how I'd ended up as a captain in the Survey Unit when I'd been in the army for less than a year. The only explanation I could give was that I'd pulled strings."

"Was it necessary to be so arrogant about it?"

Peveril felt his temper beginning to rise. "Yes. If Woolf was busy loathing me, then it stopped him questioning my story." About to add that Woolf would have loathed Cambridge-educated Cohen too, Peveril halted. Presumably, Cohen would write a report for Collingwood which might influence how his C.O. dealt with Midge. Trying to sound more emollient, Ralph added, "You see, sir, Woolf believed that public-school types could do what they wanted, so I acted according to his prejudices. I didn't want him to suspect that I was in Intelligence, sir."

"Or was it that you didn't like some peasant questioning your importance?"

"No, sir. I took his questioning very seriously. After all, some peasant arrested me last year. I had no particular desire for another one to do the same."

At this juncture, Hartismere appeared. A swift glance told him that the two officers were on the point of quarrelling, and he rapidly intervened. No matter how well Peveril had performed in the reed-beds, it would be the end as far as Collingwood was concerned if the boy were to be accused of further insubordination.

"Captain, can you come to question Mrs Serring. Peveril, will you go and speak to Miss Carrington? She's in the officers' mess. I want to know what happened to her before I came on the scene."

"Yes, sir."

When Ralph entered the officers' mess, he was shocked at how white Midge looked.

"Are you all right? I felt awful not coming to your aid. When I heard those screams, I thought..."

"Ralph, it was horrible. I know she was trying to prevent the sailors from escaping, but she just went mad and attacked them with an axe. She kept screaming her husband's name the whole time."

"She must have cared for him very much."

"Yes, but honestly, Ralph, she seemed almost insane." Midge shuddered. "She gave her bloody hands to her dog to lick and kept saying that now Trix could share in her revenge. And she was cradling the axe as if it were a baby."

Ralph's heart sank. He had put Midge through a dreadful time – could she ever forgive him?

Midge continued. "Then she wanted to throw herself into the water and die in – she said – her husband's arms. I tried every argument I could. In the end I told her that her husband had given her Trix to look after, and Trix understood Polish, not English, so she had to stay alive for Trix. It worked for the time being, but what if she changes her mind?"

"I think Hartismere warned the doctor to give her a strong sedative," commented Peveril. "Maybe you could talk to her again tomorrow."

"What about you? Are you all right?"

"Of course. Why ever not?"

"You look like you've been fighting. And you seemed a bit ill-at-ease earlier with Dr Hartismere."

Peveril grimaced. He could hardly explain that Hartismere had twice ticked him off for wanting to put Midge before his duty. That would sound like boasting. "You know Hartismere only in his Cambridge guise. He's more exacting in the field."

"Thank goodness he took charge of those men. I know that they are the enemy – Mrs Serring said that I was soft to pity them – but the hatred and the violence..." Midge bit her lip, aware that she was nearly in tears. "I hit one of them, Ralph. And, while he was unconscious, Mrs Serring attacked him with her axe. He's bound to die. I feel like a murderess."

"You aren't. You acted to save your life and Mrs Serring's life, and to help defend your country. You did exactly what you ought to have done and you were very brave to have gone out in that boat at all."

Midge managed to smile her thanks at him. "That's kind of you, Ralph, but I still feel dreadful. And I wish you hadn't been hurt; I know you don't like violence, either."

At this remark, Peveril suddenly stood up. "I have to see whether Hartismere needs me." With that he left the room. Outside, he swore savagely. Why did Midge have to say that about him disliking violence? How could he now tell her about striking Denman? She'd be disgusted with him, especially as he hadn't told her before. She'd had every justification for what she did, but he'd had none. Ralph scowled. If someone harmed Midge, he'd happily hack them to pieces, so he wasn't exactly safe to know. He couldn't expose Midge to more violence – this time from him. Hell and blast and damnation.

Peveril was still kicking his heels in the corridor when

Hartismere appeared, looking tired. "Well, Peveril, what happened to Miss Carrington?"

Pulling himself together, Ralph summarised Midge's story. Hartismere looked relieved. "That ought to protect Mrs Serring from a murder charge if the men die."

"Will they?"

"One may well. If he lives, it will only be because you summoned the police surgeon from Newton. If Fellowes hadn't been here, the man would be dead already." Hartismere regarded the younger man thoughtfully, wondering why he was not with the Carrington gel. "I imagine that Miss Carrington had a singularly unpleasant experience. She may take some time to recover from the shock."

Peveril shrugged. It was decent of the Vice-Master to attempt to help, but what did he know of this sort of situation? He wasn't even married.

The Vice-Master noted Peveril's reserve, but moved off the subject of Midge. "There are various matters we need to discuss with Cohen. Would you be kind enough to fetch him?"

"Very well, sir."

"And don't forget that you are no longer at Cambridge. Different rules apply in the army."

"I'm hardly likely to forget it, sir. I don't spend my time rolling around in the mud at Cambridge."

Chapter Sixty-Three

When Peveril returned with Cohen, Hartismere promptly introduced Midge.

"Captain, this is Miss Carrington, who was able to provide some important evidence about Cosford."

"Regarding the Latvian connection, sir?"

"Yes."

"Well, Miss Carrington, you will be glad to know that your supposition was correct. The Latvian publishing house is owned by one of the partners at Cimze et Cie – I spoke to London just now and they told me."

"So Cosford's money did pay for anti-Soviet propaganda?"

"Yes."

The Vice-Master made a further suggestion. "I imagine that our treacherous friends presumed that, if that Cosford was running an illicit gambling ring, it meant that he could be tempted – or forced – to help them in their activities. Don't forget that Woolf could have arrested him quite legitimately."

Cohen nodded. "Reading between the lines, I think Cosford guessed what the 'smuggling' was, told them to go to blazes, and only changed his mind when the Soviets annexed Latvia."

"So the gambling was a red herring?" asked Midge. "It wasn't used to pressurise men into betraying secrets if they ran up large debts?"

"No, it was a straightforward exercise in card-sharping." Cohen glanced in Peveril's direction. "I might have discovered that earlier if I'd been able to talk to some of the officers involved without them being distracted by personal wrangling."

Peveril coloured, aware that Cohen was referring to his assault on Arrowsmith.

Midge looked puzzled. "Why was Cosford needed? I can see he might have chosen to join in eventually, but surely it was dangerous for Woolf to involve another person?"

"Indeed. However, Cosford's exercise in illicit gambling must have given him a very good idea of who might be desperate for money. There was also the additional benefit that, if Cosford were the one to approach such people, that kept Woolf nicely out of the picture."

"Of course," breathed Midge. "Poole thought that there was someone behind Cosford. If he'd known whom, he might have told us in the hope of reducing his sentence."

"Precisely. Moreover, there had been talk in the autumn of siting a camp near the Hart, so they must have been desperate to find somewhere to keep the wireless, even before C Coy moved in."

"Which," commented Hartismere, "again agrees with why they began to pressurise Cosford in the autumn."

Midge suddenly sat up. "I say, do you think that Woolf didn't 'discover' the wireless when searching Cosford's shop because he wanted to use it himself?"

"Quite probably," agreed Cohen. "And when you heard him moving the furniture at Cosford's house, he may have been looking for the Cimze letter." He shrugged. "I suspect Woolf will continue to deny everything, but he'll find it hard to explain away a detailed confession from his partner in crime."

"Excellent," purred Hartismere. "It's always useful when rogues fall out. And if you are facing a firing-squad, the desire to implicate everyone apart from yourself grows even stronger."

"Quite, sir. The shock of being caught made him lose his head."

Midge looked puzzled. "I can see that Goodwin is clearly guilty, but I thought that he was a hopeless incompetent. Ralph said so. Was he really cut out to run a spy ring?"

"And who did you think it was, Capt. Thrigby?"

Peveril flushed at the ironic undertone in Cohen's voice. "Snellgrove."

"Ah, you must have been distracted by his brother's notoriety as an anti-Semite and decided that all such persons are unreliable."

"If you must know, sir, it was because he was devilish keen on following me around all the time – and he put a price on my head."

"A sensible precaution, given the information he had available about you. In his place, I should have had the saltings searched from end to end until I laid hands upon you."

Although Midge did not understand the by-play, she could see that Ralph looked uncomfortable. "Was Intelligence alerted as a result of Serring's information?"

Cohen shot Hartismere a lightning glance. When the Vice-Master nodded, Cohen explained. "Yes. Things were tightened up in January. Durrant wasn't told much – after all, he could have been the traitor himself. However, he was given very clear orders about not disseminating anything but the most essential information. That will have saved a certain amount from the Germans."

Midge hesitated. "I think it might be as well to tell Mrs Serring; she's dreadfully upset."

"Absolutely not," retorted Cohen. "Frankly, it's bad enough that you have got involved."

"But Serring died," pointed out Midge bluntly. "Don't you think that his widow is owed some reassurance that what he did was worthwhile?"

Hartismere intervened. "She certainly can't be told the details, but given that her husband was the one who first alerted the authorities, I agree that she ought to be told that he didn't die in vain." He turned to Peveril. "Did Goodwin say anything about Serring's death?"

"He claimed it was an accident – Serring saw them signalling, Woolf hit him, and then Serring drowned."

"How convenient," remarked the Vice-Master. "I think a more accurate reading would be that someone knocked him out and then they both held him under the water until he was dead."

Peveril grimaced. "Then it's just as well that Cosford claimed that he'd checked what Mrs Serring knew and that she knew nothing. Otherwise, she'd have been found dead, too."

"But Mrs Serring never said anything about Cosford asking questions," protested Midge. "All she said was that he had tried to commiserate with her."

"I thought that was a bit odd, too," agreed Ralph. "Do you think he was lazy? Or did he imagine that a foreigner would never dare to say anything to the police – or be believed if she did?"

Midge's face narrowed. "Perhaps Cosford wanted to protect

Mrs Serring and lied about speaking to her. Maybe her grief reminded him of his for his wife and child – he sounded odd when he talked about children in hospital. And maybe Mrs Serring's grief did make him have second thoughts about committing treason."

Hartismere nodded. "It is more probable that he was trying to protect her than that he was inefficient. And, as you said before, his suicide note could easily have been part of a letter telling his fellow-conspirators that he no longer wanted to be involved."

"Surely Woolf took something of a risk in killing Cosford, sir?"

"I don't think so, Cohen. As the investigating officer, he had the perfect means of covering everything up. That, of course, was why everyone was so ready to believe that Poole's death was suicide – Woolf could manipulate all the evidence, including Poole's very short suicide note."

Midge frowned. "I think that he must have hoped that the death would pass off as being the result of Poole's wound. The matron at the hospital said that that was what everyone thought to begin with." She glanced at the Vice-Master. "How did he gain access? Was it by disguising himself as a doctor?"

"I trust that some careful investigating at the hospital will confirm that someone saw an additional doctor on the ward." Hartismere coughed. "Your suggestion about policemen being invisible out of uniform would certainly explain why nobody recognised him."

"But why didn't he kill Poole before we were able to question him?" asked Midge.

Hartismere looked thoughtful. "Although Lt. Peveril clearly wanted to speak to Poole, Woolf must have assumed that he had plenty of time to act. Don't forget that the hospital had refused Woolf access earlier that day. And don't rule out your own part, my dear."

Midge looked blank and Hartismere hastened to explain. "I am not at all certain that Poole would have proved to be quite as responsive to a man in uniform. He didn't talk to Peveril precisely because he was suspicious as to who he was; the same mistrust would have applied to other officers. Again, Woolf may have assumed that he had more time to arrange Poole's death, since Poole wouldn't risk talking to any interrogator." Hartismere gave an amused cough. "Woolf's error was his failure to anticipate the appearance of a woman. And since Newnham gels are rarely to be found working with bands of cut-throat smugglers, Poole was prepared to risk speaking to you."

Midge blushed. "Why did Woolf let Ralph speak to Poole in the first place? I know Woolf had to appear to investigate Durrant's death, but wasn't there a danger that Poole would blurt out what was going on?"

Hartismere nodded. "Indeed there was, but I doubt very much whether Goodwin had trusted Woolf enough to admit that he had killed Durrant. If Woolf thought that Poole really was the murderer, he must have assumed that Poole would not confess – murderers rarely do. And Poole couldn't admit to smuggling – it would have provided a motive for killing Durrant."

"You mean the prosecution could allege that, rather than approaching Durrant for help, Durrant challenged Poole and Poole deliberately killed him?"

"Precisely, Miss Carrington. Moreover, as you say, Woolf had to be seen to investigate – it would have looked very odd if he had refused to let anyone from the battalion speak to Poole. I imagine he had expected Goodwin to appear, but he could not ignore Goodwin's representative."

Cohen frowned. "What I find very surprising is that Woolf allowed 'Thrigby' to question Poole more than once. Goodwin explained that Woolf could overhear what was said in Poole's cell, but he still took a devil of a risk and he appears to have been fairly careful in other respects."

For a moment, Peveril hesitated, wondering whether to say anything. "Poole didn't like me much. Woolf may have gambled that if Poole confessed to anything important, he would do so to him, rather than to me."

Cohen sounded suspicious. "Why didn't Poole like you? You were in the same company."

Peveril swallowed convulsively. "You see, sir, I was rather... err... rather unsympathetic in my questioning." He felt Hartismere's eyes on him. "I mean, I rather sneered at him."

"On what grounds?"

"He was clearly afraid, so I told him he was a coward. Repeatedly." There was a momentary silence, while Peveril looked away from Hartismere. "Naturally, he didn't trust me when I then offered to give him a file to hack through the window bars."

"In that case," stated the Vice-Master, "we must be thankful that Woolf decided to blow up his cell, thus allowing Poole to escape."

Peveril shifted uncomfortably. "But it signed Poole's death-warrant, sir. If I hadn't dreamt up that idea..."

"*You* thought it up?" demanded Cohen, in tones of disbelief.

"Yes."

"And you presented Woolf with the idea? What did you think you were doing?"

Hartismere saw how uncomfortable Peveril was looking. Doubtless the boy would have to explain matters to his C.O., but there were more important issues at stake. "The scheme may have been flawed, but it enabled us to acquire the necessary information. As for signing Poole's death-warrant, don't forget that he was aiding treason. He chose to play with fire; if he got burned, it was his own fault."

"Yes, sir, but..."

"Don't forget, Peveril, that Woolf had probably intended to kill Poole all along." Hartismere coughed. "Prisoners have been known to hang themselves in their cells, after all."

Midge spoke in a shaky voice. "If Poole had said something important to Ralph, what would Woolf have done?"

"I imagine, my dear, that he would have ensured that Lt. Peveril was killed before he could pass on the news. Fortunately, that did not transpire. And as for why Woolf did not kill Poole earlier, I presume that he wanted to discover Poole's reasons for killing Durrant. It must have been only later that he began to suspect that Goodwin had killed Durrant and then, of course, he had to do his utmost to cover up Goodwin's guilt – hence why he burned the notes of those who had been questioned."

"What about Trent's death?" asked Midge. "Did he get scared and want to retract his alibi for Goodwin on the night of

Durrant's death?"

Ralph nodded. "I think so. Goodwin denied bribing Trent, but he admitted that he knew about Trent's German stepfather." He winced. "Then he fell apart and refused to say anything more."

"He's probably attempting to think up a plausible lie at this very minute," commented Hartismere, before adding soberly, "I'm devilish glad you got away that morning, Peveril. I strongly suspect that you would have been 'shot whilst attempting to escape' if you hadn't. That would have prevented any counter-accusations by you."

"And the five-pound note which Ralph found on Trent's body? Was that a bribe?"

"Yes — what our American cousins term 'hush-money'. The Vice-Master paused, as if contemplating a dissertation on comparative English usage. "I should have expected Woolf to anticipate the possibility of the note being traced back to him, so perhaps he really did spend it in the mess. If so, he must have got a devil of a shock when I asked him about it."

Midge frowned in thought. "In that case, Goodwin must have stolen it from the mess to give to Trent."

Hartismere was amused by Midge's disapproval. "Do traitors and murderers object to petty larceny? However, it's more likely that Goodwin changed his own money for that note — perhaps he thought that the mess funds were a more anonymous source than his wallet."

"How did you know that it was Goodwin, Dr Hartismere? Did it boil down to the alibis for the night when Durrant was shot?"

The Vice-Master suppressed a smile at Midge's obvious chagrin at not having spotted Goodwin's guilt. "It did. However, don't forget that I had the advantage of being able to question a large number of C Coy about their alibis first hand, rather than relying on whatever Woolf chose to feed me. Furthermore, while I was able to rule out a certain percentage of the men, as Lt. Peveril had stated, an officer was more likely, because he would have much greater freedom." Hartismere allowed himself a dry aside. "Being unexpectedly assigned cook-house fatigues is liable to interfere with one's ability to signal to U-boats. Goodwin could hardly refuse to tell me his movements, since he was expected to set an example to his men. So when he presented me with a cast-iron alibi for the time covered by Trent's evidence, I was inclined to look at it askance."

"Because Trent's evidence was probably doctored?"

"Precisely, Miss Carrington. I may say in passing that your speculation concerning Poole's story proved to be of considerable use, both in relation to the timings and in relation to the motive."

"So the bullet was intended for Poole after all?"

"I suspect so. As Lt. Peveril has justly pointed out, Goodwin was not the most competent of officers. I have little difficulty in imagining that he lost his head and shot the wrong man. Quite how he had hoped to explain away Poole's body, I am unsure – perhaps a quarrel amongst poachers."

"Poachers using revolvers rather than shot-guns?"

"That's what I mean about inefficiency, Miss Carrington."

"Goodwin claims that Poole knew exactly what was going on," stated Cohen, before adding with relish, "However, your evidence will help to trip him up when it comes to a trial. Poole told you he'd offered to help crew one of the ships, but he'd hardly have offered if he'd known that submarines were involved. So that rather casts doubt on Goodwin's excuse that he shot Poole to stop him from sending information to Germany."

Midge looked disgusted. "Do you mean Goodwin's going to pretend that he was trying to protect British interests?"

"Oh yes." Cohen smiled grimly. "After all, Miss Carrington, what else can he say? 'I shot at Poole – and killed Durrant by mistake – because I thought that Poole had got cold feet and was going to expose me'? That wouldn't commend him to a judge. A desperate attempt to save important secrets from going abroad sounds much better."

"It may sound better, but it's more than a little illogical if he's also going to claim that nothing important was passed to the Nazis after January."

"Quite," agreed Hartismere. "Fortunately, the man who can

stay logical in the face of multiple counts of murder and treason is rare indeed."

Peveril shivered at the memory of the terror which had engulfed him the previous year. If he had tried to concoct a convincing story, he'd probably be buried in quicklime by now.

"But why?" Midge demanded. "Why did Goodwin get involved in treachery? Did he actually believe in Nazi doctrine?"

Reluctantly, Peveril spoke up. "I don't think his motivation was political; I think it was emotional."

"Go on," urged Hartismere.

"You see, sir, he was incompetent, and everyone I spoke to despised him – they didn't even bother to hide their contempt. At the very least, Goodwin must have known that both Durrant and Leake despised him."

"And?"

"Well, sir, if you knew that people despised you..." Peveril dried up for a second, wishing that Cohen, who definitely did despise him, weren't there. "Well, sir, I imagine that you'd have two methods of responding. Either you'd try to prove people wrong or you'd deliberately make life unpleasant for them. If you could make them look useless, you'd feel less useless yourself. And Goodwin had authority, so he could achieve that quite easily."

Cohen intervened. "Do you have any evidence for this interesting theory, Lieutenant?"

"Yes, sir. Poole said that he'd been Goodwin's whipping-boy. Chatham and Jervis stated that Goodwin made people run errands to cut them down to size. And I overheard him being vilely patronising to Snellgrove, who was the only decent soldier in the whole of C Coy." Peveril shrugged. "And then came the opportunity to make him feel powerful and important in his own eyes."

"You mean, treachery?"

"Exactly, Midge."

"But that's *silly*," protested Midge. "How could you betray your country just because you weren't prepared to accept the truth about yourself?"

Peveril could feel hot spirals of embarrassment curling up and down his torso. "Maybe he knew that the truth was so awful that he couldn't bear to recognise it. Maybe he felt less useless when he could tell himself that another state had recognised his ability, so it was clearly not his fault that he hadn't shone in the British Army. Maybe he said his own failures were all attributable to petty jealousy."

Midge snorted derisively. "The Nazis would have got rid of him pretty quickly once he'd served his purpose."

Hartismere disagreed. "Not necessarily. That sort of spineless invertebrate often proves to be surprisingly adept at office politics. They don't make the mistake of having principles, for a start. And they make themselves useful to someone more powerful, who, in return, protects them. If that means destroying people who are more competent or honest than their jackal, so be it."

Wondering whom he meant in the world of university politics, Midge admitted that there was a certain level of truth in what the Vice-Master had said. "Does that apply to Woolf as well? He doesn't sound as if he lacked faith in himself."

"Money has its attractions," pointed out Cohen curtly. "And Goodwin seemed to think that Woolf wanted to be able to convict people without the bother of a proper trial."

Peveril was disinclined to annoy Cohen further by contradicting him, but he thought that he had another explanation. "I don't think that was the only reason, sir. Caine said that Woolf failed to get a transfer to Scotland Yard, and, from the way in which Caine said it, I think that Woolf was pretty angry about the failure."

"Perhaps money wasn't the primary motive originally," suggested Midge. "He wouldn't have earned so much more in London. Maybe he wanted more interesting opportunities – or yearned for the bright lights of the capital."

"I agree that Newton lacks a certain cosmopolitan attraction," remarked Hartismere dryly, "but I am sufficiently old-fashioned to believe that boredom does not constitute an excuse for treason."

Chapter Sixty-Four

There was silence for a few moments after the Vice-Master's condemnation of Woolf. Then Midge asked hesitantly. "Will Goodwin and Woolf escape justice? It will be hard to prove that Woolf killed Poole, and if they stick to their story that Serring's death was an accident, they won't be convicted of that, either."

"Perhaps not, my dear, but they will be convicted of treason. Goodwin was caught red-handed and he has implicated Woolf. Moreover, I imagine that a really thorough investigation of Woolf's finances will leave him with some very difficult questions to answer. If he sold his country for silver, then that silver will have left a trace, however well-hidden." Since Midge looked unconvinced, the Vice-Master added. "In any case, no judge will believe Goodwin's story of how he came to shoot Durrant and – now that Woolf's no longer running the investigation – I suspect that it will be much easier to link him to Cosford's death."

Something in the Vice-Master's tone attracted Midge's attention. Cyanide took effect almost instantaneously. Cosford wouldn't have had time to leave an accusation. Even if Cosford had written something before his death, Woolf had had plenty of time in which to destroy anything of that nature. So what was left? "Do you mean a witness?" She turned white as she realised who the most likely witness was. "Do you mean that Mrs Serring saw Woolf in Cosford's house and didn't warn me?"

"Yes. I didn't find her statement that she saw only a vague figure convincing. Don't forget that she had spied on other visitors successfully enough to overhear their conversation. And she said that she saw someone in the scullery. Think about the layout of the houses. The scullery can be overlooked only from the far end of the garden or the path at the back of the houses. She must have been outside when she saw the intruder. If so, she was probably close enough to recognise him." Hartismere spread out his hands in a gesture of resignation. "Try not to blame her too much, my dear. Would you accuse the police of murder if you were a refugee in a foreign land, if your husband had died in strange circumstances, and if there was no-one to come to your aid?"

Midge attempted to pull herself together, but her voice was still shaky. "Cosford died in his shop, rather than his house. The medical evidence shows that Cosford was dead before one o'clock. So whomever Mrs Serring observed in Cosford's house on the night of his death must have taken Cosford's keys from his body."

"It could be claimed that they'd been lent to him earlier," suggested Cohen.

"Ye-es, but that wouldn't explain how they turned up among Cosford's effects afterwards."

"True."

"So if Mrs Serring is prepared to swear to seeing Woolf there, it will practically hang him."

"Indeed," agreed Hartismere. "I hope that she will be prepared to speak when she knows that the gang is under lock and key. It will be a much stronger lead than attempting to discover where Woolf acquired the cyanide."

"She wants vengeance," pointed out Midge. "Surely that will help to convince her to tell what she knows?" She shuddered as she remembered the scene on the river. "In fact, it may explain why she didn't say anything before. She insisted on going out in her boat tonight, and she was out last night long after she had taken you to meet Caine. She certainly seemed to think that it would be Woolf who was going to flee tonight. She must have wanted to exact direct, personal vengeance on her husband's killers."

"Which may explain the savagery of her attack on those sailors," agreed Hartismere. "She was keyed up to kill and those unfortunate devils happened to be in her way. Mind you, it's useful that she did stop them. Should Goodwin change his mind and retract his admission of treason, he'll find it very hard to explain why a U-boat sent a boat upstream to collect him."

Midge glanced at Ralph. "Was Snellgrove implicated at all? He seems to have been terribly keen to capture Ralph."

"I gather," replied Hartismere, tactfully rephrasing the lieutenant's comments, "that Snellgrove felt that Capt. Thrigby appeared to have a very ill-defined role within the regiment."

Peveril inspected his hands. He knew what that meant. Snellgrove thought that he was an idle hound who did no work whatsoever and who then most unconvincingly changed his tune. And, unless Snellgrove had been remarkably restrained, he had probably said so to Hartismere.

"Moreover," continued the Vice-Master smoothly, "Lt. Snellgrove had been trying for some time to improve the level of efficiency within C Coy. That is so, is it not, Peveril?"

"Yes, sir."

"Snellgrove's attempts had met with little support, but when Trent was killed, Snellgrove was determined that the investigation would not be hindered by the absence of a key witness." Hartismere gave a dry smile. "I gather that it was only Goodwin's intervention which prevented Snellgrove from carrying out as thorough a search of the mudflats as he would have liked. Snellgrove was, in fact, reprimanded for wasting the men's time when – as Goodwin put it – the murderer must have already been miles away."

Midge was momentarily surprised by this news. "*Goodwin* stopped him?" she repeated, before correcting herself. "Oh, I suppose Goodwin was frightened that Ralph might say something which made people suspect that someone else was involved. As long as Ralph was a fugitive, everyone would assume that he was the killer."

"Precisely, my dear. Doubtless Goodwin would have organised a shooting-party, had he not already decided to flee."

Midge gulped. "Then we must be grateful for his inefficiency."

"Indeed." Hartismere glanced at his watch. "Dr Fellowes has informed me that an army camp is no place for Mrs Serring. I do not wish her to be alone. Do you think, Miss Carrington, that your aunt would be good enough to let her stay with you for a few days?"

"I imagine so."

"Good. In that case, I should be grateful if you would help Mrs Serring to get ready for the journey. Cohen, could you show Miss Carrington where Mrs Serring is? Then I need to discuss a few further points with you."

"Of course, sir."

As Hartismere accompanied Cohen to the door, he glanced at Peveril. "You will remain here, Lieutenant; I should like a word with you."

Peveril attempted not to sound apprehensive. "Very good, sir."

As the minutes ticked by and the Vice-Master did not return, Peveril's apprehension grew. It was all too easy to imagine what Cohen might be saying. And, even if Cohen weren't enlightening Hartismere as to his junior's interrogation technique, the sensation of being back at school, ordered to await judgement in a master's study, was decidedly unpleasant. So was the suspicion that Hartismere intended him to feel like that. When the Vice-Master finally reappeared, Peveril was relieved that his first comment had nothing to do with Cohen or Goodwin.

"You will drive Mrs Serring and Miss Carrington back to Brandon."

"Yes, sir."

Hartismere eyed Peveril suspiciously. The boy sounded pretty low – couldn't he see that this would give him a chance to make up whatever quarrel he had had with the gel? "Doubtless you and Miss Carrington will have plenty to discuss, but don't keep her up too late. I need you back here."

"I don't suppose her aunt will let me."

'And,' thought Hartismere, 'you don't feel you've shown up very well, so you don't know whether the gel even wants to talk to you. Either that or you don't think you're fit for her because you see things. Young idiot. Mistrust me and Collingwood by all means, but why are you misjudging the gel?' Nothing of this showed in the Vice-Master's voice as he enquired, "You were disinclined to do as I asked you in the marsh. What made you change your mind?"

"I realised that you were more likely to make the right decision than I, sir."

Hartismere's eyebrows rose. "Indeed? Then there is hope for you yet."

"Yes, sir," replied Peveril despondently. It was obvious that all hell would have broken loose if he had failed to obey

Hartismere's orders, but even the thought of what he had avoided failed to have much effect.

Hartismere noticed his dejection. "You did the correct thing. Nor do I imagine that Miss Carrington will hold it against you."

"Sir."

"If you hadn't got back to camp as swiftly, the doctor would have been unable to save those sailors. Quite apart from any humanitarian concerns, their testimony will help to convict Goodwin."

"Yes, sir."

"Making split-second decisions is never easy."

"I wasn't sure whether to tackle Goodwin or not," admitted Peveril. "But I was sure that he'd spotted you. I thought he'd shoot."

"I am exceedingly grateful that you did intervene. Moreover, I happened to hear what you hissed at him."

Despite his best efforts, Peveril could feel his colour rising. Hartismere must think that he was an absolute fool. "I don't know what you mean, sir."

"Really? Now I, on the other hand, have spent years discovering what limited sense there is to be discerned in undergraduate essays, which gives me a certain advantage in disentangling impenetrable remarks. And not only do I realise what you were trying to do, I am deeply grateful. As you said, one doesn't roll around in the mud at Cambridge. So I lack the necessary training for wrestling with traitors – or boatmen of the dead – in sludge and half-submerged sedge."

"But..."

"My dear boy, do allow me to express my gratitude." The Vice-Master ran his eyes over Peveril's drawn face, wondering whether what he was about to say would prove true. "Perhaps more importantly, now that you have tackled Charon in the flesh, you will find it easier to defeat him in your nightmares."

"Sir."

Hartismere shook his head. "Carrington once told me you had an able mind. Do endeavour to demonstrate him correct by accepting the logic of what I say."

"Very well, sir." There was a pause, before Ralph looked at

his erstwhile tutor uncertainly. "Sir, may I ask you something?"

"Of course."

"I know that I'll be court-martialled for talking out of turn, and I know I deserve it, but can you do something to keep Miss Carrington from being dragged into things?" Ralph swallowed. "I should never have said anything to her, and I wished that I hadn't almost immediately. I'll take what's coming to me, but it's unfair if she suffers for my errors."

The Vice-Master's eyes raked Peveril's face. The boy sounded sincere – and scared. "That sort of admission might improve matters. However, what makes you so certain that I possess the requisite degree of influence over your commanding officer?"

Peveril shifted in embarrassment. "Well, you recruited him, sir, so he's bound to have some respect for your judgement."

"Does that follow?"

Ralph answered haltingly. "I mean, sir, I know I haven't precisely shown much sign of respect towards you..."

"Indeed – and you have shown considerably less respect to Collingwood."

"Err... yes, sir."

Hartismere continued mercilessly. "In your dealings with him, you might remember that Collingwood isn't your father. Nor is this war going to be over quickly, so you will face a number of orders which you will not like, issued by people you do not like. Your duty is to obey those orders, not to waste time arguing about them or deliberately setting out to annoy your superiors. Do you understand?"

Peveril turned scarlet. "Yes, sir." He fought to get his voice under control. "I know I was stupid. I didn't mean to let you down. And... and I don't dislike you, sir."

The Vice-Master observed Peveril's discomfiture with some sympathy. The boy really was very young. Moreover, at least he had taken the rebuke without flaring up. Perhaps there was indeed hope for him, in which case it would do no harm to give him some encouragement, even if disguised as another rebuke.

"Furthermore, it may come as a surprise to you, Lieutenant, but the majority of young officers whom I observed in the last war were very conscious of the fact that they might well die.

Contrary to what you may have heard, they did not enjoy the thought."

Peveril shifted uncomfortably. "But..."

"I do wish you would get it out of your head that I am trying to be kind to you. I am attempting to make you into a more competent operative. I cannot do that without a clinical assessment of your weaknesses."

"Sir."

The Vice-Master coughed. "Out of interest, Peveril, when I was discussing the possibility of your joining Intelligence, why did you not tell me quite how bad your nightmares were?"

When Peveril looked embarrassed, but made no reply, Hartismere sighed. "Let me guess. You didn't want me to think that you were weak or that you were inventing them?"

Peveril nodded dumbly then forced himself to speak. "You'd said I was needed, sir." He attempted to disguise his emotion. "Have you decided I'm no good?"

"I am eminently relieved that I had you in position, both tonight and to talk to Caine, whose evidence will prove vital. You also seem to have done well regarding Goodwin; Cohen thought you got the information out quickly."

Ralph shrugged. "I've had the benefit of being questioned myself and of having watched K.C.s in action."

"Are you developing a taste for interrogation?"

"God, no." Peveril took in Hartismere's expression of surprise. "I mean, sir... Well, it's a bit unpleasant setting out to break a man, isn't it?"

"A certain degree of ruthlessness is necessary at times, I am afraid. Don't forget that other seekers after the truth – doctors and barristers and researchers – need to develop a taste for blood." The Vice-Master coughed. "I have, in my own profession, needed to be less than friendly upon occasion. Undergraduates, after all, can require a blunt warning about the likely results of their folly or idleness."

"Yes, sir," agreed Peveril, realising that the Vice-Master was trying to lighten the atmosphere with a joke. "But you could develop a taste for too much blood, couldn't you?"

"Maneaters aren't inclined to worry about that," declared

Hartismere. "They bury their noses in the gore to feed without any qualms."

Peveril grimaced. He felt as if he'd had his nose rubbed well and truly in it, and that he would never be clean of the stain.

The Vice-Master decided that the boy had probably had about as much as he could endure. "You'd better go now. Please convey my apologies to Mrs Carrington for wishing an uninvited guest upon her."

Peveril seized upon this change of subject with relief. "Will Mrs Serring be all right, sir? Midge said that she wanted to kill herself."

"That was probably partly down to nervous exhaustion, but I'll send Fellowes to have another look at her tomorrow."

"And afterwards? If she does give evidence, that might furnish her with something to live for at the moment, but what will happen after the trial is finished?"

"Who knows? I shall try to persuade her that her knowledge of Polish may be of use in the fight against Hitler. If nothing else, she might be suitable for broadcasting. But she isn't going to be the only woman left alone and abandoned."

Once the trio reached Brandon, Alice Carrington promptly took over. She led Mrs Serring and Trix upstairs, leaving Midge and Ralph together. Peveril noted with concern how exhausted Midge looked.

"I say, Midge," he began awkwardly, "I'm sorry you ended up in such a beastly situation. It must have been terrifying."

Midge was horribly conscious that she wanted to burst into tears. However, she couldn't possibly do so. Ralph clearly felt guilty about what she'd been through; he'd feel even worse if she started crying. And it certainly wasn't his fault that she had chosen to accompany Mrs Serring, so she'd better sound coherent and in command of the situation.

"We benefited from the element of surprise. They expected an attack from the bank, not from downriver. In fact, it's just as well that they sheered off when the signalling stopped. If they'd reached the bank, they might have shot Dr Hartismere or Caine." She glanced at Ralph. He had taken the opportunity to wash off the marsh mud before he drove to Brandon and the damage to his face was now glaringly obvious. "Who was it who captured Goodwin?"

"Does it matter?"

"It can only have been Cohen, Dr Hartismere, or you – and you're the only one who's been in a fight."

"Well, yes... that is..."

"That was very brave of you, Ralph. Goodwin must have been armed."

Peveril flushed at the admiration in Midge's voice. "I didn't stop to think. And Hartismere had already attracted his attention. I came in unseen from the rear. I wasn't brave at all."

"I think you were." Midge suddenly grinned at him. "You said women ought to be allowed to use their brains. So you can't stop me from thinking that you were brave if I want to."

In normal circumstances, Peveril would have attempted to cap Midge's exercise in logic. However, he was far more concerned about not laying claim to a quality which he was sure he lacked than in teasing Midge. "I wasn't brave, and I shouldn't have led you into danger." He paused irresolutely. The obvious thing to say was how much he cared for Midge. But if she didn't love him, he would have asked her too soon. That would wreck their friendship, as well as any chances of her becoming his girlfriend, and, God knows, her friendship was important to him. In any case, had he any right to say anything, when he had cracked up? It was all very well Hartismere being dashed decent about it, but Hartismere wasn't being asked to tie himself to an unstable boyfriend. And it wasn't fair to explain all that to Midge because she'd probably say yes out of pity. Only a cad would trap a girl in that manner.

He turned away abruptly. "I'd better go now. Hartismere said he needed me back at C Coy." He attempted to lighten the atmosphere. "My new role is of a perfect subaltern, hence this uncharacteristic diligence."

As he opened the door, he glanced back at her. "Midge, you will let me see you if you're in London, won't you?"

"Of course," agreed Midge, suddenly deciding that her friend Jenny was overdue a visit. "And in Cambridge. It was fun when we went to those concerts."

Ralph's eyes lit up. Maybe Midge did care. There was hope. If he gave her time – if he gave himself time – then he'd be able to make things work.

Three days later, Hartismere knocked on the door of the vicarage attached to St Peter and St Paul, Newton. A scholarly old man opened the door and bid him enter.

"I gather, Mr Tobias, that you are going to conduct the funeral service for Basil Cosford."

"That is so."

"I have a request to make. Would you put this in the coffin with him?"

The elderly priest opened the shabby leather folder. His eyebrows rose as he saw the icon and the photograph of the woman with her daughter. However, he made no comment. There had been quite enough speculation in Newton without him adding to it.

"In the end," continued Hartismere, "their loss was all he cared about. It is only right that they lie with him in death, even if only in a photograph."

"The Greeks saw the dangers of love," stated the vicar in his thin, precise voice. "It can drive the healthy insane, and turn the virtuous to wrongdoing. And yet it can also provide great comfort and purpose to the purposeless. I shall see that the photograph is buried with him."

"Thank you."

An hour later, as the priest began to intone the words of the funeral service, Hartismere slipped into a pew at the back of the empty church. If his thoughts strayed to Belgium and a locked drawer in his rooms in Trinity, nothing showed on his face. But when he returned to Cambridge, he sent a message that he would not be dining in Hall that night. There were some memories which did not welcome other company.

finis

Prisoner at the Bar

In 1930s society, both Jenny and Midge face a struggle for acceptance. Jenny is trying to enter the male-dominated legal profession, while a childhood attack of polio has left Midge disabled. When Jenny's barrister father is arrested for murder, she immediately turns to Midge to help her. It seems unbelievable that a well-known K.C. could have killed a shady solicitor or extorted money from refugees, so Midge goes undercover in a desperate attempt to identify the real killer. She succeeds, but then has to convince a sceptical Old Bailey courtroom that a disabled young woman could have discovered the truth.

The first in the Midge Carrington mystery series.

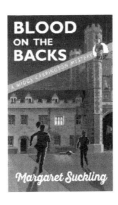

Blood on the Backs

An undergraduate crashes to his death from the roof of
Trinity College, Cambridge. Did he fall or was he pushed?
Midge's cousin John is forced to turn to her for help when
one of his students is accused of murder. Meanwhile, Midge
faces her own problems – her college disapproves strongly of
her getting involved in another murder and there is the
complication that, although she is in love with John, he loves
Jenny, her closest friend.

The second in the Midge Carrington mystery series.

22811126R00271

Printed in Great Britain
by Amazon